To
Clare

WAYWARD DAUGHTER

Love

BRENDA SQUIRES

Brenda

Enjoy!

THE EATONS Vol 1

DEDICATION

For my grandchildren Lenny and Yazz Peters

ACKNOWLEDGMENTS

To write a book, any book, is to embark on a journey. The destination may be clear but there will be roadblocks, diversions and free lifts along the way. Wayward Daughter proved no exception. In the early days I had willing readers: Carol Frances, Sally Randell, Ros Watson and James Horan. Their feedback was invaluable and gave me the encouragement I needed to continue. Anne Garside, historian, helped me enormously in the evocation of the era and she was tireless in reading drafts. She said my characters sometimes woke her up at three in the morning demanding attention! I read widely to get a feel of the era and some of the books that I found particularly helpful were: Ernest Hemingway: *A Moveable feast*, Francoise Gilet: *Life with Picasso*, David Boyd Haycock: *A crisis of brilliance*, Paula McLain: *The Paris Wife*, Virginia Nicholson: *Among the Bohemians*. The Rhosy novelists' group also has been extremely supportive in helping me work through various versions of the story. Thorne Moore, one of these writers, has gone the extra mile in formatting the book for me. And finally thanks to Richard Davies of Parthian who also helped me get the book ready for publication.
Many thanks to all of you.

WAYWARD DAUGHTER

CONTENTS

Prologue

Morwenna rifled through the wardrobe till she found the frock, faded now with age but still velvety. She fingered the fraying material, yanked it down and wriggled into the gown. Enormous on her growing body, it trailed on the ground and wrapped itself round her ankles. Almost toppling she twirled round and peered at herself in the pitted mirror. She wondered what it would be like to be a real singer.

Tonight she was allowed into the saloon bar. By nine the place was full. Morwenna circulated, collecting glasses. Froth ran down the sides of them, which made her hands sticky. 'Got her early on the job then,' said Fred, one of the regulars. 'Right looker she's going to be. Break a few 'earts I wouldn't doubt.' She clattered between bar and tables, scared in case one of the glasses slithered out of her grasp and smashed. The music started. People gathered round the piano. 'Can she sing too?' asked Fred. 'The spit of Maisy, ain't she?'

Pa, whom the regulars called Bert, was standing behind the bar, holding forth. Morwenna picked up bits of their talk.

'All over by Christmas' he said. Now look at it.'

'Too right. But we got to keep going...'

'You know what I think?' Bert leaned forward. 'They got better guns than us. They're better dug in.'

'Come off it. That's just Bolshie talk...'

'Can she sing too, this little 'un?' the man puffed on his pipe, turning towards Morwenna.

'Nothing too much for our Morwenna,' said Bert drawing a pint of Guinness and letting it stand. Morwenna went scooting from one table to the next, light as dandelion floss.

'I can dance. I can sing. I can do just any fing!' she said, bold as you like, and the group laughed and applauded.

'Cheer us up then, girly,' said another. 'We can do with it right now.'

Morwenna set down the tray. She gave a little curtsey then swirled around, pulling out the edges of her skirts. 'If you were the only girl...' she sang. Up went her little white hand and with the other she made a sweeping motion. Her voice was high, clear and bright among the chinking glasses and chatter. 'And I were the only boy!' She stopped. The words had flown out of her head. She swirled again then gave a flourish with her hand. Those around her clapped in delight, drawing glances from those further down the bar. ''Ere girlie, 'ere's a penny. You done well.'

More pennies were thrown onto the table beside her. She flushed with pleasure. Ma was staring at her. She looked annoyed. The drinkers turned back to their glasses. 'The glasses, I said.' Ma pointed to the tray. Morwenna lifted it and wove her way through the bodies, which left a heavy, lingering smell of beer, tobacco and sweat.

Pa saw her coming and took the tray from her. 'That's my girl.'

Ma was banging ashtrays onto the counter in anger as she wiped them clean. 'Don't be putting fancy ideas in 'er 'ead. God knows where it will lead.' Bert moved away, whistling, to serve three punters at the bar. 'Go to bed now.' said Ma. 'Quit prancing around, do you 'ear?'

Morwenna gave her mother a timid smile. 'Thanks for letting me 'elp out.'

'Up you go,' said Ma, not reflecting her smile.

Morwenna went up the stairs leading to the rooms above the bar. Halfway up, she glanced back over the balding heads, clouds of smoke and the quivering glow of light from the gas mantles. Her heart beat faster. In her hand she was clutching several pennies. Her mother, though, was looking more upset than ever. She seemed to hate it whenever Morwenna sang.

PART 1

Chapter One *Morwenna*

It was 1925, the year before the General Strike, seven years after the signing of the Armistice. Hemlines had risen and dresses were tubes. Women's hair was cropped, **as** if to compensate for all the boys lost in the trenches. Strikes abounded as cheap German coal flooded the market in reparation for the war. Rudolph Valentino and the silent movies held sway. People still knew their place in society, but only just, for young people, especially the rich, had started to kick over the traces. The song on everyone's lips was: *Two for Tea.*

But, at seventeen, Morwenna Dobson thought her life was over.

She still slept in the box-room above the public bar, in The Mare's Head, her parents' pub, in Hackney. Her sister Cissie had married Bob Scratton and gone to live a few streets away where she helped him run a stall in Radley market, selling clothes. Her parents thought she had done well for herself. Bob was strong and reliable. That he drank too much and had a violent streak was not talked about. Truth be told, Morwenna was glad to see the back of Cissy: she was too bossy and sure of herself, though it meant she was at the undiluted mercy of Tilda, who looked up to her, wore her clothes when she wasn't around, and pestered her when she was.

Morwenna had always felt different from her sisters. When she was eight she believed she was a princess dropped into the family by mistake. She loved music when none of them did. They might sing along at Joanna get-togethers, but with her the songs lingered on, days later. She was a dreamer, they said:

away with the fairies. She didn't look like them either: she had dark hair where they were fair. She had a quicker tongue, too, which often got her into trouble.

Every day except Sunday she went to Dukely's workshop and toiled under the fearsome Mrs Bootles, known to the girls as Bottles. The workers were crammed together in a low-ceilinged, windowless shed in a back street: twenty girls in all. Sometimes the clatter and tack-tack-tack of the machines would give her a headache. They worked a ten-hour day, five days a week and a short shift on Saturdays. They took home just enough to make it worthwhile.

At first she'd been delighted to escape school and the humiliation of not being able to spell rhododendron. For a while she worked in The Mare's Head, but was soon enticed by the idea of independent employment. Yet after a while even that palled. She could run up a straight seam. She was quick and clean and could cut material to a pattern and alter a skirt with all the pleats. And the girls were nice enough.

But something was missing.

'What's the difference between a hem and a long-distance runner?' she piped up one day.

'Dunno, what is?' answered another.

'One's got only one stitch, the other has 'undreds.'

'Ugh!'

'Hold yer tongue.' Mrs Bootles frowned at her from the centre of the room, where she kept an eye on operations.

At twelve-thirty the girls took their break and went to the local street market. Here, in true East End style, worlds collided: Mr Smolensky's herring bagels did battle with Mrs Jones' doorsteps of bread, while Mr Wong spooned out prawns from a wok and Fred White touted pork pies and chat. The girls sat in the cafe over mugs of tea, giggling.

* * *

'What d'you think happened to her old man?' As always

Bottles was their topic. To them she was an enigma. Nobody knew her family or whether she was a widow. 'You ask 'er.' Mabel prodded Morwenna. 'You're the one with nerve.'

'She'd throw me out. 'ates my guts, she does. Says I'm too lippy.'

A bet was set: if Morwenna found out her story, they'd treat her to the flicks next time they went. They trooped back into the workshop, smirking. Bottles told them to look lively and get to their places: they were five minutes late. Next time she'd dock their pay. They had a large order and there was no going home today until they completed half of it. Morwenna knew Bottles had no right to do this. In the smoky saloon bar she'd heard talk of rights and unions, of workers being entitled to breaks. The girls scuttled back in and got on without another word.

Morwenna looked at the pile lying beside her sphinx-adorned Singer sewing machine: ladies' gowns bound for West End showrooms. No shoddy work allowed. What passed muster for Petticoat Lane would not do for Regent Street. With concentration she ran up seam after seam, fixing the bobbin with silk thread and guiding the slippery material under her careful fingers.

A raiment for a lady on a luxury liner bound for New York; a man in tails guiding a slender sweetheart to the strains of a waltz or gyrating to New Orleans jazz. For a moment she was lost mid-Atlantic, and whoosh! the seam took off on its own. 'Oh no!' she shrieked, lifted the needle and snapped the threads. Bottles came rushing over. Morwenna looked up at the tight line of her mouth. 'It slipped,' she said.

'Out of the way. Let me have a look.' The other was bustling round her, pulling out the dress. 'Ruined! This order is very important. Don't you realise that?'

Morwenna burned with resentment. Though she was paid the same, she was given more complicated work than the others and rarely made a mistake.

'If it's so important why don't you pay us more?' she said before she could stop herself. She heard one or two of the other machines stop as the girls looked up. Mrs Bootles' face went from red to white and back again. She glared at Morwenna whose heart was throbbing horribly.

'What did you just say?'

Morwenna shrugged. Might as well be hung for a sheep as a lamb. 'We does our best, Mrs Bootles, but every week you want more. A lot of the girls is still learning.'

Mrs Bootles' chin wobbled. 'So you're the spokeswoman now, are you? The trade unionist? Listening too much to that publican father of yours?'

'What's my father got to do with anything?' Morwenna shot back. 'I do me best. We all do. Ain't that so?' She turned round to garner support, but saw a dozen heads bent suddenly over machines that whirred louder than ever. In another room the hissing of steam added to the brouhaha. She blinked away angry tears. Silly old crab, she thought, just look at her, what's she got that's worth writing home about? There were a hundred Bootles in Hackney and maybe twenty thousand in the world, but there was only one Morwenna Dobson.

'Sack me, and you'll never get this order in.' She tapped her finger on the table. 'I'm your best worker…' She paused. 'And don't you go talkin' about my family or I'll tell everyone your old man ran off with a fancy woman.'

The words rang out into silence.

Bottles' eyes bulged. 'Get out of here!'

Morwenna's throat tickled. Sometimes her thoughts spilled out without her say-so, as if they had a will of their own. Bottles looked about to explode. Morwenna lowered her head. 'Sorry, Miss.'

Bottles stared, her face twisting, as if weighing the likelihood of the other girls finishing the gowns in time without Morwenna. Pragmatism won out. 'Get on with your work. Not another word.' Relieved, Morwenna did as she was told.

Chapter Two

'She is watching by the poplars
Colinette with the sea-blue eyes…'

Morwenna heard on the evening air. It was a tune she recalled
from The Mare's Head, a plaintive soldier's song from the
War. It told of the longing for love and days of peace. But
never had she heard it like this. It was hopeful yet sad,
melancholic with a pure, angelic tone. How could someone's
singing evoke so much? It made her want to cry.

On her way back from work she'd taken a detour just for
the hell of it. She noticed an open door to The Queen's
Crown, once a popular Music Hall venue, and slipped inside.
As her eyes adjusted to the gloom she made out the singer
standing on a low podium in front of empty tables and chairs.

'Roses are shining in Picardy, in the hush of the silver dew,
Roses are flowering in Picardy, but there's never a rose like you!
And the roses will die in the summertime, and our roads may be
far apart,
But there's one rose that dies not in Picardy,
'Tis the rose that I keep in my heart'.

The woman came to a stop. A tall man moved towards her
from the other end of the room. He clapped slowly. 'Brava.'
Morwenna headed for the exit but brushed against a chair,
making it clatter. The two looked towards her.

'I 'eard the voice,' she said. 'It drew me in.'

'Do you sing?' asked the woman.

'Do I just?' Before she could stop herself Morwenna burst out: *Five foot two, eyes of blue, but oh what those five feet can do! Has any body se-en my girl?'* She halted, suddenly abashed.

The woman turned to the man and whispered something. They laughed. Morwenna felt awkward until the woman said. 'You've got nerve, I'll say that. But you hit the right notes. Not bad for a youngster.'

The man said: 'Let's get on with it.'

'Mind if I listen in?'

He shrugged. Morwenna sat, eyes closed, as the woman ran through the song again. Her heart grew warm as the notes seeped into her. She left just as the woman was finishing. A Hackney cab dawdled by a drinking place. From somewhere she heard loud voices, men squabbling over money. She hurried home.

* * *

At Dukely's the girls had acquired a new respect for her, but began to fear her too. She knew she had spat out and could do so again. That worried her. Bottles was strict, sometimes unfair, but she was the overseer. Morwenna could ill afford to lose her first job: to get another position she would need a letter of recommendation. For the next few days she ran up gowns in silence and watched her pile of completed work grow. Bottles said nothing. At the end of each day she came over and counted the finished items.

During one lunch break Morwenna strolled past the tubs of eels and cockles and winkles and dived into the newsagent's. Here she flicked through the magazines. In *The Tatler* an advertisement showed a blonde woman in a gown like the ones they were making. The woman was flat, back and front, and all lanky. Behind her a doting male leaned on a white balustrade above a Mediterranean garden. On another page were theatre notices. Noel Coward farces were the rage. He had just premiered his new musical revue, *On with the Dance.* Fascinated, she scanned the review. She imagined a world where women didn't have to work but could indulge in pleasure, and wondered what it would be like to be part of that world.

It was time to get back. Bottles would be counting the girls in and wondering where she was. She wanted the magazine. But it cost so much. It crossed her mind she could slip it under her cardigan without anyone noticing. She blushed. She had the remainder of last week's wages in her bag. She hesitated and then with a rush of excitement handed over the price of *The Tatler* and clutched at the magazine as she made her way back to work.

In the workshop she concentrated in her corner without looking up. After hours of clattering machines in the airless room, she longed to break out. She slid the magazine under her cardigan and went outside to the privy. Opening the shack door she got a whiff of excrement. She sat on the step waiting for the air to clear and took out the magazine. Page after page of glamour and enticement: young bodies, champagne bubbles, country estates and palaces, a trail of broken and mended hearts, court circulars, Ascot and the opening of the racing season, Lucy Baldwin, the Prime Minister's wife, playing cricket. Golden glorious days, curtailed before because of the war effort, were back in magnificent swing.

'So there you are!' The door thrust open. Bottles stood above her. Morwenna scrambled to her feet.

'I needed to go.' She nodded towards the outhouse.

'So I see. Now give me that and get back inside.' Bottles held out her hand.

Morwenna put the magazine behind her. 'It's mine. I paid good money for it...'

'You have no right to read in work time. We must be paying you too much for all this la-de-da nonsense.'

Morwenna's chin jutted out. 'Can't a body do her business in peace?'

'You weren't in the lavatory. You were on the step.'

'I was waiting.'

'Why? There's nobody in there.'

Morwenna hesitated. Her grip on the slippery magazine tightened.

'Give it here.'

Morwenna's eyes stung as she handed it over. She felt robbed. She went back inside and spent the rest of the afternoon bent over her machine. When she looked up at the clock it seemed stationary. As the going-home whistle sounded she approached Mrs Bootles. 'Could I have my magazine please, Mrs Bootles?'

The other, three inches taller, peered down. 'I'm keeping it till Saturday. I can't afford to have any of you girls slacking.'

Morwenna bit back her objection and without another word strode out of the workshop. The other girls could only stare and wonder at this new flare-up.

After the Saturday shift Mrs Bootles handed over her wages and the magazine. Morwenna clasped her by now dog-eared copy of *The Tatler* and left without a word. On her way home she stopped at a teashop. Irritated, she smoothed out the crumpled pages. She caught a glimpse of herself in the shop window and tweaked a curl on her brow. Seventeen, she thought. And what lay ahead but a life of sewing and scrimping? What was it all for: doing a boring job then handing over the bulk of her wages for her keep? Trying to dodge trouble, keep her nose clean – was that all there was? She leafed through the magazine. In one column the Situations Vacant were listed. They needed seamstresses, secretaries with Pitman's shorthand, nannies, ladies' companions, governesses and teachers. Girls who'd served in the Voluntary Aid Detachment in France were urged to train as nurses. She felt a twinge of guilt. Shouldn't she be doing her bit for others?

In one column someone was offering singing lessons. Now

that's what she wanted. Her heart raced. But how on earth could she pay for them? In small print next to it she spotted a vacancy for life class models for the Chelsea Polytechnic. Model. She could do that to pay for the singing lessons. People said she looked exotic – a nice looker, curvy but trim and a pretty face. But what did models for life classes actually do?

By the time she got home supper was on the go and she helped lay the table. As they sat over their sardines on toast her mind roamed back to *The Tatler* images: the bobbed hair of the women, the fancy champagne glasses, the elegant cigarette holder… Before she could stop herself she blurted out: 'I want to change my job. I was thinking of becoming an artist's model.'

'A what?' said Ma.

'A model for artists,' she announced proudly. Ma frowned over the teapot. Pa screwed his face up.

'No daughter of mine is going to flaunt 'erself.'

Tilda looked from father to daughter and giggled. Morwenna kicked her under the table.

'We'll 'ear no more about it,' said Bert. 'This is a respectable house. I brought my daughters up proper.'

'But why?'

'Morwenna, that's enough.' said Ma. 'Your father has spoken and you'll mind what he says.' Her father had a face like a dark cloud. She shrugged and got up from the table. Inside she was burning.

The next night she was helping out in the saloon bar. Bob, her brother-in-law, was watching her as she moved between tables, picking up glasses. He'd had far too much to drink. It was closing time. The lights were switched down as the last drinkers departed. She went to give the tables a final wipe down. From nowhere Bob grabbed hold of her and pushed her into a corner. He put a rough hand on one of her breasts. 'Great tits you've got!' She could smell the beer coming off him. His eyes were bleary and he was swaying on his feet. She slapped his hand away, but he edged her against the wall. 'You know you want it, you dark Jezebel.' The more she struggled the more he blocked her. How dare he! Just because Cissy was not around. She had been the butt of his cheeky comments before but never this. Her father would have belted him one.

'Get off!'

Just then Ma called out. 'You finished those tables, Morwenna?' The voice surprised him and he half-turned. Morwenna broke away.

* * *

Later, in bed, she lay awake going over it in her mind. The beery, sweaty smell of him, his smirking face leering at her. She recoiled at the memory. Tilda was slumped over towards her. Outside in the High Street she could hear revellers. When she drifted off she dreamt she was in a grave. A man was on top of her and others were piling sods of earth onto them. 'STOP!!' Her breath came in panicked snatches. Her ribcage heaved and she woke with a start.

Slipping out of bed she went downstairs to fetch a glass of water. She squeaked open the back door. A full moon glistened over the back yards. A lone bird piped in the sky. The moonlight made her uneasy.

Returning to bed she could not settle.

Life was nothing but indignity. She had to find something better. This week. This night. The cold voice in her head was a tyrant, brooking no resistance. These days it was always with her. It overshadowed blank moments when she had just run up a seam or was half listening to the girls' chatter in the teashop. She slipped on her clothes. She looked longingly at the dent her body had made in the bed: it urged her back under the covers against the warmth of her sister. In sleep Tilda looked frail and vulnerable. Morwenna was shot through with tenderness.

Yet the coldness of decision was pushing her. You were born to sing, it urged. If she got back into bed she would be done for: more gropings in the bar – even her brother-in-law made clumsy passes at her – endless chatter of the girls at work, Ma miserable as sin, Pa – her throat caught. Tilda shifted and turned over. Morwenna froze. Do it – commanded the voice. Time to take charge of your life. At Dukely's she'd learnt to toe the line, as Ma told her to. But the less she spoke out the more she doubted herself, and the more she doubted the more she hated. What was she there for? Just to give money to Ma and Pa, and put up with Tilda, who chomped on her brain like a little rat?

The moonlight made her restless.

She fished out *The Tatler* from under the bed, bundled together a few clothes and the remains of the money she had put by, which amounted by now to just a few shillings. She rolled them into a ball. As she crept out of the box-room she threw a last glance at Tilda, sprawled like a crab on a rock. Ignoring a rising nausea she tiptoed downstairs. In the scullery she scribbled a note and stuck it on the kitchen table. Her mother's purse was lying on the table. She took out a few coins, telling herself she'd repay her as soon as she could. Besides, they still had her keep money from her last payday. 'Off to get a job in the West End. Back soon. Morwenna.' She stuffed her bits and pieces into one of Ma's shopping bags.

Out on the street her heart beat like horses' hooves. It was April, the air was brisk in her face. She walked towards Dalston junction. An early, horse-drawn milk float emerged from the dairy, churns clunking against each other. The sky was lighting up. Already a pale sun was touching the roofs and chimneys. She walked on, losing track of time. She sniffed the air. Someone somewhere was frying bacon. It set her stomach rumbling. By now the family would be up and about. They would have discovered her note. Her feet were beginning to hurt, she could feel the pavement through the thin soles of her shoes. She leaned against a fence to rest.

By the time she reached Highbury Corner people were going about their business, bustling, chatting and buying newspapers from boys in caps, who bawled the latest headline. Horse dung steamed on the roadway and was squashed by the next dogcart. In Upper Street she caught a whiff of freshly baked bread that made her weak with hunger. She fished for coins and bought a bun, which she tore into.

All around her London was a living, breathing thing: gentlemen were off to the City and handsome, young women in striped blouses scurried in and out of Dawson's department store. Chelsea lay on the embankment. She made her way to the Thames where she gazed at the wrought iron, twisting serpents on seats and lampposts and sniffed the sea on the incoming tide. Taking a farthing from her purse she threw it into the swirling water for luck. A barge was passing by. She waved and the man at the tiller waved back. She laughed, closed her eyes and breathed deep.

Chapter Three *Derek*

In Victoria Terrace, the family home in Kentish Town he still shared with his sister, Eleanor, Derek Eaton was having a rough night. He threw off the bedclothes and groped for his dressing gown. He couldn't find it. Stumbling out of bed he crept downstairs. He lit the kerosene lamp on the table, not yet ready for the brightness of electricity. He made himself tea.

As he sipped it the dream came back to him: somebody – maybe Michael – was screeching at him that he had to wake up or they'd put him in a coffin: there were plenty left over from the war. He stared ahead, a sour taste in his mouth. The last time he'd had a similar sensation was after meeting up with Michael. He was just back from Paris and couldn't stop going on about artists grappling with the Machine Age as icons were smashed. He'd declared his urge to engage with all that movement and change.

So why was Michael intruding into his dreams now? He hadn't thought about him in an age. Michael, an older boy from school, boasted he was a born artist. Derek wasn't sure about that but he had the patter, he had to give him that. He recalled them drinking together during the war. They were in the Golden Orb in Kentish Town, when they probably shouldn't have been, hugging pints in the public bar.

Michael was frowning into his glass of mild. 'I've had enough. I'm off to Paris before I get called up.'

Derek looked at him quizzically.

'I love my country and all that, but I'm not going. Two of my cousins were killed last month.'

It was the first time Derek had heard anyone utter dissent.

It made him feel edgy. He loved his country. Isn't that what one did? At the start of the war, when young men were signing up in their thousands, Derek had regretted that he was too young. Many boys from the top of his school had gone. He'd looked up to them. Envied them. At the time he could see himself cutting a dashing figure in a sharply pressed uniform, girls flocking like gulls to a fishing boat. He'd watched his fellow pupils leaving in a fanfare of glory and patriotism.

'I'm going to paint,' Michael had stated with defiance.

'You can do that here.'

'It's not as good. Paris is full of painters. My uncle's told me about this one called Picasso. I want to see what he's up to. And the Fauves.'

'The who?' Though daunted by the older boy's sophistication, Derek could not suppress his curiosity.

'The wild beasts.'

'Never heard of them.'

'Well you should have.'

'Is that so?'

'The likes of Henri Matisse and André Derain. They value colour over representation. Even the Impressionists are old hat now... Picasso is the one.'

Derek was silenced. Though he followed what he could of the latest movements, Michael was streets ahead. He was in the know because his uncle was a painter at The Slade. Twice he'd taken Michael to Paris the year before. Michael carried on: 'They say it's the best place. And the cheapest. *The* place for girls. I'll work as a waiter. Anything to make ends meet.' Derek had nodded, pricked with insecurity. Michael downed his beer. 'Better go now. Things I need to see to.'

That evening Derek had sat at table with his family. 'Someone I know from school is off to Paris. To become an artist.'

'Paris? What about the bloody war?' snapped his father,

John Eaton.

'It hasn't reached Paris,' replied Derek with confidence, for everyone knew that when the guns of August started the French had held the German advance outside of Paris. After two years' stalemate it remained the City of Light, a beacon to artists. Derek said slowly. 'I thought I might join him after I finish school…'

'Don't talk rot!' His father waved his fork over his lamb chop, his skin so taut on his jaw you could see the bones working when he munched. 'Better a reliable post where you know where you stand.' He had the pallor of working indoors, with white hands and well-trimmed nails. 'What about doing your duty?' Months before they had introduced conscription for men eighteen and over.

'You mean joining Kitchener's army?' His mother eyed her husband in alarm. 'He's too young.'

'Many his age are enlisting.'

Derek had felt a spasm of hatred. Resistance flickered then died in him. What use arguing? His father would always have the last word. 'Another three years before he need sign up,' his mother had stated firmly and placed a dish on the table. Derek chewed the last of his chop.

* * *

And now they were both gone, swept away in the last throes of the Spanish Influenza at the end of the war. Derek coughed and tapped his chest to clear the air passages. What use revisiting the past? He sipped the tepid remains of his tea. His head was heavy with a tangle of incoherent emotions. Michael had come to taunt him, of that there was no doubt; and just when Derek believed things were getting better. He paced the room, banged into a chair in his agitation. Swore. Sat down again. Went to drink more tea before he remembered he'd drained the cup.

Patrick Shaughnessy, his mentor at art college, was always

pushing him to sound out the dark regions in himself. In the half-light of the kitchen Derek pictured Patrick's candid eyes. He shivered. It was cold at this time of night. He went to the cupboard beneath the stairs and pulled out an ancient overcoat. Sleep had flown.

* * *

'Tell me the truth.' The next morning he stood before Patrick, who in a grubby smock and with his grizzled beard springing in all directions, was mixing an array of blues and purples on his palette. Patrick had a studio in Chelsea, but now only came into college to teach the odd class.

Derek had brought a portfolio of his latest work with him.

He had not seen Patrick in months. The man always made him feel that as far as art went, he was falling short. And it was true, he was. Pragmatism got in the way. He'd painted sets for theatres, but as that work petered out he'd fished around for something else. By dint of his theatre connections he landed a job as a manager with a part share in Fingal's Cave, Purveyor of Costumes and Props. The owner, a retired actor who'd made good money in his day, allowed him a free hand in developing the business. He also had an assistant to help him. But where was that leading him? As a rule he had enough money, though not always. It wasn't just about money though, was it?

'You're interrupting me as usual.'

'I need an answer.'

Patrick heaved a sigh, replaced the palette knife on the easel ledge and opened Derek's canvas holder. Slowly he flicked through the sketches and paintings. Derek's chest was tight. 'So what is your question?'

This threw Derek, who was braced for rejection, but not challenge.

'Don't be afraid to tell me. I'll take it like a man.'

Patrick's mouth opened in astonishment then split in a wide

grin. 'What? Take it like a man? You're quite the one for posturing, aren't you? What do you think you are – some sort of pugilist?'

'No, but…'

'For what it's worth, I think you're lazy.'

Derek searched Patrick's face. 'Lazy?'

Patrick continued to peruse the portfolio then grunted. 'Much as I thought.'

Derek was unable to speak. Patrick glanced across and smeared the palette with colour, selected a brush. He screwed his eyes up and leaned back to study the canvas he had on the easel. After a moment he laid down the brush. 'You want me to say "There you are Derek Eaton, you are an artist. Just put paint to canvas and it will happen." Well, it won't. It's time you found out what being an artist is about. This work proves it.'

Derek glanced away.

'Reassurance is not the currency of artists. Unless you grasp that, you're better off sticking to selling boas.'

Derek winced.

'These are good enough for a beginner, but you've got to move on. This work is derivative, afraid to speak its mind. Artists need to be exposed to ideas besides their own. We all need that. Not a nursemaid, though, and that's what you seem to want.'

Derek went crimson.

'You close the matter before you've opened it up. You should be asking "What moves me? What do I see when I look around? How do colours affect me? Shapes? Ideas?" Then the work begins.'

'I sense the gap, the discrepancy…'

'These are too tentative. You're afraid to soar and plummet. You need to look. Really look. You need to get yourself out of the way and stop asking silly questions. Now, if you don't mind, let me get on with my work.'

'But…'

'The best I can offer is space in this studio when I'm away. Pay me what you can.'

Derek nodded acceptance of the offer and left soon after.

Chapter Four

The next day Derek took off work. He wanted to get out to the countryside. He grabbed a sketchpad and took a train heading out of London towards the west. He got down at a small station, Eynsham, on a branch line beyond Oxford. A mist lay over the landscape, moving in shrouds, broken here and there by sunlight. He walked out of the station yard and wandered down a narrow lane through a handful of cottages and out into the open fields. He lingered here and there to throw off a quick drawing.

Spring, and the fields were greening. A horse dragged a plough by a hedgerow; gulls were descending, shrieking and greedy for worms. The woodland beyond was swathed in white, which thinned to reveal a land of magic, floating before him. A cottage by the edge of the fields was smoking, the plume curling up and disappearing. He looked down: his shoes were sodden. He scribbled notes and sketched, then scratched out what he'd done.

Stanley Spencer, now renowned for his wartime paintings, had once taken landscapes such as this and transformed them into paradise. But where was Derek to derive *his* inspiration from? A glass screen stood between him and the world, between him and his spirit. Questions torrented through him, sending him from rage to despair. He climbed over a stile, skirted a field of barley, its ears moist and grey-green. He crumpled up what he'd done and threw it into a ditch.

Back in London he carried on walking. Up through Kentish Town he wandered, then through Dartmouth Park towards Highgate. He was irritated to find himself dwelling on what

24

Shaughnessy had said, his words reverberating through him. He doubled back and walked down through Camden Town again, avoiding the shop. He reached the bridge over Regent's Park canal. The water moved black and oily; he thought of the Ancient Mariner with his becalmed ship, beset by writhing serpents, and the curse of the slaughtered albatross.

As soon as he thought of her, he decided to seek out Zara. Their last encounter, months before, had been a drunken fling in Bristol, where she was visiting her ailing father. She often performed in the West End. He bought an afternoon edition of *The Illustrated London News* and scanned the listings. He was delighted to discover Noel Coward's latest revue, *London Calling!*, was running a matinée in The Athena Theatre. She could well be in it, since she'd been auditioning for Noel Coward months before. He bought a ticket, entered the darkened auditorium, buried himself among faded, plush seats and waited for the curtain to go up.

A bevy of slender girls, sparsely dressed as nymphs were at a country house party, lolling round a fountain. In bustled the young daughter of the house, telling them to clear out and get changed into suitable attire, a polo game was about to commence. Derek gasped. There was Zara, kitted out in jodhpurs that sat oh so snugly over her *petite derrière* – pointing her hand this way then that and laying down the law! Her face shone with its marble paleness and fine features. A veritable modern day Diana, mistress of the hunt, slayer of men's hearts – why ever had he let her go? Her voice was high and clear as she commanded the nymphs to get ready for the game. The curtain dropped.

From the back of the stalls came hoots of merriment. The scene changed: next to appear were a row of stenographers, hacking away at their Remingtons while a fierce-looking editor yelled at them to turn up the heat. In flounced Zara, spectacles on nose. An earnest investigative journalist, she was reporting on unemployment in the North. The editor told her to go sling her hook: the main thing was to feed the public the sensations they craved. She intoned an angry ditty, comparing the price of beer with the cost of integrity.

The scene changed again. This time Zara did not appear. While he waited to see her, he eyed the stage sets. They were mediocre: just faded bits of plywood. He could have done a better job. When she still made no appearance he grew restive. At the interval he rushed out onto the street. An alley led to the Stage Door. A porter was hovering outside, smoking. 'I wanted to see a friend.' The porter eyed him with indifference.

'Sorry sir, I'm under instructions to let no one pass until the show is over.'

'I'll only be ten minutes.'

'You won't be any minutes. Didn't you hear what I just said?' The man, five foot nine and as solid as concrete, flicked the dog-end into the gutter. When Derek saw the man would not give way, he took himself off to the bar and ordered a drink. After the show he returned to the Stage Door, now unguarded. In the corridor he asked one of the erstwhile nymphs, now wearing a long coat, where he might find Zara. She pointed to a dressing room at the far end.

Zara was sitting in front of a brightly lit mirror rubbing off greasepaint with cotton wool. The peignoir she was wearing had slipped off her shoulders. 'Derek Eaton. What are *you* doing here?'

'I came to congratulate you. You were superb.'

'Who let you in?'

'I came in by the Stage Door exit.'

She drew her dressing gown round her and continued cleaning her face. 'Well sit down, now you're here.' He sank down on the seat next to hers, watching her deft strokes.

'I thought we might have a drink together – for old times' sake.'

Months before they had parted on cool terms. Now he could not even remember why. She cast him a sidelong glance as if to ask him just what he had in mind. As she slowly brushed back her ash-blond hair he longed to run his fingers through it.

'How do you know I haven't made some other arrangement?'

'I was in this part of town...'

'Don't look so miserable. I'll have a quick snifter. Helps me come down after the show. I'm not in the mood for the gang tonight. They always want to drag me off to another cocktail party or trip down the river or something... now be a darling and step outside while I change.' Though taken aback by this spurt of modesty, he complied. She emerged in a figure-flattering pale peach frock, which made her look even more adorable as it highlighted her hair.

The King's Seal, down a nearby alley, offered the warmth and intimacy he had hoped for. Zara examined her painted nails and powdered her nose as if he were not there. She did not even bother stifling a yawn. 'Am I boring you?' he asked.

'Sorry darling. So tell me what you've been up to. The last I heard you were pursuing your love of the Modernists or was it the War Artists? You've probably moved on since then. I know I have. We went to Paris recently. There's a lot going on there. Laszlo and I go quite often.'

'So you're still together with that ...'

'Watch it! That's my lover you're talking about.'

'I thought that was just a passing fancy.' A side lamp gave her cheeks an unwonted glow. At that moment he longed to embrace her, tell her it had been too long. 'Where is Laszlo now?'

She laughed. 'Don't go getting any ideas.'

He returned from the bar with replenished glasses. 'Are you still at the Chelsea Polytechnic?' she asked.

27

He let out a sigh. 'I go there when I can. I have to run the theatre shop.'

She drew out a cigarette holder from her clutch bag, eased a cigarette into it and blew out a stream of smoke past his nose. He wondered what to say next. He felt himself growing formal, as though with a stranger. He examined his beer as though he might find inspiration there. 'I –er –I. You're as beautiful as ever…' He clasped her hand.

She moved back and gave him an appraising stare. 'You're a darling, Derek. Just don't give me any tosh about love, will you? I haven't got the energy for that sort of thing.'

'Oh,' he sat back, deflated.

'Didn't we decide we'd be better off as chums?'

'Did we? What about Bristol?'

'Bristol?' She looked puzzled then her face relaxed into a smile. 'That was fun, wasn't it?'

He was about to ask her whether it had meant anything at all to her but stopped himself. What was a chap supposed to do when a girl didn't toe the line?

'What about your art?' she asked briskly. 'That's where your real passion lies. Though even there you chop and change. One minute it's the terror of war and then you're into all the pre-Raphaelites or Arts and Crafts – curly wallpaper and flowery chimney pots…'

He stared at her, not knowing what to say. 'What's the matter, Derek? You look lost.' She swilled brandy around in her glass, sipped then swallowed the lot. 'Good stuff, that. I best wend my weary way. Got another full day tomorrow. Luckily nothing this evening.' She started gathering her things.

'Wait!' She looked up in surprise. 'Let me walk you home.'

'I was going to catch a cab.'

'Let me take you. I insist.'

They clambered into the back of a cab and were soon being dropped outside her place in Brunswick square. 'Are you going to invite me in for a drink?'

'Promise to behave?'

He nodded, suppressing a frisson of excitement. She turned the key and opened the door onto a large room of silken chairs and walls covered with paintings. She moved around, switching on lamps until the place glowed a friendly welcome. He sank onto a low sofa. She went to a corner and started rattling bottles and glasses. From his sprawled position he noticed the walls were hung with Laszlo's paintings: streaks and angles of a Modernist statement. On the mantelshelf were photos of the man himself, some with Zara beside him, some not, but all of them framed in silver. 'Is this your place?' he asked.

'It belongs to Laszlo.'

'I thought as much.' He nodded towards the creations on the walls.

'Ah those. *I* put them up. He'd stashed them away at the back of his studio.'

Derek got to his feet, suddenly animated. 'You're wasting…'

She fixed herself a drink. 'You can talk about your work if you like. But Laszlo is off limits, understand?' When she approached, drink in hand, her face was set hard.

'I'm stuck,' he said.

'What d'you mean: stuck?' She gave a little laugh. 'You could always come and paint stage sets at The Athena.'

'I want to explore my own ideas.'

She shrugged. 'If you're not sure what you're doing, you need to get away. Get out of London. Rent a cottage in the wilds. And paint. Just bloody paint…'

He withdrew into his whisky. She was right. But for the moment he was more interested in her body. He was not convinced by her show of loyalty towards Laszlo. By the end of the next whisky he was about to put it to the test. Only a growing wariness prevented him.

'Look darling, I am going to have to push you out now. Nothing personal, but I'm dog-tired. I've got another show tomorrow and a rehearsal at twelve, with new material to be squeezed in. I'll need to have my wits about me.'

Enveloped by plush cushions Derek felt his body slacken at her words. 'One for the road?' He stumbled to his feet.

'One more, and you wouldn't even recognise the road, let alone follow it. Now, come on, play the game. You said a drink for old times' sake and you've had more than your fill.'

As he stood up he caught a whiff of delicious, flowery fragrance; her dress shimmered and rustled. He had the sensation of a bright, brittle flower. She linked her arm through his. He leaned towards her, wanting to engulf her, but her arms, white and fragile in appearance, were stronger than he realised. She was propelling him in the direction of the front door and he was unable to resist. Opening the door she pushed him into the street.

He paused by a street-lamp for support. He crawled onto a tram towards Patrick Shaughnessy's studio, deciding he was not quite up to the admonishing glare of Eleanor over breakfast. Patrick grudgingly admitted him and pointed to the grubby divan in the corner of the sitting room, before shuffling back to bed.

Chapter Five *Morwenna*

The secretary at the Chelsea Polytechnic reception had a superior air about her as she looked at Morwenna through silver spectacles. 'You've come for the life model job?' Weary after walking farther in the last few hours than she would normally in a week, Morwenna glanced around to see if there was a seat. There wasn't. The other pulled out a file and leafed through it. 'Do you have any experience?'

Morwenna said she hadn't and asked what the work consisted of.

The secretary sniffed. 'Where did you hear about the job?'

Her very accent spoke of disdain. Morwenna bristled with resentment. She hesitated, then determined not to be put off she stared back at her without smiling: 'I saw the advertisement in *The Tatler*.'

The other raised her eyebrows. 'Why don't you speak to Miss Farthingale?' She handed Morwenna a card and snapped the file shut.

* * *

Miss Farthingale, generally known as Stella, was the model supreme in charge of the other girls. She was tall with long legs and a flat bosom. Her hair was cropped close to her face and she wore blue drop earrings, which matched her eyes. She looked about twenty-five. Morwenna had caught her between sessions and they were drinking tea in the canteen. 'So you want a job at the college?' Stella asked after they had dispensed with the usual niceties.

'What do you have to do?' asked Morwenna.

'Nothing. You just lie there and keep still.'

'Lie where?'

'On the couch.'

'Oh.'

'Without any clothes on, of course.'

'What!'

Stella laughed. 'Didn't you know? God, you're innocent!' Her bangles jangled as she lifted her hand to her hair. 'It's all right. They leave you alone. They draw and paint to show the beauty of the female form. It's all very proper. They set up their drawing boards and easels, start measuring and fiddling with pencils. You just lie there and pretend you're somewhere else. Main thing is, they don't see you as a person. You're more a challenge – to their drawing skills. But you mustn't fidget or sneeze or make eye contact. That distracts them. Just act dead.'

Morwenna stared down at the ground.

'So d'you want to do it or not?'

Morwenna attempted to push away the voice of her father wheedling its way into her head. Stripping off had not been her idea of being a model. No wonder Pa had objected. No wonder Ma looked outraged at the suggestion. How naïve she'd been. How stupid. 'I'm not sure,' she said in a small voice.

In her tiredness her options veered about her like drunken companions: back to the drudgery of Hackney and Dukely's, out onto the streets to do goodness-knew-what or daring this strange world where the rules were unknown? She was paralysed with uncertainty. But the main thing, insisted an inner voice, was to keep herself and pay for singing lessons. With her head swimming she reached for the last of her tea.

'What you running away from?' Stella's eyes were cool and shrewd as she surveyed the newcomer.

'I jus' wanna job.' Morwenna whispered, causing the other to give a sly smile. Then she added, jutting out her chin. 'I'm going to be a singer.'

'Is that so?' Stella paused. 'You're very young, aren't you?' When Morwenna did not reply Stella continued to appraise her. 'You have an interesting face – dark, faraway eyes and beautiful wavy hair. You'd make an interesting model. You've got a foreign look.'

Morwenna started. She was used to people referring to her dark looks, the fact she was unlike her fair siblings, but coming from a complete stranger the words felt like an accusation. She'd always banked on her good looks to get by, but did she look so very different?

'So – do you want to give it a try? You need to make up your mind. There's a session coming up this evening. The usual model is sick. I could have a word with the tutor…'

Morwenna continued to stare at the floor. 'I wanna think about it,' she said finally. 'If it's like what you say… besides, what does it pay?'

'Don't think too long or someone else will snap up the opportunity. If you're interested come back at five. You get paid by the hour. One shilling.'

Morwenna gasped. Where she came from that was not bad money.

With a swoop Stella snatched up her bag and swirled out leaving a faint trail of expensive perfume. Morwenna was transfixed. Out on the street she walked towards the river. She watched the ruffled water of high tide and a laden barge passing under Chelsea Bridge. She took deep breaths. She'd run and now here she was, faced with a prickly choice. Oh how she yearned for the wider horizon, a more glamorous life, with glitter and music. Above all she wanted to sing. But taking off her clothes in front of strangers? Lying there, like a lump of meat, not meant to move? Her heart was racing. Was this where her restlessness was driving her? One thing she did know, lodged in her body with solid certainty: she was not going back to Hackney. Not yet at least.

She turned away from the Embankment. Maybe she could find other employment. A job, after all, was only the means to an end. She passed a teashop. In the window was a notice saying they needed a waitress. Inside it was bustling: steam, crowded tables, clattering crockery and a harassed, red-cheeked manager. 'I've come about the job,' Morwenna called out above the din. The manager eyed her between supervising two trays.

'It's gone already.'

Morwenna retreated and walked for another hour, hunting out possibilities. She was not going to be choosy. She was not an idler. She was willing to put her hand to anything. She tried more shops, whether or not they had cards announcing vacancies in the window. Harrison Hats was her last port of call. Here they were seeking a sales assistant. As she entered the dark premises she could smell beeswax polish. Cloche hats and other feathered extravaganzas delighted the eye in front of mahogany drawers and cupboards ranged from floor to ceiling. This was definitely a shop fit for ladies. Summoning courage, she asked about the vacancy.

The gaunt manager peered at her for a moment and said: 'No disrespect, but we need someone who knows how to deal with ladies.' Puzzled, Morwenna stared at the pale face above the frilled blouse. The manager's lips pursed with distaste. 'Someone who speaks the King's English.'

Mo reddened. At her elementary school they'd stressed the need to know one's place. It had always baffled her. Eyes smarting, she strode out letting the door bang shut behind her. She went back to the river. She'd show them. These pumped-up petty shopkeepers, these dames with social pretensions.

* * *

At five she was back in the college canteen and had told Stella of her decision. Stella said: 'I'll show you where to go and wait for you afterwards.'

Minutes later Morwenna found herself in the large, high-ceilinged art room just before the life class was due to start. Stella showed her where to put her clothes. Morwenna shivered with apprehension. 'Come on, cheer up. It's easy.' Morwenna nodded. 'No need to worry, the teacher will tell you what to do.'

Morwenna watched Stella depart, longing to call her back.

'I'm Gillingham,' said a gruff voice. Towering down, unsmiling and stern, was the teacher.

'I'm Morwenna.'

'You're new, aren't you?' She nodded. 'We start with short poses, ten minutes apiece, for the students to warm up. We use the sandglass so we don't forget the time. Then a longer pose, for about an hour. Now go and get ready.'

Morwenna chewed her lip.

She moved behind a Chinese screen. It had a red kimono slung over it for her to wear between poses. Slowly, with trembling fingers, she started to undress. She felt dizzy with trepidation. As she undid the remaining buttons of her cardigan, she made a mental plea to her father for understanding. The room was cold. She couldn't stop shivering. She let her skirt fall till it lay like a scrunched animal by her feet. She pulled down her camisole, which she noticed was a little grubby and wriggled out of her corset. Her shoulders contracted inwards in fear, in modesty. She slipped off her cami-knickers and stared at them, a tiny pink heap on top of her skirt, before she stepped out of them and drew the kimono round her.

The paraffin stove made a whirring noise. The heat it blasted out did not radiate as far as the sofa where she'd been told to drape herself. Suppressing a welter of misgivings, she stepped out from behind the screen. As she slid down onto the sofa she noticed goose pimples on the white of her arms. She drew the kimono tighter around her. 'Weren't cut out for this,' she muttered to herself.

Students drifted in, talking among themselves. She avoided looking at them directly but estimated that there were about ten in the class. The teacher was a man of around forty with a beard and a paint-smeared over-shirt. She glanced towards the students: mostly they were men in their twenties, some with beards, others clean-shaven. There was one female student in a smock, peering around through pebble spectacles. Easels clattered as students found themselves spots to work from.

'Right then,' said Gillingham. He came over and pulled a chair in front of the sofa. 'Sit on that.'

With a rush Morwenna let the kimono fall. She felt her body shrinking into itself and sat with arms and legs folded, as if for protection. He asked her to open her arms. 'Plant your feet more firmly on the ground. The main thing is to stay still. It's irksome if the model keeps moving.' Without looking at him she adjusted her position and stared down at the floor.

Pencils scratched on paper as the room shifted into absorbed activity. After ten minutes he told her to get up and stretch. He reached for the kimono under the sofa and handed it to her. For the next pose she had to stand with her back to the students, bent over the chair. Physically it was more challenging, but she was relieved to be facing away from them. After minutes her foot went numb and she had the urge to scratch her neck. She resisted, faint with the effort. Numbness turned to cramp in one leg, pins and needles assailed the arm draped over the chair. The teacher paced around the students, muttering and pausing now and then to offer a comment. For the long pose she made herself as comfortable as she could on the sofa and spread her arms and legs as he suggested. She closed her eyes, even dozed off and woke with a start, legs jerking. A student grunted with annoyance.

At the end of the class Gillingham came over, handed her the kimono. While she was getting dressed behind the screen she heard Stella enter and exchange a few words with him. Afterwards she and Stella went to the canteen.

'Gillingham was pleased. He wants you to sit again. But 'ow about you – will you do it again?' When Morwenna stared into her tea Stella piped up. 'Look, you gonna come clean with me or not?'

'I've been in dress-making. It's boring. I hate my boss. She's got it in for me.'

'So you just pitched up 'ere? You've got pluck at least.' She paused. 'You remind me of me – a while ago, mind. My skin's a bit tougher now.' She paused. 'Will you start tomorrow? I can sort it out with the office.'

Morwenna clenched her fists in determination. 'Alright then. If it's the same as today – just sitting there.'

'Where are you living?'

At this Morwenna felt a wave of helplessness. 'My family lives in 'ackney. I can't go back there. Not yet.'

'God 'elp us, you did take a gamble, didn't you?' Stella's eyes widened with a certain admiration. Her face, despite the powder and over-plucked eyebrows, was not unfriendly. 'My landlady lets models from the art college rent, as long as they keep their rooms clean and don't bring back gentlemen visitors.' She chuckled. 'Chance would be a fine thing. They never want to come near the place. She's such a miserable old crow.'

* * *

Later, when Stella was free to take her there, Morwenna met the old crow herself. Mrs Roberts eyed her with suspicion when she said she couldn't afford the deposit. Only when Stella, her most longstanding tenant, vouched for the newcomer, did the landlady sniff, rattle off the house rules and condescend to give Morwenna a key.

While Stella went out to meet a friend, Morwenna settled into the room. She stared at the faded wallpaper where stains, springing from years of damp and neglect, formed strange, unmapped continents on the walls. She spread out her meagre belongings: a few undergarments, a couple of frocks and a favourite cardigan. In the backyard cats were shrieking. The sounds unnerved her. She lay on the sagging mattress. Better this than doubled up over a clacking sewing machine, she told herself. It was just a job, she kept telling herself, the first step she needed to make. Yet tears of doubt and confusion were swimming in her eyes. She pulled out *The Tatler,* now crumpled, and smoothed out the page advertising singing lessons.

Chapter Six

The next day she turned up as agreed and sat for four sessions. She did the same for the rest of the week; by Friday she was getting into a rhythm. She had almost stopped thinking about what she was doing. When she posed she entered another world where the students existed behind an invisible wall. One evening she was lingering over tea in the scullery at her digs in Riverton Road. Stella breezed in, all smiles, her fringe twirled in a curling rag, cold cream on her face. 'You look in need of a little uplift. Why not come to the party tonight?'

Morwenna was taken aback. 'Party?'

'One of the students is throwing it. Do you good. Chance to meet a few people.'

'I'm not sure…' Morwenna could hardly admit how numb she was feeling. Time and again she'd been on the point of returning home. She looked at Stella's puzzled expression then said: 'A party sounds fine.' She should at least try and act the part.

They went to their rooms to get themselves ready. Morwenna was still preening herself when Stella appeared. She had put on far too much powder and rouge so she looked like a screen star, only the fluttering eyelashes were missing. Standing near Stella made Morwenna realise how shabby her own clothes were. 'You can't go out looking like that,' said Stella matter-of-factly. 'Now let me see, you're a bit shorter than me but I've got just the thing.' Morwenna bridled but said nothing. Stella disappeared into her room and came back with a blue shift that shimmered as it moved. 'It'll look tiptop on you.' Morwenna could not help smiling: never had she seen anything so delicate. It reminded her of Ma's faded frocks in the wardrobe. 'And something else…' Stella moved forward and dabbed rouge onto her cheeks. 'You look too wan. Never catch a man that way. They'll say you got consumption.'

The venue was several streets away in the better part of Fulham. The tall Georgian house with railings, gleaming dark blue front door and window boxes belonged to a student's parents, away on vacation in the south of France. Stella banged down the brass lion-head doorknocker. 'Just watch me, don't say too much and don't get drunk.' When Morwenna's eyes grew round Stella laughed. 'Only joking. I'm not your bleedin' chaperone. Do as you damn well please. I always do!'

'Ah Stella! Come in. Come in.' The host ushered them in. Voices clashed and clamoured about them as they made their way through. The sitting-room, cleared of furniture, had a large parquet floor beneath a gleaming chandelier. Electricity! Incandescence. The modern era. In Hackney they still made do with gas lamps and candles. She looked up at the sparkle of crystal: never had she seen anything so luxurious. All the glowing gaslights in The Mare's Head were no match for a single bulb here. People were standing in gaggles, laughing and drinking.

'May I have the pleasure?' A young man was holding out his hand to her. 'Come on. It's the Foxtrot. Jazzed up a bit.'

He caught hold of her hand and pulled her onto the dance area.

The music picked up and soon Morwenna let it take over. She had a natural sense of rhythm, said her friends, whenever they ventured to the Hackney Empire. Now she and her dance partner were swinging to the insistent beat.

'I love this Negro jazz,' he said.

She smiled, not sure how to respond. She grew breathless as they swung and kept turning around between countless other couples. After the next number they paused. The gramophone, which had been blasting out the horn and trumpet of New Orleans music, grew silent. Someone was tinkling on the upright piano in the far corner. '*The roses of Picardy*' cut through the air. She stood stock-still. She knew this song. She started humming. Glimpses of other times and places flitted through her mind, a resonance she could not put words to. All at once she felt at ease. At the chorus she sang out loud and clear. She sang as though the vision conjured up by the words was real to her.

> *'Roses are shining in Picardy, in the hush of the silver dew,*
> *Roses are flowering in Picardy, but there's never a rose like you!*
> *And the roses will die in the summertime and our roads may be far apart,*
> *But there's one rose that dies not in Picardy,*
> *'Tis the rose that I keep in my heart'.*

Her dance partner was mesmerised, unable to take his eyes off her. The party-goers hushed to hear her. 'What a voice!' he said when she stopped. 'It soars like a boy soprano in a cathedral, but has the sensual feel of cabaret. I've heard the *Roses of Picardy* before, but never sung like that.'

She said nothing, moved by his words. 'I should be going,' she said quietly.

'Can I see you home?'

'I don't know you.'

'But still, may I have the pleasure?' He held up his arm and gave her a gentle smile. 'Or perhaps another dance?'

He looked over his shoulder as the gramophone music started up again, its loud tones in marked contrast to the piano. She hesitated. Never had anyone appreciated her voice as he had. She wanted to cling to the moment. 'Just one then.' They danced and he brought her a pink gin and then another. She searched out Stella and tapped her shoulder. 'I'm off.' Stella who was knocking back champagne cocktails and flirting with three young men, waved her arm.

'See you later.'

Morwenna headed towards the front door, followed by her admirer. They slipped out into the street where the party became a background hum.

'What's your name?' he asked.

She hesitated. Morwenna was the name from childhood. A fanciful name, some said; a name chosen by her mother, she suspected, for its theatrical flamboyance. The girls in the workshop had always called her Mo. That had verve and suggested independence. 'Mo,' she said brightly. 'And yours?'

'Derek.'

'You look familiar,' she said.

'You certainly do. You're our life model!'

She stuck her chin out, feeling vulnerable all over again. 'So you're an artist, are you?'

He shrugged. 'I have a long way to go.'

'How come? I thought you was either an artist or not.'

'I started out making stage sets but painting is my true passion.'

They walked towards the river.

'Where do you live?'

'I'm staying with Stella.'

'Aha. She rules the girls. Bit like a madam.'

'A what?' She had once heard smutty talk of madames in Paris brothels while serving in the bar.

'No offence meant,' he said hurriedly 'I was joking.'

'Dare say.'

'You're not used to all that, are you?' He paused. 'How old are you?'

'That's a cheeky question.'

'Let me guess.' He eyed her from the side. 'Not a day over sixteen, I'd say.'

She felt like a snail without its shell. 'I'm seventeen. And you?'

'I'm twenty-three.'

'Oh, quite the man then.'

He laughed. 'But you don't live with your family?'

She sniffed. 'Not right now, I don't.'

'You look like a frightened deer. The moment I saw you, draped on that couch. You had a fugitive air. A beautiful creature from the wild.' Before she could stop him he took hold of her hand. The grip was firm, reassuring and unsettling, all at once. She went to draw her hand away but he held it tighter. 'I'd give the world to capture that – that essence. And when you sang… there is something about you…' He dropped her hand and she felt suddenly bereft. 'Do you have singing lessons?'

She hesitated to tell him of her ambitions or how poor her family was. 'I'd love to…' she said quietly.

'Your voice is magic.'

As they turned the corner to the next street a dustbin lid rattled onto the ground. Light glinted here and there on the Chelsea Bridge, on the water. The breeze wafted into her face, she breathed in the smell of the river. They walked along the embankment. A launch chugged by, exuding smoke. Fairy lights gleamed from a pleasure launch heading towards the other bank. She caught the sound of a melodeon and voices raised in chorus. 'Would you sit for me?' he said. 'Privately, I mean. I share a studio with a friend.'

'I got my job at the Polytechnic.'

'This would be different. I'd pay you of course. Believe me, there is something about you…'

She was perplexed. She was two people: her father's daughter, retreating in panic, and a bold stranger, who scared the breath out of her. 'I have to go,' she said.

Chapter Seven

Mo sent a picture postcard home, omitting her address. She wrote that she had a job in a shop and would visit when she could. She recalled Pa's reaction when she'd declared her intention to model. Dropping the card into the battered post-box, she felt treacherous.

Stella invited her to another party. Stella, it seemed, knew many people. When at rest Stella's jaw was set, as though awaiting a blow. 'Don't be a stick-in-the-mud,' she said when Mo pleaded the need for a night in. They were in Stella's room, which was larger than Mo's and brighter. She held up a blouse. 'Try it on.' Mo gazed at the diaphanous green garment, redolent of waving grass.

'It's beautiful. Don't you need it?'

Stella shrugged. 'Reminds me of a time I'd rather forget.'

'Oh, what's that then?'

'There's always a man, ain't there, at the bottom of everything? And an artist to boot.' Stella was such a vibrant creature. She dropped hints of famous artists and their movements, of the circles she had moved in. 'Of course, he joined that lot in Bloomsbury eventually.' As she muttered about his bread buttered on both sides and ingratitude and him losing his way, Mo struggled to keep up with her.

She handed it to Mo. 'Here, take it. Time I moved on.' Curious, Mo fingered the blouse. Knowing it had a history Mo thought she might not wear it, but when she tried it on she changed her mind. She wore the green blouse to the party.

Derek, among the guests, took one look at her across the room and was by her side. 'Have you considered my request?'

He was leaning over her, his crop of dark hair getting into his eyes and giving him an unkempt look.

'Maybe I have, maybe I haven't.'

Truth was, she had thought of little else. Instinctively she was wary of Derek: there was something intense about him. Yet the shadow of melancholy about him made him alluring. Stella let slip that he was pining: Zara, his former lover and an ex-model, had taken up with a Hungarian artist. Devastated, he drank himself stupid. But when he offered her claret cup from a large bowl in the shape of a shell she threw him a coquettish sideways glance and forgot what Stella had told her.

* * *

The studio was a grand name for a moderate space beneath the skylight in a rundown house in Fulham. 'This is a studio? Looks more like a loft to me,' she said cheerily.

Derek shrugged. 'Belongs to a sort of friend. He teaches at Chelsea sometimes.' As he busied himself setting up the easel he told her how he ran a shop for a living, but how painting pulled at him like a tide. 'It's simple,' he said. 'If I don't do it, I cease to exist.' She gave a smile. Despite the wildness, despite the drive he exuded, there was something unguarded about him.

He pointed to a corner with a makeshift screen. 'You can put your clothes behind there.' She disappeared behind the two easels draped with sheets, and undressed. Her hands were shaking. She looked down at her pale body and was seized with shame. He wanted to paint her. Sensing the ferocity of his intention made her real. Never before had she felt so real. Yet she lingered, unable to stand before him. Yesterday this had seemed a good idea, Derek had seemed a good idea – two minutes ago even. Now she was not so sure. She stripped down to her cami-knickers.

'I'm waiting,' he said quietly.

She inhaled deeply and stepped into view. He said nothing,

consuming her with his eyes. She was glad she was not totally naked. She moved across to the sofa and plunged down onto it. He frowned, examined the paper attached to his easel and started sketching. He worked in silence and she began to breathe again.

'You have the look of a pre-Raphaelite,' he murmured after a few minutes.

'What are you talking about?'

'You've never heard of them, have you?' He handed her a dressing gown. 'Why don't you take a break now? I'll show you some of their pictures.'

In a niche of battered sofas and chairs was a table piled with old tomes. They sat together on the sofa and he opened one of the books. He flicked through the pages and there, page after page, were women with copious locks set against stone walls and casements. They had a faraway look as though they belonged elsewhere.

'Tell me about your shop.'

He sighed and leaned back, away from her. 'That's about earning a living.' This she understood: survival had been drummed into her since infancy. She felt his gaze on her face. 'You've woken something in me.' He brushed her arm gently with his fingers. 'I knew it as soon as I saw you.'

She shifted away from him. 'Tell me about your scenery painting. You mentioned that before,' she said quickly.

'I enjoyed it but I wanted to follow my own ideas. I started creating sets to escape what my father had in mind for me.'

'I see.' That, too, she understood.

'Back to business,' he clapped his hands. 'Arrange yourself on the sofa again.'

She stretched herself out. With a glare of concentration he was measuring her proportions with the aid of a cardboard frame. Nobody had ever looked at her with such focus. She heard the sound of the pencil on the paper. Her flesh tingled.

He scratched over the page, began another sheet, scrutinised her again. Minutes ticked by. She wondered when he would stop. It seemed he might go on forever. He reached across and touched her arm. 'May I?' He eased it forward. She felt a rush of anxiety, whereas he looked calm. He took up the pencil again. He murmured something she did not catch. Again he plied the page, frowned, cast aside the pencil. 'Enough.'

His eyes were grave. She grew afraid. 'Can I get dressed now? I'm cold.' He came towards her, knelt down by the sofa. She could feel the warm breath on her shoulder. So gently she could barely sense it, he touched the curve of her breast.

'Like a doe in the light of morning …' he murmured. She edged away. He had a stricken look as though she had cut him with some sarcasm. 'Will you be my love?'

'Your girl, you mean?'

'Yes, if you want to call it that.'

His hand on her arm was burning. She looked at his crumpled shirt, the wasted cheeks and blue shadows hovering around his eyes. 'I'm not sure…'

He sighed and moved back. 'Let me take you out for a drink, at least.' He stood up, lifted a rough blanket from an easy chair and covered her. The blanket smelled dank. He touched her cheek with the flat of his hand then drew her to her feet, the blanket still between them. She could not trust herself to speak.

'Well?'

'Not such a good idea,' she managed to whisper.

Chapter Eight

After her last session the next day Mo found Derek hanging around in the corridor, pretending to look at pictures. 'I've come to take you out.'

'Have you indeed?' she replied. 'How do you know I'm free?'

'Well, are you?'

'Depends where you want to take me?'

'For a walk, then I have a surprise.' He linked his arm through hers, drawing a modicum of curiosity from one or two students who were putting away their drawing materials. Outside it was blustery, sunshine coming in snatches between metal-grey clouds. They headed towards the Embankment. 'I want to make amends,' he said. 'It occurred to me I should slow down a bit.'

'I don't know what you're talking about.' He grunted as if to say it was useless to explain. They watched a boat chug by on the river. He fell silent while she became aware of their feet sounding in unison on the pavement. 'Here it is!'

'What?'

She gasped. It was Harrison Hats. In the window was a creation of net, feathers and felt sprouting in hues of blue and green like a bird of paradise.

'Blimey – what a creation!'

They went in and Derek asked the manager to fetch the hat from the window. Recognising Mo from days before, the woman struggled to contain her bafflement. Mo suppressed a giggle as she tried the hat on, viewing it from one side then the other in the tinted looking glass. 'Thank you, that's all for now' said Derek, unaware of the covert glances passing between the two women. He whispered in Mo's ear: 'That's just to whet your appetite. Now for my surprise.'

Mo threw a look of triumph over her shoulder as the disgruntled manager was left to rearrange the hat in the display window. They boarded the next bus heading north. Mo tingled with excitement, happy to be led on, willing to let things unfold as they would. From the top deck she watched the passing pageant of London's streets, taking in every corner, every blotched plane tree, and when they arrived in Kentish Town and stood before Fingal's Cave her excitement mounted.

It was decorated purple and red, Oriental hues that were all the rage; colourful stained-glass panels hung in the windows and a sign read: Turbans and sashes, gowns and bows and veils, broideries of intricate design. 'From the stage play, *Hassan*,' he explained as he unlocked the door.

They stepped into the dark interior. The space was adorned with Turkish rugs and silk throws on the sofas between rows of clothes; intricate filigree lanterns were fixed on the walls. 'Oh my – it's the cat's meow!' she exclaimed, echoing something she'd heard Stella say. 'It reminds me of Aladdin's Cave.'

'It's shut as it's Wednesday. And my assistant's not here. So we can play!' He wasted no time, fetching hats with plumes and a flowing cape, which he flourished before her. 'The finest array for the most beautiful girl in the world.' She chuckled at the excess. Already he was pulling at her jacket to make way for the cape. He put a hat on her head. It had a black veil. 'Too serious,' he said and whipped it away. Instead he placed a feathered blue and green hat similar to the one in Harrison's. 'Perfect!'

Once it was on her head she did not want to part with it. Though she had no idea of when and where she might wear it, she adored it. While she was still admiring it, Derek fetched a frock from the rail. It was the prettiest garment she had ever seen. It was sea green with silver beads sewn into the bodice. 'It's all yours,' he said. It crossed her mind that she should not be allowing this, but she was too intoxicated to stop. 'Try it on,' he said, and indicated an Indian sandalwood screen to change behind.

When she emerged his eyes lit with admiration. He held out his hands to her. 'You should dress like this every day.' She clasped them, excited, aroused, yet suddenly fearful. He pulled her towards him so she felt the length of his body against hers; his arms were around her, enfolding her.

'I must go,' she said.

'Yes,' he said, as though remembering himself. 'Let me wrap them for you.' He stood back and fetched a sheet of brown paper.

'I can't…'

'They're yours, all yours. Please. You can't be a singer and dress like a …' He hesitated, seeing her confusion. 'Tomorrow?' he said. 'Can I see you tomorrow?'

'Yes,' she said hurriedly, not giving herself time to consider. He brushed her cheek with his lips.

When she got back to her digs she ran with delight up the steps. During the night she switched on the light at intervals to check that the hat and frock were still where she'd hung them in full view. They reminded her of Ma's Music Hall outfit.

In the morning she woke to birdsong in the privet hedges. She sang to herself as she dressed. The eyes shining back at her from the cracked bathroom mirror gleamed with boldness. Later, as she posed in the life class, the hands on the clock hardly moved and the students seemed sluggish. The tutor sauntered over at the end of the session: 'Some of us are going to the pub. Care to join us?'

'Another time,' she said breezily. 'Today I am busy.' Mildly piqued, he walked away without another word. Derek was in the corridor. He was holding his hands behind his back. When the others had gone he presented her with a bunch of lilacs. She laughed and put it to her nose. It smelled of country lanes. 'How divine!' she uttered – sounding like Stella – and placed them with care at the bottom of her basket.

'Do you fancy a boat ride? We can catch one to the Tower from Chelsea Bridge.'

'What fun! I never been on a boat.'

They approached the boat pier where a boat was just leaving. They hastened aboard. From the upper deck they watched seagulls wheeling in from the sea as the boat cast off, thrusting out beige, foam-flecked water. Derek put his lips to her ear. 'I am the happiest fellow in the world.' He kissed her neck. Flustered, she pulled back.

A man with a megaphone commented on the sights they passed. As they eyed the dark hulk of Westminster Palace, Big Ben rang out the hour. Further east, the guide stressed the importance of the docks. He detailed the goods passing through the Port of London, listing quantities of Indian tea and Malayan rubber. For a moment she was wistful.

'What's the matter?'

'I was thinking of me dad, that's all. He was a docker.'

'You never told me that.'

'Now he runs a pub.'

'Once a docker, but not anymore. That's unusual.'

'You're right. It runs in families. But 'e was injured. Stumbled under a heavy load, Ma said, and ended up in hospital. And that was that. Ma said 'e was lucky. They gave him something from the Benefit Club. Not much, but Ma persuaded him to try something else...'

'Must've been hard for him.' Derek leaned over the railing, head bent towards the churning water. 'I hated my old man with a vengeance. At least I thought I did. When he went, though, I was broken.'

'He died?'

Derek nodded. 'Missed him like hell then. Wished… that I'd got to know him…' He sighed and watched a barge pass by laden with coal, black smoke billowing from behind. He turned to look at her. 'You never told me your story.'

'What story?'

'How you ended up in Chelsea.' He pulled her round to face him.

She hesitated. 'I want to sing…' she began.

'And so you shall, I'm sure of it.'

'I've got no one to help me…'

'Where's your family? You do *have* a family?'

'Don't everyone?' She was fumbling in her mind.

He laughed. 'Some choose to lose theirs. But that wouldn't be you.' She gazed into the water. 'So, where are they? You're young, aren't you, to be living away from home?' He was beginning to sound like her father. She felt some of the fizz go out of her. 'Did you leave after a quarrel?'

'No.'

'Then?'

She looked at him, his dark eyes were glowing with curiosity. The sun caught the side of his face, sculpting the cheek. She felt herself leaning towards him. 'I told them I wanted to be a model – for the money like. They said I couldn't. So I just took off.'

'How long ago?'

'Oh, days ago.'

'And they have no idea where you are?'

'I sent them a card. It's all the same to them. They don't care.'

'I'm sure they do.'

She was on the verge of tears. 'They think I should be like them. And I'm not. Never have been…' He kissed the top of her head. She stayed nuzzled against him as they drew near the

Tower of London. The boat slowed down.

'You think I should go back and see them then?' she murmured into his chest.

'At least they'd know you were alive and well. They'd stop worrying.'

Chapter Five *Morwenna*

The secretary at the Chelsea Polytechnic reception had a superior air about her as she looked at Morwenna through silver spectacles. 'You've come for the life model job?' Weary after walking farther in the last few hours than she would normally in a week, Morwenna glanced around to see if there was a seat. There wasn't. The other pulled out a file and leafed through it. 'Do you have any experience?'

Morwenna said she hadn't and asked what the work consisted of.

The secretary sniffed. 'Where did you hear about the job?'

Her very accent spoke of disdain. Morwenna bristled with resentment. She hesitated, then determined not to be put off she stared back at her without smiling: 'I saw the advertisement in *The Tatler*.'

The other raised her eyebrows. 'Why don't you speak to Miss Farthingale?' She handed Morwenna a card and snapped the file shut.

* * *

Miss Farthingale, generally known as Stella, was the model supreme in charge of the other girls. She was tall with long legs and a flat bosom. Her hair was cropped close to her face and she wore blue drop earrings, which matched her eyes. She looked about twenty-five. Morwenna had caught her between sessions and they were drinking tea in the canteen. 'So you want a job at the college?' Stella asked after they had dispensed with the usual niceties.

'What do you have to do?' asked Morwenna.

'Nothing. You just lie there and keep still.'

'Lie where?'

'On the couch.'

'Oh.'

'Without any clothes on, of course.'

'What!'

Stella laughed. 'Didn't you know? God, you're innocent!' Her bangles jangled as she lifted her hand to her hair. 'It's all right. They leave you alone. They draw and paint to show the beauty of the female form. It's all very proper. They set up their drawing boards and easels, start measuring and fiddling with pencils. You just lie there and pretend you're somewhere else. Main thing is, they don't see you as a person. You're more a challenge – to their drawing skills. But you mustn't fidget or sneeze or make eye contact. That distracts them. Just act dead.'

Morwenna stared down at the ground.

'So d'you want to do it or not?'

Morwenna attempted to push away the voice of her father wheedling its way into her head. Stripping off had not been her idea of being a model. No wonder Pa had objected. No wonder Ma looked outraged at the suggestion. How naïve she'd been. How stupid. 'I'm not sure,' she said in a small voice.

In her tiredness her options veered about her like drunken companions: back to the drudgery of Hackney and Dukely's, out onto the streets to do goodness-knew-what or daring this strange world where the rules were unknown? She was paralysed with uncertainty. But the main thing, insisted an inner voice, was to keep herself and pay for singing lessons. With her head swimming she reached for the last of her tea.

'What you running away from?' Stella's eyes were cool and shrewd as she surveyed the newcomer.

'I jus' wanna job.' Morwenna whispered, causing the other to give a sly smile. Then she added, jutting out her chin. 'I'm going to be a singer.'

'Is that so?' Stella paused. 'You're very young, aren't you?' When Morwenna did not reply Stella continued to appraise her. 'You have an interesting face – dark, faraway eyes and beautiful wavy hair. You'd make an interesting model. You've got a foreign look.'

Morwenna started. She was used to people referring to her dark looks, the fact she was unlike her fair siblings, but coming from a complete stranger the words felt like an accusation. She'd always banked on her good looks to get by, but did she look so very different?

'So – do you want to give it a try? You need to make up your mind. There's a session coming up this evening. The usual model is sick. I could have a word with the tutor…'

Morwenna continued to stare at the floor. 'I wanna think about it,' she said finally. 'If it's like what you say… besides, what does it pay?'

'Don't think too long or someone else will snap up the opportunity. If you're interested come back at five. You get paid by the hour. One shilling.'

Morwenna gasped. Where she came from that was not bad money.

With a swoop Stella snatched up her bag and swirled out leaving a faint trail of expensive perfume. Morwenna was transfixed. Out on the street she walked towards the river. She watched the ruffled water of high tide and a laden barge passing under Chelsea Bridge. She took deep breaths. She'd run and now here she was, faced with a prickly choice. Oh how she yearned for the wider horizon, a more glamorous life, with glitter and music. Above all she wanted to sing. But taking off her clothes in front of strangers? Lying there, like a lump of meat, not meant to move? Her heart was racing. Was this where her restlessness was driving her? One thing she did know, lodged in her body with solid certainty: she was not going back to Hackney. Not yet at least.

She turned away from the Embankment. Maybe she could find other employment. A job, after all, was only the means to an end. She passed a teashop. In the window was a notice saying they needed a waitress. Inside it was bustling: steam, crowded tables, clattering crockery and a harassed, red-cheeked manager. 'I've come about the job,' Morwenna called out above the din. The manager eyed her between supervising two trays.

'It's gone already.'

Morwenna retreated and walked for another hour, hunting out possibilities. She was not going to be choosy. She was not an idler. She was willing to put her hand to anything. She tried more shops, whether or not they had cards announcing vacancies in the window. Harrison Hats was her last port of call. Here they were seeking a sales assistant. As she entered the dark premises she could smell beeswax polish. Cloche hats and other feathered extravaganzas delighted the eye in front of mahogany drawers and cupboards ranged from floor to ceiling. This was definitely a shop fit for ladies. Summoning courage, she asked about the vacancy.

The gaunt manager peered at her for a moment and said: 'No disrespect, but we need someone who knows how to deal with ladies.' Puzzled, Morwenna stared at the pale face above the frilled blouse. The manager's lips pursed with distaste. 'Someone who speaks the King's English.'

Mo reddened. At her elementary school they'd stressed the need to know one's place. It had always baffled her. Eyes smarting, she strode out letting the door bang shut behind her. She went back to the river. She'd show them. These pumped-up petty shopkeepers, these dames with social pretensions.

* * *

At five she was back in the college canteen and had told Stella of her decision. Stella said: 'I'll show you where to go and wait for you afterwards.'

57

Minutes later Morwenna found herself in the large, high-ceilinged art room just before the life class was due to start. Stella showed her where to put her clothes. Morwenna shivered with apprehension. 'Come on, cheer up. It's easy.' Morwenna nodded. 'No need to worry, the teacher will tell you what to do.'

Morwenna watched Stella depart, longing to call her back.

'I'm Gillingham,' said a gruff voice. Towering down, unsmiling and stern, was the teacher.

'I'm Morwenna.'

'You're new, aren't you?' She nodded. 'We start with short poses, ten minutes apiece, for the students to warm up. We use the sandglass so we don't forget the time. Then a longer pose, for about an hour. Now go and get ready.'

Morwenna chewed her lip.

She moved behind a Chinese screen. It had a red kimono slung over it for her to wear between poses. Slowly, with trembling fingers, she started to undress. She felt dizzy with trepidation. As she undid the remaining buttons of her cardigan, she made a mental plea to her father for understanding. The room was cold. She couldn't stop shivering. She let her skirt fall till it lay like a scrunched animal by her feet. She pulled down her camisole, which she noticed was a little grubby and wriggled out of her corset. Her shoulders contracted inwards in fear, in modesty. She slipped off her cami-knickers and stared at them, a tiny pink heap on top of her skirt, before she stepped out of them and drew the kimono round her.

The paraffin stove made a whirring noise. The heat it blasted out did not radiate as far as the sofa where she'd been told to drape herself. Suppressing a welter of misgivings, she stepped out from behind the screen. As she slid down onto the sofa she noticed goose pimples on the white of her arms. She drew the kimono tighter around her. 'Weren't cut out for this,' she muttered to herself.

Students drifted in, talking among themselves. She avoided looking at them directly but estimated that there were about ten in the class. The teacher was a man of around forty with a beard and a paint-smeared over-shirt. She glanced towards the students: mostly they were men in their twenties, some with beards, others clean-shaven. There was one female student in a smock, peering around through pebble spectacles. Easels clattered as students found themselves spots to work from.

'Right then,' said Gillingham. He came over and pulled a chair in front of the sofa. 'Sit on that.'

With a rush Morwenna let the kimono fall. She felt her body shrinking into itself and sat with arms and legs folded, as if for protection. He asked her to open her arms. 'Plant your feet more firmly on the ground. The main thing is to stay still. It's irksome if the model keeps moving.' Without looking at him she adjusted her position and stared down at the floor.

Pencils scratched on paper as the room shifted into absorbed activity. After ten minutes he told her to get up and stretch. He reached for the kimono under the sofa and handed it to her. For the next pose she had to stand with her back to the students, bent over the chair. Physically it was more challenging, but she was relieved to be facing away from them. After minutes her foot went numb and she had the urge to scratch her neck. She resisted, faint with the effort. Numbness turned to cramp in one leg, pins and needles assailed the arm draped over the chair. The teacher paced around the students, muttering and pausing now and then to offer a comment. For the long pose she made herself as comfortable as she could on the sofa and spread her arms and legs as he suggested. She closed her eyes, even dozed off and woke with a start, legs jerking. A student grunted with annoyance.

At the end of the class Gillingham came over, handed her the kimono. While she was getting dressed behind the screen she heard Stella enter and exchange a few words with him. Afterwards she and Stella went to the canteen.

'Gillingham was pleased. He wants you to sit again. But 'ow about you – will you do it again?' When Morwenna stared into her tea Stella piped up. 'Look, you gonna come clean with me or not?'

'I've been in dress-making. It's boring. I hate my boss. She's got it in for me.'

'So you just pitched up 'ere? You've got pluck at least.' She paused. 'You remind me of me – a while ago, mind. My skin's a bit tougher now.' She paused. 'Will you start tomorrow? I can sort it out with the office.'

Morwenna clenched her fists in determination. 'Alright then. If it's the same as today – just sitting there.'

'Where are you living?'

At this Morwenna felt a wave of helplessness. 'My family lives in 'ackney. I can't go back there. Not yet.'

'God 'elp us, you did take a gamble, didn't you?' Stella's eyes widened with a certain admiration. Her face, despite the powder and over-plucked eyebrows, was not unfriendly. 'My landlady lets models from the art college rent, as long as they keep their rooms clean and don't bring back gentlemen visitors.' She chuckled. 'Chance would be a fine thing. They never want to come near the place. She's such a miserable old crow.'

* * *

Later, when Stella was free to take her there, Morwenna met the old crow herself. Mrs Roberts eyed her with suspicion when she said she couldn't afford the deposit. Only when Stella, her most longstanding tenant, vouched for the newcomer, did the landlady sniff, rattle off the house rules and condescend to give Morwenna a key.

While Stella went out to meet a friend, Morwenna settled into the room. She stared at the faded wallpaper where stains, springing from years of damp and neglect, formed strange, unmapped continents on the walls. She spread out her meagre belongings: a few undergarments, a couple of frocks and a favourite cardigan. In the backyard cats were shrieking. The sounds unnerved her. She lay on the sagging mattress. Better this than doubled up over a clacking sewing machine, she told herself. It was just a job, she kept telling herself, the first step she needed to make. Yet tears of doubt and confusion were swimming in her eyes. She pulled out *The Tatler,* now crumpled, and smoothed out the page advertising singing lessons.

Chapter Nine

Days later she took his advice. It was a Saturday and she had no work. She dressed carefully – no rouge and powder today – and tied her hair back so she became the picture of respectability. As the tram rattled the last few stations before her stop she kept looking out onto the street, reassured that all was as it had been but disappointed, too, that nothing had changed. As she came into the bar she saw Ma wiping down the counter. Pa was calling up from the cellar.

Hearing her footsteps her mother looked up. 'You! Where the blazes 'ave you been?' Mo went to give her a hug but Ma moved out of the way towards the back door. 'Look what the cat dragged in!' she yelled. 'She's back. Morwenna's back!'

Then came the rushed, heavy tread of her father's steps. 'So there you are!'

'What 'ave you been up to?' Ma looked her up and down. 'What got into you to take off without a word? Good mind to beat the living daylights out of you.'

'Hush now, Maisy,' said her father. 'We was worried sick, we was,' he said. 'I went looking for you. We was about to go to the police. Two days I spent wandering up and down… then your card came.'

'You never.'

'Where's your bag?' asked Ma.

'Don't have one.'

'So where are your things?'

Mo brushed the question away and walked through to the back of the pub. Her parents followed. 'Where's Tilda?' she asked.

'Out with friends.'

'Can I have a cuppa?' asked Mo, seeking distraction.

'It'll have to be quick,' said Dad. 'We're due to open and there's no-one in except us today. Unless you want to help?' In the scullery Ma put the kettle on and Mo settled into the easy chair by the range. Her heart beat erratically as her parents stared at her in bemusement. She scrambled for the stories she'd concocted for them.

'That surprises me,' responded Dad when he heard her yarn about working in a milliner's. 'As a rule they only want girls that speak proper. To deal with all the ladies what come in.' Mo went a pale shade of pink.

'Jus' thought I'd come and let you know. Sorry if you was worried about me.'

'You're under-age, don't forget. You should've asked our say-so. Barely seventeen and off you go, swanning down the West End. Anything could've 'appened to you. Anything. A good 'iding is what you need.'

'Ma, don't.' As the words whipped across her, Mo bit back her frustration. She watched Ma pushing the tea things together in readiness to go back to the pub. Her mouth was a straight line giving nothing away. Either she would never understand or understood only too well, and vowed to stand in Mo's way.

'So when are you moving back home?' asked Ma.

'Not yet.'

'Not good enough for you now, is it?'

'Oh Ma.'

'Well, what's the problem?'

'I wanted to save a bit first.'

'Save? 'Ow much are your digs then?'

Mo got up and moved towards the bar. She was getting twisted in knots. Already, after half an hour back home, she felt leaden: the place was hemming her in. She should have known not to argue the economics of it, which did not make sense anyway. Her life in Chelsea became improbable: a dream spun out of her desire for difference, as flimsy as fluff. Though Ma was furious with her for making the break, when it came to common sense and practicality, she had a point.

That evening Mo helped out in the bar. It became crowded after nine, when the beer and talk flowed. She was enveloped in a warm fug of banter and good humour. The regulars were pleased to see her and asked her what she'd been up to. Later, when there was a sing-along round Dora's joanna, she joined in. After a couple of sherries she forgot that a short while before she had been feeling out of place. That night she slept as always in the old box room next to Tilda, who kept hugging her and plying her with questions. Long after her younger sister had fallen asleep, Mo lay awake, letting sounds from the street drift over her like a tide of tepid water.

Sunday was always a quiet day except for the bells down Mare Street, summoning people to church. Already Mo was up and dressed. She wanted to get back to Derek. Now she knew that all was well in Hackney and that her parents were assured she had not been whisked off into the white slave trade, she longed to pick up where she had left off. She sat in the scullery, staring out over the backyard, evading Ma's penetrating gaze.

'Sounds too good to be true,' said Ma.

'What does?'

'A job in a milliner's, digs in a decent house.'

'These things 'appen.'

'Do they? Not in my day they didn't.'

'Things have changed.'

'Wouldn't be too sure about that.'

'I need to go now.'

'I thought you was staying for dinner? Cissie and Bob are coming over, and bringing Ted.'

Since when did Cissy and Bob want her company? Cissy

was always trying to show off in front of her and now Bob would be cagey in front of the family, knowing Mo could drop him in it if she chose. Yet part of her longed to bring everyone together round the table. Besides, she had not seen her nephew in ages.

A couple of hours later the clan assembled. The kitchen table was crowded and Tilda sidled too close, nudging her when she ate. The battered high-chair was pulled out for Ted, who was two and very active. Ma made a stew. There was too much fat on the meat and the rancid smell made her nauseous. She swallowed what she could. Ted banged his spoon on the high-chair and let it clatter to the floor. 'Stop that!' yelled Cissy. She yanked him out of the chair and paced up and down with him.

Mo looked round the table. Nobody was talking, nobody looking around as she was. Instead each focused on the plate in front of him, putting fork to mouth, fork to mouth. She had the urge to break the silence, to say something witty and sharp, as Stella might have done. Nothing occurred to her. Cissy returned to the table with Ted. Mo smiled at him and made her eyes go round, clicking them from side to side like a doll's. He went to grab a fistful of her hair.

'More stew anyone?' Ma peered into the saucepan. Tilda pushed her plate forward. Mo sank back into her chair. Ma had insisted she stay, yet not one of them expressed an iota of curiosity about her.

'Pudding?' asked Bert, rubbing his stomach.

'Get the biscuits, will you?' Ma sent Tilda off to the larder for the bag of Woolworths' broken biscuits.

Bert grunted. 'Is this the best we can manage?'

'Best I could do without Mo's money,' said Ma, while Bob was ogling Mo through heavy lids, a sly smile across his mouth.

'You're not going away again are you?' Tilda asked.

'Over my dead body,' said Ma. 'She stays here.'

Mo felt cold with anger. 'I'll do the washing-up.' She got to her feet and started piling up the plates.

'Give the girl a chance,' she heard her father say as she left the room. 'As long as what she is doing is decent...'

Bob and Cissy prepared to leave, gathering their things and saying they'd be round again in a few days. Ma came into the scullery where Mo was still washing the dishes. She stiffened as she felt her staring at her back. 'Fancy ideas you get sometimes,' Ma muttered.

Mo felt a constriction in her throat, her heart rapping in fear. She braced herself and turned round. 'Ma, please.' Ma's face was set, the mouth tight, only the eyes watered with something Mo could not quite grasp.

'You leave again and on your head be it. You won't be welcome back.' With that Ma strode out of the scullery leaving Mo on the brink of tears. She turned back to the sink, looked out through the smeared pane to the yard beyond. The door to the drayman's entrance was swinging open. It banged shut. The yard looked cramped and mean. She felt a knot in her throat. She could not stop now: she could not look into the beseeching eyes of her little sister, sense the trust mingled with fear in the eyes of her father, defend herself against her mother's fierceness. She threw down the drying up cloth and without further ado slipped out through the yard into the back alley and away.

That evening Derek called round to her digs. 'Fancy a drink?' The wind was ruffling his hair as he stood on the doorstep. 'Bit of a dragon, your landlady, wouldn't let me inside the door.'

'Shush! She's probably listening. Must 'ave decided you're up to no good.'

'I'm not.'

'There you go then.'

'Do I look like a philanderer?'

'A what?'

'A man who chases women.'

'Now you come to mention it…'

'You going to get your coat or what?'

She dashed back upstairs, heart brimming with joy at seeing him again. They settled on a nearby corner pub. It gleamed with globe lamps and a kaleidoscope of mirrors. 'What'll it be?' he asked.

'You choose. Give me another surprise.' He wended his way through jutting elbows and came back with two pints of Guinness. 'I'll never drink all that!'

'Wanna bet? Good for you. You're looking pale.' They sat in a corner with green leather sofas and an overhanging beaded lamp. She told him she'd been back to Hackney. 'They must have been pleased to see you,' he commented.

She was silent, finally sniffed and said: 'My ma was full of questions.'

'Do they know what you're doing?'

She sipped the Guinness and wiped the foam from her mouth. 'That's strong, ain't it? Like drinking soup.' The table in front of them was stacked with empty glasses. 'Not very good service in here,' she remarked.

'Well?'

'I told them about Stella and the digs and all.'

'And your work at the college?'

'Are you kidding? She would've belted me. Don't trust me an inch as it is.'

'So what did you tell them?'

'I spun some yarn.'

He pulled a packet of cigarettes from his pocket. 'Want one?'

'I'm fine. Enough coping with this, I'm not used to drinking.'

'I thought you grew up in a pub.'

'Put me off the stuff, the smell of it.'

'So do you feel better – after going home?'

She shrugged. 'Can we talk about something else?' He looked puzzled for a moment. She finished the rest of her beer and leaned back into the sofa, frowning. He had taken such pains with her, urging her to visit home and make peace with her family, and where had it got her?

He gazed at her without speaking, eyes growing moist. 'Will you come to Paris with me?'

'Paris?'

'Is that a yes or a no?'

'Yes, I will. I'd love to.'

Chapter Ten *Eleanor*

Derek's sister, Eleanor, had been working at Blundell's for nearly a decade. A small preparatory school run in a Georgian house near Regent's Park, it was one of the few London day schools that predated the Great War. Surprisingly, she was the longest serving of the staff and recognised by her colleagues as the most solid teacher.

Outside the headmaster's study she adjusted the neckline of her safe, beige frock before rapping on the oak door. 'Come in.' Roger Dawlish, MA (Oxon) was waiting for her. The headmaster was leaning back, hands entwined over his waist-coated belly, ensconced behind his mahogany desk on which she spotted a tome of Carlisle. His half-moon glasses were glinting across at her. He gave a quick smile but his eyes were wary.

'Do sit down, Miss Eaton.' She did as she was told. 'Thank you for your application,' he was saying in that dead-stick way of his. 'I have put your case to the board of governors. Much as they appreciate what you have brought to the school...' She began to feel lightheaded. 'You have produced fine results. You are well versed in educational theory...' His voice droned on. She wondered when he would get to the point. 'Then we come to the question of discipline...'

No, she was reasoning inside. This is not happening. They've made a mistake. 'So I regret to say they did not deem it appropriate to assign you...'

'But my boys do so well. You yourself said so.'

'Miss Eaton there has been a lengthy process of consideration, all factors were taken into account.'

The words flew past her. There was a burning in her gut. She thought of the weeks leading up to this moment. How she had bitten back self-doubt, argued with herself that the board, conservative as it was, dared not ride roughshod over her achievements. How they must, in their wisdom, put the welfare of the boys first.

Dawlish was getting to his feet and holding out his hand. Without thinking she shook it. The questions she wanted to put died in her mouth. She became at once the twenty-year-old longing to run her own school, her head alight with theories of the two Swiss Jeans: Jean Jacques Rousseau and Jean Piaget. She swallowed. Instead of flinging out the accusation that the Old Boys' network had triumphed yet again – learning by rote and canings would continue – she nodded and with a straight back walked from the room.

Outside she stood unable to move, then fearing Dawlish might come out and find her loitering, she forced herself back into the Common Room, where she was engulfed by smoke, chatter and clattering cups as her colleagues took their mid-morning break.

'Well?' Guy Masterson sidled up and offered her tea. 'Spill the beans.' She moved towards the far corner where two empty easy chairs promised privacy. 'Going to share your state secret then?' His attempt to amuse only grated. 'No go, eh, old girl?' She gave a brisk shake of the head and glanced at the clock on the wall, longing for the bell to summon her back to class.

Guy had already picked up everything he needed to know: the deputy headship, would go, as expected, to John Mulgrave, because he was a man. Less talented and experienced, but in the minds of the governors a safer bet.

'So there you are. Mulgrave will be appointed and the swish will go on.' She gave a bitter little laugh.

'Not the end of the world,' said Guy tartly. 'Many of us have been overlooked for one reason or another.'

Eleanor looked at him. 'I know.' She drained her cup. Just then the bell clanged to warn that recess was over. She put her cup onto the tea trolley and beckoned to Guy, who was still lounging in the easy chair. 'Come on.'

After school Eleanor and Guy sauntered through Regent's Park. A breeze was stirring the cherry trees by the zoo entrance, scattering petals over the grass. Eleanor dug her hands in her pockets. Beside her Guy was chewing on his pipe. 'Don't take it to heart.' She knew he meant well but just then she wished he would keep quiet. His sympathy brought back the bitterness of regret. Yet if she did not talk it through with him, where else could she vent her frustration? More than anyone, he understood her ambition and did not find her peculiar because of it.

'You're right. I should have known.'

'Between men and women there *is* no even playing field. Despite suffrage, despite all claims to the contrary,' he said.

'They were glad enough to snap us up when the men were away. Same old story, though. Once the men hobbled back, however unsuited or broken, they were offered the prime positions. I thought things might change. But they didn't.' Her voice cracked. They walked a hundred yards in silence, slowing as they passed deeper into the park. Ahead of them two nannies were chattering as they pushed their charges in prams, their bonneted heads nodding in unison like clockwork dolls. Eleanor watched the large wheels tracing lines as they went.

'Mulgrave is such an idiot. Thinks swishing children makes them clever. Got a cigarette?' she continued.

'You don't smoke.'

'I know I don't. But I need one now. Or a stiff gin would do.'

Guy touched her arm. 'Come on. I'll take you down West. We'll splash out on a meal in Soho. Buy a bottle of wine.'

'Thanks for the thought. Another time.' Two lovers were

linking arms before them, their hips touching. She glanced away.

Guy continued to suck on his pipe thoughtfully. 'Look, this is how I see it. Women may rule the roost at home, they may even make better teachers than men, but when all's said and done, it's about power. You can't have a woman telling chaps what to do.'

'Even when they know better?'

'It wouldn't look right. Not how I see things necessarily…' A girl with a hoop came clattering down the path, almost bumping into the couple ahead.

'Then you think I was wrong to set out my views on my form?'

'Undoubtedly.'

'But why?'

'What did Dawlish say?'

'He thanked me for the effort and said he would peruse them with care.'

Guy laughed. 'He did? What a hypocrite!'

'Couldn't wait to get me out of the room, though.'

'Probably thought you were telling him his job. He must have been furious.'

'I was only thinking of the school,' she murmured.

'School be damned. You challenged his authority. You questioned how the place is run. You just can't do that. You've got to have a bit of strategy.'

Her face was burning. Guy was giving her a lesson in reality she would rather ignore. 'It makes me want to give up altogether.' Guy stopped walking. His face grew grave. He stood a foot taller than her and she was forced to stare up at him. She felt anger and humiliation pricking her eyes.

'The school would fall apart without you.'

'Let it.' They continued without speaking. Not until that moment had she given the matter serious consideration. Oh, she had toyed with various scenarios but at bottom she knew she was a creature of habit. People depended on her stability, her predictability. For a start, Derek did. She thought of the home they shared in Victoria Terrace. Though the once parental home was in both their names, she kept it going, footing the bills when income from Fingal's Cave was meagre. Without her, he would find it hard to manage. He had ever been the spontaneous, chaotic one: the younger sibling she had to keep an eye on. She shrugged. She did not want to think about all that. Yet an image of her brother with his wide, wild eyes intruded into her mind.

'Where would you go?' Guy was asking her.

'Nowhere.' she muttered. 'I can't leave London because, well, because...'

Guy's lean face came closer. 'He counts on you too much. You do know that?'

'I could get a post in the provinces. Just about afford a cottage. To rent, at least.' An alternative life flashed before her. A thousand times she had promised herself she would hand in her notice if they refused to promote her.

'I'd miss you.' He gazed at her until she broke away.

'Guy, I'd better be getting back.' She dug her hands deeper into her pockets and shrugged. The park was full of people ambling, taking in the thin sunshine. One corner of the sky threatened rain. Guy stopped for a moment to fill his pipe. She watched his broad, lightly freckled fingers tamping down the tobacco, holding the bowl. She wondered when he had last been with a woman. She knew he'd had a liaison with the former French teacher at school. And there had been others. Many women found him attractive. The thought shocked: she had not viewed him in that light before. There seemed to be something inexorably self-sufficient about him.

A wind had blown up, tossing branches of the willows by the water's edge. They arrived by some giant chestnut trees.

She looked up. A week ago they had still been bare, now the sprouting buds were open. She looked across at Guy. He was watching her carefully. She was caught by a gust of wind and had to pull her skirt around her.

'It's getting cold. Maybe I will take up your offer of tea.' She glanced up: rain clouds were thickening, the sky suddenly dark. People were scattering in all directions, the paths suddenly emptying. The Tea Garden gazebo lay across a stretch of lawn, behind a cluster of shrubs. Not far away in the zoo enclosure birds were squawking. An elephant trumpeted. 'Even the animals know there's going to be a downpour,' she said. As the rain came down they ran as fast as they could towards the teashop.

Guy went to the counter while she found a corner table. He placed a pot of tea between them. 'Drink up! You look frozen.' She was shivering. She put her hands to the pot for warmth but quickly withdrew them. 'You okay? You look like a drowned...'

'Rat. Go on, say it.'

He laughed. 'Here, let me.' He started rubbing her hair and neck with a tea towel he'd requested from the manageress. She took it from him and continued to dry her head and then her legs. He smiled towards her. 'The wet look suits you but I hope you don't catch your death... you need to get out of those wet clothes.'

'Yes,' she murmured. She paused. 'It wouldn't surprise me if Dawlish went ahead and implemented my ideas and then claimed them as his own.' She watched Guy's hands as he played with the sugar bowl.

'You're very brave,' he said quietly. She sniffed. She downed more tea and gazed out at the dripping rhododendrons, the silver of raindrops lighting the deep crimson blooms. 'You need to put it behind you. There'll be other opportunities.'

'Yes,' she said flatly. She could hardly admit she was feeling sorry for herself. So many women were in the same boat. It was the chorus of her generation. Some partied into the night, scuffing over the traces, with jazz till dawn and fancy dress dos on the Thames. Why couldn't she join them? Why couldn't she forget and adapt?

'So, how about dinner? Cheer you up. I know a really nice place in Soho. It opened a few months ago. It's been a roaring success. They have live jazz and dancing. It would be a lark.'

'Another time perhaps. I've got too much schoolwork to do. Marking to catch up on.' Guy shook his head in disbelief. They sauntered back through the park and stopped outside her house. He moved towards her and kissed her lightly on the cheek.

'See you tomorrow!' she called with forced cheerfulness and walked away. Slowly she turned the key in her lock, relieved to be back home on home territory. She lit a lamp and pulled a pile of books towards her. She flicked through the first exercise book, but she just wasn't in the mood.

Chapter Eleven *Mo*

'Paris was held by the Romans and then by the Franks, who established it as the capital in 987 under Hugh Capet. During the reign of Philippe-Auguste from 1180-1223 it was organised into three parts: the Ile de la Cité which we are now passing …' Mo peered at the grey stone above as the heavily accented voice of the steamboat guide drifted over her. These boats had first come in the exhibition of 1867 and were growing popular with visitors. The speech droned on, but she had ceased to listen. Once she'd read about the plague in Paris. As the Ile's towers glided by she imagined alleyways thronged with rats and piled corpses.

How thrilling to be so close to all that history – so different from the Tower of London. Here everything was charged with the boldness of her decision. Not only was she travelling alone with Derek, she was in *Paris* of all places, without her family knowing. It made her dizzy and terrified in turns.

Beyond the Ile the boat turned and thrust back in a wide arc towards the starting point. The sun broke through a bank of grey and sparkled on the water. People were wandering the banks of the Seine as the boat slipped under the bridges and docked. They alighted amid chatter as people regrouped on the landing stage.

Derek took her for a meal to what he called a Left Bank bistro. It had dark green awnings, which fluttered in the wind. A pungent aroma of butter and garlic pervaded the place. People were laughing and some were shouting above the din, others gesticulating. Families and raucous students heaped together, cheek by jowl, in a fever of conviviality. Derek's eyes glinted. She could tell he was delighted to be in Paris. He said he'd been longing to travel here for months. 'It's not called the City of Light for nothing!' he beamed.

When she said nothing, he continued in a rush. She had rarely seen him so animated. 'It's the fulcrum, the place to be. And Patrick told me about this restaurant. Artists come here. So do students from the Sorbonne and lecturers, philosophers, followers of Kierkegaard…' She had little idea who he was talking about.

The waiter came to the table and announced the dishes of the day. 'Fish stew or rabbit fricassée,' Derek had a quick exchange with the waiter and she was amazed how fluent his French seemed. He had not mentioned that he spoke it so well.

'Rabbit?'

He laughed. 'Don't look so appalled. It's a delicacy here.'

'I'll stick with the fish stew.'

The waiter approached with bread and pâté. They tore off chunks of light, white bread, smeared them and tucked in, speaking of whatever came into their heads. Never had she felt so free, never so vibrant. Any silly thing she uttered he seemed to find amusing. 'Let's stay here forever,' he said. 'We'll live in a garret. I'll paint and you'll sing. We'll become famous.'

'And what about money?' she interjected.

'Who needs money when you've got love?'

It made her heart soar when he spoke like that. It also made her afraid. She just laughed and told him he was crazy. Afterwards they ambled, arm in arm, by the Seine. At the Pont Neuf he slowed down: 'There's a woman here, an American, Gertrude Stein, who helps artists. She and her brother used to buy their art. Now it's just her and her companion, Alice Toklas.' There was a catch in his voice as he spoke. Before them loomed a huge pointed church. 'That's Notre Dame,' he said. Mo stared up at the vaunting arches and high steeples.

'So is that the real reason we're here – you want to go and

visit her?'

'You need to know somebody… You can't just turn up.' He sounded ill at ease, irritated even. She was puzzled. From her short time at Chelsea she gathered that artists no longer stood on ceremony as their parents had done. 'She's fierce and knows what she likes. She is a fan of Henri Matisse and Paul Cézanne but has less time for Pablo Picasso. They say she collects people the way others collect objects…'

'You brought some of your sketches with you, didn't you? Do you know where she lives?'

'In the end I decided not to bring anything.' He peered at her from under the mop of straying back hair, his face touched with self-doubt.

'Why ever not?'

He stared at her intensely then broke away. He grabbed hold of her hand and started running over the bridge, dragging her along. 'Derek, don't! Doooon't!' He stopped and looked down at her, his eyes wild.

'Art is about life. To see the world as it is, sun on water, perfect verdigris of a duck's wing. Right now, you are all I need.' He laughed and gave her a kiss of such tenderness she felt her will melting.

Later they went to a Montparnasse gallery, which housed the early work of the artists who had come into vogue. In the second room he lingered by a painting: *A glimpse of Notre Dame in the late afternoon* by Henri Matisse. The colours on the canvas were faint, as they swirled around the renowned church. A sense of emptiness pervaded the frame. It had no figures just two blunted towers in the distance, pale blue in the mist.

'It reminds me of a nightmare I had,' she blurted out. When he looked curious she carried on: 'It's foggy and I'm on top of a horse-drawn carriage. I gee the horse up but I can't see a bloomin' thing. I sense something up ahead and scream. We're going to crash into it. The horses rear up. I wake in a cold sweat…'

He stared at her. 'Dr Freud says the mind is an iceberg. We only see the bits above the surface… dreams tell us more.' He carried on gazing at the picture. 'And artists live closer to the rocks.'

She'd never heard about Dr Freud but was prompted to ask: 'You think artists are different from other people, then?'

He shrugged. 'We can't stay in the upper regions. We have to keep going below. We're driven to.' Mo walked on. All this talk of icebergs and treacherous rocks was beyond her.

Towards evening they headed up through the narrow streets towards a cabaret in Pigalle. She did not know what to expect. Already she was feeling way out of her depth. Apart from the Hackney Empire she'd never been near a nightclub in London. It was just not something girls from her background would do. Derek carried on chatting about it as though it were the most natural thing in the world. 'Not quite *Le chat noir*, but they get good singers here and it's cheap.' She could tell by the zeal in his voice that he wanted to impress her.

The cabaret was tucked away in a small, ill-lit square off Place du Tertre. Inside they squeezed in among a crowd already high on wine and music; they were not speaking French. Everybody looked much older than she was and far more worldly. After listening for a moment Derek nudged her. 'I think they're Russians,' he whispered. 'Who knows whether White or Red? Thousands flooded into Paris after the Revolution and during the Civil War.' It felt as though she had stepped into a play from the West End. She watched and waited, taking in as much as she could.

The tables were filling fast. A slow, syncopated melody was snaking its way from the small band of musicians on the makeshift stage. The plangent bluesy sound vibrated through the room. The saxophonist fronting the ensemble was pouring all his own longing into his horn; it was slow-churning and unutterably beautiful. Faces were caught in the rays of a glittering, rotating globe, which highlighted an arm, a whitened cheek of a dancer, a waiter crossing the room with a tray. In the cramped dancing space couples were gyrating. The women, older than Mo, with bobbed hair and slinky gowns, exuded glamour from head to toe. Derek went to the bar to order drinks. Mo felt suddenly young and inept. What madness had she let herself in for? What if Derek disappeared and left her alone in this place? Ma was right: she was nothing but a dreamer, a spinner of fine tales.

It had been a long day. They had caught an early morning ferry and stopped at the hotel just long enough to register and drop off their bags. Yet despite her exhaustion she was taut as a spring, not wanting to let slip one moment in this maelstrom of a city. As soon as they'd stepped off the train at Gare du Nord she'd sensed something so quickening and racy in the air that she longed to take it all in.

The music grew louder and more insistent. Every fibre in Mo's being longed to move with it. A singer had joined the band, a sturdy woman in a shimmering blue gown. Mo looked down at the beaded blue-green frock Derek had given her. It fit close to the body and it, too, shimmered in the light. She could feel men looking at her with unbridled interest.

The voice of the singer was full of love's pain and depth as it slid up and down the cadences of the song, unwilling to let them go. Though Mo did not understand the words, the passion reverberated through her. She was tinged with an elation bordering on fear. She watched couples spinning round the dance floor. Derek returned with the drinks and pulled her up to dance. The music segued into an upbeat smooch tempo. He was guiding her from his pelvis. The deep voice of the singer in the glowing blue frock flowed over them like warm water. Mo felt herself responding, almost on the verge of tears. Things were happening too fast. She was losing control.

'I so want to sing,' she murmured.

'Then you must,' he whispered fiercely into her ear. 'Set your course and follow it.'

The band struck up a lively tune drowning out his voice. He grabbed hold of her two hands. There was a rawness about him that made her nervous. They moved to the rhythms, at first bumping into others until they found space. Again the music shifted its mood. Derek took her in his arms and they moved to the tempo of a slow foxtrot. She closed her eyes and leant against him.

The evening was not over.

* * *

'I got tickets for Josephine Baker,' said Derek with glee. They entered the brightly lit foyer of the Folies Bergère. Mo was agog at the people milling there: flappers and flat-chested women, well turned-out men in white spats with slicked down centrally-parted hair. She was dazzled by the glitter of pearls, the turn of a delicate ankle, the dress suits and multi-coloured evening wear. Derek led her towards the bar and ordered two champagne cocktails. She tingled with delight. *Siren of the Tropics* a poster proclaimed, showing the long-legged crop-haired black woman who had danced her way into the hearts and lusts of half the population. They took their seats and the curtain rose.

Dancers in petal formation bowed and lifted their heads like opening buds. Mo watched their lithe legs, their sparkling pink and blue costumes. They fluttered fans, bent and waved their limbs as they formed another constellation. Next scene was a jungle: musicians banging on drums, fronds of artificial palm trees, waving, rippling, pulled by hidden levers. A staircase spiralled up to a higher level where dancers were strewn like boa constrictors or tree sloths. And then the star slunk onto the stage, shimmering in a clinging gown of gold.

This she discarded to reveal the skimpiest of garments

beneath, a mere covering of the genitals. Her breasts were bared for all to see. What a beauty! What a bold, outrageous creature! She moved to the pulse of the music; as it grew ever faster she shook, coiled, swayed her pelvis in alluring, suggestive movements. It took Mo's breath away. The music got faster and faster. When would it stop? Faster and faster. Surely it was too much for the suave Parisian audience. But no. Derek was smirking with pleasure. Josephine Baker's face was lit by inner fire, vitality, self-assurance. She was moving every muscle of her body. People behind them started clapping in rhythm to the music. Josephine Baker glanced from left to right, swivelled her knees, hands on both, in an energetic Charleston. One could see her breasts moving. Everything stirred up, quicker and quicker. Derek's cheeks were flushed.

'Never seen anything like it. Nothing vulgar or contrived, just animal beauty and grace.'

'Has she been in Paris long?' Mo asked when the dance ended.

'She came on a tour and decided to stay. There are too many restrictions in America.' Other dancers were surrounding the star as if to pay her homage and shield her from the hunger of the audience, who were hooting their glee. Seeing Josephine Baker sent a shock wave through Mo. Derek was as enchanted as the rest of the audience. Mo was forced to reappraise herself: she was not like Josephine Baker and never could be. She could appeal to an audience but never lose herself to the music in that way. The energy of the sun and the south rippled through Josephine Baker's body like a wave of the sea, a gust of fierce desert wind. 'Quite something,' muttered Derek as they wound their way back from Pigalle. 'No wonder the Parisians are bowled over.'

Mo had to agree. There was something of the goddess in Josephine Baker: something so explosive, joyful and dangerous that it pushed all other women into the shadows.

In the lobby of Hotel du Cygne a single bulb burned in the high ceiling, emitting a feeble light and casting shadows about the well-worn furniture. In the hotel, close by the Gare du Nord, there was a cage of a lift, which rattled and creaked to the upper floors. Derek swung open the door onto a small room, which smelled of dried lavender and nicotine. 'Ah Gaulloises,' he exclaimed. The sidelights, when he switched them on, created a pink glow and revealed a print of Delacroix's *Entry of Crusaders into Constantinople*. The bed had a beige eiderdown, folded back, and a long white bolster. On the side table were an ewer and basin from Provence. Derek moved towards her, removing her jacket and dropping it onto the bed.

'Careful, it'll get creased.'

'Come here,' he commanded.

'Come where? I'm already here.'

'Next to me.'

'How much nearer can I get?' He snorted and moved away.

'I'm going down to the bar. Want to join me?'

'I'd like to hang up my jacket first.'

'I'll see you down there then.' He shut the door firmly behind him. She sank onto the bed, kicking off her shoes and letting her head sink into the bolster. Impressions of mottled plane trees, wide boulevards, endless paintings, teeming cafés and smoke-filled bars came crowding in on her. She fingered silky folds of the eiderdown. She wriggled her toes, tinged blue by the dye in her shoes. She choked back her confusion. Was she afraid? She had willingly come to Paris, buzzing with the audacity of it, the modernity of it; but nobody knew where she was or what she was doing. She had the image of the drayman's gate banging shut at the back of The Mare's Head; she saw her mother's tight mouth summoning her to stay. She gave a little gasp, brushing them away. She viewed herself in her beaded blue-green frock. It had been just right for the jazz club. She stared at her image in the pitted bathroom mirror: she looked so alive, so full of herself; her dark eyes were gleaming at her in defiance. This is what you are choosing, they said. This is what will take you forward.

Downstairs three men hunched over beers at the opposite end of the bar. 'Ah, there you are,' said Derek. They settled onto a shabby sofa. The barman wiped the table in front of them and put down two beer mats, glancing with indifference towards them. 'Monsieur?'

'Beer?' Derek turned to Mo. The waiter brought the drinks. Derek moved towards her. Lightly he touched the back of her hand. 'You have beautiful hands, you know. Long fingers. Denotes a refined sensibility.' Again, fleetingly, she asked herself what she was doing here, in an ill-lit bar in Paris. She regarded her toes, encased once again in her blue, strapped shoes, as if they could provide the answer. Her body was saying one thing, while the voices of her family squabbled inside her head. Derek held her glass to her mouth. She drank. He kissed her on the mouth. At once she soared, her whole being filled with light. She leaned towards him. He glanced over his shoulder at the men.

'Derek – I – will you do that again?' He put the glass on the table and kissed her again. She drew closer to him, causing the sofa to creak. The men in the bar looked towards them with mild amusement. Her head was back in the smoke-filled jazz bar with the slow and fast transfixing sounds of its music working through her, the wailing of the horn ringing in her ears. She was watching Josephine Baker's sinuous movements. 'Shall we go upstairs?' She nodded.

In the darkened room they slid down onto the bed. He smothered her mouth with kisses so she could hardly breathe. He was kissing her cheek and throat and fumbling to undo the back buttons of her frock. They were small and fiddly and she heard him groaning in exasperation. She giggled, turned away and deftly undid them and slipped out of the dress, flinging it in a careless arc onto the floor. For a second a shadow flitted by. Did she know what she was doing? There would be no going back. The shadow banished like mist before the sun, a strain of saxophone music blasting it away. She felt Derek's arms around her, her body responding to his with a will of its own. Her eyes closed and all her senses focused as she slid out of her undergarments.

'You all right, my sweet?' he was whispering into her hair. She tensed for an instant, then murmured assent. He was easing himself ever closer towards her, so it seemed he was surrounding her. She felt herself opening to him. Then he was moving inside her, gently then ever faster. She gave a half cry before her body took over with its own longings.

Chapter Twelve

The next morning, while Derek was still dozing, Mo prised open the stiff shutters and peered out across the tiny balcony, surveying the grey roofs and steeples of the quartier. The sight of the higgledy-piggledy tiles and rounded corners of apartment blocks thrilled her: so unlike the smoky terraces of Hackney. Colours were brighter and the sky wider than she had ever known. The voices of her family had faded to a murmur. She wanted to be nowhere else this bright May morning. She started humming, then as she caught the tune she sang out loud. No matter that it was a corny song broadcast every day from the wireless. It suited her mood of the moment.

'You made me love you, I didn't want to do it, I didn't want to do it.
You made me want you, and all the time you knew it, I guess you always knew it…'

She heard him shift behind her, he murmured: 'Come back to bed for a while.' She turned and smiled, held out her hands in a gesture of expansion, as though she could embrace the whole world.

'You made me happy sometimes, you made me glad
And then approaching, kneeling within reach of him, she crooned:
But there were times, dear, you made me feel so bad.
You made me sigh, for I didn't want to tell you, I didn't want to tell you.

I want some love that's true, yes I do, indeed I do, you know I do…'

Before she could finish, he had pulled her towards him and given her a lingering kiss on the mouth. 'My beautiful song-bird.'

'Just five minutes then,' she whispered.

He was still sleepy, giving off an aura of muskiness. She lay against him, nuzzling her cheek against his back. 'Glad you came to Paris?' he murmured. She murmured back. Warmth surged through her just being at his side. They made love again. She slept a little until she felt the bed stirring. He was getting dressed. She watched the curve of his back as he bent to tie his shoelaces.

Downstairs they took a breakfast of coffee and croissants in the poky dining room. He spoke of all the places and people he still wanted to see. He rattled off names but he caught only a Pablo here and a Matisse there. Wasn't it thrilling to know they walked the same streets they themselves had tramped the day before – by the Seine, the Left Bank and La Bourse? In the past the greats distilled from what they saw: society dames at the opera, dancers frozen in movement, prostitutes waiting in the rain. Now the new ones shocked and enchanted, with their cubes and abstractions, sending seismic waves to shake the complacent.

Mo could only nod, bemused, as she sipped her milky coffee. For her it would be enough for them to stroll together through the city, enough to admit that her world had been turned upside down.

Michael, Derek's artist friend from school, had disappeared down to the Midi to paint, but Patrick Shaughnessy had given Derek the address of another friend in the Marais district. They followed a cobbled narrow alley until they came across an old run-down *hôtel particulier*, shrouded by bushes. The ancient street door was ajar. Derek pushed it open and they came upon a courtyard surrounded by three wings, split into ateliers. In one of them someone was hammering metal; from others wafted the pungency of linseed oil and paint. A lanky man in his forties was crossing the yard, whistling. When Derek asked him where he could find Pierre Leclerc, the man shook his hand. '*C'est moi.*'

They followed him into his workshop, a large, echoing space, shallow at one end under a sloping roof. Here were stacked canvases of all shapes and sizes. Derek stared at a canvas on an easel in the middle of the room. Splashes of red and orange streaked across a metal blue background. Mo stared at it. The painting drew her in, its vortex of dark, pulsating energy almost tactile, colours and shapes colliding. 'I feel I'm being sucked down a well,' she said.

Pierre moved towards a bench cluttered with palettes and tubes of paint. He started screwing the tops back onto the tubes. 'Now people want stability. They've had enough of Surrealism.' He shrugged his right shoulder. 'When I struggle I think of Henri – always experimenting, passionate about colour from the day his mother gave him a paint-box.' Pierre was a disciple of Henri Matisse and had worked with him at the *Académie*. 'Madame, do you paint?' She looked at him for a moment; he had an air of inwardness.

'I model,' she said and realised it no longer caused her shame. She was one of the artists now, one of the Free Spirits.

He looked at her with a measured eye. 'You permit?' He put his hand under her arm and led her towards a sheaf of paintings leaning against a wall. He flicked through them. An array of haunting, vibrant images flashed by, across many streaked the jagged black of barbed wire. Pierre had seen action in the war, Derek had told her that morning. His face was lean and his eyes tired. No doubt, the experience had taken its toll.

'Have you seen *Paths of Glory* by Richard Nevinson?' asked

Derek. 'Like these, it shows the true face of war.' Pierre said nothing, his dark eyes searching Derek's. Mo moved away from the paintings and looked up through the skylight. Clouds were driving in from the west. She felt exposed. Every time Derek spoke his voice went through her.

'A Modernist?' asked Pierre

'He started with Cubism then got more realistic. He was an official war artist. Worked as a stretcher-bearer. Some of his paintings show dead soldiers in trenches. That got him into trouble with the War Office.'

'Now it's all Modernism and clear-cut shapes,' Pierre said. 'Nobody wants to recall the carnage.' He walked over to a dusty dresser where he stored his brushes. 'And how is my old friend Patrick? What's he doing these days?'

'Prolific and crazy as ever.' Mo could not keep still. The pictures disturbed her. Being with Derek disturbed her. Her eyes watered.

'Tell me about your painting, Pierre.' She attempted to blot out her thoughts. 'What were you thinking when you done this?'

'The secret is not to think, Madame. I do my thinking elsewhere. I go round observing: the light, shapes, people. Feelings come and go, rise and sink. I roam at night, in the rain, in unlit places, by the river when other people are asleep. I let the day crash in on me. It all goes round and round. When I come to paint I am calm. I stand in front of the canvas and just wait. The impulse takes my hand and moves. I surrender.'

Madame, he'd called her. Madame. She was a grown woman worthy of respect. Inside she could feel she was smiling.

Pierre suggested they meet up with some of his friends. They crossed the Seine and walked towards Montparnasse. It had become the new hub, he told them. Here, beyond the boulevards, workers, artists, writers and Bohemians rubbed shoulders, drank, conversed, ate and slept together. There were all sorts in Paris these days: Jews still fleeing pogroms in Eastern Europe, Greeks and Armenians escaping Turkish massacres, Arabs moving to France from Francophone colonies in northern Africa. 'Not only that – it's a witches' brew of political parties,' Pierre went on, 'with every shade of radical, liberal. Monarchist, anarchist and revolutionary…'

They entered the smoky atmosphere of a *boîte*. Talk was loud, shot through with laughter and occasional squabbles. Through a fog of blue smoke the copper counter glimmered, and above it, a motley display of coloured bottles. The smell of cheap tobacco mingled with a meaty aroma from the kitchen. Already Mo felt different from yesterday. Though still dazzled by all about her, she carried within her another knowledge. She knew what it was to be loved, to love, to merge and become part of something beyond herself.

On a makeshift rostrum a young woman was wailing. Wearing a short black dress, her lips were vermilion and her face plastered white, making her look consumptive. Mo could not take her eyes off her. The voice was husky and sounded of whisky and cigarettes. '*Chanson réaliste,*' Derek whispered in her ear. 'Street songs about hardship and undying love.' The words were sliding over each other in a throaty mix of sentiment and sensuality. Pierre leaned forward and attempted to translate.

'It's cost me a lot
but… one thing… I've got
It's my man.
Cold and wet, tired you bet
But… I soon forget
With my man
He's not much for looks
No hero out of books
Is my man.

Two… girls has he
…he likes as well as me
But I love him!'

To Mo it was wild poetry. The woman in the black dress had her lips pursed for a lover's kiss as she sang. If I could that, thought Mo, I could find my way in the world.

Around the table they started discussing art. Pierre gave them the gist. Mo was more intrigued by their faces than by what they were saying. It reminded her of Friday nights in The Mare's Head when men aired opinions about the aftermath of war or the price of meat rising, with nobody paying much heed to anyone else.

'After photography what's left?' asked one. 'Even in the *Belle Époque* painting was on its last legs. Degas knew it. The Impressionists knew it. Everything was dissolving into light.'

'What about the masters?' butted in another. 'I come from Provence. I was attracted by the old traditions. What about universal truths?'

'What truths?'

'You're saying we have to start from scratch? Where does that leave me?' Short and stocky, the speaker reminded her of a wrestler. His shoulders slumped, exuding dejection.

Pierre gave up trying to translate: the arguments were becoming too embroiled. These men like the sound of their own voices. Surely truth was more like that rotating globe in the nightclub with its thousand glittering facets? Even as they talked about smashing it, she sensed that art was crucial to these men. Come the morning she guessed they would be in their studios, setting up easels, ready to get on with their trade.

The singer reached a crescendo. The voice was deep for a woman and the number an alluring mix of jazz and ballad. Derek's head was cocked to one side as he struggled to keep up with the art debate. His leg brushed hers under the table, sending a wave of warmth through her. Chatter around her faded to the voice of her own mind. She longed to be alone with Derek. To unravel their story, enter ever deeper into it.

The pianist skimmed over the keys and ended with a flourish while the singer inclined her head. Those clustered round the tables roared their approval. The singer smiled, a little sadly, and left the stage. The eyes of the men followed her then they reverted to their glasses and talk. Mo watched her, this magical creature, plunging into the dark blue sea between the sunlit peaks of the iceberg.

They caught a ferry back to Dover as daylight dimmed. Mo insisted on staying outside on the boat deck as the air in the bar was tinged with the stench of vomit. The rolling sea made her stomach lurch until she feared that she, too, might join the ranks of the poorly. A wind stirred the water and rattled metal fittings on the vessel. Lights from the upper deck glinted on the swell of the water. Through her coat she felt the lash of wind against her body; she snuggled closer to Derek.

'Did you enjoy the trip?' he asked, his breath against her cheek.

'It was perfect.'

'No regrets?'

As she watched the toiling water she grew tense, wondering what her father would say if he knew about the weekend. Derek put his arm round her and started humming. She sank against him, imbibed the warmth from his body. There were questions she would ask him but she did not know where to start. Once she would have blurted out her concerns, now she was learning to wait.

'We didn't get to the Theatre Elysée,' he said. 'Pierre told me it's a great place for dancers…'

'Is that so?' Mo wondered with irritation just why he was listing something else they might have done, as though her company were not enough. Stars were becoming visible in the sky. The wind was just starting to drop.

'Shall we go inside?'

'Derek?'

'Yes?'

'What...' she hesitated.

'Go on, old thing, say it, whatever is on your mind.'

'What – what happens next?'

'What do you mean?'

'With us?'

He put his arm round her and pulled her close, kissing her forehead. 'Come on. Let's go inside. It's getting too cold here.'

Chapter Thirteen

Back in her London digs Mo and Stella were having breakfast together. Mo was full of her time in Paris. Stella fumbled in her bag for an early morning cigarette, put it in a holder, and blew out a long stream of smoke past Mo's nose. 'Don't forget what I told you.'

'I forgot already.' Mo waved the air to disperse the smoke.

'I said not to get involved with any of the students, especially *that* one. He's still burning a candle for his old love. Zara, that is.'

'No, 'e's not,' retorted Mo.

'Suit yourself. Men are all pretty much the same. They're only ever after one thing. They like the challenge, see.' There was something hard about Stella this morning, as though she might be capable of cruelty. Mo had not noticed it before.

'What time is it? I got a class at ten,' said Mo.

'Did you even hear me?'

Mo got to her feet and took her plate and cup to the sink in the scullery to rinse them. The cold water splashed over her hands and stung them. Stella was beginning to sound like one of her parents.

At Chelsea Polytechnic there was no sign of Derek. Even later in the week he did not appear. Mo convinced herself that he would turn up soon: had he not said he wanted to go off to the country to paint? He'd also mentioned that he needed to earn money. Yet when after two weeks he was still nowhere to be found, she began looking out for him in every corridor and room at the college. During one class, spread out on the sofa with head reclining and eyes closed, she took flight. She was back in the Paris hotel, their softly lit room…. Her mouth dropped open. She jerked awake, startled. The students were staring at her behind their easels. The sudden sight of them shocked her.

And then he was there. One day after class she found him mooching around outside. Her heart leapt. 'Where've you been all this time? I thought something was wrong.' It was hard to keep her agitation to herself. He smiled, shrugged off her questions and insisted on taking her to a teashop a few streets away. He poured her tea, his dark eyes searching hers. He had not shaved in a week.

'Derek, you look terrible. Where have you been?'

He shrugged off her question with a wave of the hand. 'Tonight I'm taking you to the Café Royal. I won some money on the gee-gees.'

'I thought you was working.'

He pulled out his wallet, displaying a wad of bank notes. 'I was. But I had a flutter and I got lucky. And today I'm going to buy you a frock.'

'No, you ain't.'

'Why ever not?'

'Because…'

'See, you don't have a good reason to refuse. I can spend my money as I choose.'

He took her to Regent Street where he bought her a delicious cream frock with a drop waistline and beaded bodice. She had never owned anything so fine. As she clutched the expensive-looking box she quashed rising doubts. How much he paid for the garment she did not want to know; besides, it was rude to ask.

They arrived at the Café Royal after nine – it was not worth going earlier, he said, as nobody would be there. They took a table by the main entrance so they could catch sight of people coming in. 'It's is a watering-hole for artists. The odd aristocrat turns up, rebelling against the rambling pile in the Home Counties. A clique has formed around Augustus John …' he spoke in a hushed, reverential tone, which struck her as exaggerated. 'You can live more cheaply in Paris,' he went on. 'But I have better access here.' She took that with a pinch of salt. 'What would you like to drink, old thing, wine or champagne?'

'Very lucky on the gee-gees then, if you're offering bubbly?'

The waiter, a middle-aged man with bulbous eyes, was obsequious. Mo wondered how much it cost him, day in day out, to serve young upstarts without getting cross. Her father would not be so patient. The place began to fill. Taxis and horse-driven carts rumbled up and down Piccadilly. Lights blinked out from cafés, restaurants and nightclubs. As she sipped the bubbles tingled in her mouth. Derek was gazing round with a nonchalant air. A crowd jostled in, pushing wide the glass doors and spilling with exuberance into the café.

'There he is!' whispered Derek. She looked around to behold a rotund, bearded man sporting a flamboyant green jacket and knickerbockers. 'Augustus John.'

'What a get-up! Does he always dress like that?'

'Shshsh. He likes to make out he's got Romany blood, but actually he's from Pembrokeshire.' Admirers were clustering round the maestro like royal retainers. He seemed more actor than artist. 'Art,' said Derek, 'is as much about how you live as what you put on canvas.'

'So does all this improve their work?'

Derek looked at her askance and laughed. 'Not necessarily!'

He ordered poached haddock and spinach. Around them people were growing wilder, shouting and slamming down glasses. A skinny girl in a blue, fringed dress danced between the tables, swivelling hips in a provocative stab at the samba. A cheer rang out and they clapped madly. The band in the corner played louder, a trumpet blaring out.

Derek turned to her. She swallowed hard. There were questions she would put to him if she could find the words. What had been true just a month ago had shifted into a grey unknowing. She recalled a recent dream. Her father had drowned at sea and was frozen beneath the ice. Then he turned up for tea in Hackney. At table, he was relating his experience then he stopped and asked Mo: 'So what's your story, Morwenna?' She was about to answer when she woke up.

She considered her half-finished glass of champagne and glanced up at him. 'Derek I've missed you…'

'I've missed you too.'

'Why have you stopped coming to the polytechnic?'

He sighed. 'Too much distraction. My tutor agreed I could work elsewhere on my portfolio. I've been focusing on landscapes. Or trying to…'

She only half believed him and when he told her he'd booked a room in the Imperial Hotel at the back of Oxford Street, she demurred: why should she fall in with his plans when he came and went as he pleased? But her body was already singing another song, which had no use for reflection. Already her head was on his shoulder. She longed to escape this mêlée of noisy artists and their hangers-on. While she went to the Ladies, he settled the bill and fetched her jacket from the cloakroom. They wandered down Piccadilly, leaning against each other, laughing, gazing in shop windows and canoodling like any other lovers.

Hotel Imperial did not live up to its name. It bordered on the tawdry, with a broken sign and façade in need of paint. Yet she did not care. It was just a place where they could be together. He had already explained to her that he lived with his sister, who was a teacher and quite strict. They laughed and bumped against each other as they went up the narrow staircase. 'Not quite Hotel du Cygne,' he said.

'Hotel of Sin?' she queried.

'No, Cygne means swan. Don't you remember the sign outside?'

The room, it turned out, was adequate: clean and rendered familiar with sepia photos of London sights. Above the bed loomed an image of the Tower of London. 'I didn't bring no toothbrush or nightdress,' complained Mo, but Derek only laughed and covered her mouth with kisses.

'No need.'

It felt so natural to her when he slipped her dress over her head and started kissing her neck and caressing her breasts. She sighed and fell back on the bed. 'I miss you like crazy when you're not there,' she said as he lay nuzzling into her, drawing his hands in long strokes along her legs. She wanted to ask him what it meant to him, what... but already the questions were growing weaker and her desire stronger. Champagne and her longing for him were mingling, confounding her, making her bolder. She lay on top of him. He groaned in pleasure. Their bodies moved in unison, making passionate love.

Afterwards she leant against him then propped herself onto an elbow and watched him dozing, tracing her fingers over his face, hardly daring to believe she was here beside him. Tears were streaking down her face. She put her fingers to her cheek, tasted the salty water and could not stem the tumult within.

Chapter Fourteen

'It's a long way to Tipperary…It's a long way to go' rang out in the Chelsea street. Mo recalled it from The Mare's Head: a common soldier's song from the Great War. And here it was again on the night air. It was a banal, popular tune that had done the rounds, but for all that it still caught her by the throat. It was song of exile and longing, like so many Irish songs. The words faded. She was on her way back from work, bracing herself for yet another evening alone in Riverton Road.

There had been no sign of Derek in a week.

'If singing's what you want to do I might know someone could help you.' Mo and Stella were in the scullery at Riverton Road. Mo was wearing the old silk dressing gown Stella had cast her way. In the cramped space at the back of the house there were draughts and creaks as an early summer wind rattled dustbin lids and wafted through the few trees in the back yards. She caught a glimpse of a half-moon through the grease-smeared window.

'I've wanted to ever since I was little. But my Ma was against it.'

'Why?'

Mo pictured the pinched, disappointed face of her mother. Not a good idea, she'd told Mo when she'd first confided her desire to be a singer. 'She danced and sang in Music 'all herself. I reckon she still gets the yen. But she won't talk about it. Whenever I try, she buttons up.'

'Not much of a life if you ask me,' commented Stella. 'Singing for your supper in all those noisy bars…'

'If that's what you want to do.'

'So you're a born performer, are you?'

Mo was taken aback by the tone of light sarcasm. 'I never said that, but I want to try at least.'

'Doreen's her name, this friend. Doreen Delange. She's a friend of a friend. She sings in The Cockerel Tavern, at the end of King's Road. You could always go and ask if they have any evenings spare.'

* * *

One evening after work Mo went to the pub. Stella had promised to go with her to make sure she got a hearing but then dropped out at the last minute. The saloon bar was swirling with smoke, laughter and talk. Through the uproar she spotted Doreen, who stood out on account of her brown satin outfit. The robe clung to her shapely if plump body; her face, powdered and rouged, was lit by an unrelenting smile. She was singing to her admirers with arms outstretched.

'Don't 'ave any more, Mrs Moore…' she bawled out to the merriment of those around her. There was a burst of applause as she hit the top notes then bent her head in mock humility. Men were hovering near, pressing her with compliments and offers of drinks.

'Miss Miss Delange…' Doreen Delange turned her head as Mo pushed towards her, the cluster thinning as men took their drinks from the bar and sat round the small tables. One or two hung on beside Doreen.

'Have we met?' said Doreen to Mo.

'I'm Mo. Mo Dobson. My friend … I have a friend called Stella. She was going to come tonight but then couldn't. Said she'd introduce me to you. She thought you might show me the ropes like. See, I want to sing. She said … there might be a chance.'

'Did she indeed? What's her name?'

'Stella. She is a friend of yours, ain't she?'

Doreen sipped the large gin and tonic a man had just

handed her. 'Can't say the name rings a bell. So many pass through. What was it she said again?' They were being jostled as a new burst of people came in from the street.

'I want to sing. Like you.' Mo sounded childish now, even to herself. She was finding it hard to breathe, hard, too, to stand her ground and not push back out of the pub in embarrassment.

'Look girlie, why should I want to queer my own pitch?'

'Pardon?' The question startled. She merely wanted a few tips, an opening. Seeing her air of surprise Doreen Delange laughed.

'Hard enough to make a go of it myself without encouraging others. Have you got a repertoire even?'

'Of songs, you mean? Not really. Only the ones I 'eard at home.'

'And where's that?'

'Hackney. My Ma was in Music Hall.'

'Was she?' Close up, Doreen was less sure of herself. Mo could see droplets of perspiration on her upper lip and dark roots showing through her dyed, blond hair. When her face was at rest lines ran by her nose and mouth. She must be well into her forties. 'You need to put together an act,' the woman advised. 'Songs you're good at, that you can make your own.'

'If – if I practised and come back…' A man put his arm round Doreen and was steering her towards a huddle by the darts board. Mo stared at her retreating head then looked around. People were busy talking and drinking, far too engrossed to give her the time of day. A solitary drinker propped himself up by the counter, looking doleful. Much as she was familiar with the inside of a public house, this was no place for her. She sniffed away her disappointment and headed for the exit.

It was after this encounter that Mo determined to find a singing teacher.

WAYWARD DAUGHTER

Chapter Fifteen   *Derek*

In Victoria Terrace Derek was having another sleepless night. He stared into the darkness: what had he let himself in for? A frivolous weekend in Paris was turning into more than he had bargained for. Paris and Mo had confounded him, jolted him out of his complacency. It made him realise that everything he undertook was mediocre, all was procrastination and muddling through.

Paris was the fount of new ideas, movements and protests. Yet at the crucial moment he had backed off. He could have gone alone, stayed on, found a studio. Even sought contact with Gertrude Stein. Instead he'd taken Mo with him and now even that bit of fun was getting complicated. Patrick was right. He should rid himself of distractions and devote himself to his art. (But Mo – the sweetness of her, her verve and spirit, her sheer unconscious beauty: how could one *not* be distracted by her?)

Later in Fingal's Cave, he was sorting through a batch of boxes sent by a colleague in Manchester. The shop was the most practical venture he had ever embarked upon. With his share of the parental legacy – which all told did not amount to much – he'd persuaded the owner to grant him a fifteen-year lease. This he hoped would tide him over until he established himself as a painter. At least that had been the plan. He employed an assistant three days a week to allow him some leeway.

He attracted custom, but not enough.

Now in the storeroom, which was warm and cramped – only eight feet by six – he felt choked by clutter. Every week he bundled together the rejects into sacks. Some went to the rag-and-bone man. The rest he donated to the Sally Army.

He wrenched open a box. It was crammed with shoes and belts, gathered from an old market. Black, high-laced boots and several pairs of men's brogues: brown, solid and uninteresting. He rifled through them with a growing sense of dismay: how many stage directors would buy brogues? Audiences hardly looked at feet unless the actor tripped over. The next box he opened gave off a whiff of staleness, reeking of unaired back rooms in some big old house. He pulled out a fox cape. The eyes of the animal stared at him: black, glassy, unreal. The fur stank of mothballs.

He threw open the door to the store, dragging out three sacks of detritus. Inside he heard the shop bell ping, announcing his first customer. He heard the swish of material and caught sight of a deliciously carved ankle. With an impatient swoop its owner was rummaging through the frocks. She took one out, held it against her body, clucked her tongue then pulled out the next.

'Good...' The words stuck in his throat as he beheld the woman before him. She was staring at him in consternation. He moved forward. Her hair, escaping the current trend for bobs and shingles, touched the edge of her shoulders. It was hair a man could lose himself in. Her cheeks were pale, tinged with rouge, her eyes dark green.

'Oh, I didn't see you.' She had a penetrating gaze.

'Madam,' he said. 'Can I be of assistance?'

'I'm not sure you can,' she answered in such a matter-of-fact way he felt his insides shrivel. Her sculptured face melted into a smile. 'I'm auditioning for a part in Noel Coward's play, *The Vortex*. Have you heard of it?'

'I keep my theatrical items back here.'

'I don't want anything theatrical. This is a contemporary piece.' She laughed. It was a distinctive carefree laugh. 'You must get a lot of wardrobe people in here.'

'Not enough,' he admitted with an honesty which surprised him.

'Is that so? Then perhaps not enough people know about you.' She pulled a boa from the hat corner, laid it on her shoulders and tilted her mouth towards the looking glass.

'This is the first time you've been in here, if I am not mistaken?'

She turned on her heels and sauntered towards him. On the way she had to step over a couple of boxes. 'Stock taking, are we?'

Derek cleared a path for her. 'Your face is familiar – would I have seen you in a recent show?'

'Maybe.' She gave a nonchalant shrug. Her face was carefully made up, bordering on the obvious, but with a hint of restraint. He had work to be getting on with: more boxes to sift through, but he stayed put, watching as she preened herself.

'I'm playing the part of the adulterous, fornicating mother. A bit young for the part but it's a wonder what face paint can do. Provided I get the role, of course.'

'I'm sure you will,' he replied without thinking.

She looked at him askance. 'So you think I look the part?' She smiled at his embarrassment. 'You know the play, I take it?'

'Actually, no, I don't.'

'She's frightfully vain and preoccupied with her own appearance and her ability to charm and seduce. She's oblivious to all else, to the detriment of her son. But her role is fascinating – I love playing wicked women.'

I bet you do, he thought. Suddenly the shop seemed too small. 'If you'll excuse me, Madam, I'll look out the back. We have more in storage.' He went to pass her but she laid a restraining hand on his arm.

'I'm sure there's enough here,' she paused. 'I hope I didn't shock you?'

'Not at all.'

She released his arm. 'You must be used to loose talk. Working with theatres.'

'No one quite like you has ever been in here,' he said and then wished he hadn't.

'Most wardrobe mistresses would love it. Do you place advertisements? Are you well connected? Do you go to the right parties?'

'Can't say that I do.' He reflected that since he'd abandoned stage set work his contact with the world of theatre had dwindled.

'Well, you should. You have a veritable treasure trove here. A bit chaotic, I agree, but a wide selection.'

'Well thank you, Madam.'

'Oh do stop calling me that. You make me feel like a governess or something.' Again she laughed. 'Now be a darling, and fetch that black dress at the end of the rail. I meant to pick it out when you arrived and interrupted my train of thought.'

He brought it to her. 'Would you like to try it on?'

'I can tell by looking.' She held the dress up to the light where it appeared a little faded. 'Mmm. Not quite the goods, I don't think.'

'I'll give you a discount.'

'Pack it up with these.' She handed him the boa and a pale peach shift embroidered with shimmering beads. He extracted a few sheets of tissue paper and folded the clothes carefully into them before putting them in a flat box, which he tied with a bow. 'One guinea please.'

'A guinea! That's robbery. It's not as though they're new.'

His mouth dropped open. The audacity of it – he was giving the best price he could. Did she have any idea of the value of these hand-sewn garments? When he looked up he saw she was smirking.

'My, you're so serious. I was joking. Can't you see that? You know, I think you would do better if you widened your circle of acquaintances. Would you like to come to one of my parties?'

He thrust the box towards her. Was this woman in earnest? Fifteen minutes before she had walked into his shop, a complete stranger, and here she was inviting him to a party. In some circles girls still went chaperoned. She fixed him with her dark eyes. 'By the way my name is Isadora Fonthill. But my friends call me Issy. Here's my calling card. In case you change your mind.'

Chapter Sixteen *Mo*

After the let-down at the Cockerel Tavern with Doreen Delange, Mo decided lessons were the way to go. By now she had enough money. The day before she'd spotted a notice at the art college: 'Singing and elocution lessons at reasonable cost.' She bought herself a songbook. When class was finished she set off in pursuit of the teacher.

The terraced house was rundown, with a dark stain from a leaking gutter. A severe-looking woman, with eyebrows that threatened to meet, answered the door. She peered at Mo and introduced herself as Miss Dawson. When Mo explained what she wanted Miss Dawson led her into a room that smelled of cats. In one corner an upright piano was cluttered with sepia photographs. The room felt airless.

'What do you want to sing and why?' asked the other. Taken aback by the abruptness of her manner, Mo hesitated. For her singing needed no justification. 'You are afraid, I can tell you that much.' When Mo continued to say nothing, Miss Dawson declared: 'Either afraid or nervous, I hear it in your voice.'

Something about the woman reminded Mo of Bootles at Dukely's. She felt herself go hot and cold. She suppressed the urge to lash out, told herself it was just an unfortunate manner the woman had. 'I brought a book…'

The woman approached the piano. 'Sing me a song – any song – and I'll see if I can tell what you need to do.'

Mo had rehearsed one or two and now sallied forth. *'Yes sir, you're my baby…'* She noticed immediately that she had pitched her voice too high. After a few bars she faltered. She excused herself and began again.

'Stop!' ordered the woman. 'Come here.' Mo paused, then moved forward. 'Allow me.' With fingers that were unexpectedly gentle the woman touched her neck and shoulders. 'Breathe. You're forgetting to breathe. Breathe in down here.' She laid her hand on Mo's diaphragm. 'You're holding on too much. Now sing and imagine you are alone.' Mo felt the impossibility of doing this. Every fibre in her was straining.

'Singing is as natural as breathing once you let go. Breathe deeply. Ten times. When you have done that you will sing.' Under such scrutiny nothing seemed simple. Mo attempted the scales. Uncharacteristically, her voice sounded shaky. 'Again.' Mo repeated the exercise. 'And again.' By the time she had done the scales four times she was exasperated.

'Now I better let you go,' said Miss Dawson. 'You have talent. You need to work.' Mo reached for her purse, wondering what the payment would be. 'Today is free,' said the other. 'I charge eight shillings for four lessons. You can come again next week.' Mo gave a quick smile and left.

* * *

In college several students were missing. With the changeable summer weather came a rash of colds. Mo kept expecting to see Derek rush in, canvas and brushes flying around him. His absence puzzled and saddened her. She told herself not to be silly. In the long pose she got pins and needles in her arms. She wriggled discreetly to get the circulation going. She glanced at the clock: the hands seemed stuck.

The next day, which was sunny, she arranged a second singing lesson. Miss Dawson showed her into the cat-smelling room with the upright piano and waved her hand. 'So, we shall see how it goes.' She hummed a high note. 'Repeat after me.' She picked other notes as if from the air. Mo sounded the notes: she had practised the scales. To her music was magic;

but like magic sometimes it visited and sometimes eluded her. Miss Dawson asked her to sing another song of her own choosing.

Mo had been waiting for this. She had heard *'So this is love'* by Irene Bordoni on the gramophone at college – sometimes tutors brought in discs to play during the breaks. She repeated what she had learnt by heart. The musical from which it came, *Little Miss Blue Beard,* had swept Broadway. Miss Dawson stopped her halfway through. She broke down the song into bars, which Mo had to repeat until the teacher was satisfied. 'Enough for one day,' she said at length. 'Practise at home.'

Mo took her leave. As she went home through the bright streets, she hummed, felt herself growing lighter and freer. Something was kindling in her. Her mind reverted to Derek: buoyed by excitement she longed to tell him all about it. There was no way of knowing whether something had happened to Derek or if he'd just gone off without bothering to tell her.

On Saturday she took a bus up to Fingal's Cave. His assistant, Mrs Bradley, a rotund woman with frizzy hair, was just pulling down the shutter. When Mo asked after Derek she told her he'd gone off to paint for a few days. She had no idea where. Mo returned to Riverton Road and busied herself in a frenzy of cleaning, erasing balls of fluff from the corners of her room and tea stains from the linoleum with Vim. She opened the window and let the air blast in, like Ma did at home to give their box room its weekly airing.

No time to mope, she scolded herself. She struck up and sang the scales with more zest than ever. Miss Dawson's words of encouragement, however few, echoed back to her. But Derek – where was Derek? By the afternoon she could stand the sight of her stained wallpaper and battered wardrobe no longer. She left the house.

A market was in full swing two streets away. 'Penny a pound! Penny a pound!' yelled the barrow boy, holding up potatoes. She bought some vegetables to cook a stew. Stella was nowhere to be seen, no doubt off enjoying herself somewhere. From above Mo heard faint sounds of her landlady's gramophone. Someone was singing an Italian aria; the voice was high, clear and impassioned. She hummed along, scraping the potatoes and carrots in the sink. She thought of the wireless they'd acquired in the saloon bar in The Mare's Head – a novelty when it arrived and the wellspring of so many songs.

After eating she strolled by the river. Large barges crossed, trailing shallow wakes. She found a café to sit in. She ordered tea and watched people in the street going about their business, shopping and chatting. Later, in her room, she lay on her bed and tried to read. Sadness settled on her like a blanket of smog; it took all her willpower not to succumb to it.

The next day, a Sunday, church bells rang out, summoning the faithful to services. She got dressed and caught a tram to Hackney. But would she be welcome there? On the way she rehearsed what she was going to say to her family. Ma would be furious with her for leaving the way she had. Would she even let her in? One moment Mo longed to fling herself back into their midst, forgetting the madness of Derek, modelling and Paris; the next, she shrank in fear. If she gave in now, while she was feeling low, they would get the better of her. She would never discover what lay outside their tight circle.

She alighted two stops sooner than she needed to, at Dalston Junction. She had drunk several cups of tea before leaving and was now dying to spend a penny. She dived into a rough-looking pub, one of the few open on a Sunday because of a nearby market. It was packed. By the bar was Sam Tyler, who had been working the streets for scrap metal for as long as she could remember. 'Any old i-iron? Any old i-iron?' He had a limp and some of the kids took cruel delight in hobbling after him. He glanced over as he swigged his pint. She ducked behind a group of vociferous stallholders and scuttled down to the Ladies.

By the time she'd re-emerged she'd decided that today was not the day to go back to the Mare's Head. She caught a tram in the opposite direction, brushing away the misgiving that she was betraying her kind, burning a lifeline even. As they rattled through the junction she saw the crisscrossing lines of tram tracks and thought of swords clashing in battle. She almost cried out. Why had she been so rash? Why had she placed so much trust in Derek? Why had she allowed herself to fall for him? She suppressed a sob, pinched herself. Where's your grit, girl, she almost spoke out loud.

That calmed her, and by the time they'd reached the pillared entrance to Islington Town Hall she started to imagine herself singing, not in a smoky pub like Doreen Delange, but on a stage lit by footlights. And by The Angel a life of performance beckoned. Miss Dawson would help get her voice into condition before she launched herself. Then there would be no stopping her!

In Riverton Road she prepared herself a frugal meal, making do with remains of stew. With elbows propped on the ancient table she gazed out onto the backyards. 'How is it going, Mo?' she heard over her shoulder. Hands on hips, the whisper of a smile on her face, Mrs Roberts, was staring at her from the scullery threshold.

Mo was startled into honesty: 'I'm not sure.' She blinked fiercely, chatting about this and that while the landlady made herself a cup of tea.

'It takes time,' said the landlady. 'Learning to live on your own.'

Mo nodded and continued eating. Sunday, she realised, was the worst day to be without a family. The rest of the day she spent mending clothes and then settled down to read the Marie Corelli novel Stella had lent her. She began to wonder if she would ever see Derek again.

Chapter Seventeen   *Derek*

Derek went to Patrick's studio and asked if he could stay overnight in order to capture the first light over the Thames. Patrick grudgingly consented. True to his word the next morning Derek was up at dawn. He made copious sketches of the river at high tide, caught in pure white light before the sun was too high and the traffic started up. Later he set up an easel under the studio skylight and worked the best sketches into a composition, which he daubed in charcoal. He was pleased with the result.

He made himself tea. He sat, hugging the mug and eyeing his effort, wondering whether to use watercolour or oils. He watched a glaucous cocoon of spider's web, dangling from a beam and catching sunbeams, which filtered into the room. Inside a knot of spiders was growing; he could see their dark forms glistening through. He looked around: a patina of dust lay over everything in the studio, every ledge and shelf now illumined in the light. Oils would be better: more resonant, he decided.

Patrick was gurgling and spitting water as he did his morning ablutions in the freezing bathroom next door. The Ascot exploded into life as it delivered its first hot water of the day. When Patrick came through into the studio, Derek pushed a steaming mug towards him. The other grunted. At bottom the man craved solitude. In the past Patrick still had access to his ex-wife's shed in Barnes when he needed a change of scene. Now that opportunity had vanished.

Derek was paying a pittance for the use of the studio; he knew the older man was just doing him a favour. They went back a long way. Patrick had picked him off the ground when he'd been flapping and floundering as a young student. He knew about the death of his parents, how it had dragged the ground from under him. He'd told him to paint his way out of the gloom he was in danger of sliding into. 'Never mind style. Never mind trying to please others. Just get it out there onto the paper, onto the canvas. Make art your friend. Your confidant. The rest will follow.'

That was years ago.

Derek felt a tingle of envy. Why couldn't he be more like Patrick? Of mediocre talent – in his opinion – Patrick carried on, come what may. Trailing disastrous relationships and one failed marriage, the man went through life in a daze, always yearning to get back to his work. Obsessed, even as he ate and drank. It gave him a reason to get up in the morning, a reason not to get tied up with paraphernalia. Without it, Patrick grew as tetchy as a penned animal. There had to be relief, in surrendering to obsession as Patrick did. Though he hated to admit it, in comparison he himself was a fair-weather painter, one ear always cocked to the wind, courting distraction.

After the Zara episode he was forced to admit that he'd been chasing a chimera. He'd made a damned fool of himself. She'd been right to sling him out on the street. With her willowy beauty and self-possession she'd excited him, she was the latest cry. But she was no more than a stopping stage, a cracked mirror to show up his gloomy corners. He had been strangely relieved when she shrugged him off.

But Mo? Where did Mo fit in to all this?

Mo was another story. He could not get her out of his mind, even though he'd distanced himself of late. He thought of her when he woke in the morning and last thing at night. He was constantly on the point of rushing to college to find her. But he sensed he would only be pulled in deeper. And what good would it do her, when she was trying to find her feet?

They were too young for commitment. He needed to establish himself as an artist. She needed to … There were so many things they needed to do, but when she intruded into his mind he grew confused.

Patrick had started creaking over the floorboards, frowning. Derek got to his feet and started putting his sketches together. 'I'm heading off for a while,' he said. Patrick looked across and nodded. 'I need to get out of London. My assistant is minding the shop. I've got the loan of a boat shed in Henley.'

'Good. Let me know how you get on.' Patrick had placed an old boot by a pile of crumpled newspaper, which he was arranging into a still life. He couldn't take his eyes off it.

'I appreciate…'

'Yes, a good idea for you to get away. You've been too – too befuddled of late.'

* * *

Grey roofs and chimneys gave way to leaves, meadows and hedgerows brimming with willow herb and buddleia. Derek caught a glimpse of his reflection in the train window. All at once it became Mo's beautiful oval shaped face, her dark searching eyes. He grunted with impatience. He would take leisurely walks by the Thames and its water meadows. He would contemplate wild copses and the tangled profusion of foliage and flowers; watch light playing on water and catch a riot of greens against the umber of heavy mud. He would sketch madly, spontaneously, freely; make notes on everything from hues of the undergrowth to the angle of branches and slant of summer shadows. In the isolation of the boat shed he would set up his easel and work on his observations. He was an artist, not a lover. An artist. But he was filled with the sweet memories of their love-making, he yearned to see her again. He sighed deeply. This would not do. He was becoming a slave to his imaginings.

He needed to paint. Paint. Just bloody paint, as Zara had

said.

When he arrived in Henley, Peter Burnington, the owner of the shed and an ex-student from Chelsea, would not leave him alone. Starved of artists' company since he'd abandoned his course, Burnington barely let Derek out of his sight. Derek had forgotten how tiresome he could be. At first he humoured him, but when it became obvious there would be no let-up in the trite anecdotes, Derek plotted his escape.

Now he was in a pub, looking out over an expanse of flat fields through the smoke-stained window. He'd only managed a few meagre and banal sketches. He put them to one side. He was not in the mood.

Before leaving London he'd spotted notice of a house contents' auction in a town further west: if painting was no longer an option, making a few bargains might be. Yet the morning sale had disappointed. After two hours he'd done more than enough turning over bundles of clothes, inspecting of hairline cracks in ancient teapots and holding up of silk shawls to inspect for flaws.

He salvaged a box of scarves, gloves and cravats; there was nothing else suitable. The West Country was drying up. Whether because he lacked hunger for the hunt or because the better stuff was snapped up by eagle-eyed stall-holders from Bristol, he couldn't say.

He was ensconced in the inglenook of the Duck and Drake in Gossington, a non-descript village strung out along a minor road leading nowhere. The ploughman's lunch, put on for the sale, had been edible and the chat round the bar convivial enough. He recognised faces from previous house sales. One or two of the men chatted, asked how things were in Kentish Town.

But now, there was nothing for it but to return to London.

The train back to Paddington was crowded. He squeezed into an overstuffed Third Class compartment with his crate.

The ticket inspector said: 'That should go in the guard's van by rights.' Derek said nothing, proffering his ticket and wedged himself into a window seat, tucking the crate under his legs. The rhythmical clattering over sleepers made him drowsy.

As he was sinking into a light doze an image of Issy flashed through his mind. She'd called back to Fingal's Cave days after her first visit. She had got the part she was after and was in high spirits. 'You brought me luck!' she beamed. 'This place brought me luck.' He'd been delighted to see her, started offering her all the latest and most glamorous outfits in the shop. She'd laughed. They'd laughed. It was like meeting up with an old friend.

Again she invited him to one of her parties – she seemed such a sociable creature – and again he demurred, certain it was just part of her patter. When she discovered, while they continued chatting over a rail of satin evening gowns, that he was an artist, she became ebullient.

'A real artist?' She went on to say that the least, the very least, he should be doing was painting scenery for the stage. Nowadays, in this era of Modernist design, with musicals, farce and variety all the rage, it was hugely creative. Why oh why was he hiding his light under a bushel? She knew plenty of people and could furnish him with introductions. 'You should definitely come to one of my parties. The West End is blooming…'

Though he had made a pact with himself that Fingal's Cave was about earning a crust and painting for its own sake was where his ambition lay, he began to reconsider. By the time the train had reached Paddington he'd resolved to call round to Issy's house. He fingered the blue Modernist script of her calling card, then put the crate in the left luggage depot and caught a bus to Primrose Hill. She lived in a well-appointed Georgian house in Remington Square, he discovered. Framed rectangles of light gleamed out. The house radiated warmth and excitement. He walked across the street, steps slowing as he approached the wrought iron railings of her house.

Three men, in evening wear and sporting white gloves, approached from the other direction. Toffs out on the town, he thought. One was telling a story, the others bent in to catch the drift. One looked across at Derek and nodded. They came to a stop outside Issy's house. The front door was thrust open. There was Issy, all smiles, hair caught up in some sort of twist, a blue dress down to her knees, beads shining, a band of blue framing her face. She laughed, with that light throwaway sound she made, as she took one of the men by the arm and led the way inside. Hidden in shadows, he realised she had not even seen him. Now the door was closing, shutting him out. He looked down at his workaday clothes, his dusty jacket and shabby trousers and decided he was wasting his time.

Chapter Eighteen *Mo*

Over the coming days Mo's life took on a blurred aspect. She had not seen Derek in weeks. There were fewer courses during the summer months, but one-off intensive sessions were always in demand. The college never shut its gates and she was never short of work. Meanwhile she turned down invitations to join the tutors and students at the pub, and went for more music lessons.

She and Miss Dawson worked on recitation: Miss Dawson had told her rather sharply she needed to lose her Cockney accent as fast as she could. Mo bristled, but took note. Miss Dawson did not approve of her material nor her wish to sing in bars. She was, Mo decided, a prude. It was too much like being back at school. She decided that when the next stint came to an end she would call it a day. Besides, her funds were dwindling.

But she was in for a surprise. At the end of her final session Miss Dawson handed her a card. 'Try this place. The Fox's Den. They've got a small nightclub. I know the pianist.'

Mo decided to give it a try. She encouraged herself by buying a red beret, but when she put it on it reminded her so much of Paris that she thrust it to the back of the wardrobe. She grew impatient with herself. Blast Derek. Damn and blast him. He would turn up sometime – when he felt like it. He was an artist: he had to paint. She must not begrudge him that. For her part she would make her life happen as she wanted it to. Heated debates did not help artists, and fruitless mooching would not help her, Mo Dobson. She had a silk blouse and close-fitting skirt Stella had cast her way. These would come in handy for performance.

* * *

Students and tutors often frequented The Fox's Den. It was lively enough and they had an almost-in-tune piano stashed in one corner. She'd been there once and knew they often had singsongs. She studied herself in the mirror. She was looking blue round the eyes and a little drawn. *I shan't have him haunting me;* she resolved to exorcise her preoccupation with Derek. Yet time and again her mind reverted to Paris. She asked herself what it had all meant to him. For her, it had been a watershed. If you loved someone surely you wanted to be with them as much as you could? Yes, you had to work, but that aside, love pushed all else into the shade.

It was after seven when she arrived at the Fox's Den. The saloon bar was half empty. The Fox's Den had pretensions to Variety; formerly it hosted Music Hall and an aura of razzamatazz still clung to it. On one wall faded posters harkened back to the pre-war days of Marie Lloyd. At the bar a lean man with hairy arms was serving pints. 'I'm a singer,' she announced. 'I've come to offer my services in the nightclub.'

He eyed her and smirked. 'Have you indeed? And what do you sing?'

'Popular stuff. Variety. Musical songs.' She reeled off the names of a few tunes. He raised his eyebrows.

'Another barmaid is what we need.'

'I can do that, too. I was raised in a bar.'

'And where would that be?'

'In the East End,' she said. The bell clanged in the other bar. 'My parents run a pub there.'

'That so? It can get pretty rough round here.'

'Nothing I couldn't handle.' She sounded cockier than she felt, but he was heeding what she said. 'So where's the nightclub? Is it every night of the week?'

'I don't think it's for the likes of you.'

'You need a barmaid and I can sing and all. You'd be stupid to turn me away.'

'Is that so?'

'If you won't speak to your boss then I will.'

Seeing she was not to be deterred the man hesitated. She could see the bar was in disarray. 'I'll 'ave a word with the publican then.' He disappeared and returned in the company of a short bald man who eyed her with suspicion.

'I hear you want to sing? But a barmaid is what we need.'

'So where is the night club?'

'Through there.' He jerked his head to the side where a narrow stairwell led down to a basement. Now he was watching her: appraising her appearance. 'Experience. Any experience?'

'I can sing like a bird.' Her cheeks coloured as she gave him a bright, brittle smile.

The round-faced man with the shiny pate seemed uncertain. She searched in her bag for the card Miss Dawson had given her. 'She recommended me to you,' she said. 'I'd be good for business.'

He turned Miss Dawson's card over in his hand. 'She's the old bird what gives singing lessons, I suppose?'

'She's a professional,' said Mo with a touch of haughtiness.

'I'll tell you what. You 'elp out in the bar for a couple of hours then I'll try you out downstairs. As an also-ran. Our regular singer's got a bit of a bad throat.'

Mo considered that this might well be the best offer she was going to get. 'You've got a deal.'

'Tidy up that counter then, will you!'

'Right, yes.' She sprang to it. She laughed. She could do this. No need for her to put on airs and graces. She would be among her own kind. She adjusted the belt of her skirt. 'Er – Mr?'

'Bates.'

'What time do I get to sing?'

He puffed on the cigarette dangling from the corner of his mouth. 'Round nine o'clock,' he muttered. 'And what's your name?'

'Mo. Mo Dobson.'

She busied herself tidying up the stack of glasses left on the counter, pulled together a few more, found a dishcloth and swiped it over the tables. She emptied the overflowing ashtrays. There was a smell of stale beer and nicotine-drenched air. Though she should be used to them, it made her nauseous. This was a chance she must take. For the next couple of hours she was lost in the hubbub of the crowded bar. Arms reaching onto the copper surface, smoke swirling up amid clinking glasses with voices getting more raucous.

She glanced up at the clock behind the mirrored wall. It was almost nine o'clock. She'd caught sight of people in the street crowding down to the basement club. In her head she'd been running through her repertoire of songs. Bates signalled for her to leave the bar. Another barman had arrived to relieve her. 'You better be good,' muttered Bates leading the way down the creaking stairs, 'our reputation depends on it.' He introduced her to the pianist, who was smoking and strumming the keys as people settled in. When Mo mentioned Miss Dawson he said the pianist who'd known her had moved on, but he knew his stuff. He had sheet music for all the latest West End Shows. They agreed on a couple of songs.

It took her a minute to adjust to the dim lighting. Several tables had elaborate art nouveau lamps on them, others had candles. There was a hum of chattering and muted laughter. In front of the tiny podium a space had been cleared for dancing. Bates introduced Mo as a promising new star from the East End. There were hoots of encouragement and wolf whistles. Mo stepped forward, heart beating wildly. Memories of Paris flashed through her mind – those exotic wailing singers who poured their souls into their music, those travellers of the dark regions. The piano started up, cheery and just about in tune.

> *'The world to me will always be a gamble,'* she began.
> *I don't care if I win or if I lose*
> *The straight and narrow path is such a scramble,*
> *And is such an unattractive life to choose.'*

She and the pianist had chosen a song from Noel Coward's *'On with dance.'* It fitted her current mood. The more she sang the more she entered into the spirit of it. Something in its studied carelessness made her feel free.

> *'I'm a cosmopolitan lady*
> *With a cosmopolitan soul.*
> *Every dashing blonde*
> *Of the demi-monde*
> *Starts to quake when I take a stroll*
> *As my past is incredibly shady,*
> *And my future grows more doubtful every day*
> *Though determined to be pleasant*
> *I shall utilise the present*
> *In a cosmopolitan way.*
> *I much prefer a flutter at the tables,*
> *I treat my whole existence as a game*
> *And if I end up in sackcloth or in sable,*
> *I shall not have lived for nothing, all the same.'*

As she finished there was applause and hands banged on tables. Bates, from his corner, nodded to her to carry on. She sang more from the same show. And then in deference to Music Hall tradition she sang Marie Lloyd's *'I'm just one of the ruins that Cromwell knocked about a bit...'*

Afterwards the landlord handed her a shilling. 'You was

good for business,' he said. 'Come again.'

'Is that all you're giving me?'

'Tonight was a trial,' he said. 'You can come back.'

'When would you like me?'

'Whenever you can,' he replied. He gave her a sly look, his hand rubbed her arm, remaining there rather too long. She brushed him off with a tight smile and walked up the stairs and out into the night without looking back. Her step was lively. She had won them round, the audience lapped up the magic of her voice. She could hardly sleep that night. She dreamt of world wide audiences, of admirers with eyes gleaming as she gave them song after song. The future was beckoning.

Chapter Nineteen

But the next day she had no energy; in fact, she was feeling quite unwell. She had a pain in her lower abdomen. Her period was due. It was weeks late. As a rule that made her tired and she took extra rest where she could – though Ma insisted it was better to carry on moving around to keep your mind off it. After a day's modelling she retreated to her room where she lay on her bed. Later she bumped into Stella on the landing. Stella was looking cheerful and bright-eyed in a lace blouse and pencil skirt. It transpired she had been away for a day or two. Mo did not press for details, enough that the chief model was less sharp-tongued than normal.

'There was something I wanted to ask you.' She hedged around the subject before blurting out: 'Do you ever have days off – from modelling, I mean?'

Stella looked mystified then laughed. 'Oh, I see - times of the month and all that? No problem. You just say – 'This week I am resting.' Everyone will know what you mean. Make sure you let the office know though.'

Yet despite the pain, no blood came. After a day off she returned to work. They were slipping into autumn and more students were pouring into college. Summer courses, sporadically attended, gave way to the structure of term time. When, two weeks later, there was still no sign of Derek, Mo began to panic. 'What's up?' said Stella over tea and toast in the scullery. 'You look pale as a sheet. What's the matter?'

'Nothing.'

'Do you want to tell me about the nothing? Something's obviously eating you…'

Mo twisted her handkerchief into a tight ball in her fist, then released it. 'Derek's disappeared and I haven't had my monthly for weeks now.'

'I often miss mine when I'm travelling or upset,' said Stella.

'Derek said he'd be careful.'

'Oh lawdy, you better get yourself sorted out. I've got a friend who knows somebody, if you need help in that department.'

'What sort of help?'

'What d'you think I mean? You can't very well work as a model if you're pregnant, can you?'

'But I can't be.'

Stella eyed her sceptically. 'So where do you think he's gone?'

'In Paris it was all hunky dory. He talked about going off to paint. But I don't know where…'

Stella was silent, her crystal-clear gaze unnerving.

'I've tried his shop. His assistant says he's gone off for a while, but she doesn't know where either.'

'It might be he don't want you to find him…'

'Stella – how could you?'

'As I said, there's this woman who 'elps out girls who've got themselves into trouble. She's reliable and doesn't charge too much.'

'I won't be needing all that Stella.'

In her room Mo curled up in a ball on her bed, drew the old blanket over her head, felt her face wet with tears. For the last few weeks she'd been living and moving in a bubble of unreality, swept up in it, so every day concerns were set aside. She'd kept her family out of her mind. They made her feel that whatever she was doing was wrong. Ma had said she would not be welcome home if she left again. And she had! She had defied her, walked out without even saying goodbye.

She felt so tired and drained she could have slept for a

week. Yet despite her physical exhaustion she slept only fitfully, taunted by nightmares: she was on a train going too fast and without a driver; she was hanging over a precipice clutching a tree root; there were rats loose in the house.

The next morning she decided she could put if off no longer: she needed to get herself checked by a doctor. There was a surgery near the college. She scraped together what money she could for a consultation, bought a brass ring in Woolworth's and called herself Mrs Eaton, which gave her a secret thrill. She spent an anxious couple of days before her appointment, distracted herself by going back to work, but felt so awful she had to excuse herself and go home early. The doctor asked to do an internal examination. Mo could not stop shivering and shaking on the examination table. The doctor said he couldn't be certain but he thought she was about eight to ten weeks gone.

Mo wandered out onto the street in a daze, feeling sick and very alone. Words ran through her head: plight, fallen woman, Magdalene, unmarried mother – ominous words, which reeked of wrong-doing. She could not help herself, but caught a tram back to Hackney, though she knew she could no more face Ma and Pa than fly to the moon.

They'd say she had it coming, what with her headstrong ways.

She could not bear the look of anguish in her father's eyes. She could not bear her mother's shoulders sinking under the burden of it. She could not…And Derek? Where was Derek in all this? In Paris he had spoken of love, of living in a garret like something out of romantic novel. And now? He came and went at will. Did he have any regard for her at all?

The only person in the family she could possibly admit anything to was Cissy. She resented her older sister's bossiness, yet she knew that Cissy kept her feet on the ground. Besides, she had to confide in someone apart from Stella.

She hesitated before she knocked at the terraced house. Cissy gaped to see her standing there. 'What the blazes are you doing there! I thought you was dead!'

'Can I come in?'

'Where 'ave you been all this time? Not a word in weeks. Ma will bloody kill you.' Yet despite the harsh words Cissy stood aside to let her pass. Thankfully Cissy's husband, Bob, was out minding the market stall. The little one was having a nap.

'Thought I'd call by,' said Mo. ''Ow's tricks?'

'Just like that? You've got a bleedin' nerve!'

'Okay, Cissy I know. Can I have a cup of tea?' She followed her sister to the back of the house. The cluttered room gave off a mixture of overused air and the aroma of a lamb stew simmering on the hob. Cissy cleared a space for her on one of the worn easy chairs, stared at her, waiting for answers. Mo longed to open a window to let in fresh air. Cissy placed a large, brown teapot and cups on a low table between them. 'We was worried sick. You've no idea. Pa went looking for you again,'

'He never.'

'Anyway, 'ow's your new job?' asked Cissy handing Mo a cup of tea.

'All right. Making enough to get by.'

'Selling hats?'

'Mmm?'

'Hats. How many do you sell in a day?'

'What are you talking about?'

'You work in a milliner's, don't you?'

'Oh yes, of course.' Mo sipped the strong tea.

'You all right?'

Mo shrugged.

'You look a bit peaky to me.' Cissy reached over and stuck another lump of coal into the burner, which burned winter and summer to counteract the dampness. Ted stirred in his crib. Cissy picked him up, nuzzling her face against his and whispering sweet talk into his ear. Mo stiffened. Why were things so complicated? Before she knew it a tear was sliding down her face. She brushed it away.

'Cissy, I don't know what to do. There's this man, see, and we went – we went to Paris and now he's gone away and I don't know where. 'E's a student at the college.'

'Paris? What college are you on about?'

'Where I work.'

'I thought you worked in a milliner's.'

'I do. I did. Oh Cissy I'm in such a mess and I don't know what to do…'

'Well, go find 'im if 'e means that much to you.'

'That's not all…'

Cissy stroked the top of her son's head without looking up. 'You're not...?' She placed the toddler back in the crib. 'He's still sleepy.'

'I think so.'

At that moment they heard the front door go and Cissy's husband came striding into the room. 'Look, what the river's washed up,' he said with a smirk.

'Just a social visit,' said Cissy quickly. Mo recovered herself sufficiently to fetch a cup and saucer for him. 'Morwenna was telling me about 'er new job.'

'Oh I see. So 'ow's it going?'

'Be a love – could you go down to Downe's and fetch something. A couple of Bath buns would do …'

'I just got in.'

'Not every day Morwenna calls round, be a love…'

Bob grunted his displeasure but when Cissy pleaded that Ted was about to wake up, he did as he was asked. When he had disappeared Cissy banged her palms onto her thighs. 'Father will kill you if he finds out. Break 'is bleedin' heart, it will.'

'Don't I know it?'

'So who's the lover boy who's gone off and left you in the lurch?'

'He may come back.' Even as she spoke Mo realised how desperate she was feeling. For a few short days her passion for singing had blotted out all else, but talking to Cissy forced her back to reality. She was in a minefield. Cissy was right: father would never forgive her. She knew from Ma that when he worked at the docks he'd come across women living on the streets and he'd vowed, then and there, that his daughters would grow up decent.

'You could always get rid of it,' said Cissy. She went and picked up Ted who had started crying. She held him close to her. 'Or stay away long enough and then give it up for adoption.'

She sounded so sure of herself. Mo detected a little malicious pleasure at her news. But she couldn't blame her. She had brought it on herself. No one had held a gun to her head. Yet now as Cissy cooed baby talk to Ted and prepared to change his nappy, her air of superiority grated. The front door slammed as Bob came back from the bakery. 'If I was you,' added Cissy hurriedly, 'I'd find him quick and see what 'e has to say. You say you love him and all, but what about him - how serious is he?'

Mo let out a sigh. 'I think – I thought he was.' All confidence deserted her. She sounded gullible and lacking in backbone. Today she didn't have the slightest clue what Derek's true sentiments were.

Bob put the Bath buns onto the table. 'There you are, girls. Now do I get to finish my cuppa in peace?' Cissy handed Ted over to Mo while she went to fetch plates and pour Bob fresh tea. The toddler's milky, soft baby smell caught Mo by the throat – this living, breathing being...

Cissy cut up the buns but Mo found she had no hunger.

'So 'ow are the titfers going?' Bob asked. Mo blushed. She had never been a good liar. 'You gonna see the old folks then?'

'Don't 'ave a lot of time today but I'll be back soon.'

He bit into the bun and slurped his tea. As always, he disgusted her. Perhaps it was because he acted as though his brawny body and large hands were a source of fascination to all women. Besides, she hated the way Cissy went quiet in his presence as though she secretly feared him.

'How's business?' she asked.

'Same as always.' He looked at her from the corner of his eye, slyly, provocatively. She got to her feet.

'Need to be getting back. Thanks for the tea.'

'You haven't finished yet. What about eating yer bun? I went out extra to get it.' Mo took a quick bite but the dough lodged in her throat. She bade them a hasty goodbye. Heavy with a sense of betrayal she went nowhere near The Mare's Head.

Back in Chelsea she fretted until Stella came home. No point driving herself crazy with worry, she kept telling herself, but as the minutes passed she grew slowly frantic. She could not get out of her head the delicious milky smell of Ted and his cheeks so plump and unmarred by life, nor could she suppress the welter of fear going round and round. Towards nine, more restless than ever, she decided she could not give up Derek so easily. The least she could do, the very least, was to seek him out and speak to him. Give him the benefit of the doubt. Yet tracking him down would not be easy: he had always just appeared, as if from nowhere. Fingal's Cave was a start but often he was not there. The assistant, who'd only been there weeks, did not know where he lived.

Now she could hear Stella shifting about in her room. She banged on her door. 'Can I come in?' Stella looked taken aback. She'd been out wining and dining and had a mellow, satisfied look about her.

'I went to see my sister.'

'Derek still not turned up then?'

Mo sank onto the end of Stella's bed. 'I need to speak to him, that's all I know. I've no idea how to get hold of 'im.'

Stella slipped off her coat, throwing it over a chair and lit a cigarette. 'Want one?' Mo declined. Stella gazed at her. 'The college ought to know. In the office they'd have his address and whatnot. Next-of-kin's details.'

'I went to the doctor.'

'And?' Mo stared at the row of scent bottles, all colours, pointed and flat topped, on Stella's cluttered dressing table and nodded.

'I told you I knew someone.'

'You always do, Stella. But it's not that simple – just – just getting rid of it.'

'I suppose you could always try the natural way…'

'Meaning?'

'You know – running up and downstairs, hot baths, lots of gin.'

'Sounds revolting.'

'Better than bringing a brat into the world without a father.'

Mo felt pain in the solar plexus. 'At least the father has a right to know,' she whispered.

'He's an artist. Or had you forgotten? They believe in taking love where they find it. They don't give two hoots about commitment. Believe me, I know.'

'Speaking from experience, are you?' Mo spat back.

Stella stabbed her cigarette into an overfull ashtray then sat next to Mo on the bed. 'Yes, Mo, as it happens I am. You see I got pregnant, twice in fact. I had one, aborted the other.'

'Oh, I didn't know.'

'So now you're in the picture. You see, I *do* know what I'm talking about.'

Mo stared at her in silence. 'I'm sorry, Stella. What happened?'

'Look, it's the past. I can't – I don't want to be forever looking over my shoulder.'

'But what happened? Was it a boy or a girl?'

'It's over, Mo, I said.'

'Sorry.'

Stella gave a sigh. 'Don't keep saying that. It's not your fault. It was a little boy. Rupert I called him, though they may have changed 'is name. I kept him for a week while I was in hospital and then…'

'Do you ever see him?'

'Of course not, I gave him away.'

'Oh!'

'I thought – and I still think it was the right thing to do. At least they were able to give him some sort of life.'

'What about…'

'Mo, it's over I said. I don't want to talk about it anymore. Don't you understand? I'll give you the address of this friend and then it's up to you. After all, you can't say I didn't warn you.'

Chapter Twenty

When Mo woke up the next day she decided that though Stella might be older and supposedly wiser, she was too hard-bitten. She refused to take the route Stella was advising: downing masses of gin and jigging up and down stairs was too revolting for words. So, too, was the visit to the woman 'who sorted girls out'.

Derek had gone to paint, as he said he would: he would return in his own good time, and there was an end to it. She scrubbed her teeth over the chipped hand-basin and ignored the desperation in her eyes. The last thing she felt like doing was stripping off to pose for students. But what other option did she have?

She forced down a breakfast of porridge, which made her feel ill, and then pushed herself through her daily sessions. It was not as onerous as she feared. By now the students were so used to her that they paid her only as much attention as their work demanded. She felt drained and dozed off during the long pose, but nobody seemed to notice. It could be worse, she told herself: she could be on her feet all day as a waitress or stuck in Dukely's with the constant clack-clack of machines.

She resolved to track Derek down. She went back to Fingal's Cave but found only the assistant. In the college office she told the receptionist she needed to contact him urgently in connection with a painting he was selling. The woman shuffled through an index-box and handed her a card to copy down his address.

* * *

Nineteen Victoria Terrace in Gospel Oak was far primmer

than she would have expected. It was a neat, terraced house behind iron railings with shiny windows and freshly laundered net curtains – certainly not the Bohemian dive she would have associated with Derek's wilder tastes. A bread delivery van passed in front of her. Thompson's Fresh Today she read with a jolt. The same company serviced The Mare's Head. Her diaphragm trembled. She banged down the doorknocker. The sooner she did this the better.

The clang echoed through the house, meeting no response. She was on the point of retreating when the door opened. Before her stood a woman in her late twenties. Puzzlement battled with curiosity on the woman's face. 'Good afternoon,' said Mo, though every inch of her longed to flee. Derek had spoken of Eleanor, his schoolteacher sister. The face before her was lightly lined about the mouth and eyes, but not hostile. 'You must be Eleanor?'

'I beg your pardon?'

'My – my name is Mo. I don't know whether Derek mentioned me?'

'I can't say that he did?'

'Is he… is he at home?'

'No, he's not, I'm afraid.' They hesitated. Having come so far Mo was not about to give up so easily. Eleanor stared at her, bemused.

'I need to see him.'

Eleanor looked at Mo so gravely she felt she could see right through her. 'I see. Then you had better step inside for a moment. He's been away. But coming back today.'

As Eleanor led the way down the hall Mo glanced around, avid to take in every detail. The worn Persian rug and old brown prints of the Thames hailed from another era, no doubt hand-me-downs from Derek's parents. The house had a front parlour, visible from the street, a back kitchen and scullery, where they now were. Derek had spoken of his parents' house as if it had little to do with him. Now she understood why. The solidity and thrift of their hard-working lives seeped from every fibre. The back kitchen had a fire grate on one side and a range on the other. A row of socks and stockings were drying on a clothes jenny.

'Sit down, won't you?' Eleanor indicated an easy chair. Mo was dumb with confusion. So determined had she been to pursue Derek that she had not counted on meeting his sister. Eleanor made tea. She served it from a rosebud tea set complete with silver tongs. She offered Mo a plate of ginger biscuits. The more hospitable she became, the more Mo shrank into herself.

The clock struck the hour solemnly.

'Is anything the matter, Miss…?'

'Dobson. It's just… it's just I need to see him.'

'You're a student, are you, at his college?'

'No. I'm a model. And a singer.'

'Oh, I see.'

It was time to go. Either that or come right out and say what she was here for. Damn Derek, damn him a hundred times! 'There's something he and I need to sort out,' she said.

'He doesn't owe you money, does he?'

Mo reddened. 'What d'you take me for?'

'I wasn't … I know he's borrowed money in the past. He sometimes forgets to pay it back.'

Mo sank back into the easy chair, shoulders sloping down.

'Do tell me if anything is wrong. I may be able to help.'

She stared at Eleanor's impassive face, wondering what to do or say next. She felt stuck to the chair. 'I've been there a few months now,' she murmured. 'At the college…'

'Would you like some more tea?' Eleanor replenished the rose teapot. The more Mo looked at her the more she discerned a reverse image of Derek. Where Derek was unpredictable and intense, Eleanor appeared to take it everything in her stride. Just then they heard the key in the lock and the door thrust open. Mo's heart banged. Before she saw him she knew it was Derek. He came whistling down the hall and halted on the threshold of the kitchen. Slowly she turned towards him. He looked as though he hadn't slept in a week.

'So there you are,' said Eleanor. 'I was wondering when you'd put in an appearance… we have a visitor.'

'So I see.'

'I was wondering where you was.' Mo got up and moved towards him. Derek flicked the hair out of his face. His eyes flashed at her and she drew back, uncertain. He threw a duffle bag into a corner and pulled out a chair.

'Sorry. I've been very busy.'

Eleanor looked from one to the other. 'I have some shopping to do. I'm going to pop out for a while.' Derek nodded without looking at her, while Mo went back to her chair. Eleanor walked to the cupboard beneath the stairs and fetched her coat, 'I won't be long.' The door shut behind her, leaving the two in silence.

'You must have been pretty determined to flush me out.' He stared at her with that fierce air he sometimes had.

'I have my reasons,' she said.

How often in recent days she'd pictured this reunion, yet there he was, frowning and looking as though he'd been living in the park. 'You don't seem very pleased to see me.'

He broke into a smile. 'I'm shocked to find you here. That's all. How did you find out where I live?'

'From the office.'

'Well, now you have found me …' He leaned back and stretched out his legs, brushed her arm with his hand. 'What happens next?'

'I was beginning to think you was avoiding me.'

'It's true, I was.'

'Oh!' she recoiled as if punched.

'I'm joking. I told you I had stuff to do. I've been away – painting.'

'What stuff?'

'Money. I need to earn some money. And painting.'

'But you weren't in your shop…'

'You came to Fingal's Cave?' He paused. 'To tell the truth I wanted to get on with my painting. I needed to get away. I was getting… I felt stuck. First I went to Henley. When that didn't work out I went further afield.' He poured himself tea. 'Want more?' She shook her head. He looked across. 'So how have you been getting on? How's the singing?' he paused again, searched her face. 'I've missed you.'

Did he mean that or was he just trying to placate? A window shuddered as a car passed by. She tried to calm herself. Her mind was fumbling as she felt the situation slipping out of control. 'Nice place you have here.'

He gave a nonchalant shrug. 'Not quite to my taste, but it's a roof over my head.'

'Quite a roof,' said Mo. 'It's well kept.'

'We have a char comes in once a week. More tea?'

'I just said no.' He seemed distracted, which made her feel she was in the house of a stranger. She could stand it no longer. 'Derek, I'm pregnant.'

He stared into the empty grate as though he had not heard. She folded her hands. At that moment the front door clicked open as Eleanor returned. She walked through with her bundles of food. 'I bought some bacon. We were getting low.' When neither spoke she dropped the goods onto the kitchen table. 'Shall I go out again?' she asked.

'I was just telling him I'm expecting his child.'

Eleanor gaped. She walked through to the larder and started tidying away the groceries, banging things about on the shelves. Derek slumped in his chair. Eleanor came back from the scullery, stone-faced. Eleanor turned to him. 'Surely not,

Derek?' She turned to Mo: 'Are you certain? How long have you known? Have you been to a doctor? Are you sure it's Derek's?'

Light-headed with anger Mo got to her feet. 'You said I was your love. I was your girl. I trusted you. What sort of man are you? Ain't you got no sense of decency? Where I come from if a man gives his word he keeps it!' Even as she let fly these sentences she knew they were only half true. Derek looked surly, brow-beaten. Where was the advocate of passion now?

'Derek, did you make promises?'

Derek got up and strode about the room then sat down on the arm of the chair opposite Mo.

'Well?' said Eleanor.

'It's true enough,' he said at length. 'We went to Paris. We stayed together. We…'

Mo's eyes blurred with tears. She glanced at him but he had lowered his eyes and was staring at the ground. She gulped back her turmoil. The mere sight of him made her feel so many things all at once. She longed to seek the shelter of his body. 'I don't know what to do…' she mumbled.

'I'm not ready for this,' he said, still staring away from her. 'I'm too young… so are you.'

Tears trickled down her face and she made no attempt to stop them. Eleanor got up and walked out of the room. Mo sniffed loudly and searched in her pocket for a handkerchief. Derek was quite white by now. 'If we rush into anything we'll end up hating each other,' he said at last.

Mo had a moment of piercing clarity, which shocked her with its coldness. She picked up her things. 'I'm going now.' She moved towards the hall.

'No, wait.' He caught her arm. 'Let's talk about it.'

She shrugged him off. 'What is there to say? I love you Derek. I love you more than I ever thought possible. But I'd rather jump in the river then beg you to marry me.'

'Wait.'
But already she had reached the front door.

Chapter Twenty-one *Derek*

Derek heard Mo slam out the front door and march down the street, her heels clicking on the pavement, hurrying her away from him. He chewed the corner of his thumbnail. At the time of their Paris trip she had said her period was due and he had taken security from that. He stared at the scrubbed floorboards, heard Eleanor shifting about, and decided to get out of the house.

In the corner pub he sat over his pint of ale and ruminated, but not for long. A couple of regulars came over and sat down at the table without being asked to. They joshed him and bought him a pint. Shocked beyond words he gave no sign of it, laughing with the rest of them and standing the next round. When he joined them at darts his arrows flew all over the place, causing a fellow player to remark: 'Don't have your eye in tonight, mate, do you?'

He was on his fourth pint and the floor was swinging like a boat beneath him. He belched quietly and felt unutterably sad. Why were things going so badly? What was a man supposed to do? It was the way of nature for men to find women delectable and to want to get as close to them as possible? But marriage! That was something altogether different. The throbbing increased. In his mind he saw Mo's sweet oval face and gave an unbidden sigh. She was adorable. He lurched towards his beer, realised the glass was empty and ordered another. He watched the barmaid drying off glasses and stacking bottles of ale in neat rows. She caught his eye in the mirror. He looked away. He drank another two pints and sloped off home when he guessed it was late enough for Eleanor to have gone to bed.

The next day he returned to college, expecting to see Mo. When she was not at any of her classes, and had not turned up the day after, he began to worry. In the intervening hours he had thought about nothing but their time together in Paris. It had been sweet, so sweet. If only there was not this complication. She had opened him up so he became a stranger to himself: someone light and full of hope, someone who could climb mountains at dawn, someone who could paint until the paint ran dry.

She would say it had been unfair of him to stay away, to put his painting first. But it was a proof of what she had unearthed in him, of the depth of feeling she had stirred. Now he was driven. He couldn't help it. She'd bitten deep into him, making him afraid, making him both more and less than he had been before. She, of all people, would understand that; it was the same with her singing. But even as he tried to persuade himself that he was not in the wrong, he knew he had let her down. He had wooed her, won her love and then played hard and fast with her, making an appearance only when it suited him.

Something had to be sorted out.

On the third day he became agitated. He went to her digs. Stella looked at him with a sour look and told him she'd never seen Mo in such a state.

'So where is she? I've got to see her. It's urgent.'

Stella gave him a cold, hard stare then shrugged and looked away. 'I haven't a clue. She hasn't been here for days.'

When he realised he was wasting his time at Riverton Road, he nodded and went on his way. 'Tell her I want to see her. As soon as possible.' He ambled by the river, watching the ceaseless traffic of coal barges and goods vessels. It was high tide. A chunk of wood was buffeted along, dipping up and down in the waves. He followed its course until it disappeared under a bridge, caught up in other flotsam. He reflected on their last meeting: her pale face spoke of helplessness coupled with indomitable pride. She was nobody's fool. She had stated her case, declared herself without embarrassment or guile. When she didn't meet like for like she had made a lightning decision. Not stopping to plead or persuade, she had simply fled.

This steeliness he had not till then encountered in her. For him she had always been this highly attractive, pliable though spirited creature – more girl than woman – naïve, impressionable, unworldly. Now he was forced to concede she had a core of integrity far surer than his own.

He went back to Victoria Terrace, hunted out the flimsy sketches he had done over recent weeks. He examined them. They were facile, immature. There was something he was evading. He could not commit, neither on the page nor in life. He reneged, withdrew, disappeared and distracted himself. The sketches mirrored his evasiveness. In a fit of self-loathing he began to rip pictures from sketchpads. He wrenched others from the drawers where he'd stored them, crunching them into an untidy heap and taking them into the back garden. Here he set fire to them. Flames licked round the sheets where he'd scratched his images; he watched them ignite and curl in flames, roar into life and drift skywards as blackened bits on the up-currents of hot air. He wiped a sooty hand over his cheeks, stamped on the smouldering embers until nothing remained but charred ash under his feet.

The next day he resolved to find Mo, come what may. In a more buoyant mood, he set off: he would go again to the polytechnic to check if she had turned up to sit. If she hadn't, he would seek out information in the college office: they would have more details about her than he did. With determination he walked down Kentish Town Road towards Camden Town. Ahead of him a crowd, bunched around the hump-backed bridge by Camden Lock, was blocking the pavement. A police cordon marked off the area. There was a buzz of activity, voices muttered while police officers were moving people out of the way and putting up more tape. He asked one of the bystanders what was going on.

The sturdy man next to him said he worked the canals and owned one of the barges further along. The way was currently blocked to the public. 'A woman was out walking her dog. She spotted something in the water. Thought it was a bundle of rags. When she got nearer she realised what it was. The police ain't letting nobody through. But I've got a living to make…'

The police were taking no chances. Though it could well be just an accident, they were determined to seal off the area and prevent the curious marauding over the ground. Onlookers were being pushed to one side, told to go about their business. Derek walked on, disquieted. Further down the road he glimpsed a headline in the afternoon edition of the London Evening News. He rushed to buy it. 'Unknown woman fished out of Camden Lock.' Mo's parting words came back to him. 'I'd rather jump in the river and drown than beg you to marry me…'

Suppose it was Mo? Just suppose. The hurt look on her face haunted him. He caught a bus to college. He stared at his image in the window as he went, his eyes glared back in accusation. He almost missed his stop. He dashed into college and enquired after Mo in the office. The receptionist raised her eyebrows in amused disdain. Derek could barely contain himself. He strode out and walked towards the river, smoked a cigarette, threw the butt in the water and paced back inside the college again. Stella looked surprised to see him.

'I haven't a clue where's she's gone. As I said last time you asked, she was in a proper state. But then you know all about that...' She looked at him with a mildly flirtatious air, which riled him.

His stomach was churning in anxiety. He turned on his heels and retraced his steps to Camden Town, where he approached the police station and addressed the officer-in-charge. In a voice shaky with emotion he told him he wanted to report a missing person. A domestic strife, asked the duty officer, looking wary: the Force did not take lightly to police time being wasted. Derek stated his concerns and mentioned the body in the canal.

The officer considered him for a moment and started another column. He wanted to know what Mo had been wearing and the circumstances of their last encounter. Eventually the officer advised him to go to the University College Hospital morgue where the body had been taken to await identification and the coroner's report. Derek broke into a run, by now light-headed. He found his way to the hospital and through various corridors to the morgue, located in the basement. The mortuary attendant told him to sit down and wait.

After some time a lanky individual in a white coat nodded at him to follow him downstairs. In the basement Derek could not stop shivering. The overhead electric light glimmered on the slate floor. Steps came towards them, echoing down the corridor. It was the keeper of the morgue. He led them into a small room that was even colder and where the body had been laid out on a rubber sheet. There was a tag tied to its protruding blue left toe. The keeper pulled back the sheet covering the woman's face. Derek stopped breathing and felt the floor veer towards him, his bloodless legs about to collapse beneath him.

It was not Mo.

He staggered back and the tall man grasped his arm, steadying him. He laughed, a strange laugh that was almost a shout as it rebounded from the walls and startled the other, who looked at him as if he was crazy. 'It's not her,' he managed to say, and rushed out onto the street where the light was dazzling after the gloom of the nether regions of the morgue.

Veering between desperation and elation, he headed for Hackney. He would find her. He would. The girl on reception had had no address for her, apart from Riverton Road. All he could recall was the name of the pub, The Mare's Head. Must be in Mare Street, he reckoned. But it was not. He walked and walked, searching every pub, asking in every corner shop where it might be. He wasn't even sure what Mo was short for. Was it Molly or Miranda, Maureen or perhaps Morwenna?

The brush with death had cleansed his vision. Fate had spared him, given him another chance. He would find her. Marry her, if necessary. He would concentrate on what was important. All else was diversion. He thought fleetingly of the funeral pyre of his sketches. Phoenix will rise from the ashes, he laughed at the absurdity of himself and his behaviour. What an effect she was having on him!

Chapter Twenty-two

In the end he came across her before he located the pub. Tired of trudging down Mare Street and all the streets off it, he'd wandered into a pocket of green. Here he sat and considered his next move. Sparrows were scratching and squabbling over crumbs thrown by an old girl standing beneath a slab commemorating the Great War. Pigeons were flapping and cooing on the ground. And there, ambling by, alone and looking very weary, was Mo. He rushed up to her.

'Mo!'

She turned. She went scarlet.

'Mo, please forgive me...'

She put down the shopping bag she was carrying. He took hold of her hands, which were frail to the touch.

She pulled back. 'What do you want?'

'You,' he said. 'You.'

She stiffened. 'I don't believe you.'

'Mo?'

'I don't trust you. Not a word you say.'

'Marry me.'

'Marry you? Marry you! What for?'

He stepped back. 'Mo, I love you. I've been stupid. And the baby...'

'The baby's gone.'

'What do you mean, the baby's gone?'

'As good as – I am going to see someone Cissy knows. Tomorrow.'

'No, Mo. No, Mo. Don't do that. Don't.'

Mo looked paler now than he had ever seen her. 'If only I

could trust you,' she said in such a small voice that he was filled with a chaos of guilt and fear.

'At least come into a bar with me so we can sit down and talk in peace.'

Her eyes twitched in anxiety. Just looking at her turned-down mouth and wan face made him ashamed. He could not let her go now, to walk away to a botched abortion and out of his life. She was biting her lip as if in two minds whether or not to go for a drink. She was shaking, though the tremor was barely perceptible. Overcome by tenderness he kissed her. She stifled a gasp. He sensed there were too many things going through her mind right now. She was floundering, sinking.

'Derek...' she began. Relief mingled with rage in her face. At the next corner they went into a small smoky pub with a line of drinkers lingering by the bar. He found them a table and fetched some drinks. He tilted her chin towards him, forcing her eyes to meet his.

'I've been looking for you for days. You led me a merry dance. I was convinced you'd jumped into the river...'

'I led *you* a dance!'

'I thought you'd drowned.'

'I nearly did. I was that mad with you I didn't care anymore.'

'So what changed your mind?'

'I just didn't believe you could be like that... after Paris and all.'

'I owe you an apology.'

'You owe me a lot more than that.'

'I know.'

'What are you afraid of?'

'We're too young. Especially you.'

'I said I won't force your hand – even if I could. I just thought you should know. That's all.' She looked away at two men playing dominos. 'Why have you come to say the same

149

things as before?'

'I'm not prepared to let you go so easily. It's a mistake. We're not ready… but it's happened. I'm willing to make a go of it if you are.'

'Is that what you want?'

'Yes Mo, that's what I want.'

'Derek, there's never been anyone else as far as I'm concerned.'

'I should hope not. You're only seventeen.'

'Where I come from many girls are married by then.'

'Not where I come from.' He emptied his glass and went to fetch another. Mo straightened her blouse, which had ruffled up. Her cheeks had gone quite pink. She gave him a knowing smile as he returned from the counter.

Chapter Twenty-three *Mo*

Later they went together to The Mare's Head. Ma looked as though she wanted to hit Mo till kingdom come. She held her tongue. Pa looked pale and worried. All they knew was that Mo had been staying temporarily at Cissy's and had been unwell, though Mo knew Ma would have had her suspicions. Derek cleared his throat, summoning courage, and told them he and Mo wanted to marry.

Alone with Ma in the scullery, Mo fiddled with the crockery and tried to avoid her gaze. 'Do you realise what you've put us through?' Ma hissed.

'I'm sorry Ma. I really am.'

'You in the family way?' she accused her, taking a cloth and drying the cups. When Mo said nothing but turned away, she went on. 'Would've broken your father's 'eart if the man had gone and left you in the lurch.' Mo gazed at her reflection in the window and sniffed back a tear. Ma waited till she turned back to face her. She gave her a strange, penetrating look, which made Mo afraid. She seemed to be seeing right through her. 'Blood will out,' she said quietly.

'What do you mean, Ma?'

Ma shook herself slightly as if chasing off a shadow. 'Headstrong you are. Always have been. I tried to protect you. Now look at you.' She paused. 'Do you love him at least?'

'Oh Ma, more than all the stars in the sky.'

'Then 'eaven help you. There's no more I can do.'

* * *

Three weeks later she and Derek were married. Mo was still seventeen and they had known each other less than a year. It was a hastily put together affair, both the ceremony and the party. The Church was St Mary's where her sister had wed four years before. The party was held in The Mare's Head, not dissimilar to Cissy and Bob's do. Mo detected an undercurrent of hostility darting between father and Derek, or more precisely from the whole family towards Derek. Tilda was outraged that her older sister and support were departing for good. Ma hardly spoke to her. Only Cissy treated her with understanding. When her parents gave their consent she realised they felt they had no choice. Friends of the family and neighbours swallowed the tale of a whirlwind romance, though Mo knew romantic yarns cut little ice with Ma.

At the end of the evening, when she was a little tipsy, Ma came over to her. 'My little gypsy,' she said. 'My exotic musical creature. May the angels protect you from what's in store.'

Puzzled, Mo broke away and went to seek Derek who at that moment was downing pints of ale with Pa. She was glad to see that they, at least, were getting on.

PART 2

1927

Chapter Twenty-four *Mo*

Almost two years had passed.

In that time the Germans applied to join the League of Nations. Savage riots rocked India. An Irish woman took a pot shot at Benito Mussolini and Ali Khan, a former Cossack cavalryman, crowned himself Shah of Persia. In Britain the General Strike came and went, splitting the country: Welsh miners gave concerts to support soup kitchens while Cambridge undergraduates rode in chauffeured Bentleys to work in the docks.

The Surrealists held their first exhibition in Paris: 'Pure psychic automatism, free of all control by reason.' Claude Monet, the first and last of the Impressionists, died, aged 86. Coco Chanel revolutionised women's clothing, making it simpler and more sporty. Riots broke out in Dublin at Sean O'Casey's play about the Easter Uprising. Joan of Arc won the Nobel Prize for G B Shaw. Fred Astaire and his sister, Adele, delighted London in George Gershwin's: *Lady be Good.* Noel Coward produced *The Marquise* and *Sirocco,* which audiences booed.

While all this was happening Mo and Derek settled into a mundane routine. They lived in Victoria Terrace with their son, Timothy, and Derek's sister Eleanor. Derek focused on earning money in Fingal's Cave while Mo became a fulltime wife and mother.

Every day Mo took Timothy for a walk. Today they were in Waterlow Park, where ducks were scooting over the pond. As soon as he saw them Timothy squealed 'Ducks! Ducks!' and beating his feet against the pushchair, demanded release. He ran in a crazy zigzag amongst the pigeons waving his arms and shouting in glee. The sun caught the curls of his dark brown hair, his plump legs striding towards the water. Not yet two and already with a mind of his own.

She caught up with him as he reached the reeds. Impetuous as ever he was about to plunge into the water to join the ducks. Alarmed, they paddled off. She chuckled. There was no stopping him! Such a zest for life he had, such joy in all that surrounded him. More than anyone he could lift her out of herself. 'Here, I brought some crusts.' He clutched at them, lost some and scattered the rest towards the water. The ducks came gliding back. He giggled and clapped his hands, ran up and down beside the water. A dog was wading in. Timothy squealed as he watched its head bob up and down. He loved animals. When he'd had enough of chasing up and down he settled back into the pushchair. They went up through the copse and over the slope.

As they did so Mo's mind reverted to Derek. A heaviness came over her. He seemed to be slipping away, slowly, quietly – like water filtering through her fingers. Where now were the sweet words he'd used to win her over? She recalled his vagabond eyes entrancing her as she lay stretched before the sputtering gas heater in his draughty Fulham studio. At times they'd been unable to finish a studio session without touching each other. He'd join her on the divan where they'd tumble into the joy of each other's bodies in the dying afternoon light. Together they'd mixed with his friends in Paris, eyed the Bohemians at the Café Royale, shimmied to jazz or decked themselves in flowing kaftans. This is my tribe, she'd thought. These people put freedom above convention, beauty above security. It was for this she had left her family in Hackney.

She sniffed. It was time to be heading home.

At home, while Timothy was taking a nap, she tackled the ironing. Derek was back from Fingal's Cave and sat brooding over a cup of tea. When he got like that he reminded her of the worst of her father. She went in search of the flat iron and found it on the corner of the draining board. 'D'you want more tea?' she asked, keen to show she could rise above his sullenness.

'What about Timothy? Hasn't he been asleep long enough,' he said.

'Can't you see I'm busy?'

Derek opened his mouth to protest then closed it again. His hair was falling across his forehead, making it hard to read his expression. He rarely touched Timothy, never played with him. As she lifted the pile of crumpled shirts and blouses onto the table, Timothy started whimpering. Derek leaned over the pram. 'Poor kid,' he muttered. She caught only half of what he was saying. He was rattling the pram, trying to get Timothy to sleep again. She crossed the room.

Derek slunk back to the table, watching her. She picked up Timothy and held his face against hers. She gave a little gulp. The softness of that skin against hers was sweet. So, too, the milky smell of him. But now she was getting another smell. He had filled his nappy and needed changing. She scooped a blanket around him and clattered up the stairs. The sudden noise set him off. A second later he was yelling his discomfort in her ear.

With Timothy slung against her shoulder she rummaged in the airing cupboard for a clean nappy then took him through to the bedroom and laid him on the floor. She pulled apart his chubby legs and undid the pin to reveal a mass of soft yellow faeces. He was yelling full throttle now. She scooped up the mess with a wad of cotton wool. When had Derek ever changed a nappy? Got up and rocked Timothy back to sleep in the night? Her fingers worked deftly and she turned her face to avoid the smell. Timothy was inconsolable. 'All right Timmy, all right.' She started humming to calm him. She sang, but to no avail.

Derek was standing in the doorway. 'What's he upset about?'

She looked across at him. Help me, she longed to say, but the words stuck in her throat. 'He just won't stop,' she muttered. Derek said nothing but came and stood by her side.

'All right, Timothy.' She cleaned him with water and applied balm to his reddened thighs. She dusted him with Johnson's baby powder and dressed him in clean leggings and a jacket. By now Derek had gone back downstairs. She started humming gently into Timothy's ear. She sat on the bed with him in her arms. There were moments like this when she could stay quietly next to him and she would have been content enough. She walked to and fro with him. He started grizzling again. What more could she do? He was dry now and clean. Maybe he was teething? She paced the room hugging him to her shoulder. His cry pierced her, stirred her, made her feel desperate. She had done her best. A tear ran down her nose and clung there. She sniffed it back. Downstairs she could hear Derek moving around.

Later that night she sat up in bed, propped by pillows, flicking through an old theatre magazine. She got up to fetch another from the pile just as Derek entered the bedroom. She sat down on the chair by the dressing table and glanced up at him. 'So how were things in the shop today?' she asked. He muttered something she did not quite catch. He seemed preoccupied, distant. Her eyes sought his but he shifted away, as if not wanting to engage with her.

She re-immersed herself in the magazine: the smooth skin and shiny seal heads of the women filled her with yearning. This was the world she'd once dreamt of. Her eyes clung to the pages, unable to let go. Suddenly something in her broke like a stick of chalk. To the surprise of both of them she began to cry. Once she started she was unable to stop. 'Derek, I'm not happy.' She cast aside the tattered magazine.

'What's the matter, Mo?' Through a film of water she saw he was staring at her, baffled. He paused. 'You know what I think?'

She gazed up at him. 'What?'

'You need to concentrate on what you've got. Timothy. The house and all.'

'I adore Timothy. You know that. But sometimes it all seems too much…'

Derek clucked his tongue. 'It would only take a minute to clear things away.'

'It all gets messed up again straight away. It's tedious.' Tedious was a word she'd taken to using a lot of late.

'You've got to get a more of a grip.' His voice sounded harsh. It cracked through her like a whip. She turned away from him. Why was he talking about tidiness? It was the least of her worries. Right now he seemed evasive, hard: a stranger almost. He was mumbling inaudibly.

'What did you say?'

He went to hang up his jacket in the wardrobe. 'I said we can't carry on like this. Eleanor does more than you do and she has a full time job.'

'Don't you ever consider what it's like for me?' She stared at him, wiping away the tears with the back of her hand. 'I had ambitions.'

'You can't be a mother and an artist. It just doesn't go.'

Mo bit her lip. Where did that come from? Once he'd encouraged her on her journey as a singer. Had he forgotten? She wanted to pick up a shoe and aim it at his head cocked so arrogantly to one side. He threw himself down onto the bed and tucked his hands behind his head. 'Look, I'm just asking you to make an effort.'

'Don't you think I do?'

'Come here,' he said roughly, patting the bed beside him.

She stayed where she was. He got up and walked over to her. 'Look at me.' She stared at the buckle of his belt, refusing to raise her eyes to his. How often did it come to this? The acid comment followed by the plea to make up, Derek ever eager to brush aside the hurt burning inside her. 'Mo,' he pleaded.

She sighed in response, softening towards him despite herself. She fingered his belt, holding back her helplessness. They said such cruel words to each other these days. She looked up at him. Once he had been her Adonis, her beacon. She'd loved to take off her clothes and lie before him on the divan, ignoring goose pimples and the stench from the gas fire and the dusty windows giving a smeared view of the Thames. He'd led her to believe she was born for a wider horizon, to live the life of the artist, to be his helpmeet and lover.

Now a light from the street was crossing his face, turning him into some strange animal. A centaur. 'I hate it when you treat me like a housewife.' Her voice was so faint she hardly recognised it. Let it be over, she thought, this silly squabbling. He touched her lips with his. 'Sometimes I feel lost,' she said, resting her head for a moment against him. He moved away and pulled off his shirt, throwing it onto the chair amongst her things.

'I want you to help me,' she said.

'I don't understand what's wrong.'

She cried out. Surely he should know what it was to have a gift and not use it? The noise woke up Timothy who was sleeping in a cot in the corner of the room. He started whimpering. She got up and crossed the room, rocked the cot gently, encouraging him to go off again. 'There now,' she murmured in his ear. He showed no sign of settling. She placed her cheek against his. Derek was watching, willing her, she felt, to fail.

'Now you've woken him, he'll never get back to sleep,' he said.

159

She patted Timothy's back. 'There now, pet. Hush. Mummy's here.' She walked up and down the room with him, weaving her way through scattered garments. She snatched words from a song she'd heard on the wireless. *'My bonny lies over the ocean, my bonny lives over the sea. Bring back, oh bring back, bring back my bonny to me…'*

Timothy's crying dwindled. 'Leave me alone,' she muttered as Derek brushed her arm after she'd laid Timothy in the cot. Did she mean it? Did she really want Derek to leave her alone? A tumult of instinct bound her body to Timothy. Sometimes she grew confused so it clouded her mind: a bright idea in the morning would turn to ashes by noon. Timothy was quieter now, fingering her hair with his stubby little fingers as she leaned over him. The sweet milk smell of him, the softness of his skin calmed her. He gurgled even as he plunged into the security of her nearness. She bundled him down, covering him with a light blanket.

She slipped into her side of the bed. For now she wanted some of that same oblivion. She heard Derek shifting beside her, the mattress creaking as he moved. He touched her arm. 'Sometimes,' he began and she heard his voice catch. 'I don't know where you are. You seem so...' Exhaustion was seeping into her body like night over land. He was rubbing her neck, seeking response but a stone inside her refused to be lifted. 'Mo?' The hand was moving slowing, pausing, unsure of its effect. She kissed it lightly.

'Sorry but I'm tired,' she said flatly. Derek gave a grunt, withdrew his hand and turned away from her.

Chapter Twenty-five   *Derek*

The next day Derek woke early and left for the shop. He knew Mo was struggling and that he was not helping matters; he wanted to, but did not know how. At the moment he seemed to make matters worse. There were times he feared for Mo. When she teetered on the brink of these dark moods he wanted to stay put on the opposite shore. He hurried out of the house, closing the door quietly behind him. He glanced up at the sky, which was dark but shot through with silver where it was clearing. He swept aside a flicker of guilt. He'd been working in Fingal's Cave such long hours, in the shop and at auctions, that he rarely saw Mo, let alone Timothy.

By mid-morning he had had his fill of being a shopkeeper. Over recent days he'd sold well and he'd done enough stock-taking. Besides, it was one of Mrs Bryant's days and she always declared herself ready to hold the fort if need be. He boarded a bus towards Fulham. The bus chugged between cars and the odd horse-drawn vehicle; bicycles and delivery vans wound their way through. Derek stared out of the window. Well-kept squares and elegant Georgian facades alternated with pavements thronging with students, businessmen, flower girls and newspaper vendors. Down-at-heel unemployed men in shabby boots loitered on street corners.

This was London, his city. How could he have forgotten these fragments of a huge canvas? They reached the river. A passing boat discharged a black pall of smoke. He was an artist, whatever the world might say. But artists painted, didn't they? They didn't sell boas and top hats to actors. The conductor was whistling cheerily as he clipped tickets.

In Fulham Derek got down and walked. The streets were shabbier than he remembered, with some shop fronts boarded up, while others displayed the latest frocks behind curved glass. He stopped by a side door next to a tobacconist's and rang the bell. A man thumped down the stairs and flung open the door. Patrick Shaughnessy stood before him. His forehead and hair were spattered with paint and his hands and clothes were grubby. He looked surprised, annoyed even.

'What are you doing here?' Patrick turned and went upstairs. Derek followed. They entered Patrick's studio, as cluttered as ever. A line of enamel mugs was strung out on the floor next to palettes, caked with paint. A well-worn easel stood next to a pell-mell of canvases and thumb-smeared jam jars with brushes. Splashes of paint streaked across bare floorboards. Smells of linseed and drying oil paint pervaded the air. Derek sniffed.

'Ah, it's good to be back here!' He moved around the room, inhaling. Patrick was watching him.

'So what do you have to say for yourself? Disappearing for God knows how long and then just pitching up like a lost pigeon.' Patrick looked more dishevelled than ever. His hair stood out like a windswept bush. Some said he was crazy. By now he'd stopped teaching at Chelsea Polytechnic altogether.

'What are you working on, anyway? Show me,' said Derek.

Patrick flipped through a stack of canvases. 'Take a look for yourself. Urban scenes mainly – I'm experimenting with tonality…'

As he glanced at the paintings, Derek asked himself how he could he have stayed away so long. Patrick's colours had grown more vibrant and his shapes stronger. There was no holding him back. Now his work issued more from a teeming imagination than from observation. Bright orange suns burnt over desolate blue-streaked landscapes of factory stacks and barbed wire. Midnight seas toiled in slashes of violet and magenta. The anger and irritation Derek had been holding began to dissolve. 'I need to work again. It's been too long. When can I start?'

'Start what?' Patrick looked disgruntled. 'You had your space here.'

'Sorry to burst in on you…I was feeling kind of...'

'Desperate?'

'It must be the spring.' Derek sprawled onto a battered sofa.

Patrick laughed. 'It's true. The light is getting better.' He turned back to his canvas and holding up the paintbrush to measure against the square. He squinted and turned the brush sideways. Derek glanced at the canvas. It was a mass of bright streaks with the skeleton of a blue chair set to one side.

Now Patrick was taking a flat knife – much like Eleanor used to ice a cake – and was flattening a splodge of white into a dark brown, blending in ochre. His head tilted to one side as he assessed the effect.

'This place might not be much to shout about but at least it's here and you can come everyday,' said Derek. When Patrick said nothing he went on: 'You have a system that works…'

Patrick grunted impatiently. 'As usual you're talking too much. You think I sit around and wait for the muse to strike?'

Derek stared at the vivid tones on Patrick's palette. No longer the drab hues of the previous years when his works recalled the Camden Town group. The renown of those Bohemians of North London had fizzled out. They'd revelled in the subdued browns and beiges of workmen's clothes, nicotine-stained bars and the beleaguered look of anaemic landladies. Derek had missed out on them much as he'd missed out on the War.

Patrick was mumbling to himself: 'Not quite brown, not sepia, not ochre, terra cotta. I've been after it for days. What is it you were saying?' Patrick dipped a thick brush into the mixture and started dabbing one corner of the picture. 'Sad really when you come to think of it.'

'What do you mean?'

'You just walked out on your whatever you like to call it. Your gift, I suppose. It's not a question of talent. You just don't have the stamina.'

Derek grunted and took his leave soon after. But not before he'd arranged with Patrick to resume where he'd left off, using the studio at least once a week. Returning to North London on the upper deck of a bus, his eyes could rove and feast. The river was glistening. The sun caught the tangle of branches turning from winter to spring, iridescent, wild with crossing shapes and spaces. There was a world here awaiting him: raw, urgent and infinite in its variety.

* * *

When he returned to Fingal's Cave he felt lighter, in a mood to tackle the clear-out he'd been putting off. Mrs Bryant had left by now. The renewed arrangement with Patrick would set him on the right track. Even a glimpse into that other world edged him nearer to it. He would be there when Patrick was not, to avoid any clash of space or tempers. He would buy new art materials. After the ritual burning of his drawings he needed to start afresh. He whistled as he glanced over the rail of vintage velvet frocks, selecting those that had found no buyers to be bundled off to the Sally Army. Into the same heap he cast footwear that had likewise found no takers. He gathered up anything that had been sitting for more than three weeks.

A ping of the bell announced a late customer.

It was Miss Isadora Fontane. Issy. He slowed to a halt as he looked over at her. He had not seen her in well over a year. In a dark blue caped coat and with her hair cropped in the latest gamin shingle, she looked ravishing. Although he regretted the loss of her rich tresses, he was captivated by the cheeky, direct look it gave her. Seconds later he realised she was in the company of a tall, aristocratic-looking gentleman.

'Ah there you are!' She came towards him and grasped his hand warmly. 'Just passing. I wanted to see what you have in stock. I am up for auditions again. It always helps to show willing, even though every theatre has its props department ...' Already she was running her expert eye along the rails, fingering items. The man behind her looked at his wristwatch. 'I shan't be long. I couldn't bear to walk by and not to look in...' She turned back to Derek. 'How is business?' Derek muttered something non-committal and busied himself ordering a row of cloaks.

'So-so, eh?' She pulled out a pink shift and held it up against herself. 'I'll take this one.' Derek wrapped it up while her companion gave one last look around before striding out into the street. She laughed. 'Typical man – can't bear browsing.' Derek handed her the parcel and the change. 'Look, do come to one of my gatherings. I'll introduce you to some theatre people...' She scratched something on the back of a card. He took it without smiling. Long after she had left the premises he caught the fragrance of her in the air. He tidied up the bundled items and took them through to the back storeroom before locking up for the night.

Chapter Twenty-six *Mo*

Mo was standing before the tall Hampstead house. It was like ones she'd seen advertised in *The Tatler*. There were window boxes bright with pansies on the sills and striped canvas curtains instead of the usual nets. She hesitated, tempted to hop onto the next bus going down to Camden Town.

She recalled her recent meeting with Stella. Over tea and cake in Kentish Town Stella was fighting off Timothy, who was pulling at her skirt. 'Give it a try,' she'd said. 'Jonathon Knighton is a director at The Athena Theatre. He does these performance classes in his house. He's good. Go. You've nothing to lose.' One look at Stella's fine, pencilled eyebrows and painted nails made Mo feel dowdy. She'd pulled Timothy onto her lap and given him a bite of her cake. 'It's just an hour or two. Your sister-in-law will mind Timothy. She doesn't work Saturdays, does she?'

And so here she was. Eleanor had readily agreed, for she adored Timothy.

Before she could change her mind Mo lifted the doorknocker and let it fall. The door opened. 'Come for the class?' A slender woman in a white turban and green silk jacket with a white dragon stood before her. Her crimson lips were pursed over a jade cigarette holder.

Mo nodded and the woman motioned for her to enter. The woman introduced herself as Zara. Zara, thought Mo. That name rings a bell. The woman swung open another door onto a large room of dazzling white. Inside, people were gathered in a circle in thrall to a man who was striding up and down, holding forth.

He stopped, mid-speech. 'Come in, come in. I'm Jonathon Knighton. Welcome to our midst.' Mo sidled down onto an empty chair. 'We will start with movement.' His voice boomed around the room. 'Mostly we have forgotten how. So we need to remember.' He paused, looked around.

Mo was intrigued. Knighton came towards her and gently took her hand. Confused, she pulled back. 'See!' he cried out. 'This delightful creature – one of nature's talented ones. I can tell.' Coming closer he whispered. 'Don't be shy.' He asked aloud. 'Have you ever danced the Shimmy or the Snakehips?' Mo shook her head. Now was not the time to admit how she loved to dance or that her mother had performed in Music Hall.

'The polka was once the most revolutionary of dances,' he continued. 'Such contact. Such distance. Discipline mixed with wildness. Music please.' Zara went over to the gramophone and placed a disk on it. Zara. Zara, thought Mo. Zara was the name of Derek's ex-lover. Could they be one and the same? With growing curiosity she watched the willowy woman drift across the room. She felt a stab of envy. 'But we have moved beyond that,' Knighton was saying: 'Ours is the jazz era. Would you like to dance, Miss?'

He pulled Mo to her feet. As the beat of New Orleans throbbed through the room they started swinging up and down. He moved freely then grasped hold of her hand again. They turned and turned. The room was flying by, so she could hardly catch her breath. She laughed, flushed and surprised, but kept to the beat. At last he led her back to her place.

'So you see,' he was saying. 'In art as in life we must push against the limits. This is less a classroom, than an experiment where new things can emerge.' Mo began to wonder what she had let herself in for. Freed from his imperious hold, she took a good look at the man. Of above average height, he exuded magnetism. With a mop of unruly, grey-black, slightly frizzy hair, penetrating brown eyes beneath bristling brows and hands as large as bear paws, he resembled a corsair.

'Now it is your turn. Find yourself a partner. Gender is of no concern.' Some moved to find a partner while others hugged the edges of the room. The few men in the room were soon spoken for. Zara put on another disk. 'Forget you are in a class. Let the music take you over, body and soul. Cooperate with your partner – but without words.'

The music started up: strident, broken up and sure of itself. Pervasive awkwardness gave way to laughter. Mo's neighbour nudged her. Mo got to her feet. Slowly at first then ever faster, the couples moved around the room. The floorboards creaked with the sound of their feet. The room grew warmer. When the music stopped the dancers looked around, smiling, then wandered back to their seats.

'Now you are warmed up we will consider where drama comes from.' He stalked around. 'Who knows anything about the ancient art?' Expectation rippled through the room. Mo looked around at her fellow participants. Seven women, she counted, and four men. Most of the women were older than her. Clerks and shop girls? Housewives? She could not be sure.

'Drama came from Ancient Greece,' piped up a skinny woman rattling huge silver bangles on her arms. She hesitated. 'That's all I know...'

Knighton stopped and turned on his heels. 'The word drama comes from the Greek *drao* It means to do or act. Drama presupposes a collaboration, in other words, an audience...' Mo's head was spinning, absorbing what he was saying. 'The two masks you see in theatre foyers depict the division of drama into tragedy and comedy. Melpomene, with the weeping, downcast face, is the muse of tragedy. Thalia, with a smiling face, is the muse of comedy. In the early days – we're talking five hundred BC – drama was a genre of poetry.'

Mo had never met anyone quite like him before. 'But that's

enough history. You came here not for academic knowledge but to learn about yourselves.' He paused, assessing the impact of his words. 'We choose to be only half awake.'

Mo could hear herself breathe.

'I repeat. We choose to be only half awake. Why would that be?'

Silence spread around the room, thick as snow. She looked round at other blank faces. Mo sank into her chair. When no one dared a response he continued: 'Because' – and now he was striding up and down again – 'we are afraid.' A girl alongside Mo sniffed nervously. Tension mounted while he looked at each person in turn. 'We fear our own power,' he said with a glint of triumph. 'Especially if we happen to be female.'

Mo glanced around. Several people were staring at the floor. She noticed the walls. They were bare and white whereas the entrance hall had been lively with bright, unsettling pictures. As if reading her mind Knighton said: 'Even the walls are blank so you can project your inner pictures outwards.' He came to a sudden stop. 'Now we will form a tighter circle.' There was more jostling as people fell in with his command. 'Look round the ring.' They eyed each other furtively. 'These are your companions on the journey.' More shifting. 'Each of you will now say what has brought you here and what you want to discover about yourself.' Then he added in a lower voice. 'Those who wish to leave may do so now.'

One young man stepped forward. 'Excuse me, sir. This was not what I was expecting.' Another man joined him. 'Pretentious bugger.' Mo heard him utter as he passed. Others tittered.

'Quite all right, old chaps' said Knighton. 'This is not everyone's cup of tea.' They heard the front door slam. 'Performance is not for the faint-hearted,' said Knighton. Now people dared not look at each other. Mo's heart was throbbing erratically. Should she bolt too, she wondered, hearing the men's steps fade away? Or else laugh? She could not help seeing the funny side of it. Knighton took himself very seriously.

Zara spoke up. 'Anyone else want to leave? No one can say you are not here of your own free will.' She spoke in a deadpan way as though exhausted. Her skin was porcelain pale beneath the turban, which now half covered one eyebrow. Had she and Derek really been lovers? Mo could not stop looking at her, wondering. Zara waved a long arm towards the circle. 'Let us start with the newcomer.'

Mo looked around as though someone else were being spoken of.

'Come now,' said Jonathon, 'no need to put the girl on the spot.'

'You just have!' Laughter filled the room.

Mo swallowed, then thought: what the hell. 'I've come here to – to see if there's anything besides washing nappies,' she blurted out. Several people giggled.

'Quite right too!' called another.

'That's why I came an' all,' whispered a woman nearby.

'Let's hope you discover that something else here,' said Jonathon.

'Anyone else?'

'I always wanted to act,' said the girl with the bangles. 'I love a good story. I work in a lawyer's. Good job, you know. But's there's no fun in it.' Others volunteered their reasons. As they spoke Mo found herself relaxing, she was not so strange after all.

Jonathon Knighton looked around, frowning. 'Another word about drama.' Several fumbled for their notebooks. 'In Athens competitions took place for the festival of Dionysus. Now who knows anything about Dionysus?'

Again the bangles' girl arm up shot up. 'We know him

better as Bacchus, the god of wine,' she said.

'Mmm,' he muttered, looking at his shoes, then above their heads. 'He was the god of nature itself. There were rites in his honour – wild rites. More importantly he was known as the liberator, Eleutherius. He freed you from your normal, everyday self. Ecstasy. That's where the word comes from. Being outside your self.' Mo suppressed a tickle in her throat. She was dying to cough. He glanced towards her.

'He could move between worlds. He presided over the spirit world. His mission was to make music and bring to an end all care and worry. Later, in Rome, there were bacchanalia – frenzied orgies. These were for women only. Imagine that. This was because they believed women had better access to his realm.' He stopped as abruptly as he had started and walked around the silent group.

Mo coughed. 'Would you like a glass of water?' he asked.

'Perhaps it is time for a tea break?' suggested Zara.

Knighton nodded then gave a rare smile. 'For those of you new to the group, Zara is my assistant. She keeps me sane.' People laughed. It surprised Mo how Knighton could switch so swiftly from one mood to another.

The circle broke apart. People wandered towards the kitchen beyond. Here the housekeeper was wielding a hefty teapot. Zara handed Mo a cup of tea. 'So, is this what you expected?'

Mo shrugged. 'I'm not sure.'

'Will you come again?'

'Why not?' Once the words were spoken she knew them to be true. She caught Knighton's eye. He pushed to the front of the queue, exchanging a word here and there. No wonder they regarded him with such awe: he lifted them clean out of their shops and sculleries! A chubby girl jostled against her.

'Beryl here,' he said, 'works in a milliner's. How about you? Did you work before you became a mother?'

'I was an artist's model and singer.' She met his eyes for the first time. And what eyes he had! They burned right through her. She caught a whiff of tobacco and muskiness from him. He was, she guessed, old enough to be her father. Taking her tea she moved to a clear space where she could view him from a distance. It was a while since a man had so unnerved her.

On the kitchen wall were notices of dance venues and plays in London and Paris. Just looking at them filled Mo with longing. As Beryl came and sat next to her, a shadow fell across them. When she looked up Zara was looking down at her. The teacake Mo was crunching broke apart. Mo brushed herself down. 'Ever been to any like this before?' asked Zara.

'Can't say that I have.'

Zara moved away and others gathered round her in the corner. Mo was curious. When she approached she saw large deck of cards with strange images laid out on a small table. 'It's the Tarot,' whispered Beryl.

'Pick a card,' said Zara

'Don't start on that malarkey,' said Knighton, who had wandered over. He turned and walked away. Mo watched his solid retreating back.

'She's good, you know,' volunteered Beryl.

'I don't believe in all that.' Mo was about to move but curiosity overcame her.

'Just pick a card,' said Zara.

Mo hesitated then selected one from the centre. Zara drew in her breath sharply. 'It's the Tower,' she said. Mo gazed at the image of an ancient tower spitting fire, people spewing from its ramparts, as lightning struck. Zara spoke slowly. 'You're about to undergo a sea change.'

'And that would be?' Mo was torn between fear and excitement. What did this flamboyant and annoying woman have to say to her? 'It's a load of old tommyrot if you ask me.'

'It's the Tower,' repeated Zara.

'So what does that mean?' Mo peered again at the disturbing image.

Zara demurred.

'What is it?

'It denotes great change. Upheaval.'

'Rubbish,' said Mo, heart racing.

'I think you should be careful,' said the other.

'About what?'

'You need to watch it. That's all I can say.'

'See. Told you it was all baloney.' Mo pushed away from Beryl and Zara. Jonathon was waiting by the threshold of the reception room. 'Time to re-gather,' he said.

Chapter Twenty-seven *Eleanor*

Eleanor returned from a stroll in Parliament Hill with Timothy. Walking him in his pushchair and seeing so many young mothers and nannies about made her wistful. A wind had blown up, tossing branches of the skimpy trees by the water's edge and shaking their tight green buds. Although May, it was colder than expected. Timothy's cheeks were red, his eyes watery: it was time to get back inside. She opened the front door and dragged the pushchair into the house, its wheels snail-trailing mud and grit.

She made up a fire. As she watched the crackling, dancing flames and savoured the smell of burning wood and coal she hummed to herself. For a second she imagined what it would be like to have a husband and a child to look after. Brushing away the thought, she began to wonder when Derek would return. No sooner had he entered her mind than she heard the key in the lock and there he was, bundling into the room, hunched up in a padded jacket with a cap on his mass of curly black hair, forever the look of a wild gypsy about him. He seemed surprised to see her.

'Wotcha sis. So what's this? Where's Mo?' He threw his shoulder bag onto a chair. She moved towards the sink to fill the kettle.

'She's gone to Hampstead. I thought she told you about it?'

He slouched down at the table and cast off his cap. For a moment he looked exasperated, helpless. There was so much she needed to teach her younger brother. She pushed the mug of tea towards him. He got up and fetched the sugar bowl from the larder. 'What did you say it was?' There was a querulous tone to his voice, as though, somehow, wherever Mo had gone, she was in the wrong.

'A performance class for singers and actors.'

She came back to the table, glanced across at Timothy, who was lying sprawled on a blanket by the fireguard, rubbing his eyes. She lifted him up. 'Time for a nap, I think.' She settled him into the pushchair and he was soon dozing. She came back to the kitchen table, pulled her mug towards her and observed Derek as he scanned the room, eyes restless and vacant. For all his bluster at times he came across as unsure of himself. She recalled he'd said something about auction items arriving from Bath. 'Get a good haul?'

He shrugged. 'Mixed bag. Lots of rubbish, a few good bits.' He went on to tell her about the run-of-the-mill garments that had been on offer, describing one or two frocks in detail. He had always had a good eye. After a few minutes he went upstairs. She pulled out a heap of exercise books from her bag and started correcting them. Pleasantly drowsy, her head dropped onto her chest.

The latch rattled and there was Mo, her face was glowing with enthusiasm. She retrieved an exercise book that had dropped from Eleanor's lap into the grate. She warmed her hands then turned to the pram to check on Timothy, who was still asleep. At that moment Derek came thundering down the stairs.

'Hello there!' Mo looked over her shoulder. 'I went to the class. They made us dance and talk about ourselves…' She had a rushed childish excitement as her words tumbled over each other.

'Why didn't you mention it this morning, Mo?'

'You weren't here when I left, were you? Besides, I told you a couple of days ago.'

Eleanor examined her fingernails. She reached for the teapot and poured Mo a cup of tea. Mo sat down at the table, the light of excitement leaving her face. 'Tell us about it,' said Eleanor.

'Nothing else to say really.'

'Who were the other people? In the class, I mean?'

'Oh, shop girls and the like. People like me. Misfits, I suppose.' Eleanor and Derek glanced at each other then back at Mo, whose eyes were fixed on the table as she sipped her tea.

'What makes you think you're a misfit?' asked Derek. When Mo shrugged he went on: 'Look, I'm glad you went. You saw something different. Another world.' She looked up and smiled at him until he added. 'I'm glad you found the time...' He scraped back his chair.

Mo flashed him a look. Lightning streaking across a dull, cloud-laden sky. Eleanor got to her feet, fearing the worst: another fierce row, followed, most likely, by another noisy reconciliation. It was becoming a pattern. Someone's stomach rumbled. Eleanor was tempted to laugh. Earlier she'd put together scraps of ham and a few potatoes and carrots, none too fresh, which she'd found at the back of the larder: a stew of sorts. 'Do you want to eat?' She went to the dresser and took out the striped bowls, which had belonged to their parents.

'I'm not hungry,' grunted Derek.

'I'm starving,' said Mo.

'I'm sure you can manage something,' said Eleanor to her brother. She lit the gas under the saucepan and watched the stew bubble and coalesce. She stirred slowly. Stews were for the dead of winter, times of chapped hands and draughty schoolrooms. But that was all she'd been able to scrape together, given the near empty shelves. As she dislodged lumps from the bottom it occurred to her that she had already done her bit for the day, in fact, more than enough. She wanted to get out for a while.

'So.' She rummaged in the kitchen table drawer for cutlery and filled a jug with water, laying the table as though nothing were amiss. Derek looked ill at ease and Mo, hurt. Eleanor ladled out the soup and pushed the bowls towards them. Neither reached forward. Neither thanked her. Timothy stirred, giving a little whimper. By now he had been sleeping well over an hour. If he carried on he would give them no peace at night. She glanced towards him. 'I fed Timothy earlier,' she said to Mo. Mo got to her feet and approached the pushchair. Timothy murmured and carried on sleeping. 'It might be better to wake him now,' Eleanor said.

'Let him sleep,' replied Mo and went back to the table. Eleanor shrugged. She was not the mother. She was not their mother, either. Outside it was still light, people would be walking, talking, visiting teashops and art galleries.

'I had some soup earlier when I fed Timothy.' Neither Derek nor Mo responded. 'Right, well, I think I'll leave you two love birds alone.' She went to the cupboard under the stairs. 'I'm going out.' She buttoned up her waterproof jacket and gave them a fleeting smile as she left.

Chapter Twenty-eight *Derek*

Later that week Derek ventured to Remington Square where Issy was throwing a tea party to raise funds for destitute actors. He found it not only a peculiar notion – he assumed most actors preferred hard liquor – but an even more peculiar cause, given how many others were down on their luck. Surely an actor could always turn his hand to something? After all, he had to. By now he had decided he needed to broaden his theatre contacts. Whether this was to increase the flow of customers to Fingal's Cave or to explore the chance to create stage sets he could not say. All he knew was that Issy represented a glittering world that enticed him.

A young man with slicked back hair was tinkling on a piano. Nearby a group of men were smoking and joshing each other. A blonde woman placed a tiered plate, piled high with scones and fairy cakes, on the dining room table, while another rattled a tin: 'Cough up what you can.' Someone dropped his cup and saucer, causing an outburst of mirth. The whole thing seemed more about fun than fund-raising.

'I'm Jonathon Knighton. At The Athena.' Derek turned towards an intense-looking man with the darkest eyes Derek had ever come across. 'Issy told me about your shop. She says you sell good stuff.'

'Ah yes. My wife went to your class, I believe,' said Derek, a little taken aback by the sheer presence of the man.

'Is that so?' Knighton looked puzzled. He paused. 'I'll get the wardrobe people to come round to Fingal's Cave and have a look. You don't do sets, do you? Scenery?'

'We specialise in clothes and small props.'

'Our last designer left us in the lurch. I don't suppose you are able to help us there? Issy mentioned you were an artist.'

Something in Derek quickened. Why not? He had done it before. 'As a matter of fact I *can* do sets.'

'Really? You have experience, do you?'

Derek outlined the projects he had been involved in.

'Could you come round to The Athena?' Knighton reached into the breast pocket of his jacket and handed him a business card. 'And bring some sketches of previous work?'

Derek said he would. Knighton nodded and moved off: there were other people he needed to talk to. Derek watched him go. Luckily he'd not torched his stage work when he'd burnt his other drawings and paintings. Surely Mo had said more about this man, when they'd talked about her class, once they were back on reasonable terms? He couldn't remember. He'd been half asleep. Knighton seemed a man with many strings to his bow, as the saying went.

* * *

Issy called round to the shop two days later. She needed head-ware for a specific role as the wardrobe mistress had not come up with anything suitable. A silk turban for another Noel Coward role was what she needed.

'I might have just the thing,' said Derek, delighted to see her again. Together they rummaged through netted skullcaps and cloche hats until she found what she was after. Her eyes glanced across the cash register at him, full of mischief and promise.

Chapter Twenty-nine *Mo*

Mo could hardly keep still. Once she'd breathed that special air of Knighton's Hampstead house she knew she was more than just a mother and sloppy housewife. She started singing the scales again. Things were opening up for Derek, too. He had told her about Patrick and the studio and she'd been delighted for him.

Eleanor said she was happy to take care of Timothy if she wanted to go again. By Saturday an unusual peace had settled on the house. Mo stirred, watching Derek move around in the dawning day. 'I'm going to the class again today,' she said.

'The one with Knighton?'

'Yes.'

'I told you I met him at a theatre party two days ago? I'm going to see him at The Athena. I might be doing some stage set work for him.'

'Oh.'

'I think you need to watch your step with him.'

'What do you mean?'

Derek shrugged 'Just a feeling,' he said. 'Anyway, enjoy yourself.'

Minutes later he banged out of the house.

Timothy wriggled in his cot and gave a whimper. Soon he had pulled himself up and was staring at her over the rail. 'Mummy. Mummy. MUMMY!'

'Alright, you little scamp. I'm right here.' She brought him into bed with her and he tugged at her hair and patted her face with his palms, demanding attention. 'I know. I know. It's time to get up. You must be hungry.' He screwed up his nose and started shouting: 'Gagagagaga.' She kissed him on both cheeks and pulled back the covers.

Later, after she'd fed Timothy, she and Eleanor were sitting together over porridge and toast. To her mind her sister-in-law was looking drained. 'Eleanor,' she said, 'you look a bit peaky.'

Eleanor looked up. 'Me? I'm fit as a fiddle.' Mo shrugged and chomped on her third slice of toast. She spread a blanket on the floor and placed Timothy in the centre, surrounded by a heap of bricks. These he sent flying with a shriek of delight, gleeful at her reaction. She sat down next to him. 'Look Timmy we can build a castle.' He clapped his hands. 'Give me the brick,' she pointed to one next to him. He eyed her with curiosity and passed it over. She glanced up at the clock on the wall and realised she needed to be on her way.

Knighton's class was depleted: even as they moved into late May, influenza still lingered. It had been a cold spring. Mo was relieved to discover a few familiar faces. Beryl was there, as was Zara, sporting a long scarf with silver threads. It *was* the very same Zara Derek had once pined over. He'd admitted it in one of their closer moments. 'All said and done, just a figment of my immature, artist's imagination,' he'd said with a laugh. Watching Zara's affected manner and hearing her pinched, high-pitched voice, Mo was inclined to believe him. She did wonder, though, what was it was about Zara that attracted him in the first place?

'Today we will be looking at Realism,' Knighton was saying. 'Does anybody know what I'm talking about?' An embarrassed silence descended. Few had done the suggested reading.

'Ibsen,' piped up a pale-looking woman at the other end of the room. Eyes swivelled towards her.

'Who is Ibsen?' responded Knighton, walking in her direction. Today Mo was reminded of a lion, his hair a thick mane.

'Henrik Ibsen was a Norwegian playwright. One of the first

to put the conflicts of ordinary men and women onto the stage,' continued the pale one, as if from rote.

'Quite right,' he said. 'In the nineteenth century playwrights begin to deal with the dilemmas of ordinary mortals, people like you and me…' He glanced around the circle, scanning each person in turn.

Beryl whispered. ''E's like a lion on heat.'

Mo burst out laughing. He stopped by her. 'So, Miss, Miss?'

'Mrs,' she corrected. 'Mrs Eaton.'

'Do let us share the joke.' She went crimson. 'Do tell what is so amusing.' She studied a stain on the floorboard. He was standing right in front of her. She could almost feel his breath on the crown of her head.

To her relief someone else spoke. 'Ibsen wrote about women, didn't he? In *The Doll's House*, for instance.'

Knighton grunted and moved on. 'Now I'd like you to do a bit of work. You can break out of the circle for this. Move the chairs. And there's an ottoman over there.' There was a spontaneous eruption of movement, all thankful to be shifting and unfocussed again. 'You need something to write on. We have spare pads and pencils on the table.' There was another rush as they reached for these. Mo settled herself against a cushion in a corner.

'Imagine you are a dramatist. Look at your life. At the conflicts and characters in it. What would he say? What would he want to draw out and exaggerate?' Mo's heart was banging against her ribcage. What horrid questions. She was being asked to look over her life as though she were separate from it. She had come here to get away from all that. What was this impossible man doing to her? She raised her eyes and saw him staring in her direction.

'Derek,' she murmured. She felt a flash of anger mixed with longing. She scratched his name then scribbled all over it. There was so much she could write about them, but she did not know where to start. She stared at her feet in shabby shoes, looked down at last year's faded dress.

Across the room Knighton continued to focus on her. His eyebrows twitched. 'However ordinary you think you are, however run-of-the-mill your concerns, your life is the stuff of drama…' She dropped the pencil and it clattered away from her onto the floor. 'The secret,' he added in a quiet voice, 'is to listen to yourself.'

She struggled to contain a wave of mounting emotion. Around her people were scribbling away, no doubt penning their riveting lives. She made a sudden dash for the door, staring ahead and ignoring gasps of surprise. But before she reached it she felt a hand on her arm. 'Mrs Eaton,' said the familiar voice. 'Can I have a quick word?'

'I'm a singer, a SINGER – not a bleedin' writer. I'm going home!' She almost shouted.

He did not release his grip. 'Please stay,' he said. 'Surprised, she looked at him. The brown eyes gazing into hers had an almost vulnerable air about them.

She walked back into the room with him.

Chapter Thirty *Derek*

Derek was with Issy in a Soho restaurant. Issy had said she wanted to thank him for the costumes he'd found for her: they'd made all the difference when she went for an audition. He had told Mo he was going to a late artists' talk with Patrick.

It was around eight and La Baguette in Soho was half full. The interior was dark, illumined only by up-lights and flickering candles. Somewhere at the back a fiddler was scraping a Hungarian gypsy air. Issy called the waiter and ordered oysters and champagne. 'My favourite.' She smiled at the astonishment on Derek's face. 'I want to celebrate.'

'What about? If I might ask.'

She shrugged. 'Does there have to be a reason?'

'Usually, yes.'

'Not with me there doesn't.'

His eyes caught hers and she held the gaze. She'd swept her hair back off her face, which showed off her high forehead and sculpted cheekbones and enhanced her elegance. Her eyes continued to challenge him as the light from the candle flickered over her face. They raised glasses, clinked and sipped.

'Here's to friendship,' she said with a laugh. 'And to getting good roles.' There was a glint of anarchy in her. As a girl she would have been a tomboy. She exuded nonchalance, not giving a fig for convention. The oysters arrived on a large silver-plated platter. Derek stared at them. She laughed. 'You've never eaten them before?'

'No.'

'Here's to a new sensation then. Watch!' She drew the oyster off its shell with a small fork added a dash of piquant sauce, tilting back her chin to reveal more of her creamy neck. He watched the oyster slithering into her mouth and down her throat. 'Now your turn.'

He hesitated, at once the new pupil being tested by an older classmate. He pulled the platter towards him and struggled to pierce the oyster.

'It's still alive, you know.' Her generous mouth was curving towards him. He slid the oyster onto his tongue. It was a slippery slimy thing with a tang of the sea. He gulped it down. 'You see. I knew you'd like it.'

Within minutes they had finished the platter and emptied the champagne bottle.

'Who was that man in the shop?' he asked. Her eyebrows shot up in a moment of alarm before her face assumed its habitual good humour.

'Arthur. Arthur Bonnington. A good friend,' she said and added. 'And yes, in case you're wondering, I do sleep with him.' Derek's fork rattled on his plate. She looked across and gave the wisp of a smile. 'I knew what was going through your mind so I thought I'd save you the trouble...' He struggled to contain himself. Like Zara she seemed unfettered by custom. He wanted to ask what it was between them, this Arthur and her, but his mind baulked.

She smoothed out her napkin and looked across at him. 'On another tack, I've been thinking. As far as Jonathon's concerned you should strike while the iron's hot. He is desperate. His set designer has done a moonlight flit. He needs someone who can work quickly – someone with flair. I saw you talking together at the party...'

'What sort of stuff does he need?'

'There's a lot on about country houses at the moment. You know, salons, dining rooms, vistas through French windows over lawns rolling down to tennis courts. The ruling classes at play...'

'I see.' He looked at his watch. 'It's getting on. Shall we go for a walk?'

He fetched her wrap from the cloakroom, but felt wrong-footed when she paid the bill in his absence. 'I wanted to pay,' he said weakly.

'My treat,' she said crisply. He was both relieved and stabbed by guilt: only the day before he'd told Mo they could not afford a new outfit for her, oddments from Fingal's Cave would have to do.

They sauntered towards Leicester Square. The lights above the Empire cinema winked down on restaurants around the green. 'You must come and watch me rehearse. That headgear gave me confidence to play the part.'

He took hold of her hand. It felt warm and fragile in his, like a small animal. They ambled on towards the Strand. 'I've been waiting for someone like you.'

'What about your wife?'

'That's different.'

'Don't, Derek.' She freed her hand.

'Why not? When the spirit moves you.'

'*Someone like me.* Could be anyone. You're just wanting to get out of the impasse you're in.' He glanced at her. He was sure she was dissimulating. He could tell by her pink neck. Her sudden clipped tones reminded him of Eleanor. As they passed along the back of the Savoy Hotel strains of a dance band playing jazz drifted through the evening air. For a moment he pictured women in long silken backless ball gowns and men in tails.

'I want to paint you.'

'I don't have time. Besides I could never sit still without fidgeting.'

'You have such light in your eyes...'

She laughed. 'Derek behave yourself. The champagne is going to your head.'

She pulled away from him, walking quickly towards the water. He caught up with her, grasped her arm. She went to pull herself free but again he grasped her. He kissed her on the mouth.

* * *

Derek met Knighton at The Athena as arranged. He had dug out some old stage sketches and worked on new ones along the lines Issy suggested. Now from the stage he gazed over the plush red chairs in the auditorium. Here he'd seen Zara perform and just days before had come to see Issy. He trod over creaking boards, peered up at gantries and fresnels and rows of arc lights, the heavy drapes drawn back from the podium. Here is where it all happened. Where illusion and inspiration collided; where words, music, and face-paint were brewed into the heady elixir of theatre.

Knighton was brisk and clear in what he wanted. He took a quick look at what Derek had brought and grunted approval. Then he strode round the stage, pointing out here and there, currently blank spaces, but where the vistas and trees and bay windows of mansions were to be conjured. He needed stage flats showing a country house in the heart of the Home Counties. Glad of the money it promised and the break from routine, Derek was delighted to oblige. They shook hands on it.

Derek returned to the studio and carried out more sketches of a country house. These he worked up into water colour vignettes, hoping to catch the leisure and elegance of such an ambience. In general he was pleased with his efforts. At the theatre he met Mr Garfield, stage manager and general factotum. He was a tall, thin man with a sinewy neck and hands, and a habit of looking past you rather than at you. They stood side by side on the empty stage in The Athena theatre. Derek had propped his work on an easel and Garfield was eyeing it. 'Mmm. The colours don't quite work, do they?'

'What do you mean?'

'They're too dim. Can't you come up with something a bit brighter? The set needs to suggest midday mid-summer in a sunny room. Here you have too much brown. If you stick to lighter shades the footlights and spotlights will do the rest. See what I mean?' Garfield stepped nearer to the canvas and pointed to the bookshelves depicted there. 'This is fine for early evening. It would blend in with the sidelights, but it's too dismal for other times of the day.'

Derek stood back and studied his sketches. He had to admit his efforts came across blander than expected. The luminosity created by the studio skylight made hues more vivid. 'I did what was asked of me,' he asserted.

Garfield gave him a sideways glance. 'You'll be part of a team here – working alongside carpenters and stage-hands.'

'Is Knighton around? I thought I'd be seeing him...'

Garfield shrugged. 'He's working right now, seeing actors. He expects the stage to be fully primed and ready to go. So we need to be doing our jobs. Don't we?'

Derek stared at the ground. 'When do you need them by?'

'As soon as possible – by the end of next week?'

'Can I work here?' He glanced around at surrounding drapes and gantries.

'Normally I'd say yes, but for the next day or so there's going to be too much going on. If for now you do the panels for the side flats in miniature in your studio – that would be a great help. We have access to a bigger space round the corner in Covent Garden in one of the old warehouses. When it comes to the main drop with the vistas and garden, you'll be able to do that *in situ*. You will need help there. It's a lot of square feet to be covering and time will be pressing.'

Garfield was looking past him, making a sign to one of the stagehands: he had work to be getting on with, other things to do. Derek gathered his portfolio and took his leave. He pushed out into the street; outside the light dazzled him. Though disgruntled at the criticism, he relished having a concrete assignment and was impatient to get back to the studio. He called at Russell and Chapple to order more canvases, more poster paint. He needed to re-accustom himself to using the stuff for that was what they would employ for the flats – buckets of it. Garfield said they bought in bulk but for now Derek could get what he needed, on account. Shaugnessy had cleared out of the studio and gone to the South of France for a few weeks. Derek longed to lose himself in activity.

Back in the studio he paced up and down kicking out at dust motes, muttering to himself, thrusting open the door to the stairs to allow in more air. He put his hand to the canvas, tested its strength, its suppleness, its ability to absorb paint, to take the flying figments of his fitful imagination and turn them into something visually pleasing.

Chapter Thirty-one *Eleanor*

Eleanor was woken by a noise coming from downstairs in the early hours. When she went to investigate she found Derek stumbling around in the kitchen. It was the third time in days that he'd come home late. He looked across at her. She drew her dressing gown tighter round her and sat down at the table. 'Sorry. Did I wake you?' he said.

She looked at him keenly. She hoped she was doing the right thing in supporting Mo to fly the nest now and then. Her animated face on returning from Hampstead that first week had told its own tale. Though subsequently Mo seemed pensive, unsettled even. Faced now with her unkempt brother, Eleanor feared she was stirring a snake pit. There was a restlessness eating away at him. These days he flew off the handle at the least thing; he had an irritation with life in general and with Mo in particular. All this petty fault-finding was unlike him.

Mo was right: she herself wasn't feeling at her best. And for that reason alone it was bliss when she was alone in the house without doors slamming and sullen exchanges. She could smell the whisky on his breath. 'You seem – you've been drinking again.'

He laughed. 'What if I have? Is there a law against it?'

'No, no,' she said quickly.

'Cup of tea?' He lurched towards the range.

'I know it's none of my business and I don't want to interfere between you. Heaven forbid, the last thing a sister should do is meddle in her brother's life...'

'Well don't then!'

She was taken aback by his vehemence and sought another tack. Days before he'd told her about painting in Shaugnessy's attic. 'Have you been back to the studio lately?' He turned the tap and water splashed noisily into the kettle. He started whistling. 'Well?'

'Yes, I've been going there. I've got a commission.' He leaned over the sink and for a moment she thought he was going to pass out.

'Are you all right?'

'Not really.'

'Derek, I'm worried about you and Mo.'

He blew air through his teeth. 'Stop being such a busybody!' She began to wish she'd stayed upstairs.

'I'm concerned about Mo.'

'Don't you think it's a bit late for this sort of talk?' he said.

'What other time do we have? All I want to say is that I don't think Mo is coping. It's hard on a young girl to break with her family like that...'

'It didn't hurt her to fall into my arms.' He hovered in silence by the kettle, waiting for it to boil, filled the teapot then placed a steaming mug in front of her. 'Stop looking at me with those headmistress eyes.' Tiredness was haunting him now.

She sipped and screwed up her face. 'Tastes like ditch water, Derek. And you forgot to strain it. Why don't you learn to make a decent cup of tea?'

He shrugged. 'I'm off to bed.'

Eleanor pushed the mug away. He got up from the table scraping back the chair. It toppled and banged to the floor. He muttered something then trudged upstairs. On the landing she heard him come to a standstill before fumbling into the bedroom.

Over the next week she found herself replaying the scene. Something was amiss. A rift was growing between Derek and

Mo. What if their relationship was no longer tenable? She pushed away the notion: it was just young love struggling to find its way. There were times they had eyes only for each other, when you couldn't have a slid a sheet of paper between them. When Mo said very little about the class except that yes, she would continue to go, Eleanor encouraged her, and when Mo complained she didn't know what to wear she urged her to visit Fingal's Cave or ask Derek to bring her something back. Everyone was imitating Bakst and the *ballets russes,* said Mo, and she longed to do the same. It occurred to Eleanor that Mo had not been to Fingal's Cave for months: it had become Derek's sacrosanct domain. Knowing this, she called by one day and persuaded Derek to pick out some frocks for Mo. For a while this seemed to lift Mo's spirits.

The possibility of estrangement between the two set Eleanor pondering her own situation. She thought she was resigned to her fate. Yet there was less joy in everything she did. She had even shrugged off Guy, for that friendship felt too complicated. He wanted far more from her than she was able to give. He said nothing, appeared cheery enough, but she could tell. She could read it in his eyes.

One day even her beloved teaching let her down.

The boys were at their desks, seated according to class ranking. On the walls were posters of spring fauna and lists of Britain's kings and queens. Suddenly the space seemed cramped and sweaty. She caught the reek of feet. The faces set towards her were sunny and anxious in turn. Did fear have a smell, she wondered. One of her objections to the regime was the use of corporal punishment to inculcate learning. How could it possibly work? It made timid boys cringe. It encouraged bullying. It made the bolder, brighter ones fixate on nothing but results.

She surveyed the upturned faces, heads propped on hands behind inkwells. 'Who can give me the dates of the

Plantagenets?' Blank faces met her question. It was the first period after lunch when concentration was weakest. As she turned to the board she heard a shuffling and tittering behind her. Two boys were fighting over a comic. She swooped down and wrested it from them. The others watched, amused. She prided herself on the class's grasp of history, but now all interest had flown. She caught a restive, insolent air.

What am I doing here? An inner voice whispered. All at once she had no spirit for the fight, no urge to assert her authority. Instead she would march unannounced into the headmaster's office and hand in her notice.

'Miss,' said one of the boys. 'Are you ill?'

Several boys were staring are her. She snapped to. 'Turn to page ninety and refresh your memories.'

Chapter Thirty-two *Derek*

Without Patrick the attic studio seemed huge. The enamel tea mugs, once littering the floor, had been washed and placed on the shelf. Patrick had even tidied his canvases along one wall. But Derek still sensed the man striding around, throwing paint at the canvas, cajoling an image from his fiery brain. Every surface, object and paintbrush spoke of his presence.

Derek threw down his canvas bag and pulled out one of the easels from the pile by the door. He searched out his sketches and notes. He would plot out the ideas running through his head. To aid the flow he'd bought some glossy magazines as these nudged him towards settings and voguish designs he could work into line drawings.

Hours later he looked up at the darkening sky through the dusty skylight. On the ground were the bruised fruits of his labour: a wad of drawings, some rough and scratched over, one or two larger pieces. Colour could come later. Garfield had said the scene sets needed vibrancy. He sifted through his day's work, took out the best of his efforts and the rest he heaped together.

He was starting to get hungry. But more than that he had an urge to see Issy. He wanted to talk to her about his work. She seemed to understand it and be curious about it in a way that Mo was not. There was no harm in it. Of course he still loved Mo, but right now he needed to enter more fully into his creativity.

That morning he'd told Mo he might have to leave London for a day or two: a manor house was being emptied near Cheltenham with possible rich pickings. The lie slipped out easily enough. It was more a fib really, just enough to gain him leeway. He wanted to explore himself as an artist: for two years he'd played the dutiful husband and father and the restrictions were choking him. Half asleep, Mo had murmured her assent. For days now she'd been excited about Jonathon Knighton's class in Hampstead. Knighton, it seemed, was opening doors for the two of them.

By the time he'd finished for the day he'd made up his mind to call round to Remington Square. As he walked by the river, he chewed over what it meant to be an artist and why it had always been a source of conflict for him. Issy believed in him. He might love Mo, but Issy would release the artist in him.

He glanced at his dusty trousers. He stopped for a moment to brush them down and checked his image in a corner shop window. Reaching Issy's square he looked across at her house. Framed rectangles of light gleamed out; the place radiated warmth and excitement.

She was having a party!

Dismay mingled with anger as he watched the translucent curtain of her bedroom, half-expecting to see her there. His steps slowed as he approached the wrought iron railings. He heard a Hackney cab chugging nearby. It halted outside Issy's house and two men in evening suits emerged. The front door opened and there was Issy, delectable in a beaded pink frock with a floating shift swathed over it. She laughed – that light throwaway sound – as she greeted the men and invited them into the house.

Derek stared at the gleaming lion's head door-knocker and before he knew it he was banging it down. The door flew open. He caught a dazzle of lights, a buzz of voices chattering, laughing. 'Derek!' Issy was standing in the doorframe, a champagne coupe in her hand, eyes wide with disbelief. 'Why... do come in!' He stepped into the hallowed bright circle. A few people gazed in his direction and taking in his worn clothes, smiled with indulgence.

She guided him down the corridor. 'How delightful to see you!' Forever the actress, her voice sounded high and bright. He watched her moving ahead, the gentle curve of her hips encased in the shimmering, slippery gown. The shift swished as she walked. He wanted to catch up with her, force her to look into his eyes to see what was going on with her. But she slid away and now, at the far end of the lobby, she was turning to him. 'Come, my dear. It's just too exciting that you are here tonight.' She was looking around the tight huddles. 'I'm not sure who you know here. You came to the tea party, didn't you?'

Derek sipped the champagne she'd handed him. He felt a burning in his stomach: why hadn't she told him about the party? He recalled one or two people from before. Most of them were dressed up to the nines in shiny suits and gleaming, beaded dresses. He noticed he was drawing glances. She introduced him to a couple of people. 'And you know Jonathon Knighton, of course,' she said. 'He's in the other room.'

'Issy!' whispered Derek, touching her arm. She looked at him in alarm. 'And you met Arthur – Arthur Bonnington. We came to your shop.' She turned to smile at the tall, imposing man who had just appeared. Bonnington was wearing a dark lounge suit with a dark blue tie. He was handsome in a cold, austere way. Arthur gave what Derek considered a supercilious smile. 'How do you do?' He extended his hand. The smile on Issy's face segued into anxiety. Derek turned to her.

'How's the play going, Issy?'

'Ain't easy, being an artist,' said Bonnington. 'How ever talented you are. You must have seen our Isadora tread the boards.' Bonnington touched her shoulder, which seemed at once captive beneath his large hand. Derek had the urge to slap it away. Bonnington moved in closer behind her.

'Mr Eaton – Derek, you must come and see me perform again.'

Derek raised his glass. 'All the best,' he said gruffly and barged towards the far end of the lobby, hardly seeing where he was going as he bumped against people.

'Strange fellow,' muttered one.

'Maybe he's a resting actor.'

'Lost his way.'

'One of Issy's protégés,' said another.

'That's what I love. She knows where to find 'em.' They chorused in laughter.

Derek let the words slide off him. He glanced back at the shiny round heads of the women with their shingles and head-bands, and at the plastered down hair and patent leather shoes of the men. They might embrace the latest craze in daring clothes, but when it came to it they were terrified of stepping out of line. Ahead of him was the kitchen. He caught sight of heads bent together round a table with a large vase of sprawling red tulips and blue irises. On the wall was a painting of a similar vase painted in bright reds and blues. A man was holding forth while others leaned towards him, intent on every word.

It took Derek a moment to realise it was Knighton. And there beside him was Zara! Derek winced, again wrong-footed. Knighton was expounding to the eager circle. 'Drama should be the stuff of every day, heightened of course...' Was the man an idiot to be spouting on at a party? Knighton spotted him from the corner of his eye and nodded an acknowledgement. Zara spotted him too, blew him a kiss and sidled away into the other room. He did not have the energy to pursue her.

He glanced over his shoulder. Where was Issy? Who *were* all these people and why in the blazes had she not told him about the party? Now Knighton was standing opposite him, his listeners drifting away to find drinks or start dancing. 'I gather you saw Garfield. He said your stuff was promising. Needed work, but good.' Derek felt suddenly naked: did the man have no tact? 'Would you like another drink?' Knighton asked, spotting Derek's empty glass. 'Try the claret cup.' He passed him a glass.

'I didn't quite like Garfield's attitude.'

'Don't be aggrieved, my good man. He has stringent standards...'

Derek nodded. He sipped the claret cup. It had a warm mellow taste. Somebody had shaken in more than a drop of port. Maybe brandy, too. He eyed the man in front of him. He had a broad, lightly lined face and wild hair. There was a fire and unnerving intelligence in the eyes. Beyond that he had the air of someone who was used to getting what he wanted. Not a man to be thwarted. He wondered whether he had been Issy's lover. He coughed again and looked past him. 'How long did you say you'd known Issy?' he could not help asking.

'I told you. We go back a long way.' Knighton gave him a shrewd look and laughed. 'I see the wonderful Issy has you under her spell.'

Derek stepped back. 'In case Issy didn't give you the name of my shop: it's Fingal's Cave on Chalk Farm Road. I got some new stuff in yesterday.'

'Good. Good. I'll send our wardrobe mistress. And now perhaps you'd like to meet some of my students?' Knighton beckoned to a young woman. 'Allow me to introduce Miss Beryl Dunstable.' Beryl Dunstable's face was red, her nose far shinier than it should have been.

'Delighted I'm sure,' she said. Squiffy, thought Derek. He shook her hand, exchanged a couple of sentences then walked through to the larger reception room. He felt the girl staring after him. Why waste time talking to lesser creatures when Issy was only yards away? But where was she? Not still being commandeered by Arthur, that upper class bore? He brushed past couples locked in huddles. Some were shuffling to the slow, smoochy music while others loitered in corners, smoking.

As he entered the salon he froze, blinked hard. There, throwing back her head in laughter was none other than Mo. Her dress, which was more than familiar to him, was from Fingal's Cave. It was red and mauve velvet and glittered as she moved. It showed off her dark, bobbed hair to perfection. Her cheeks were rouged and her lips tinted. She'd put a dark band on her hair, which gave her an older, more sophisticated air. She was even smoking, a habit she'd never taken up. She must have felt the power of his gaze for she twisted round. Her mouth dropped open. 'Derek!' she shrieked. 'What on earth are *you* doing here?'

He felt the blood ringing in his ears. He strode towards her. Like the Red Sea people parted, clearing a space around them. They stared at each other.

'I thought you was in Cheltenham.'

'I *was*,' he lied. 'And now I am here. But you?' Her eyes flashed up at him. Her painted mouth was half open. He grabbed her hand and pulled her towards the hall. For a tense moment people watched then resumed drinking and talking. The music drowned out what they were saying.

'What?' she protested as he continued to pull her by the wrist. When he'd found a quiet enough spot he edged her against the wall. 'Stop it! You're hurting me.'

'How did... What are you doing here?'

'I was invited.' Cornered, her eyes were filling with tears. She looked young, helpless. He stepped back, pulse racing. 'Derek, why are you being so ghastly? Eleanor said I should go with the group if they asked me. They're people from my class. We got invited. You're always going out. Why shouldn't I?'

Derek did not know what to say. Her eyes were glistening up at him. His breathing became ragged. He had to get her out of here. 'I think we should go home now,' he said as steadily as he was able.

'I only just got here.' She jutted out her chin. He had the urge to smack her face. How dare she defy him? The moment passed. He was behaving like a brute, and he knew it.

'Look, I think it's late enough already.'

'What are you talking about? It's only ten o'clock. The party's barely started. I'm staying put. Especially while you're being so – so beastly.'

His jaw was working. It was just too much to have Mo and Issy at the same party. He could not stand it. 'Have it your way,' he said coldly. He turned and walked away from her. As he passed the open door of the cloakroom he caught sight of Issy, who was alone and gazing towards a looking glass. He watched as she adjusted her hair. She looped up a stray curl and smiled at her reflection.

She looked over towards him. 'Derek,' she said nonchalantly. She straightened her spine as if to announce the cool-headed hostess tending her guests. He stepped towards her, throwing a glance over his shoulder to make sure Mo was not around. Issy's eyes darted from side to side. For a moment she looked trapped. She went to sidle past him. 'Issy!' His voice grew urgent. 'Why didn't you tell me?'

'But your glass is empty. Let me find something for you.' Her head was high, her voice once more bright and in control. She shot him a dark glance. He heard the rustle of her dress, caught a whiff of her mimosa perfume and then she was moving towards her other guests. He checked again to see if Mo were anywhere in sight, then paced towards the kitchen. Damn these women. He dived towards the punch bowl, wanting to get drunk, but his mind was stone sober. He did not want to talk to anybody. He emptied his glass in one gulp. Best to get the hell out of there. He walked through to the entrance lobby, banged the front door behind him, strode down the steps and across the square, putting as much distance as he could between him and this infernal party.

He gained the main road within minutes and caught a bus heading south towards the river. The din from the party, with the clamorous voices of Issy's irritating retainers, still rang in his ears. He felt acid in the pit of his stomach. He pictured Issy at the party: the softness of her skin and the flashing of her green eyes, earrings dangling like shards. He pictured Mo defying him, eyes bright with determination. She looked prettier than she had in a long while.

Ice was shattering his chest. He had to keep moving. He squashed an errant scrap of paper fluttering down the aisle. The bus was almost empty. Two lovers, heads bent together, sat at the front. A bent old man muttered nonsense to himself. The bus clattered over cobblestones. Half an hour later he got down from the bus and wandered along the Victoria Embankment. Hulks of boats slid by on the water. There was the famous floating restaurant, pennants flying, throwing pillars of light across the water. Sounds of jazz and dancing drifted across. He sniffed. He'd often walked here with Mo. Hand-in-hand spinning dreams, telling each other silly stories. The temperature was dropping. A tramp shuffled by, nodding a vague greeting. Another misfit: some shell-shocked wretch unable to slot back into civilian life. Derek looked at the gleaming black water. The tide was out, exposing the grey clay bank with its scattered debris. A barge was chugging by. From it came the sound of someone strumming a guitar. It pierced him through.

Chapter Thirty-three *Mo*

Mo was shaking as she heard the front door slam, knowing it was Derek striding away. Never in her life had she been so afraid and never before had she been so resolute. She would not give in to him. Now she knew he was being unfair. No one had ever spoken to her in the way he did. Not recently anyway.

She looked around. Right now the last place she wanted to be was anywhere near her husband. She would go home in her own good time. He kept her hanging around waiting often enough. And what was more, he had lied to her. He said he'd stop over in Cheltenham – for a house contents' auction or some such. At the time she'd hardly heeded him. But now she determined that for the next hour or so she would give him a wide berth. She breathed deep, sensing she was crossing into new territory.

'Your glass is empty,' said a low male voice, somewhere behind her. Startled, she turned and almost bumped into a tall, distinguished-looking man with a strong jaw and shock of blond hair. She had seen him earlier and assumed he was attached to the lady of the house. 'May I help you to more champagne?'

She nodded, not quite knowing what to say. He seemed awfully important and she was baffled why he should be bothering with the likes of her. He approached a maid, who was circulating with a tray, and returned with a bubbling glass. 'You're new here, I think. I haven't seen you at one of Issy's parties before.'

'I came with Mr Knighton's class.'

'Ah, the thespians!'

'I beg your pardon?'

'The acting class he holds in his house?'

'Yes, that's right.'

Mo sipped the champagne and hoped the man would shift away. She was finding his presence hard to cope with, and now to cap it all she was feeling lightheaded. 'Very well, thank you. Mr Knighton is very – inspiring.' She gazed into her glass. The ideas in her head had dried up: she had nothing to say. But the man was not about to give up.

'By the way, my name is Arthur Bonnington. I'm a good friend of Issy's.'

'I'm Mo.'

He was gazing at her mouth. She twisted it, biting her lower lip. 'You're delightful,' he murmured. She cocked her ear, listening for Derek's voice. It would not do if he came back and discovered her talking to this tall stranger.

'I better be going.'

'But why? I wanted to dance with you.'

She began to think he was making fun of her. She looked past her velvet gown to her worn shoes and considered her lack of jewellery. Why would anyone of his ilk want to dance with her? He took the glass from her hand and placed it on a nearby mantelshelf. He was leading her by the hand to the centre of the room.

'Thank goodness it's not jazz. I don't do the Charleston. Far too energetic.'

'Me neither,' she mumbled.

They glided round the room, her mind humming. Now and then she looked up at him. His lips were straight, his eyes resting on her face. It made her feel beautiful. She would show Derek. Teach him to lie to her. She threw her head back and laughed. 'You know I do so love to dance,' she said, imitating the high, bright way Zara had of speaking. Some from her background took on a different way of speaking, just to fit in.

So far, despite Miss Dawson's elocution lessons, she had not done that. What's the harm, she now thought.

'Then we shall dance until the sun comes up, my delightful, beautiful creature.'

'It's the quick step, is it?'

'It's whatever step you want to make it.'

One or two people glanced in their direction. They're jealous, thought Mo, to see me on the arm of such an elegant man-about-town. She was losing her breath. When would they stop? The three glasses of champagne were making her head pound. She didn't care. Tonight she would enjoy herself. Tonight was hers. Tomorrow might bring regrets, remorse even, but tomorrow was a long way off. She caught sight of Zara coming into the room, followed by Knighton. They, too, took to the floor.

Bonnington looked down at her. 'You're very light on your feet, my girl.' Her face was pink by now, she was sure, and her nose in need of powdering. The music swelled to a crescendo. It was the Ragtime sound from America she'd often heard on the wireless. As it came to a stop couples moved off towards the edges of the room. Bonnington led her back to her space by the mantelshelf.

'You're looking hot and bothered, Miss Mo. Shall we step outside?' She looked down at his shiny patent leather shoes.

'Fresh air would be a fine thing,' she said, a touch haughtily, and emptied her glass. He strode ahead and she followed in his wake, glancing to left and right. A back door led onto a quiet patio area with potted plants. Concealed beneath an overhanging miniature willow was a curved stone seat. She sank down beside him. His hand traced the curve of her elbow, which sent a tingle through her spine. She moved away from him. 'Can we go back inside?'

'Already?' He paused. 'Only when you've given me a kiss.'

'The cheek of it!'

'Just a little one to show there's no ill feeling then I'll release you from my clutches.'

'No,' she said.

Somewhere she heard a glass smash. A horse was clip clopping in the square out front. Her head was reeling. She wanted to laugh out loud. It was a long time since she had felt so fizzy and full of fun. Nor had she ever seen anyone quite so handsome, quite so commanding. Slowly he touched the side of her face, drawing her round to face him. His lips brushed hers, sending a rush of sensations through her.

'No!' she said, moving further away.

Someone was opening the back door, breaking into song. *'Daisy, Daisy give me your answer do-o.'* He pulled her towards him, crushed his mouth against hers. She got the tang of tobacco, alcohol.

Startled, she pulled away from him and looked across. Just then more people broke away from the party and wandered into the garden. A figure was silhouetted against the doorway. 'Issy,' called Bonnington, getting to his feet. 'We were just taking the air. Splendid party.' He walked away from the bench towards the house. Mo made out the hostess framed in the doorway. Issy waved at them, laughing.

'I just came to gather the troops. Miranda is about to sing. But if you'd rather stay and admire the stars that's fine by me.'

Bonnington glanced back towards Mo. 'Shall we, Miss Mo?' he called in a jocular voice. Slowly Mo got to her feet. Issy was watching them, a light smile playing around her lips.

Along with the others Mo jostled into the main salon. Chairs were dragged from the back room and placed in a row. A standard lamp with tinted shade provided an improvised stage light. The maid cleared away bottles and empty glasses from the mantelpiece and the room took on a purposeful, anticipatory air. People stood about, sipping their drinks.

Issy was beaming at her assembled guests. 'Tonight we are

privileged to have in our midst a principal from the English National Opera, Miss Miranda Caitlin.' Cheers rang out as people crammed together. 'Please give her a warm welcome!'

A dark-haired woman in a knee-length silver dress stepped forward. Her voice, when it came, filled the room. Mo could not take her eyes off her. The person, who minutes before looked like any other, was swaying her hips in sensuous imitation of Carmen, the fiery gypsy tobacco worker. She cast alluring glances to all and sundry, she strutted and coaxed, flirted and disdained. Her voice was strong, pure and clear. Transfixed, Mo took in every glance, every movement and inflection.

Miranda plucked a flower from a vase as she ended her song and tossed it towards one of the men. He leapt to his feet and caught it. 'Encore! Encore!' they shouted as she swept out of the room. She returned. 'Now I bring you: '*If I were a blackbird,*' a traditional Irish folksong. Now the singer transmuted into a demure, lovelorn young woman yearning for her sailor sweetheart, her voice poignant and sad as she began: '*if I were a blackbird, I'd whistle and sing and follow the ship my true love sails in.*' Mo's eyes were glistening.

When it was over, chairs were put back where they had been and the gramophone was reinstalled. Issy selected the discs. Jazz alternated with band music, crooners with tunes from Viennese operettas. Dancers took to the floor with renewed vigour, weaving in and out.

Mo wanted to be alone: she wanted to savour the effect the singing had had on her. Looking at the tireless partygoers she longed to slip away. In the cloakroom she fished out her black coat from a pile that had landed on the floor. She was about to step silently out into the night when she spotted Bonnington by the front door.

Before she had time to escape, he'd caught sight of her. 'Ah Miss Mo.'

'I'm going now. It's getting late.' Her voice was more determined than she felt.

'So soon? Well, I suppose if you have to get up and work tomorrow.'

'I don't work.'

'Oh? A woman of means, I see.'

'Stop making fun of me,' she said, quite cross by now. She had had enough. She was going back to where she felt safe. Even if Derek had a filthy temper at least she knew where she was with him.

'I wasn't. I assumed you had a job. You have that air of independence about you.'

She could smell his condescension. She threw back her head. 'I have a son to look after.' She thought of Derek. Her hand fluttered to her throat. Somewhere at the back of her head an insistent voice was nagging that she should cut and run. Scenes flashed through her mind like a passing train: the bright-eyed fourteen-year-old, cramped in the back bedroom, sisters squabbling over clothes... herself in the workshop, machines clattering, windows shut tight, women running up seams, 'Over my dead body!' threatening Ma, Timothy chasing ducks in the park, clapping hands in delight – Derek thundering away from her.

Who did she think she was?

The words echoed like a chorus. People always said that to her. Everyone wanted to keep her in her place, like the salmon in aspic she once saw at the Café Royal. Derek came and went as he pleased. And lied to her. But she had caught him out, hadn't she? He'd looked shifty. Embarrassed. Guilty. He knew he was in the wrong. And so he should.

'A penny for them?' said Bonnington. His nose was pinched and his cheeks glowing. His blue-grey eyes had a sharp, direct look about them.

'Why should you be interested in what I'm thinking?' She

was exasperated. Sometimes she wished she didn't have to think at all.

'Let me get you another drink.'

'I've had enough. I'm leaving. It's getting late.'

'Look, I'll make no bones about it, I find you attractive. I'd like to see you again.'

'Would you indeed?' she retorted.

'Damn minx,' he muttered. She tilted her chin towards him. 'You lead men a merry dance, I can tell.' The sudden sternness in his voice made her afraid. 'You see, I'm not often in town. You understand I'm a busy man.'

'Oh, I'm sure you're very important.' She heard her high-pitched voice utter. He looked mildly shocked. She should stop now before she did or said something she would later regret. He caught her wrist.

'I'm in town till Tuesday,' he said.

'So what?' She shook herself free. 'I am a married woman,' she said fiercely.

'But are you happily married?'

She stared at him. What sort of a question was that? 'Of course. Isn't everyone?'

He laughed. 'You are such a sweet naive thing.' He paused. 'If you would allow me I could drive you home.'

'Out of the question. I can catch a bus on the main road. They're still running.'

'I am a friend of Mr Knighton's. I may be able to help you … with your career, that is. You said you wanted to sing…' She hesitated. Looked up into the blue-grey eyes and felt her resolve weaken. She was losing the thread of her thoughts. 'We could take tea together. Here take my card.' He bent his head and picked up her hand and brushed it with his lips. She said nothing but took the card and opened the door onto the square.

'Goodnight.' She walked briskly away into the night, not

daring to glance over her shoulder.

Chapter Thirty-four *Eleanor*

When Eleanor reached the staffroom her colleagues were bunching around the tea trolley. Eleanor took her place in the queue. Mr Dawlish was sitting in one corner, puffing on a pipe. 'Miss Eaton, could I have a quick word?'

Eleanor suppressed a surge of irritation: couldn't she even drink her tea in peace? She followed him down the corridor. In his study he motioned her to sit in the large leather armchair opposite his desk. 'This morning I received a note from John Mulgrave. He's been called to Manchester at short notice. His mother is ill. He was hoping to start the new timetable. And well, now he can't...' Dawlish began tidying his already tidy desk. So that was it! No need to guess further: more duties were to be piled onto her but without change of status or financial recompense. 'There are several curriculum matters...' His gravelly grey eyes met hers, asserting authority.

'I'll see what I can do,' she said brusquely.

* * *

She met up with Guy after school and they took a bus to the centre of London. Though there had been a cooling between them over recent weeks after she repeatedly turned down his offer of dinner, he'd persisted. One day after a particularly gruelling staff meeting he'd told her she looked cross enough to explode. He made her laugh, when no one else could, and she realised just how much she'd been missing him.

In Trafalgar Square they came across a Trade Union Council rally. They sat on the upper deck of the bus and watched dozens thronging towards the gathering. A man was yelling indistinctly through a megaphone. She caught odd words. 'Bolshies … ruin the economy!' yelled one heckler. 'Uncaring Capitalism!' countered another. Words clashing, voices getting more abrasive. The country was being sold down the river, shouted one speaker: the bosses were only out to line their pockets.

For a while the bus was unable to move forward. 'I'm sick of Baldwin's platitudes,' Guy said. 'The man is out of touch.' He went on to say that the General Strike had been a close call, paralysing the country. It could happen again. The school had been shut for several days. Dawlish had sided with the government, of course. She eyed him with curiosity: she'd never marked Guy down as a political creature. The suffragist in her agreed, the brokers of power had had things their own way for far too long.

'The trouble got worse when Britain came off the Gold Standard. The pound is too strong. Our exports can't compete.' She murmured in response. The man had a good head on his shoulders. All too often she'd viewed those shoulders merely as a place where she could seek sympathy at the injustice of her life.

They got down from the bus in a mounting clamour. A rival bunch of demonstrators were brandishing banners in support of King and Country, yelling that the unions were rabble-rousers in the pay of the Soviets. Eleanor was jostled by one of these. Others followed in his wake, thrusting towards the hub of the meeting. A police van appeared from Pall Mall. Several constables leapt out of it, forging their way through the milling crowd. 'They're going to break it up!' she called.

And then they were in the thick of it, more protesters rushing in from every side. She couldn't tell who was who. Suddenly she felt a jolt in her back and was shoved forward. Guy was pushed to one side. She stumbled and fell to the ground.

'Eleanor! Eleanor!'

A boot caught the side of her face. Her leg was trampled. She shrieked in terror, tried to pull away. And then Guy was there, beating off forward-lunging men, dragging her to one side, sheltering them by a lamppost. She felt herself grow faint.

'Let's get out. This is getting ugly. Some of them have coshes. They mean business.' He looked over his shoulder. 'Over there.' He nodded towards the Lyons Corner House. Shielding her with his arms he directed them to the café. Inside it was bristling with life as others took shelter from the turmoil. She sank thankfully onto a seat. She closed her eyes, letting the sounds and sights pass by.

'Eleanor – are you…?' He touched the side of her face. She winced.

'Nothing serious.' She stared at the ground. The constant swinging open of the door reminded her of a hotel foyer. Guy ordered tea and cakes and gradually she felt normality return. Outside the police were trying to restore a semblance of order. Many demonstrators drifted away.

'I shouldn't have got you into that,' he said.

'Wasn't your fault.'

'Tensions are running high.'

They drank several cups of tea. She had no desire to move until the rally subsided. Outside another man was calling out through a loud-speaker. He was outlining the conditions in his factory. How so many had been laid off, how the bosses were considering a cut in wages.

Over more Darjeeling and another round of rock cakes she mentioned Dawlish's request, adding that she was tired of being used. Guy's lightly freckled face was earnest as his sharp blue eyes challenged her. 'I think it's time you dropped your resentment.'

'Oh you do, do you?' she snapped.

He laughed. 'You're like a porcupine these days.' She could not help but smile. She knew it was time to move on, but she was just not sure how. Disgruntlement had become a habit of mind. 'Eleanor, going over old ground is not doing you any good.' She glanced away. She, too, disliked self-pity but it perturbed her that Guy was no longer allowing her that rut. He looked across at her.

'On a lighter note did you hear what happened in the General Strike when Dawlish went to join his son down from Cambridge as a Plus-four volunteer? The two of them tried to drive a bus. It ran slap bang into the barbed wire that had been put up in Hyde Park.'

She gave a hearty laugh. 'I would like to have been there. He's such a pompous twit. I can't stand the man.' She gave Guy a sudden bright smile. 'Anyway enough of all that – what's been happening with you?'

'Mother's been sick again. Can't seem to get rid of her cold.'

Just after your attention, she was on the point of quipping. The few times she'd met Mrs Masterton she'd been unable to shake off a distinct dislike of the woman. She knew Guy was sensitive where his mother was concerned, but could not resist remarking: 'A dose of castor oil should do the trick.'

He bent to sip his tea. 'And how are your two lovebirds getting on? Still squabbling?'

'Actually Mo's turned over a new leaf. She's started scrubbing floors. I think she's plotting something. But she never tells me much. Thinks I'm on Derek's side.'

'So it's battle lines drawn, is it?'

'I think she still misses her family.'

Guy took her hand in his, rubbed the back of it. 'You know it's something *they* have to sort out. You can't play the big sister all your life.' Eleanor was startled by a surge of emotion. She pulled back her hand, took up a knife and cut into a rock cake. When it resisted her effort, she stabbed at it until it broke apart. A chunk landed in Guy's lap. They laughed. 'Such aggression against the poor cake!'

213

'It's probably days old.'

Guy looked at her intently. 'I think you need to get away. Forget about your role in school and being a surrogate parent…'

'I can't just up sticks and take off.'

'Well,' he paused, again stroking the back of her hand. 'You know what? I think we should both go away for the weekend. I could borrow a friend's motor. We could flee the city. Would do us both the power of good. What do you think?'

Flustered, she poured more tea, eyes down. 'Your mother would have a heart attack. Her darling son out of her sight for five minutes…'

He frowned at her.

'Sorry.'

Something somersaulted within her – it was an age since she had done anything spontaneous. A ray of sunlight peeked through the gloom of a dark cloud outside and she found herself imagining a springtime meadow. Now it was late May, the time of flowering and village dances. She longed to feel grass about her ankles, to swing along a country lane where hedgerows brimmed with purple campion.

'Anything is possible if you want it to happen,' said Guy slowly.

Eleanor looked up in surprise.

'But…'

'Don't worry. I'll be the perfect gentleman.'

'Can I be sure of that?'

'The choice is yours.' He called the waitress and asked for the bill. The police van had left and the gathering seemed to be simmering down. 'Think about it though. Life is too short for procrastination.'

Chapter Thirty-five *Mo*

Mo would continue going to Knighton's classes, no matter that she did not know where they might lead. Knighton knew Issy who knew Miranda Caitlin who could sing like a lark and soar above the petty, grinding, narrow, sad and unhappy things of life. Knighton would lead her out of the dark tight corner she had been pushed into.

She decided to strike a deal with Eleanor: if Eleanor took care of Timothy on Saturday she would do a pile of mending, which Eleanor had stashed in the corner. She knew Eleanor did not like needlework. She could hardly blame her. Though she herself detested ironing, she knew she could run up a seam in no time once she put her mind to it. In this respect Dukely's had served her well.

Eleanor had sheets of paper spread out in front of her on the table. Mo looked down at the top page, full of arrows and crosses. 'Doing your marking, are you?' She pushed a cup of tea towards her sister-in-law.

'I'm just trying to work a few things out.'

'Eleanor?' she said. Eleanor looked up, a perplexed expression on her face. 'There's something I wanted to ask you: a favour, if you like.'

Eleanor seemed mildly disgruntled as though she resented the interruption. 'Go ahead,' she said.

'It's that performance class. Last time they said something about openings in theatre. Possible auditions... I really want to go this week.'

'Oh?'

'I was going to offer to do your mending. In exchange, like.'

'In exchange for what?' Eleanor pushed away her papers. For a moment she stared at Mo.

'For minding Timothy.'

'This Saturday is not a good one for me. Why not ask Derek? Maybe he can get his assistant to do an extra day in the shop.'

Mo suppressed the irrational annoyance she often felt in her sister-in-law's presence. She pulled out one of Eleanor's garments from the pile and held up the frayed sleeve of a well-worn cardigan: grey in colour and shapeless, the garment was ready for the scrap heap. 'Do you really mean to wear this again?'

Eleanor laughed. 'You're right. I should throw it out.'

'There's good stuff in there. I had a look. I could mend them.'

Eleanor raised an eyebrow. 'Look – any other Saturday. But not this week.' She turned back to the papers she had pushed away. 'By the way, Mo, I meant to ask – have you had Tim inoculated?'

'What do you mean?'

'They'll do it for you – in the clinic, if you ask.'

'Against what?'

'I don't mean to alarm you. Just as a precaution I think it would be a good idea. There's been a case of diphtheria at school. I made sure all the parents knew and got their sons injected.'

Mo turned away. 'Derek and I will discuss it,' she said crisply and left the room.

In fact, Mo and Derek had barely spoken since the party. He seemed busier and even more remote than usual. She was seized by an unbounded fury with him: for his bare-faced lies, the unfairness of their life together, his ingratitude, his arrogance – the hardness of the one who called himself an artist. Everything about him was now subjected to a horrid, glaring light. You can live so long in a cheerless place without knowing what you are missing, Mo thought, then one day a beam shines into a corner and shows up all the dark, nasty things lurking there. Now not only do you see the gloom, but you long for more light.

The trouble was, she could not stop loving him. Not stop thinking about him. She scolded herself, telling herself she was weak, stupid, to be so susceptible. But the truth remained: all the other men, at the party, in the drama group, on the street, only whet her appetite. Even Bonnington. Derek remained the one. But oh she was furious with him. She could have killed him. Certainly she would not let him see how much power he wielded over her. She would strike out on her own: carve a track through the jungle of her tangled emotions. She bided her time, unwilling to be the first to break the uneasy silence. But as the days went by she realised it could not continue.

They would have to have it out. But it had to be the right moment.

Afraid she was going mad, she took care with everything she did. For once, the kitchen sink was spotless after she'd scrubbed it with soda. Every day she made sure the cupboards and pantry were replenished. The linoleum on the kitchen floor showed patterns never seen before. Even the front step gleamed a dark red with cardinal polish. She took down the nets and soaked them, then hand-washed them until the grey sludge sluicing down the plughole told her they were ready to be dried and rehung. She even took out the Singer sewing machine, stashed under the stairs, and hunted through old patterns to see what delights she could create for herself from the surplus of Fingal's Cave.

Timmy thought all this was great fun. He smeared red polish all over his hands when she buffed up the step, slid around in the suds when she scrubbed the floor and generally took delight in this new set of activities. His antics made Mo laugh. All the while, as she scrubbed and polished, she sang snatches of songs she heard on the wireless. She opened the windows and let her voice fill the street, startling passers-by, causing the milkman to wink at her and say: 'Who's ringing your bell then?' She laughed and called out at him.

'On your way, mister.'

When she was not doing this, she was picturing how she would break free and run off with another man when a suitable one appeared. Only, well, she didn't want to. Or she plotted revenge. She would break into Fingal's Cave, tear up all the boas, snip the nicest frocks from top to bottom. When she realised how that would harm her and Timothy – where, after all, did she get the money for the groceries? – she smirked to herself.

After a day or two of the new regime Eleanor noticed and made encouraging remarks about her spring-cleaning and letting the air in. She even helped Mo hang the clean curtains. As for Derek, he noticed nothing. He just came and went. He mumbled about putting in time at the studio and working on more flats for the theatre – apparently Knighton and Garfield had approved his revised sketches. Often he returned so late she had already drifted off. She would thumb through her disintegrating magazines and shift, disconsolately, to her side of the bed. Often he was away by first light.

One night she had a strange dream. She and Derek were in a clearing deep within an ancient forest. It was night. A wood fire smouldered and sent up a plume of sparks and curling smoke. Voices drifted from the distance together with a strange, haunting music, which filled her with longing. Derek took hold of her hands and swung her round, his eyes glinting by the glow of the fire. She was wearing a heavy skirt with layers, which flared out as they danced. He was pulling her, urging her to jump over the flames with him. The fire beckoned and menaced at the same time. They circled the flames and leapt across. Others, who had been murmuring by the trees, gathered round clapping in rhythm and laughing.

It was after this dream that she decided to ambush him. She drank strong black coffee to stay awake. Eleanor had long since retired for the night. The key turned in the street door and he shuffled into the room. 'So *there* you are. Another auction in Bath, is it, or Cheltenham?' He threw down his folder of sketches and looked across at her slyly before slumping onto a chair. His dark eyes gleamed, a half-smile shadowed his mouth. He had been drinking: she caught a whiff of whisky. He looked like he needed a shave, there were dark rings under his eyes and his hair touched the collar of his none-too-clean shirt. His appearance reminded her of the time when she first knew him and he'd been forever disappearing.

'You're up late, aren't you?'

'Only way to catch you, my sweet.' She moved towards him, stood in front of him, her legs against his knees. She leaned in towards him, her breasts brushing his arms. He sighed deeply and gave her an intense stare. 'We need to talk,' she said. He continued to stare at her. 'The party – we've barely spoken since then.'

He looked thoughtful, gazing down at the floor. 'I am sorry, Mo. I was an idiot. I behaved like a...'

'I know you did.'

'I was shocked. I didn't expect to see you there.'

'But you – what were you doing there? You said you were going to be staying in Cheltenham. What's going on?'

'I was. Well, I thought I might.'

'You wanted to keep your options open, sounds like.' He shot her a sharp look. Looked around.

'Place is looking good,' he said.

'Don't dodge the issue.' She hesitated. 'Derek, I want you to tell me the truth...' Her throat caught. She found her eyes watering. Did she really want the truth? He was staring at the ground in front of him as though examining every line and swirl in the lino. He seemed afraid to meet her gaze, just as she was afraid to continue though she murmured: 'Derek, tell me what's going on.'

At last he raised his eyes. There was so much there she could not decipher. Her heart was beating erratically. She wanted to fling herself at him, almost as much as she wanted to strike out at him. She breathed deep. 'Oh Derek, why has it got like this? Is this how you want us to be?' Moving swiftly he got to his feet and took hold of her hands, drawing her towards him. He fingered her hair gently, smoothed his fingers over the nape of her neck.

'Mo, I'm a fool. Sometimes I just don't know what comes over me.'

'So are you my husband or some stranger who turns up now and then?' she said quietly. He kissed her gently then ever more urgently on the mouth. She felt his abrasive bristle on her face, was filled with a desire to punish him, control him, be controlled, overwhelmed by him. She wanted to destroy the space between them. They stumbled up the stairs, into the bedroom, clasping each other, collapsing onto the bed and into each other. They made passionate love. Without words. Without regret. Without thoughts of the next day, or the one after that.

Chapter Thirty-six *Issy*

In Remington Square Issy switched on her beaded side lamps in the back parlour as evening drew in. It was days since the party and order had been restored. Knowing Arthur liked the place to look lush as well as inviting, she did her best to fall in line with his wishes. Everywhere, in runners and wall hangings, were voguish purples and acidic green. Vermilion curtains glowed against the throws and shining cushions heaped on the divan. It was vital, she reminded herself, not to let herself or the place go.

She heard Arthur's Rolls draw up in the square then the front door was banging open. Her breath deepened. Already he was pulling off his white tie, looking around in expectation, wide white forehead gleaming. As he stood before her, a tall, blond aristocrat with chiselled features and the long bony look of his conqueror forebears, he looked too large for the room. He glanced around, then threw himself down on the ottoman and yanked off his shoes. 'Damn boring dinner,' he said. 'Port. Have you got any port?'

'Port? I've run out.' She extricated him from his jacket then moved towards the door. 'But I put some champagne in that ice contraption you got me.'

'Champagne, then.' He undid the top button of his trousers. 'Come here woman and give me a hug.' He pulled her down and kissed her roughly on the mouth. 'Beautiful as ever,' he murmured. His right hand was roaming freely over her neck and breasts.

'Wait. Can't you wait?' She pulled herself free, skipping towards the door.

He groaned. 'As you wish.'

Outside in the corridor she ran her hands down the green silk of her dress, bunched at her hips. She needed, as always, to adjust to him being here. There were days, weeks even, when he never came near the place. Then she would slip into her own rhythm.

The second stair to the cellar creaked as she walked down. A year ago now Arthur had set her up in Remington Square, but always she felt unsettled when he first arrived. She scraped her foot against a mousetrap. Last week she'd caught a musty smell down here so she'd laid traps, but so far not even a whisker. She fumbled towards the switch. She put her hand into the coolness of the icebox and took care to extract a bottle without upsetting the others.

As she picked her way back up in the semi-dark she thought about how they first met: not the detail of it, but the coincidence of them both knowing Jonathon. Jonathon Knighton seemed to know most people; he was always reaching out, eager for novelty. She'd been in a theatrical revue, which Jonathon was directing. He'd thrown a party for the cast in his Hampstead house to celebrate the run. There she had been introduced to Arthur.

Back upstairs she put the champagne on the sideboard. As Arthur came towards her she smelled the brandy and gamey tang on his breath. She snaked her arms around his waist and pressed herself against him. She murmured in his ear, her body responding to him even as her eyes flitted about the room to make sure everything was in order. She registered, as if through his eyes, the sparkle of the funny French chandelier she'd picked up on the Caledonian Road. She, too, liked to have things that were good to look at. Arthur had given her oil paintings of ancient seascapes, which made the house look more like a home.

He pulled away and threw himself down on the divan while

she poured the champagne. When she looked over at him his head was tilted back and his mouth open. He was dozing. She tweaked his toe and his eyes shot open as though he'd forgotten where he was.

He was up in town on business. 'Tedious affair,' he complained, but did not elucidate. He'd visited his banker in Chancery Lane then attended an early session in the House. 'They're still harping on about the price of coal. Obstreperous miners are threatening to strike again.' With a wave of the hand he mimicked and dismissed. He took none of it seriously. A peerage had come to him by dint of family. His duty to King and Country was lightly done. He attended the Upper House when asked to. After all, one had to show willing.

'They caved in last time. Had to. Can't keep up with or rather down with the price of German coal flooding the market.' She'd heard all this before. How since the Great War the gentry were overtaxed, their estates depleted. It went without saying that last year at the time of the General Strike he had supported the colliery owners, and would do so again if need be. She held her counsel, not wanting to antagonise. What use pointing out he was damned lucky to have what he had and should he not sometimes put himself in the shoes of a working man down on his luck?

He'd been in the war, he liked to remind her, though she knew for a fact it had been behind the lines and for a short time only. But for all that he had got off lightly, the war cast a shadow over him. Many of his company had perished or were blighted through shell shock. Sometimes, out of nowhere, moroseness would cloud his bright, determined mind.

Now his head was lolling on the cushions, his mouth drooping. She touched his fine blond hair, traced her finger along the line of his jaw and slipped to the ground beside him, placing her head close to his. She stroked his leg. It twitched in response. He murmured and pulled her towards him, caressing her head as he drifted between sleep and arousal. She nuzzled her head into his hand, enjoying the wide spread of his fingers like a cat stretching itself into her master's reach. At times like this she was almost fond of him.

'Your champagne?'

'It can wait.' The desire for sleep was winning out.

She put the coupe to her own mouth and sipped, relishing the lightness and subtlety of the vintage. She would wait here while he dozed, then they would put a jazz record on the gramophone. They would dance and cling to each other until one of them starting loosening the clothes of the other. They would end up, as always, in the luxury of her wide, silk-sheeted bed with curtains still open to look down on the square. But was this love? She pushed away the question. Who was she to go looking for the moon?

* * *

Tonight after they had made love he seemed deflated. She ran her finger along the side of his face. 'What's up?'

He grunted and turned away from her as he sometimes did. 'Nothing.'

'You seem a little gloomy,' she persisted.

He let out a long sigh and then another. Finally he faced back towards her, speaking into her hair. 'It's Dorothy.' She groaned lightly: he knew he could speak his mind without danger. She said nothing. Often he poured out regret or sadness to go away cleansed and ready to take on the world. 'Two miscarriages in nine months. She just doesn't seem to be able to carry. The doctors say everything is normal. Down there, I mean. She's seen umpteen Swiss doctors. Done spas and sanatoriums. You name it. They can't find anything wrong.'

She felt herself go flat. All this talk about babies was no concern of hers. She propped herself on her elbow and glanced back at Arthur, trying to gauge what it all meant to him. She was trying to feel sympathetic but something in her refused to respond.

'You don't want to hear all this,' he said, but so mournfully she began to stroke his shoulder. 'She's a good wife. But you know, men often need more than that.'

'Someone like me you mean?'

'Exactly.'

She turned away and snuggled down under the covers. We clutch at straws, she thought. We make arrangements and then have to live with them.

'She probably needs to get away. The pressure is building...'

From the square Issy heard late night revellers, someone singing: '*Show me the way to go home,*' then titters and laughter reverberating around the houses. Within minutes Arthur was snoring. She lay on her back gazing up at the ceiling.

Chapter Thirty-seven *Derek*

Derek was catapulted back into reality. The episode at the Remington Square party had given him the measure of his relationship with Issy. She had the arrogance of a woman desired by too many men. She gave the impression she could call or dismiss him at will. For all that, he knew it to be a game. Underneath, she was as fragile as the rickety relationship she maintained with Arthur Bonnington.

She had bided her time then breezed into Fingal's Cave one dreary afternoon, asking if he wanted to come and see her in the West End: she and Zara were in a version of *Hay Fever*. After the initial shock at the prospect of seeing the two together, he agreed. Besides, he wanted to see his artwork. Knighton had asked him to produce more flats for the production, which he'd done: it would be good to view them under stage lights in a live performance. He wondered what Issy was after. By now he doubted any affection towards him on her part. She collected men like Christmas baubles to dangle and flash together.

He knew the plot: a silly tale of a rumbustious weekend party at a country house where each family member invited a guest and these got horribly and hilariously entwined. The houseguests were left to fend for themselves as the eccentric family unravelled before the audience. He took a seat sat at the back of the stalls: he had no desire to bump into Arthur Bonnington, who sometimes popped in to see Issy in a matinée. Issy entered first and Zara soon after. Issy was playing the part of the older, wily vamp, invited by the son but with designs on the father. Zara was the guileless, dim flapper, in frills and flounces, who couldn't work out the rules of the simplest parlour game. Issy was several inches shorter than Zara and somewhat thicker of waist. She had a more intense, mysterious face, which had a glow about it, whereas Zara looked pale as silk.

He sank into his seat and let the words roll over him.

As he watched them he began to feel uneasy. Why the dickens did Issy want him here anyway? She and Zara knew each other quite well, he gathered. They often played alongside each other. Both were protégées of Knighton. Was it all some sort of tease? Was he some sort of mascot for them? Women like these, who prided themselves on being free and easy, were hard to interpret.

Zara's voice rang out, tight and high, like a debutante. Issy's was deeper, befitting the role of the more sophisticated woman. After a while he lost track of what they were talking about or where the play was headed. He concentrated on the flats he had produced. He had to admit they were fetching, definitely in keeping with smart, moneyed people at a weekend party.

Out of the blue he thought of Mo, which gave him a knot in the throat. Of late she had become so fiery she scared him. Something in her had sprung to life. The house in Victoria Terrace was looking cleaner, and for that he was thankful. Yet some daemon was driving her. He had been caught out in a downright lie. She had scored points there and she knew it. He couldn't blame her. He'd been an idiot. No two ways about it: an outright idiot. After their night of unexpected passion he was unsure of his footing with her.

One night soon after, he'd been unable to drift off. He watched Mo as she slept, her face lit by the wan gaslight from the street. To look at her made him heavy with responsibility: in sleep there was such a beauty in her, tenderness and resolve strangely mixed. He'd pulled back the curtain to illuminate her more. She was an extraordinary creature whose essence he could never capture. It made him doubt whether he knew her at all.

Her lips had quivered, as if to speak. He'd waited, but she carried on sleeping. His thoughts had gone round and round. At first it had been such fun: in the early months of marriage there was no end of gatherings in dingy studios and raucous public houses. Poor though they were, they'd had good friends and with them they'd rant about God, atheism, revolution, what the artists in Paris were getting up to, the price of canvas, who was flying high or throwing the craziest party. She'd looked up to him, hung on his every word. And he'd found her a source of constant delight. He worked long hours and in all lights. She encouraged him. He loved to paint her, in all her moods. Afterwards they would traipse round pubs, drinking and singing till the early hours. Sometimes they'd stroll down the Embankment to catch dawn over the Thames. Sometimes, when business at Fingal's Cave was good, he took her to the Café Royal or the Café de Paris. Such fire they had then he thought nothing could extinguish it.

In the early months of her pregnancy she'd continued to sing at the nightclub of the Fox's Den. Often he'd go and watch her, marvelling at her growing stage presence. The richness of her voice shot him through with longing. But as she grew heavy with child, she retreated, no longer wanting to perform. He, too, turned away and concentrated on Fingal's Cave.

* * *

The curtain came down for the interval. The aisles filled with people wanting ice cream. He knew better than to traipse round to the Stage Door to make his presence known. In fact, he didn't even want to see them at the end of the play, so he stayed only ten minutes of the second half before creeping out of the theatre. Later he called round to Remington Square as he knew Issy was not needed for an evening performance. 'Ah you,' she said. 'Come in. We were talking about you. I wondered where you'd got to.'

'We?'

'Zara and myself.'

'She's here, is she?'

Issy laughed. 'No, she's gone off to help Knighton with auditions.'

He followed her into the sitting room. The last time he'd been here the furniture had been pushed back to make way for dancing. With its sofas and bookshelves it was now a different place. 'How's Arthur?' he asked, despite himself. She served tea from bone china. She was wearing a bottle green shawl over her shoulders. Her hair was swept back and her face was clear of make-up. There was the lightest of shadows under her eyes. 'I can't say I enjoyed bumping into him. And I certainly didn't enjoy your party...'

'Derek, I'm sorry. I was taken aback that's all – you springing up like that...'

Derek studied the sugar bowl. She sighed and for a moment he had the sense that she was struggling to tell him something and did not quite know how.

'Arthur has given me my marching orders,' she said at last. He felt a jolt: something shifted in him, a strange flash of fear and relief. He studied the strained expression on her face as she said, 'I shouldn't be surprised. We both knew it was a sort of – of deal for want of a better word.'

'I don't even know how you two met...'

'It's not important. It was through Knighton, if you must know. Jonathon's been brilliant at getting me parts. Has kept me in work for a long time now. It's such a competitive affair. A while back I broke my ankle doing a dance set and couldn't work – about fifteen months ago. I know we actors like to talk about resting, but I had no choice. There was no money coming in. And well… Jonathon introduced me to Arthur, at some party or other. Arthur invited me to go away for the weekend. I liked him.' She gave a little laugh. 'Perhaps it was convenient for me to like him. No matter. He was fun. He took me on a shoot now and then, when he could get away with it, and there were parties in town. He had to be discreet. I knew there was a wife somewhere, and I had no intention of interfering with any of that. She often visited her family, for days on end. That suited us …'

'And now?'

'He has decided to spend more time at home. Apparently she is finally carrying their child and he wants to be around to see it through. Quite honourable, I suppose.'

'And that leaves you…?'

'It leaves me contemplating my future. I have no excuse not to work. He says he needs the house back – not straight away, but soon. She wants to accompany him to town when he comes up here for business or to attend the House. At least, that's what he says.'

'You sound like you don't believe him?'

'Look, I have to be a realist. This is not something I can fight.'

She stared at him so directly he faltered: he was unsure what she was asking of him. 'So you invited me to the theatre to let me know your – your protector, let's call him, has thrown you over…'

'I just wanted you to know.' When he glanced down he noticed her hands were quivering, which evoked in him a mixture of fear and concern. Another time he might have tried to jolly her along, but not now. He felt wary, uncertain, but drawn irrevocably towards her. She brushed out a wrinkle on her dress and stood up. As she walked with the tray towards the kitchen he observed her back. Something in the way she held her shoulder blades and the softness of her neck struck him as vulnerable. Yet there was steel there, too. There was an essence of the true artist in her, impossible to grasp.

Later, he watched smoke from his cigarette spiral up against the dark velvet curtains in her bedroom. He closed his eyes. He could not believe this had happened. He had not willed it, despite how often in recent days he might have dreamt it. He had pushed the notion of it away. Thought it right that she had rebuked him, shunned him.

Now she stirred beside him, her skin silky and cool against him. He reached towards her. 'Issy,' he murmured. She shifted at the sound of his voice and opened her eyes.

'What?'

'I need to go.'

'If you must.'

'This can't…' he whispered.

'We both know that. You have your obligations.' She sighed. 'We both know this should not have happened,' she said.

He faced away from her.

The room came back to him as a stranger. It had silver-framed photos of a younger Issy and a late Victorian seascape – no doubt one of Arthur's – beside bright splashes of a Matisse print. She laughed – her light careless tinkle of a laugh. He turned back to her. She had rolled over and propped herself up on her elbows. Her short auburn hair caught the late morning sun. He noticed a dusting of delicate freckles across her nose. Her green eyes sparkled at him, in defiance.

'But we had a choice,' she said.

'I know.' His voice was thick. He did not want to talk or think any more about it. 'But it must never happen again,' he muttered.

She smiled, clutching the sheet up to her chin. He felt a stab of annoyance. He pulled away from her, put on his trousers and buckled up the belt. He left the room without looking back at her.

Chapter Thirty-eight *Eleanor*

Early Saturday morning Eleanor, only half awake, wriggled into her clothes: a grey wool skirt, which clung to her slender frame, and a blue jumper, kept by for an occasion such as this. And what was the 'this' she was about to embark on? The question wormed its way into her mind as she struggled with the skirt fastening. She gave an impatient little snort: why not? She spent too much time pondering what she should or should not be doing.

She tilted the swivel mirror upwards, painted her mouth a muted pink and twisted it in a half smile. She was looking pale, her oval face grave. She pinched her cheeks. Her *joie de vivre* was not totally lost, only buried. Recently, at a school fête, she'd heard someone murmur that she was a handsome woman. She grimaced at her image, poked out her tongue and peered coquettishly at her image. Nobody really knew her.

Outside she could hear the first workmen underway, scraping flagstones with heavy boots. One was whistling *'Yes sir, you're my baby.'* An early mist shrouded the rooftops while the roadway glistened with moisture. Soon the sun would burn through. She took a jacket from the wardrobe and shook it out. It was part of a worsted, checked two-piece but she had long since discarded the skirt. She stared at herself, turned this way then that. It was the sort of thing a county set woman might wear for walking dogs. Mo was right: she hadn't a clue. She draped a light blue silk scarf round her neck for good measure. She loved its softness against her skin.

Guy would be waiting for her. Sure enough, as she rounded the bend there was the Austin Tourer, borrowed from a friend, lurking in shadow like a barge on dark water. Propped behind a newspaper, he had not seen her.

She tapped on the window, startling him.

'You're early! I wasn't expecting you for another ten minutes.'

'Shall I go away and come back then?' She laughed as he leapt out to take her case from her. He busied himself pushing it into the boot along with a woollen travel rug. As she settled herself into the front seat he gave her a sly, sidelong glance.

'Madame is ready to take to the road then?'

'Let's get going before the shops open and everyone starts coming out.'

He got out and yanked the starting handle. The engine gave a splutter then the ignition caught and the engine burst into a steady chug. 'We'll head out west along the A40. Stop where we fancy. The country's lovely that way, out towards the Cotswolds. The world's our oyster...' He took his hand off the steering wheel in an expansive gesture that made her giggle. She watched his hands grasp the wheel again. He had strong, slender fingers, the hands of a musician. All at once she felt curiously awkward. She stared at the passing houses.

They left the terraced streets of north London and were swinging round the North Circular towards Hangar Lane. There was little traffic, only the odd tradesman's van. She opened the window and loosened her scarf so it fluttered in the wind. Exhilarated, she watched buildings and the greening trees flash by. Something in her cried out, longing for Guy to go faster, to overtake vehicles chugging along – faster, faster, as fast as they could. Then they were off down the tree lined A40 leaving London behind, speeding west. 'How fast can it go?' she called out above the din of rattling parts.

'I could get her up to fifty I reckon.'

'Go on then!'

When he grinned at her she asked: 'What did you tell your

mother?'

'A conference. A very important meeting that all teachers of the school have been summoned to. Can't possibly miss it.'

She laughed. 'Mo wanted me to babysit. I almost caved in but then something in me refused to budge. After all we made a pact.'

The Austen Tourer flew by hedgerows and fields, skirting villages, leaving the dust of the city far behind. If Eleanor pictured Victoria Terrace and its residents she soon dismissed the image: Derek and Mo must be made to realise she was neither their mother nor their keeper. High time for them to account for themselves and their darling Timothy, who seemed to figure last in their equations.

'Getting peckish?' asked Guy.

'I should have packed a picnic,' she responded.

'I was thinking of something more interesting.' He was frowning slightly as his hands gripped the steering wheel. 'Like a riverside pub where we can quaff cocktails and watch swans float by.'

This nonchalance from Guy pleased her. She needed a little luxury in her life. 'Beats a meal in Soho.'

'We can do that, too.' Weekends in the country, meals in the West End went way beyond their usual exchange. As his eyes lit up and his face broke into a slow smile something in her stirred. Confused, she stared at the road ahead. 'And later I know the perfect place. It used to be a coaching inn,' he said.

They did indeed stop for cocktails at a roadside pub. A stream rippled nearby under a humped-back bridge. They sat on a bench overlooking the constantly churning water while people came and went, calling in for a drink or cycling by. From there they continued deeper into rural England, winding their way down narrow country lanes to Castlecombe, in the western reach of the Cotswolds. 'The prototype English village,' he said cheerily. And indeed it was, with its squat stone church, minute post office and general store. Moss-covered cottages faced onto a short, cobbled street, enfolded in turn by sloping hills and farmland. The place was bright with flowers: packed into window boxes, sprouting where they shouldn't out of crevices. Beside the church was The Castle Inn. Grey-green with slated roof, wide chimneys and low eaves it seemed as sunk in the ground as the nearby trees. Outside was an old mounting block and standpipe.

They had an early supper of lobster and champagne in a candlelit bar where the waxed floorboards glimmered and the low ceiling gave a snug, intimate feel. She could imagine generations of lovers sneaking away to such a place. The thought only unsettled her. Every time she looked up Guy was gazing at her. 'Shall we take a walk before it's completely dark?' she asked.

They glanced out through the window. Already the sun had sunk behind the trees, casting long shadows. Inside a gas lamp was glimmering faintly. 'The street's not well lit. You could stumble and twist an ankle. Let's have a glass of port instead.'

They shifted to easy chairs beside the grate, which had one smouldering log, more for cheer than heat for it was the first week of June and not cold. The smell of the smoke reminded her of orchard bonfires. She gazed as a solitary flame licked round the log. It was possible, she thought. Another place besides London was possible.

'What are you thinking about?' asked Guy. 'You look wistful.'

'I hardly know…' The further they drew away from the staff room at Blundell's the more her friend and colleague was transmuting into a stranger. She no longer sensed what she could or could not say. 'Guy,' she started. He folded his arms and leaned back. There was a glimmer of naked affection in his eyes. 'You know what I said about leaving Blundell's?'

He nodded.

'Coming here makes me realise anything is possible. I'm tired of being there at everyone's beck and call. It makes me feel so – so sensible.'

'You are sensible.'

'I know. Damn it. But that's not all I am.'

'Steady on!'

'I'm tired of being a goody two-shoes.'

He laughed. 'You're hardly that.'

'Dawlish and his ilk can go hang. They don't care about the boys they teach. They just care about making money and keeping their reputation. Even my own brother takes advantage and as for that dreamy, immature wife of his – I could bang their two heads together.'

Guy gave a belly laugh. 'Good to hear you vent a bit of spleen. You've been so subdued lately…'

'You're even worse. Your mother runs circles round you. You can't see it. She wheedles her way in so that every time you have to sacrifice what you want to do…'

'I didn't know you felt so vehemently about it.'

Eleanor waved to the barman to bring more port. Guy watched as she drained it in one swig. 'I'm sick to the teeth of doing what people expect of me.'

The log shifted sending up a spiral of sparks.

'I love your spirit,' said Guy. 'I always have done. But you always…'

She looked at him fiercely. 'I always what?'

He said nothing, tapping the side of the armchair with his fingers.

'Say it. Say it.' She had raised her voice and drew a glance from a couple sitting by the bar. Guy leaned forward to speak as if mindful others were listening in. From one moment to the next she was on edge, fearing what might follow. 'Just say it Guy,' she said slowly.

'Very well, I will. You keep people at arms' length. You give the impression that no-one is ever good enough for you.'

She sat back as if punched in the stomach. She felt like crying. The alcohol was making her maudlin. The truth was: nobody was good enough. Life was one disappointment after another.

'You're buried in the past,' Guy was saying. 'You cling to a rigid view of how things should be. You're in danger of becoming…'

'What? Go on say it.' Her voice was calmer now, her eyes perusing ancient floorboards. Who else but Guy would dare tell her what she could not bear to hear.

'No man will ever measure up to your darling Lance, the man who captivated you in your youth, the man who stood head and shoulders above all others, and always will. Even in death.'

'I'm tired,' she said. 'I think I'll turn in now.' He touched her hand lying in her lap. She pulled away from him. 'You've got the key to my room, have you?'

He handed her the key. 'Let's not part like this. You're angry with me.'

'Right now,' she said, her voice as clipped and precise as though she were addressing a school assembly. 'All I want to do is sleep. We had such an early start.'

With that she levered herself out of the chair and headed, rather unsteadily, towards the staircase, which led to the two adjacent rooms under the eaves of the old inn. She clung to the banister and ascended the stairs with care, aware Guy and several others were watching her.

Chapter Thirty-nine

Upstairs she was unable to sleep. She was tired, excited from the journey, but more than that Guy's parting words about her and Lance reverberated through her. She drifted off, woke again. She had a pain in her chest, a rising nausea. She sat up and sipped some water, snuggled down under the covers again. It was useless; she was breaking open, the past leaking into her.

A scene flashed through her mind.

* * *

She had travelled up to Cambridge to be with Lance and they'd planned a bike ride. As they set off from Cambridge it was late morning, the sun already high in the sky. He cycled ahead. She took pleasure in watching him. His back was strong and his arms well-muscled from all the rowing he did. Now he was tackling a slope in an otherwise flat landscape. The sun caught his hair. She pedalled faster. He turned round and smiled encouragement; she waved back. These days she was always impatient to see him. She could tell him whatever she wanted to, and he never judged her. With him she felt like a peach in the sun.

Now he was waiting at the brow of the hill. When she reached him she was panting. 'Not much further,' he said. 'I know a lovely spot by a stream.'

A mile further on a track led off the road, winding through trees of acid green. Underfoot it was soft from recent rain. 'We can leave our bikes here. No one comes near the place.' She took out the picnic hamper and blanket from the panniers and handed him the hamper as they set off deeper into the wood. He clasped her free hand and started singing: *You are my sunshine, my only sunshine. You make me happy when skies are grey…'*

She heard the rush of water, looked up at light dappling through the canopy of branches. 'Here we are.' She spread out a tablecloth and arranged items from the basket: Norfolk ham, Stilton and freshly baked bread. He tucked in straight away. 'We'll need to be quick. I saw some ants.' He pointed to a line of them, inching towards the cloth. He wolfed his food while she picked at hers, twirling a lettuce leaf. She had butterflies in her stomach.

He was watching her. His smile faded. He looked at her with such ferocity she could barely breathe. With one movement he swept aside the cloth and remnants of food, rolling them into a heap. His hand ran over her foot, light as a feather and caressed her ankle. 'There's something I need to tell you.' She searched his face. He took a deep breath and sighed. 'I've been called up.'

'What do you mean?'

'Lord Kitchener – you've seen the poster?' There was a sense of purpose about him she had never seen before. She struggled to contain herself. Weekly, and sometimes daily, reports were coming back from the Front. Field hospitals had been set up near Dover. Thousands had died within hours in the north of France. Thousands. Early optimism was being acknowledged as wishful thinking. The Huns knew how to build deeper trenches and their soldiers were as brave as any.

'What about your education?' she asked in a weak voice.

'That can wait. Most of us are off.' He moved towards her, ran his hand over her knee, her thigh. She quivered, assailed by confusion. 'I want to know you're here.' He struggled to speak. 'When I get back … I want to carry your photo.'

'Lance…'

'So I remember why...'

They lay down on the grass. She was in his arms. She wanted to battle against him, against what he was telling her, but her body was no longer under her control. She could feel the dampness of the ground seeping into her. He pulled at the blanket, folded nearby, and smoothed it under them. He kissed her. She wanted to draw away, lash out at him. She wanted to drag him to her, keep him safe.

'Will you wait for me?' he whispered.

She nodded, too troubled to speak.

'Will you?'

'Yes,' she murmured. 'Yes, I will.'

Afterwards it seemed like an oath, binding them.

She longed to blot out the darkness of what he was telling her, even as they were clasping each other. She longed for oblivion. She pulled him towards her, clear what they both longed for. She murmured into his shoulder. For her there was no going back. Afterwards, they lay together, the blanket cocooned around them.

'When are you leaving?'

'Next week … I think.'

'We don't have much time.'

'Can you come and stay?'

'At your college, you mean?'

'That's not possible. We'll find a place. We can tell our families that we have an understanding...'

'You don't know my father,' she replied, smiling to herself. More than anything, she sensed the pledge their bodies had made.

* * *

The telegram arrived, weeks later, addressed to Lance's mother: it said it was with deep regret that the AIF Administrative Headquarters had to convey the very sad intelligence that No 4123 Lieutenant Lance Golding 22nd Battalion, had been killed in action on the 10th June 1917, whilst serving with the British Expeditionary Force in France. No further details had been received respecting the circumstances surrounding this most unfortunate happening, but in the event of any news coming to hand they would communicate with her immediately. They said they were directed to forward the enclosed message of condolence from Their Majesties, the King and Queen. An impersonal telegram like thousands of other birds of death flying through the land: its terse sentences changed her life overnight.

Chapter Forty *Eleanor*

Eleanor opened her eyes. There was a creaking near to her head. When she turned and looked across the pillow she saw a branch scraping the casement window. It cast strange shadows. The twigs of the bough were the tight claws of a midnight creature, scratching its way into the inn. She pulled the covers up to her chin. A gentle wind blew round the eaves and down the gutters into the deserted street. Gaslight glimmered between the heavy William Morris curtains she had not quite drawn and threw a jagged streak across the ancient Persian rug. The place had been around for centuries. It had the endearment of bent walls, creaks and uneven floorboards.

Guy had chosen well.

She pulled the sheet up to her mouth. Breathed in the freshly starched smell of laundered linen, tinged with a whiff of lavender. The sheet was slightly stiff to the touch, cool against her skin. He was trying so hard to please her. She thought back over his words and her hurried exit. That had been ungracious of her. He was only trying to get her to … But that was it, wasn't it? He wanted to draw closer to her, make a friend out of her. No, they were already friends. He was beginning to treat her like a woman.

She'd stopped herself considering men in that way. She turned over on her side. The blankets fitted tightly across her, as in a hospital bed. She pulled at them. She did not want to be in a straitjacket. They refused to give. She pulled again, dislodging the pillow so it slipped to the floor. She retrieved and puffed it up, yanked at the coarse blankets until they were forced to yield and slip out from under the mattress. They lay heavy across her legs. She kicked them off. Outside the branch scraped again against the pane in a gust. The window rattled. She stared up at the ceiling.

The alcohol was taking its toll. Her throat felt parched. She got up and poured herself water from the ewer, gulped it down. The room was cool. She slipped back into bed and drew up one of the blankets she'd cast off. She lay on her side, willing sleep.

A few minutes later there was the lightest of taps on her door. She started. Was she imagining things? The tap repeated: two, three times. She groped for her housecoat and undid the latch to the door. There, in striped pyjamas and looking taller and leaner than she remembered him, was Guy. He looked at her intently.

'I heard you get up. I wondered if you were all right.'

'I got up for some water.'

'Look, can I come in?'

Confused, still half asleep, she moved back and switched on a side lamp. She sat on the bed. The lamp shed a soft light over the lumps and shapes of the room. He sat beside her on the bed. 'You must be cold,' he said, placing his arm gently round her shoulders. She sniffed, unsure what to say. He pulled her towards him. For a moment she was unsure where she was, what time of the night or day it was. He spoke again, shocking her into wakefulness. She felt herself resist his voice. He was saying he cared about her, always had done. She shifted away from him. She wanted to be alone. She did not want the complication of this. She wanted to avoid… She wanted… But she no longer knew what she wanted.

'I watch you get more and more unhappy,' he was saying as he rubbed his hand over the top of her arm. 'Taking on more responsibility. Not taking anything for yourself. I can't bear to see it. I want – I want to show you something different.'

'Guy …I …Guy.'

'I know,' he hesitated. She drew in a deep breath, dreading what was coming. 'I know how hard it is for you. I know the sadness you've had to endure…'

'Look, isn't it a bit late for all this.'

He drew her round and kissed her. She pulled back, felt something like anger rising in her, wanted to push back, push him away.

'Eleanor, Eleanor. If only you knew…'

She broke away and stood up. 'No Guy, I don't want this.'

He took her hand. 'Sit down.'

'No!'

'Please.' She sat down and drew the housecoat tighter around her. 'If only I could believe you,' she heard him say. 'But I think you've made yourself blind, deaf… You've built a wall around yourself. You loved and lost and so you decided you would never love again.'

'It's not like that.' Her voice sounded faint.

'Eleanor. I'm here. I'm real. Your memories can't keep you warm. You can't continue to live in the past. You'll just dry up.'

Something in the word dry caught in her gullet and made her want to crash the ewer onto his head. He had no idea. Dried up old spinster. It was the cliché of the times, the way of writing off a whole generation of women. No one knew what she had gone though. No one could possibly know.

'Eleanor… you mean so...' He pulled her towards him on the bed. 'I'd like to hold you. That's all.'

'I –I...'

'Eleanor,' he said hoarsely.

She was confounded with a tangle of emotions and sensations. She wanted to slap him for what he was saying. Yet she was shocked by the truth that knifed its way into her. He was the only one prepared to be honest with her. Others took careful steps around her, made appreciative noises of what she offered, but passed swiftly on.

Now she was taken aback by the warmth spreading through her body, by her longing to be held close, so close. He was stroking her cheek now. She let her head sink onto his shoulder. She could hear him breathing more heavily, drawing near to her. Was it true she'd slipped into an arid rut? But Lance is dead, she argued inside, so romance is dead. The matter was settled, once and for all.

'It's easy,' Guy was whispering in her ear. 'If you let yourself...'

There was comfort in distance. You knew where you were. No more disappointments. No more catastrophes... Possible to observe all encounters from the sidelines, happening to someone else. Never having to take risks, test yourself against an opponent... but never, whispered another voice, able to surrender, engage, let yourself desire.

Guy kissed her. An awkward, clumsily executed kiss. It misfired because she'd turned her face away and he caught her neck. He gasped in exasperation while she was surprised by the gentle moistness of his mouth on her skin. It startled her: this feeling of flesh on flesh. So natural. She wondered what she had been so fierce in resisting. Protest died in her throat. Nervous, she wanted to laugh: she did not know how to conduct herself.

In her mind she had rendered Guy safe. After all, he lived with his mother, though she knew for a fact he had had love affairs. He appeared without ambition. All this now evaporated. Guy was not the man she'd taken him for. She had chosen not to see him, not to let him impinge on her. At once she was curious: angry, but curious. Stung into wakefulness by his words, aroused by his nearness. He placed his hands firmly on her shoulders and gave her a long passionate kiss.

This time she did not pull away.

Chapter Forty-one *Mo*

It was after eight when Mo surfaced from the scrambled bedclothes and her even more scrambled dreams. The house was uncannily quiet. From the street she could hear the whirr of the milk trolley and its colliding milk bottles. In the corner Timothy was snuffling, sleeping longer than usual after waking at midnight. Mo felt beside her. The bed was empty, the sheets cold. Derek had long since gone. She vaguely recalled him shuffling into the hallway.

Now she sat bolt upright. Today was the day. She had promised herself she would not let the chance slip her by. Jonathon Knighton was summoning her away from a life of nappies and professional despair. She threw off the covers, padded over to Timothy's cot and assured he was still not awake, went to get ready for the day. As she passed Eleanor's room she noticed the door was open. She peered in. Eleanor was nowhere to be seen. Her bed had been made and her books were neatly stacked on the table. Mo pulled the door to. Eleanor had been adamant she could not help out with babysitting. This, in itself, was out of the ordinary. So Eleanor had planned something all along and wanted to keep it secret. Mo was intrigued.

She gave herself a quick wash-down and decided what to wear, opting for a red cardigan and black skirt. Half an hour later she was spooning a mash of milk and rusk into Timothy. He was more lethargic than usual and dribbled out the food. She pulled his foot. 'Come on, you scamp. Get this down you like a good boy.' He pouted at her.

The day before, after Eleanor's refusal to help and when

Derek said he was too busy, she'd called round to ask a neighbour. Now she made Timothy presentable and marched out of the house with him before she could change her mind. She'd packed his favourite wooden bricks in a canvas bag. He was quieter and less chirpy than usual. Once she'd deposited him, she hurried to the bus stop without glancing back. Sometimes, she told herself, you have to be ruthless. Her strap shoes clicked on the paving stones, sounding uncommonly loud, as though declaring to the world that she was abandoning her child.

A bus arrived within minutes. As she boarded it she allowed herself a backwards glance. Victoria Terrace looked as it always did. She smiled at the conductor. Timothy was in good hands. Clare Constable could cope: Mo could tell that by the way she handled her twins.

She began to think about the class to come. She remembered Zara's words about The Tower the first time she went there. Upheaval, she'd said. Certainly Mo was wiser now. Above all, she was doing what Pa always told her to do: 'Take stock of your life and count your blessings.' Ma would never, ever approve of what she was doing and Mo had given up trying to figure out why not. Now she had taken stock and decided that no one would dictate her life to her.

In the Hampstead house Knighton threw a glance at the latest person to arrive. 'Most of you came to learn about performance, especially singing, so you may ask why we've focused on drama?' He paused, looking round the group. 'The answer is atmosphere. Atmosphere. It is vital whether you sing cabaret or musical revue that you get under the skin of the character.'

Mo twisted the ring on her finger. Zara was staring towards Knighton, a dutiful, slightly bored attendant. She and Zara had barely acknowledged each other at the Remington Square party.

Knighton continued: 'Today is the last drama session. After this we concentrate on singing. Today, then, we look at atmosphere. And for that we'll work on Macbeth. How many of you know the play?' One or two hands went up. Mo had once seen a touring company perform it at the Hackney Empire. One of her school friends was an usher and Mo had crept into the back stalls, illicitly. To her astonishment she'd been drawn by the sheer power of it.

'The play portrays the evil of ambition from start to finish. It is vital to grasp the thrust of Macbeth's ambition. But also Lady Macbeth's. In many ways she is the driving force. She urges him when he falters, pushing him to murder so he can become king'.

'Zara has typed out three speeches. We'll divide you into groups. I'm not expecting you to learn the lines by rote. I'm looking for interpretation, a stab at imagining the situation,' he paused. Mo went cold. She was bad at reading. Words still danced on the page in front of her. She was so much better at learning by ear.

'Or, if there is a song you can sing or recitation then you can do that. Above all, I am looking for you to engender presence on the stage.' Zara was walking around, handing out sheets. Mo noticed her long fingers, nails painted bile green. She was such a curious creature. Watching her move with the slightest swivel of her hips and her head bent to one side, Mo guessed, with a pang, that Derek was probably still attracted to her.

'So?' Knighton asked. 'Which group are you in?'

Mo started and hurried off to join her huddle, where someone was declaiming lines from Macbeth's encounter with the weird sisters.

> *'Double, double toil and trouble*
> *Fire burn and cauldron bubble.*

Fillet of a fenny snake,
In the cauldron boil and bake…'

'Bubble bubble toil and trouble.' The words swirled in her head: they had such venom, such music. 'Another three minutes.' said Knighton. In all corners people were murmuring lines. Mo wanted to run from the room almost as much as she wanted to slither around as a snaky, wicked witch beguiling the ambitious Macbeth.

Bubbles, she thought. I can do bubbles. She laughed out loud. A girl beside her was whispering the words. Mo tilted her head and listened carefully. She could hear the quiver of fear in the girl's voice. Knighton was walking towards the centre of the room. 'So, who would like to start?'

Mo pushed herself forward, propelled by she knew not what. She took up the piece of paper and placed it at his feet. She took a deep breath, paced away and then back towards him. 'I offer another sort of bubble…' Then she started singing. Her voice rang out, loud, pure and clear, sure of its journey, its melody.

'I'm forever blowing bubbles,
Pretty bubbles in the air,
They fly so high,
Nearly reach the sky,
Then like my dreams,
They fade and die.
Fortune's always hiding,
I've looked everywhere,
I'm forever blowing bubbles,
Pretty bubbles in the air.

I'm dreaming dreams,
I'm scheming schemes,

I'm building castles high.
They're born anew,
Their days are few,
Just like a sweet butterfly.
And as the daylight is dawning,
They come again in the morning.'

Here she twirled, eyes brimming with joy, face glowing. Knighton was staring at her. Others were laughing out loud at her audacity. Zara was glaring. Knighton held out his hands in bewilderment. She had listened to the song on the wireless and bought the sheet music, simply because the song was hers more than any other it told her story. Little had she realised that she would get the chance to perform it so soon. Several people started clapping. Knighton was still staring at her.

In time, others did their pieces. Over half read from the given texts. All this passed Mo by, she was floating somewhere up by the ceiling. After the break Knighton introduced the next part of the session:

'You've heard a summary of the plot. In some theatres actors refuse to call the play by its name. They refer to it as the Scottish play. Why so, do you think?' There was a mumbling of uncertainty. Knighton was always testing the group.

'Witchcraft,' offered Beryl, the shop girl. 'I saw a performance in the town hall. The witches frightened me something rotten. I felt they were calling up the Devil.'

'Summoning the dark powers?' Knighton took up the theme. 'For many it arouses terror. Lady Macbeth pushes Macbeth to become king so they can reach an unassailable position. But from the outset they are doomed to fail. He burns. Lady Macbeth burns. They are obsessed and so become *possessed.'*

Silence followed Knighton's stentorian pronouncement.

'Shakespeare,' continued Knighton, 'holds up a mirror. We

see how murderous, unfaithful and disloyal we can be, but also how mighty and gracious and free.' Tension mounted. With Knighton one never knew what was coming: it was like teetering on the rim of a volcano.

'I want you to create a scene. This is not a test of how well you know Shakespeare. You have just heard Lady Macbeth's speech urging him to kill Duncan. You are Macbeth. How do you respond? Quickly write down key words, phrases. Above all, picture the scene, hear it, smell it. Feel rather than think your way into it.'

People took up their pads and wrote. Mo closed her eyes, letting the scene unfold before her. From an early age she could do this. She'd shut her eyes and stories would roll out, characters taking shape to become more real than her family. She saw Macbeth recoil at his wife's ferocity. His eyes flickered, unsure he had heard right while her eyes were black, glittering with passion. She wanted power. Nothing less would satisfy her. Macbeth was alight with an inner force. His wife reflected his unbending ambition. After a moment's doubt he confirmed his direction. Nothing would stop him now. Mo did not need to write down the words. She carried the impact of the situation in her body. It made her twitch with discomfort.

Knighton was watching her out of the corner of his eye while others scratched at their pads. He told them to put down their pens. 'Mrs Eaton!' he nodded towards her. 'Show us what you have discovered.' Mo blushed to the roots of her hair but quickly got to her feet.

She moved around, displaying Macbeth's intent. Reason was unable to stem his lust for power. 'Now is the moment. I will not stop. I will not shirk...' Words came to her from the air, from the ground. She was no longer in control. His madness was seeping into her. She stopped for breath. As she returned to her seat the eyes of her classmates followed her. Stunned by her vehemence, they said nothing.

When it was time to go Knighton drew her to one side. 'I'd like you to come to the theatre with me. You know I'm a director at The Athena? Your husband has done our scenery.' She nodded. 'As I said last week, we are looking to fill certain roles.' Mo grinned, unable to suppress the delight surging up in her. An image of Timothy flashed across her mind. She should be going home. She bit her lip. She was not a bad mother, as Derek claimed when he was angry with her. Timothy would be fine. Mrs Constable could be relied upon.

'Of course,' she said. 'I'd be delighted to.'

Chapter Forty-two *Derek*

Derek was surprised to find Victoria Terrace swallowed in shadows when he arrived home. He supposed Mo had put Timothy to bed and was lying down next to him, trying to catch up on sleep. He was conscious of the noise he was making as he walked down the hall, across to the kitchen: the house seemed eerily quiet.

'Mo? Eleanor?' he called up the stairwell. When he entered the bedroom he discovered it was empty. The blankets were pulled back from Timothy's cot, their own double bed was a knot of sheets and blankets. What on earth was going on? He had left so early that morning he had not had enough time to talk to anyone. Perhaps Mo had said something to him the night before and he'd been only half listening. He sat on the edge of the bed and fingered Mo's nightdress, which was slung over the bedstead.

He put it to his nose and caught the faintest whiff of her. He shut his eyes. For some reason it made him want to cry. These days they were leading each other a merry dance. What was it about the daily grind that made them bait each other? Perhaps it was just that: the daily grind. Once they had relished the freedom they saw reflected in the other. Now that freedom was fled. He held the nightie to his cheek absorbing the silky feel of it, then put it to one side and stood up.

Someone was banging at the front door: loud, insistent knocks that betrayed urgency. He rushed downstairs and thrust open the door to a middle-aged woman with a shopping bag in her hand and a stern expression on her face. It took him a moment to piece together that this was Mrs Constable, the woman from three doors down. Normally she was hemmed in by children and had a permanently careworn look.

'Derek,' she began then corrected herself. After all, he was a grown man now with responsibilities. 'Mr Eaton, I came as soon as I could. It's Timothy. 'E's poorly. Right poorly. I had to take him to the hospital.'

Derek felt himself weaken. He leaned against the doorframe. 'Where's my wife?'

'I don't know.'

'What do you mean, you don't know?'

She blinked in consternation. 'Mr Eaton I…'

'Sorry,' he said. 'I didn't mean to snap.'

'I was looking after him, see. He took poorly. He looked a bit floppy when she dropped him off. But then he got worse …'

'Why? I mean why was Timothy with you?'

'She came round yesterday. Said she had to go somewhere today and would I have him for a few hours. 'Elp her out like. Said she'd be back by five. But she never come. I waited and waited. As soon as Bert got back I took the lad off to hospital. Thought it was for the best. He was running a fever…'

Worry knotted her face. She was close to tears. Derek felt ill. He had barely exchanged the time of day with Mrs Constable in recent years, though he knew her from childhood. She'd been one of the kindly souls who stepped in when their parents died, a pie in one hand and cast-offs from her brood in the other. In his youthful arrogance he'd brushed aside all her offers of help. He knew her to be a placid, maternal type with a wealth of experience of children and their ailments. What she didn't know about measles or scarlet fever wasn't worth knowing. If she had concerns about Timothy then so should he.

But where the blazes was Mo? He looked about him wildly.

'I should get down there as soon as you can. If you like I

can wait 'ere and tell 'er when she turns up…'

'Right. Where?'

'University College. In the emergency…'

'I'll get a bus.' He went back inside and grabbed his coat. 'Yes, please Mrs Constable. I'd be grateful… make yourself a cup of tea. What do you think it is – with Timothy? Was he still awake when you left him?'

''E was hot. He was lying there like a rag doll, his arms and legs. But it was the cough that bothered me. He was barking like a dog, clutching 'is throat. I don't know what it was. But I wanted 'im seen by someone. You know, a medical person. Children get ill and then better. You can't always tell. The nurse took him in straight away. Said the doctor would see him.'

Derek was barely listening. His heart was beating strangely. Where was Eleanor? 'Was my sister there? I haven't seen either of them.'

'Nobody was here. I thought it strange your wife didn't come back when she said she would.'

'So you don't know where she went?' Derek tried to keep his voice as neutral as possible, though the world was careering around him. Rarely had he felt so helpless. Rarely had he felt such rage towards Mo.

'You best get on. The doctor will want to see you. He may – he may be better by now, little Timothy, and ready to come home.' She gave a quick smile but he could tell that she was attempting to reassure. Her face was glum. She herself had lost two children, one stillborn, the other at eighteen months from pneumonia. Such a woman would know the lie of the land. 'I'll be on my way then.' She waved him off.

Derek ran through to Kentish Town Road and hopped on a passing bus.

Chapter Forty-three *Mo*

Mo was intrigued by this business of auditions. When Knighton had told them to read and then interpret lines, she feared he would catch her out. Yet when she'd decided to do it her own way, a new power had surged into her. More than anything she longed to dive into that other realm, that place of the imagination. It was in her blood to do so. Ma might hate her for it, but it was there, plain as day: the passion to perform. This was an opportunity, which she must not mar.

She thought of Timothy and wished she could get on with the audition to get back to him. His little face rose before her inner eye and she was stabbed with tenderness. He was the dearest thing in her life but she could not live just for him. She needed to breathe. She needed to fly. Derek came and went. Eleanor had ambition. Why not her? She'd be the happier for it. Timothy could only benefit from having a smiling mother instead of a grumpy one.

Knighton invited her to come with him to The Athena theatre after class. 'I'd like to try you for a small part.' She had talent, he'd repeated. Others from the group gaped in envy, Zara scowled.

'Why not?' she asked herself. This might be her only opportunity. And what if Derek objected? How would she manage with Timothy? Shows went on at night, didn't they? Timothy slept then and Eleanor was always in the house by five. It would not be a problem. Zara could scowl all she wanted to. Did she fear Mo would usurp her precious position beside the maestro? That was laughable. Mo had no such pretensions. Knighton was just a means to an end. She was no more interested in him than she was in that other chap, what was his name – Arthur Bonnington?

She brushed away any lingering doubt.

Knighton told her to enter via the Stage Door. She walked down round the building twice before she came upon the dimly lit sign. She eased the door open. The walls smelled damp. It reminded her of Hackney Public Baths when the tiles streamed with water. She walked along the corridor, which gave onto the auditorium. Above she saw giant lights across a bar and gantries for lifting flats. Some were already in position. This was surely Derek's handiwork. She peered at it, admiring the shading as the light caught it, colours streaked to resemble bookshelves, cabinets and windows. There was no doubting Derek's talent. She felt her heart widen with pride. And now, here she was in the same space. She wished Derek were here to sit in the stalls and watch her perform.

Several people huddled at one side of the stage. Others took up seats in the front rows. And there was Knighton looking over and beckoning her to approach. 'Ah Mo, there you are.' As she neared them he said: 'I'd like you to do the same as you did earlier.'

'You mean to sing or the Macbeth bit?'

'Sing. Let them hear that voice.'

'I could have a bash,' she said cheerily.

'That's what I like to hear. You're the best of the bunch. Schooling or no schooling.'

She flushed with pleasure.

'Mo Eaton?' A woman with a clipboard approached. Mo nodded. She walked up the side stairs to the stage, her legs threatening to give way. There was an accompanist. She glimpsed him in the shadows. He was hovering over the keys with an intense, expectant air. He looked familiar but she did not know where she might have seen him. In the front row people were making notes. She must do this. It was what she wanted. It was what she was capable of. She centred herself as Miss Dawson had taught her and nodded to the accompanist. He stared at her without smiling and began to play. Her voice when it came was calm and pure. She sang the Bubbles song, smiling as she allowed herself to move, to feel the dream of the song, its longing, a bubble drifting up to the sky, bursting, dispersing in air.

And then it was over. She moved off to the wings where she could just make out Knighton. He was beaming. 'You did well. Really well.' He grasped her arm. She winced. 'Are you all right, Mo?'

She started as if from a dream. 'I'm relieved that's over. I didn't think there'd be people taking notes.'

'Mo, there are things you need to acquire – Stage English, et cetera , but that can be fixed. You learn quickly. The main thing is – you have raw talent.'

A shiver ran down her back. 'Someone just walked over my grave,' she said.

He looked at her quizzically.

'What do you mean?'

'I don't know.' She could not explain it, this sense of terror, a quaking in her stomach. She had the sudden image of a lightning-struck tower.

'Here, this is my telephone number. Can you call me in two days?' he said. This was all getting too much. It was time to retreat and think it over. She needed to talk things through with Derek. Her mind began to tumble. Knighton's face was glistening in the shadows. The accompanist was watching her.

She headed towards the exit. The world was light under her feet, she could barely contain her elation. Now she knew she was born to perform. Her mother had denied her her birthright, pretended she had never trodden the boards nor sang to the delectation of all. Mo could set that right. She was more than a bar room singer or a Music Hall artiste. Knighton had chosen her above all the others. Outside in the street she glanced at a clock in a pub. Goodness, it was so late! The time had just flown. She hastened towards the nearest bus stop.

Chapter Forty-four   *Derek*

Derek sat in the chilly corridor nursing the cup of tea the lady almoner had given him. It had gone cold and a coat of dark khaki floated on top. He didn't know how long he had been there, hours perhaps: time was stretching in and out like a concertina, seconds ticking slowly, years colliding.

He felt very alone.

The walls and linoleum floor dully reflected the overhead lights. No daylight penetrated here, no sign of passing seasons. Now and then one of the hospital personnel bustled through, bearing notes or other paraphernalia. But it was never for him. He was in limbo, exiled to a place outside normal existence.

They said they were doing tests. The croup and the swollen neck and throat concerned them. The men in white coats spoke of infection and contact. They wanted to know where Timothy had been in recent days. Most illnesses had an incubation period; children passed things on very easily. Had Timothy been inoculated? They were skirting around saying the word, but Derek heard their asides and had read enough about epidemics and horse-derived toxoids to know they were talking about diphtheria, just as clearly as he knew that Mo had not had Tim injected.

Until now it had all seemed academic. The diphtheria epidemics of the Victorian era were long since past. Eleanor had warned them. He remembered now. She was all for taking Timothy to the clinic herself, but they had told her not to interfere. Infection was such a remote possibility, he'd argued, as the illness was in decline. But there had been a case at her school, she'd countered. The other boys had been done – as a precaution. When Mo demurred, Derek had not insisted. Besides, mostly Timothy was in Victoria Terrace or the local park, decreasing the risk of picking up anything nasty.

And yet here he was, laid out on an operating table being poked and examined, while Derek waited in the corridor and that blessed wife of his was nowhere in sight. Powerless, he could only hang on until someone saw fit to make a proclamation about the welfare of his son. A door swung open. An anxious-looking nurse stood before him. He noticed her breathing was a little ragged. 'Mr Eaton,' she began. He nodded, fearing what was to come.

'Yes,' he said.

'It's Timothy.'

'He was struggling with his breathing. It became critical. The doctors needed to carry out a procedure. To help him…'

'What is it? What did they need to do?'

'It's called a tracheotomy.'

'They punched a hole in his throat?'

The nurse looked uncomfortable. 'His breathing was restricted. They tried opening the air passage, stemming the swelling. It was the only way. There wasn't time to come out and tell you. It became an emergency. They had to get directly into the windpipe.'

Derek had heard of it in wartime cases when men were choking on mustard gas. 'And now?'

'That immediate danger is over.' Her voice was steady but dull. Her face was impassive. She was at pains not to offer false hope. Heavy with misgiving, he sat back down. 'A doctor will be out presently to speak to you.'

She folded her hands over an ample stomach, looking resigned. What a thankless task, he thought: dealing with illness and diseased organs. She had been on her feet too long and looked weary. But she smiled then, taking him by surprise, and patted him on the arm. 'We have the best team here. I'll get you another cup of tea. That one's gone cold.'

'That would be nice,' he replied, perfunctorily.

'You must be peckish too. I shall ask the ward orderly to make you up a sandwich. The ward is quiet at the moment.'

'That won't be necessary,' he said, the thought of food abhorrent.

She gave another smile and was gone, the starch of her uniform making a crisp, snappy sound as she moved. Derek walked up and down the corridor, his fear for Timothy growing. He felt hollowed out: too exhausted to be angry and too worried to think straight. He caught sight of the hospital clock. It was past seven. Where the hell was Mo?

Just then from the other end of the corridor he heard a rush of feet. Someone was running. He recognised the sound of her steps. There, with hair flying about her face, pale as death, looking as vulnerable and afraid as he had ever seen her, was his wife. 'You!' he said.

'Timothy?' Her voice was a hoarse whisper. She looked about to collapse.

'They're doing tests. He couldn't breathe. They had to…' the sudden image of Timothy's vulnerable little throat caught at him. 'A tracheotomy.'

'A what?'

'It's a medical procedure. His throat was blocked. The air passage…'

He caught hold of Mo as she slid to the floor. He guided her to the bench where he'd been perching for the last hours. He left her for a moment and hurried to find her water. When he returned she was leaning forward, head between her hands.

'He was fine when I left him, a bit sleepy that was all,' she murmured, almost to herself. Derek was too tired to fight with her. He quelled reproaches building in his mind. 'So – what?' she turned her face towards him. Her eyes were moist. It was the face of a child. Her cheeks were podgy, her mouth down-turned. It struck him more than ever how young she was. Right then he felt as callow and as much at sea as she was. All that he had wanted to say to her dissolved. He took hold of her hand.

'It could be diphtheria,' he said as calmly as he could.

'Is that what they said?'

'They haven't said as much, but that's my guess – from the questions they asked.'

Steps echoed elsewhere in the building. Someone laughed, the tea trolley clattered and someone whistled. 'Oh Timothy,' she whispered. 'Timmy.' He felt the tremor that took over her body. He put his arm around her. He wished there was something comforting to say. Of survival rates from the illness he knew little. He did not even know how advanced the illness was in Timothy's case. The medical staff seemed reluctant to say much.

He did know death from the malady could not be ruled out.

He rubbed the skin on the back of her hand. 'These things happen,' he said.

'Do they?' she replied weakly.

We should have had him inoculated: he bit back the words. He was just as careless as she was, just as much caught up in his own story. Eleanor had warned them. He remembered how vehemently they had resisted. If there were a question of culpability he was as guilty as she was. He got to his feet unable to sustain that line of thought.

A tired-looking doctor came through the door where the nurse had just exited. He looked very care-worn. 'You'll be Timothy's parents?' Derek nodded while Mo continued to stare at the ground. She was shaking. She dared not look up. 'I'm afraid. I'm afraid he didn't make it. We did all we could.'

Derek heard a sound like the howl of an animal as Mo crumpled onto the floor. The doctor bent to help lift her. The howl grew louder, echoing down the corridor. Sobbing racked her body. Derek bent down, attempting to put his arms around her, wanting to enclose her, afraid the sobs would destroy them both. His head was spinning. This could not be. Only this morning... this could not be.

The doctor sat on the bench beside them. 'I'll get the nurse to bring something,' he said and disappeared. Men always have to move and act, he thought. Only women allow the pain to go right though them, clean as a knife. In that moment he envied Mo's ability to surrender to the anguish. He stood up and hovered above her, reflecting on what the doctor had just said: so few words to impart such weight.

Mo was on the seat, rocking to and fro, cradling her elbows in her hands. The sobbing grew quieter, turning to a wail. He touched her back but she drew away, wanting nothing. She averted her face as if she would be consumed by her grief, uninterrupted by anyone or anything.

The same nurse as before hurried in, harassed. She had a couple of tablets in her hand. 'The doctor said to give your wife these and asked if you would like to see anyone – the chaplain perhaps?' Derek shook his head. She held her palm out towards Mo. 'Mrs Eaton? Mrs Eaton?' Mo ignored her. The nurse sighed. 'I'll leave them with you, Mr Eaton. I'll get the ward orderly to make tea.'

Tea, he mused. It's going to take more than that: a dose of opium more like. He attempted a smile, which came out as a grimace. There would be all sorts of practical things to see to now, his mind hopped from the pragmatic to the surreal. The nurse was hesitating, unsure what to do next. Hearing the door open behind her she took her leave and hastened back to the ward. Derek sat down beside Mo. His head sank into his hands. He had never felt so old, never so young. What he would not have given to turn back time and heed the counsel of his sister.

He did not know how long they stayed there in the corridor before the machinery of death kicked in. It brought a busyness around them, which distracted. The chaplain came. He stared at the ground, thinking perhaps it was too soon, too delicate, to discuss funeral arrangements. The tall man shook their hands and nodded in sympathy: he said he was there for them if they wanted to talk: the ward sister could fetch him at any time. He had the gravity of office about him. When Mo asked to see Timothy, Derek grew tense: he was not ready for this. Nor was she. She looked as though she might crumple onto the floor all over again. Nevertheless, he led her through as she requested. The chaplain accompanied them.

A screen had been drawn round the little hospital cot. Timothy was stretched out on his back. He looked pale, the face small and pinched, as though he were still sleeping. For a moment Derek thought it was all a cruel joke; he only need pick Timothy up to hear him chuckle. But when he looked closely there was an unearthly stillness about him. He was a rag doll before them: an empty form. Derek could not see the hole in his throat where they had performed the tracheotomy; it was covered by a bandage.

He felt a stab in his chest. This was not happening. He looked up: three nurses and a ward orderly stood by. They kept a respectful distance and bore solemn expressions. One of the nurses, who could not have been much more than twenty, looked as though she had been crying. The others, despite professional impassivity, looked shaken: the death of a child could never be easy.

The ward sister pulled him to one side. 'I think it better if you took your wife home now, sir. We'll get the undertaker in and see to the practicalities. She needs to rest.'

Derek barely took in the words but did as he was bid, grasping Mo under the elbow to guide her out of the ward. He was asked to sign a form, but could barely read the words. Mo was clasping her hands together and staring down at the floor. The ward sister ordered them a taxi. Derek helped Mo into the back seat and stared in silence at the passing streets. When he tried to hold her hand she pulled away from him.

Chapter Forty-five *Mo*

Mo felt the presence of Derek beside her. He was a warm, dark shadow, which she wanted near but could not engage with. Sounds and sights moved past her as disembodied bubbles; she, too, was in a bubble. The bubble had been there when she needed to evade the taunts of her sisters, the ugliness of the world, the disappointments which piled onto her: it was her Jules Verne protector, the means to negotiate outside demands. She could choose what crossed the barrier; at will could she thicken or weaken the membrane.

The shadow that was Derek had led her up the stairs and into the bedroom where he had pushed something into her hand: little white things to swallow. He was urging them onto her, saying they'd make her feel better, help her sleep. He was tugging at her coat, loosening the buckle. She let him. He had made her a cup of tea but it looked too strong and the mug was not clean. She wanted to push him away, push everything away. She wanted to be tired, wanted waves of darkness to wash over her.

Greedily she crunched the tablets with her teeth. They had an acrid taste. She wanted to spit them out but more than that she wanted to be carried away. Her head was pounding. There was something kept wanting to push into her mind and she had to keep it out, away from her. She was feeling ill. She was numb. Why hadn't he removed her cardigan now she was lying on the bed? Downstairs she could hear voices. Surely that was Clare Constable. Was that Ma's voice? What was all the fuss about? Was one of the children sick or something? She wanted to laugh. Why was she upstairs on the bed only half undressed?

What had happened? What was it that kept pushing, pushing itself into her mind?

The bubble burst.

The image of Timothy laid out on the hospital cot penetrated her. Her mind could no longer swim away: his little fists were curled up; his mouth was slightly open. But he was white so white. Where had he gone? Where were his smiles and fumbling words? Where were the wide-open vistas of his eyes, the joy in them? She heard a scream, a woman's scream, so close, in the room even. It pierced her. She wanted to shut her up, the one creating the commotion. She looked up. Derek was staring down at her.

'Oh Mo,' he said.

* * *

She wanted to have Timmy buried in the church where she and Derek had married. For months she had had little contact with her family and now she wanted them around her. They rarely ventured to Kentish Town and she had only occasional trips to Hackney. She'd insisted on having Timothy christened there when he was a few weeks old. Whether out of fear he might not survive the rigours of childhood or a desire for roots and tradition, she had not stopped to question.

Now Derek indulged her, saying it mattered little to him where his son's remains were laid to rest. His voice broke whenever he said the word 'son'. Mostly he just said 'he'. Derek told her he would sort out the practicalities. He promised to contact everyone they thought should know and would deal with the family. She took to her bed. For hours she did not emerge. What was there to do or say? She requested more sleeping tablets and got them. Ma and Cissy came to visit. They stood over the bed and yanked back the curtains letting daylight flood in; Ma's voice was sharp but the eyes full of pity. Mo could not bear to be pitied by Ma or her older sister or anyone else. She knew it was time to move. Besides, the sheets were beginning to smell and her body ached from lying too long.

'I'm getting up now,' she said and was as good as her word. Eleanor had the bath filled and pulled out a dress from the cupboard. When Mo put it on her shoulders stuck out and it ballooned away from her waist. Ma left, saying she'd be back soon. Mo and Cissy went for a walk in the park. The cold weather, which had hung on for far too long, had lifted. Blossom had long since given way to leaves. Mo was leaden as she wandered beside Cissy, who could not stop chattering. She was full of talk of what had happened at the market stall and who had come and gone, what their plans for the next year were. Mo nodded now and then. She knew it was just nerves, her sister did not know what else to say. Wanting to distract her, Cissy even took her to the gazebo café in the park and bought her tea and a cream cake, which she left uneaten. 'You've got to eat. Keep your strength up.'

* * *

The funeral was a week after the death. Mo let Eleanor, Ma, Cissy and Tilda choose the hymns. The only one she insisted on was *'All things bright and beautiful'*. She had never taken Timothy to church in Kentish Town. She recalled the few times she'd gone to church in her Mare Street days. Then she knew she'd always bump into someone from The Mare's Head or Dukely's. It was worth putting up with the boring sermon just to spend time with them afterwards. In north London she knew no one.

The night before the funeral they stayed at Cissy's place. Eleanor and Guy arrived in a taxi an hour before the service. Mo let Ma and Cissy dress her. She hated black, she declared, as Cissy inspected the dress and jacket she'd managed to procure from a shop near the market. Mo stared at herself in the mirror. The clothes hung off her, making her look wasted. Only the round cheeks remained, though less full than before.

She had the haunted eyes of a vampire. She just had to get through the day, she told herself. Surrender and be drawn along on the current of words, condolences, flowers, faces full of sympathy, faces she could hardly recall, faces from her childhood, well-wishers, the curious. Who had invited all these people anyway? Ma came close, gave her a hug, suppressed her sobs and pressed her hand for support.

The church was full. The organ started up and with it the first of the hymns: *The Lord is my shepherd. I shall not want, He maketh me down to lie…'* She remembered it from Sunday school. Her father was looking scrubbed up and spruce in a striped suit. His face had grown thinner. It made her realise how he was ageing. Ma looked the part in a feathered black hat and veil. Her eyes were puffy.

The size of the coffin caught Mo unawares. She knew it would be small - but not *so* small and white and covered in white lilies. It was too much. Her legs turned to water. She leaned sideways towards Derek, clutched at his arm, saw the world swirl around her. There was a clatter of people, arms reaching down, concern on people's faces. She could see the enlarged pores on her father's face as he pulled her up by the arms. He held her by the waist. 'All right, love,' he whispered. She straightened herself and looked towards the altar.

The vicar continued. She didn't recognise him: he must have been new to the parish. He was talking about Jesus suffering little children to come to him and about the Risen Christ and life eternal. Then they started singing again: *All things bright and beautiful. All creatures great and small, All things bright and beautiful, the good Lord made them all.* The words went round and round in her head. Now they were leading the coffin out, candles on either side, for committal in the churchyard. There were altar boys in white surplices. How did they get off school, she wondered.

Derek led her out. Everyone seemed to be wiping eyes,

snuffling. She felt as dry as bone. Over the grave Derek gave her a trowel. She stared at him. Why was he doing that? He took it gently from her hands and filled it with earth from a nearby heap and cast the soil over the coffin, which had been sunk on ropes into the gaping hole. She did likewise. For a moment, looking down, seeing the white box covered by soil and lilies she wanted to throw herself down into the pit and never come back to the surface. Derek steadied her. He never left her side, never let go of her arm.

Ma and the neighbours had laid on tea at The Mare's Head. A huge urn sat on a trestle table, borrowed from the local carpenter's. Rows of cups and saucers stood at the ready. Sandwiches piled high next to Victoria sponge and scones. The small round tables of the bar had been bedecked with frilly white tablecloths. Someone had put a small bunch of roses on each one. People came into the room. After a hesitant moment when they removed hats and coats, the chatter began. They shuffled around between tables, piling up food on their plates, slowly taking up conversations, which over time grew louder and bolder.

Mo sat in a corner next to Derek, with the family. People came over to shake their hands muttering words, which she barely heard. She nodded and smiled, nodded and smiled, wanting them to go and leave her in peace, wanting them to stay because she dreaded the void that would follow. It was ten o'clock before the last of the mourners disappeared. Mo let herself be taken back to Cissy's house for the night before she and Derek set off for Kentish Town the next morning.

PART 3

Chapter Forty-six *Derek*

Derek found it difficult to stay in Victoria Terrace. He went back to work as soon as he could. Before Timothy's death Knighton had let it be known he needed even more interior salon settings and more country house façades. Derek scouted around for photos of debutante parties and threw himself into painting flats for The Athena. It gave him the focus he needed and as the days went by he became increasingly engaged and confident in his sketches. At first he roped together two easels and when this proved insufficient, he leaned a large piece of flat wood against a wall and painted directly onto it.

At home he watched Mo. It was like observing a dazed animal: she shifted around with sluggish movements and glassy eyes. He told himself it would pass. He tried to talk to her, but she asked to be left alone, complaining of a headache or vague stomach pains. She needed rest, she insisted. She ruled out seeing a doctor though she did ask him to procure more sleeping tablets. He demurred, but in the end agreed. He felt ill equipped to deal with the situation. Eleanor advised him to give her more time. Eleanor herself looked pale as a sheet. Mo's mother and sisters came to visit but did not stay long.

Only after a few weeks did the mist seem to lift, but then Mo talked non-stop about such inconsequential things he wanted to block up his ears. She started to berate him for not mending the garden fence when they didn't have one. After that, she descended deeper into silence. She refused point blank to sort through Timothy's things or to enter the little box room, which they'd decorated in preparation for his next birthday. He had to move Timothy's cot out alone. He bundled together his clothes when she was downstairs. Eleanor then saw to it that these things were laundered, stuffed into pillowcases and trawled off to the Sally Army.

Mo refused to eat the meals Eleanor made for them. Instead she set about discarding her possessions. This she did in odd spurts of fury, which were at variance with her dreaminess. She began to alternate between stupor and an angry restlessness on an almost daily basis. Derek did not know which state he preferred; he no longer knew what was going on in her head.

First to go were her magazines: she piled her treasured old theatre things together and set light to them in the backyard. She stood before the fire, hair awry, in an old skirt and jumper, gazing into the flames, not stepping back when billows of black smoke threatened to engulf her. Before he could stop her, she gave away most of the chic dresses and skirts she possessed. She tied them together and took them along to the Church bazaar. This worried him even more. These had always been her pride. He himself had fetched the best of them from Fingal's Cave. At the time she'd so delighted in them she'd twirled and hugged him, saying they would stand her in good stead for her stints on stage.

Of theatre and singing there was no more talk.

'I don't know what to do for the best.' Derek was lingering on Clare Constable's doorstep as he returned a dish. He moved from one foot to the other, awkward in front of his bulky neighbour. She had been a stalwart from the start. In the days after the funeral she'd made them pies and brought them round. Now she looked at him with pity.

'It's hard losing one, you know… specially if it's your first… to lose one at all is bad… but your first and only one …' He said nothing: no one knew grief over a child more than she did. 'Give her time, Derek.' By now Mrs Constable had reverted to calling by his Christian name.

'That's what my sister says.'

'Wise words.'

'But she worries me. She's not making any effort,' Derek echoed what Eleanor had said the day before.

'As I said, it's early days...'

'It's impossible...' he hesitated.

'...for a man to understand what goes on in a woman?' Clare Constable shocked him by completing his sentence. That was not what he'd been about to say, but it fitted. She nodded sagely. 'If I was you I'd just make sure there's food on the table. She'll come round. And...' she glanced at him, 'a bit of affection would go a long way.' Derek recoiled before the knowing look. Talking about apple pies was a lot easier.

Issy was not a good idea right now. Everything in him shrieked that it was the worst possible idea to go anywhere near her. For her part, Issy had kept a respectful distance. Along with others she had sent flowers to the church for the funeral.

It was the end of a dreary afternoon. He had completed the last of his sets for Knighton and was in Fingal's Cave, where he had seen only three customers in three hours. Even these seemed reluctant to part with more than a few shillings. Exhausted from the lack of business and his ever-circling, sad thoughts, he decided he'd had enough for one day. He could always start afresh the next morning.

Later, he blamed the cloud of ennui, which was beginning to settle on him. He blamed his grief over Timothy. He blamed his growing fear for Mo's sanity. He blamed the sun, which broke through cloud when he was on his way home. For instead of returning him to Victoria Terrace where every other part of him had every intention of going, his body took him elsewhere. It had a will of its own. He realised, even as he was knocking on Issy's door, what a stupid thing he was doing. He was about to retreat when she opened.

'Derek!'

'It's good to see you!' he said, and it was. It was evident she was not expecting visitors. Her hair was unkempt and her face free of cosmetics. She looked younger and more guileless than he'd ever known her. Her eyes lit up with genuine warmth on seeing him. Something in him leapt up to the surface, a diver gasping for air.

'Derek I was so, so sorry to hear about your son.'

'Knighton told you?'

She nodded.

'I shouldn't be here.' He sat opposite her in her sitting room on one of the two pieces of furniture not shrouded in dust covers.

'But you are.'

'On the move, I see.'

'Arthur's given me two weeks to get myself sorted. He wants the place refurbished. All this is going into storage.'

'Where will you go?'

She raised an eyebrow as if to ask: what's it to you. 'Can I get you a drink? Tea? Something stronger?'

'A glass of water would do me.'

He watched her make her way towards the kitchen. When she came back there was a gentle smile on her face. Her brittle, social manner had dissolved. She seemed altogether simpler, more open. She was bearing up well, taking the fact of her altered circumstances with an equanimity which astounded him. She handed him the water, took a sip from her own glass and looked at him directly. 'How is your wife?'

'My wife... Mo is... quite frankly, I think she's in a bad way.'

'Can hardly blame her.'

'I don't.'

'I'm tired of wives,' she said and stood up, pacing towards the window. She drew back the curtain and gazed out over

Remington Square. She continued without looking at him. 'At least I'm tired of men with wives who come running round me when they feel the need.' She turned to face him.

He winced as if winded. Observing his reaction she grimaced. 'There I've offended you. I don't mean to be harsh. God only knows, it's a hard time for you too.'

'You sound so…'

'Hard-hearted? Many a woman in my position might get vengeful but I don't want to get into all that.'

'I can understand you being upset. But I thought you and Arthur were finished.'

'We are. I'm no longer at the beck and call of that erratic, vain, selfish, lascivious man…'

He laughed. 'Said with feeling.'

'I don't want any more to do with him. It was always a one-way street. Who do you think called the tune?'

'You held complete sway over him. I saw it with my own eyes.'

She sighed. 'What does that mean? He's fickle. He likes variety. But he can be pretty ruthless…'

'Where will you live?'

She came and sat back down, running her palms over the velvet arms of the chair. Now her look was fierce. 'Did you come here out of concern for me?'

Derek looked down at the dusty floorboards and the rolled carpet. 'I came because I wanted to see your face.'

'So, now you've seen me, what next?'

'Issy – not so angry.'

She leaned back, extending her feet before her with a sigh. 'You came to talk, I guess. You look terrible.'

'It's not me. It's Mo. She's stuck. I don't know what to do. She's always had a tendency towards – introspection – but now she seems lost. I'm at my wits' end.'

'So where do I come in? As you just said, you shouldn't

even be here.' She frowned at him.

He got to his feet. 'Look, if I'm disturbing you, I'll go. I didn't come to cause you annoyance. I just wanted to see a friendly face.'

'All right, all right. Sit down. We're both in a bad way. Would you like a whisky?'

'Not really, but if you're having one I'll join you.'

She disappeared back into the kitchen. He could hear the tinkle of glass as she moved bottles. When she came back bearing a tray with a bottle of Glenfiddich and two crystal glasses, she was looking calmer. She poured him a decent measure while taking a small one for herself. She added water to hers.

'Time to reassess,' she said. 'I've known for weeks I have to get out there. Salvage what I can from my patchy career. Think about getting more work. Jonathon has said he will help me.'

'You trust him?'

'Trust is a big word. Do I trust him to find me work? Perhaps. Do I trust him not to exploit the weakness of a woman down on her luck? No. Do I trust him to come clean with me? Well yes, I suppose I do. We're nothing if not old friends.'

'Can he get you more work?'

'I'm still on the cast of the Coward revue I did months ago. It's coming back. A few bits have been changed. Zara will put me up – for the time being. And you?'

'Me? He's giving me plenty of work. He's been a good contact.'

'Oh Derek, for God's sake you look terrible. Go back to your wife and try and make a go of it. She needs you now. I don't.'

Derek could not take his eyes off her. Despite gnawing doubts about the future, she was glowing with determination. She was spirited. The break from Arthur had done her more good than harm. He adored her honesty even as he flinched from it. Talking to her was like talking to a man. With her he need never hold anything back. She was as resilient as she was flexible, a sapling to bend rather than snap in the wind.

For the next hour they mulled over recent days. She even told him Knighton had been on the point of offering Mo work, which he had not known. Now that was all swept away. He grew sadder than he knew he could be, falling into morose silence, allowing himself to feel what he felt. Bit by bit. Timothy he could not talk about. Even as the whisky flowed and he was feeling ever freer to empty himself out, Timothy was a constriction in his chest, somewhere he dared not go: the ache of him beyond words.

'Don't look at me like that!' Issy scolded as she noticed him eyeing her.

'I can't help it.'

She in her turn looked at him over her glass.

'It wouldn't do any harm, would it?' he said.

'What wouldn't?'

He sat on the arm of her armchair and started stroking the back of her head, the nape of her neck, down her shoulders. She moved slightly, accommodating herself to his touch. 'If we consoled each other...'

'Derek, you know as well as I do that's not a good idea.'

'Why not?' He mumbled into her hair.

'It'll get complicated.'

'Life is complicated.'

'Not if we don't want it to be.'

'Shshsh. You talk too much.' By now his hands were doing the talking for him, exploring the fastening of her blouse, prising open the buttons, running gently over her breasts, his fingers, deft, urgent. He met no resistance. She gave a deep sigh. He lifted her to her feet, clasped her in an embrace, their bodies close, warm. He pulled her mouth towards his. Kissed her passionately. Her skin was soft as silk under his fingers. He wanted to bury himself forever, never to re-emerge. He wanted the darkness of her. She broke free, looked at him through her eyebrows, her eyes softening.

'Just this once then,' she murmured. She led him into the bedroom, which was crammed with boxes and covered lumps of furniture. He almost tripped over a chest by the bed, causing her to laugh. 'Derek, this way.' She stepped out of her skirt and threw off the opened blouse and stood before him in her pale pink chemise and camiknickers. He gave a sigh of longing then hurried to discard his trousers and shirt. The two of them fell onto the bed laughing, scrambling, pulling at each other's undergarments and then before he knew it, they were making love.

Afterwards they curved into each other, like folds in a drape. For a while they dozed then he woke with a start, realising where he was. He threw back the covers and grabbed his clothes. She watched him through drowsy eyes.

Chapter Forty-seven *Eleanor*

Eleanor could not wait to see Guy's cheerful face. The last weeks had been a tornado. Losing Timothy had seared right through her. When she saw the little body laid out in the Chapel of Rest the blood had drained from her head; she'd had to clutch onto Guy to stop herself collapsing. Only then did she realise just how much the little chap meant to her. For him alone had she been willing to put up with the volatility between Derek and Mo. The only positive to emerge from the cataclysm was her attachment to Guy. In her wretchedness she'd allowed the closeness to grow, previous assumptions exploding as grief rendered her raw.

He was waiting for her in the staff common room. He looked up as she entered. 'There you are!' His face lit up. Most of the other teachers had already gone, one or two lingered by the wall timetable. It was nearing the end of term, the time of sports' days and fêtes. As Guy helped her on with her jacket, she wondered if it was becoming obvious that something had shifted between them.

In the park he took hold of her hand. He entwined his fingers with hers. She had a moment of tension when she felt herself stiffen. With her history of fighting her instincts she knew these traces of resistance would not leave her quickly. 'You all right?' he asked.

'I feel like I'm leading a double life,' she said.

'You are, in a way.'

'None of their business really, but I feel on tenterhooks.'

'Why?'

'Dawlish would dearly like to be shot of me. I don't like

that uncertainty …'

'Oh that! It's never bothered you before.' He swung her hand gently.

'I feel I've just woken up. It took Timothy's death to do it. I guess I was holding on, trying to create stability …'

'You have more talent then the two of them put together. I've seen some of your sketches.'

She laughed. 'When did you get to see them? Ah yes, my notebook. I shouldn't have shown it to you.'

'You should do more. You have a real gift.'

'Sketches don't pay grocery bills. Sketches don't buy clothes, pay for visits to the doctor...'

'It's time you started thinking less practically.'

They walked for a while in silence. Emotions were tumbling through her, the glacier of past certainty shifting into ice floes.

'Marry me,' he said.

She started 'What?'

He tugged on her hand, making her run down a slope of grass towards the water. 'I want to show you the ducks. I spotted them again this morning.' He led her over a small bridge above the canal. 'Look in the bulrushes.'

She was reeling from his words.

'There – a whole family of them! I noticed them a week ago. The ducklings are big enough to survive but there are always foxes about. If they stay on that island they'll be all right. Foxes hate water.' The mother duck was waddling from the bank into the water, trailed by four ducklings. As they entered the water they started splashing and dive-bombing each other.

He continued in a low, matter-of-fact voice. 'I think we should leave London. Let Roger Dawlish go hang. We could set up our own school in the West Country.'

She stared at him with incredulity. 'Are you off your head?'

His eyes widened with tenderness. 'I've never been more

serious.'

'What about your mother?'

'We'd find a way. Property is cheaper out of London. The house is in my name. If I sold it we'd be able to afford a cottage and have somewhere alongside for her.'

'You want me to come and live with your mother?'

'Not in the same place. Nearby. Would that be so terrible?'

'Guy – I…'

'Look, I'm serious. I don't expect an answer straight away. But I love you Eleanor. I always have done…'

'Guy…'

'You always seemed … so I held back. I didn't think I had enough to offer you. But I've changed my mind. I have my strength, my youth, everything I have is yours. If you want it.'

'I don't know what to say.'

'Don't say anything. Go away and think about it.'

'I wouldn't know where to start.'

'I don't want to stand by and see you lacerating yourself for others. I don't want to see you waste yourself…' He paused, took her chin in his hand and forced her eyes to meet his. 'I've thought about it long and hard. It won't be easy. I have responsibility for my mother, but she can't consume all of me. I want to be there for you. I want to share my life with you…'

He had run out of words. He stroked her cheek, pulled her towards him and kissed her passionately. She struggled. 'Not here,' but he was not listening to her. His mouth was hard on hers, his tongue pushing into her mouth.

She was hot with confusion. She wanted to draw back, run as far away from him as she could, block up her ears; but even more she wanted to bury herself against his chest. It was all too much. She turned to face the water. The ducklings were still splashing around. Their effervescence reproached her. Life was all about her, breathing through the landscape, transforming fruits into seeds, breaking out of constricted forms to create anew. She was afraid. She ached with longing. Her body was in pain, her mind in denial. She did not want to be here. She did not want to be anywhere. She wanted to escape into her dreams, into the security of a memory which could never be questioned or violated, a pledge which could never be broken, a relationship that would be sacred as long as she breathed.

Yet, beyond all that, she wanted to live.

Chapter Forty-eight *Mo*

'He thinks I'm crazy,' Mo paused and stared at her one-time colleague, Stella. 'Perh'ps I am.'

'We all know what you've suffered and that, but even so, there's a limit. You've got to pick up the pieces.'

It was weeks now since Timothy's funeral. It was high summer, the trees heavy with dark green foliage. One day Mo had woken and been inordinately hungry. Even after trauma the body has a way of re-asserting itself. Her stomach had grumbled. She was weak with the pangs she'd been trying to ignore; they intruded into her thoughts. She roamed around the rooms at Victoria Terrace, yanking open every cupboard door. She found nothing to snack on, just dried lentils and rice. Not enough to feed a mouse, or so it seemed to her, suddenly ravenous. Eleanor's food she'd been unable to stomach: she knew her sister-in-law cared, but it only made her feel worse. If only she'd listened to Eleanor they would not be where they were …

From one day to the next she could not bear to stay in bed nor mooch round the rooms. Besides, it was too stuffy indoors. She had to get out. She had to take in fresh air. The first day this restlessness hit her she just put on her coat and left the house. She walked and walked until her feet grew sore. She found a cheap café where she huddled in a corner and stuffed herself with bacon and eggs. She was loathe to encounter people she knew, but this place was off her normal circuit. Condolences she wanted none of, nor advice, nor smiles of sympathy. So a sullen waitress plonking down a plate of greasy, midday breakfast in front of her had been just fine.

Stella she could just about tolerate. She had not seen her for months, except at the funeral. Since Timothy, their ways had diverged and they used to meet only once in a while to catch up. With her mixture of brashness, fellow feeling and practicality, Stella seemed the best bet right now. So here they were, in The Cockerel Tavern, the mirrored, old Victorian pub in Chelsea, over a midday drink. Mo was building herself up for another encounter with the clan in Hackney.

Stella pulled out a packet of Players and lit up. 'I came to visit more than once and 'e said you weren't seeing no one.'

'I didn't know till later.'

'He wouldn't let me near you.'

'Wouldn't 'ave been much point.' The two women were sitting near the impromptu stage where Mo had once accosted the singer, Doreen Delange, in the hope of getting 'a leg-up' in the trade. All that belonged to a different era.

'You look pasty,' said Stella.

'I *feel* pasty,' Mo retorted, giving her friend a wistful smile. She was glad she'd made the effort to see her.

Stella blew out a stream of smoke, which clouded the air between them. Someone was hammering on the out-of-tune piano; a couple of drunk women were leaning in towards each other, attempting a desultory love song. 'I wish they'd stop that bleedin' racket,' moaned Stella.

When Mo remained silent Stella went on. 'I'm glad you decided to poke your nose out. Another week in that house and you'd be going round the twist.'

'I did a bit. I thought I was back home and was worrying about some stupid fence. I 'eard myself ranting and thought: you've got to get a grip. Derek has been dead worried, I can tell you that much.'

Her friend reached over and touched Mo's hand. 'Let me get you a stout. That'll make you feel better. I'll get a ham sandwich and all. You could do with a bit of fattening up.' She wound her way through people bunched round the piano and pushed towards the bar. Mo was left staring at the heaped-up ashtray. The smell of cigarettes was nauseating, the smell of the beer sloshed onto the floor even more so. Stella had raised the possibility of her returning to work. At first the prospect shocked, yet the more it sank in, the more it appealed.

'Work might not be such a bad idea. I'd have to convince Derek though.'

'He can't very well stop you, can 'e? He didn't object to you singing.' Stella sounded petulant.

'That was before Timothy.'

'Come on Mo, where's your spirit?'

After the pub they strolled for a while along the Embankment. Outside the sky was patchy with clouds. Mo watched pleasure launches passing, churning foam, going places. She heard a Cockney voice telling tales of the river and Port of London over the loud hailer. She caught Stella's arm and linked hers through it. 'I 'ave to start all over again,' she said.

'That's more like it.'

They walked in silence. Mo was studying the ground. 'I was a bad mother,' she murmured and gave a loud sniff.

'No, you wasn't.'

'I was.'

'What makes you say that?'

'I was never content. I got bored.'

'*Normal,* you was. You listen too much to what people tell you.'

'There's more to it than that. I should've 'ad Timmy inoculated.'

'You weren't to know. Diphtheria is so rare these days…'

'That's not the point.'

Stella pulled forward, towards the water. She leaned over the railing. 'Water's high. Tide must be in. 'Ave you ever seen all that gets carried in on the river? Planks, chairs, bicycles. You could start a business from it if you had the mind to.'

The clear air was having a bracing effect, the more Mo walked the more the haze in her mind disappeared. As it lifted her options became stark. She dreaded returning to Victoria Terrace. It felt good to be with Stella, dawdling by the Thames and watching its ruffled water. It reminded her of when she first came to Chelsea.

Stella said she had to go: she was sitting at five in one of the smaller studios for an advanced class in life drawing. There would only be a handful of them, thank goodness, and then she was off to a party she'd been invited to. Would Mo like to join her? Mo shook her head. It was time to be getting back home. The two parted company and Mo caught a bus back to Kentish Town.

As she put the key in the lock the silence folded round her. She caught her reflection in the hallstand mirror, a dark figure in dark clothes, a pale, defeated, lonely face. Her steps echoed as she went upstairs. She stared at the door of the little box room they'd decorated for Timmy's next birthday. She caught her breath. She did not want to be here. She did not want to sit waiting until Derek came home. She did not want to seek Timmy in the corners. The few photos they had taken were kept in a box. One day she would have the courage to peer inside. For now the lid was tightly closed. Timmy's clothes had been laundered by Eleanor; for all she knew they had left the house by now. She could not bear to smell his smell on them, nor could she bear to finger them, imagining them around his chubby limbs, remembering how she pulled them on and off. And a pile of his freshly washed clothes would be anathema.

There was a visceral sorrow she was not ready to explore, not ready to part with. The ache, the dull ache of his absence was the fiercest presence she had ever known. Who was there to understand any of this? It should be Derek. It could only be

Derek. Yet where was he? Where was he? She needed him and she needed him now. She went back downstairs, switched off the gas where she'd started to boil water for tea and banged the door shut behind her.

Chapter Forty-nine

Mo took off with determination down the road. Earlier in the week there'd been a spell of warm, sunny weather, now it had grown dull again. If she hurried she would catch Derek before he shut up shop. He said few people came in after five unless by special arrangement. Her meeting with Stella had given her the courage to stand up for herself. If she stayed at home any longer she would lose her way again, forget that she had once earned her keep and was now resolved to work again.

As she came within sight of the bow-windowed Fingal's Cave, her heart beat faster. She had to do this. She was clear something needed to change: in her, in the house, between her and Derek. Only movement and effort could save her from the blackness of despair. Her steps slowed over the cobblestones. She pulled down the flyaway skirt of her dotted dress and settled her hair. He may have customers present and, despite all, she would not want to show him up.

The door moved. Someone was leaving the premises. What sort of people came here to shop? Women mostly, she knew that: but what sort of women? Until now she had only been to the place two or three times for it was Derek's work domain, which in its day-to-day activities had little to do with her. She heard the clatter of a shutter being drawn down and the door being locked, saw the back of a figure. It was Derek. She froze, caught her breath. She watched him as she might a stranger, incapable of calling out to establish normality between them. He was whistling and seemed carefree. Something in Derek's manner linked with a dull awareness that something furtive was going on. He started walking down towards Primrose Hill. She ducked into a shop doorway, telling herself she was being ridiculous, but unable to do otherwise. It was early yet. He never came home at this time. There was no out-of-town auction, nothing to pick up from one of the train depots. He'd said he needed to trek round West End theatres to re-establish contacts with other stage managers and he'd mentioned painting more scenery for The Athena. She'd started when he'd said that. The notion of Knighton and her audition reverberated through her. But all that belonged to a Mo that was gone. She'd let the familiar name fade without response.

Now something felt amiss.

His mind was elsewhere. He flicked back his head, sauntered, still whistling, hands in his pockets. He seemed almost jaunty, blissfully unaware she was only yards away. Where was he going? He was heading south instead of north. She crept behind him, taking care to keep at a safe distance. A bus swept down the roadway. A woman with two children crossed the street, shooing them over before the traffic. Two workmen were jostling down the pavement, joking. They passed him by. Derek was striding now, eager to be somewhere. She had a job keeping up with him. He passed made a long diagonal across the road and took a footbridge across the rail tracks.

As she entered the square behind him she knew where he was headed. She gave a little gasp: Remington Square. It seemed an age since she'd been through that door into the party with Jonathon Knighton and his protégées. True enough, Derek was now making for that same royal blue door. A removals van was parked outside and workmen were hefting pieces out of the Georgian house and loading them onto the van. There was a ramp to aid with heavier items.

And there was Issy Fontane or whatever her name was. Her hair was scooped into a silk turban and she was wearing floppy trousers. She held out her arms towards Derek. He ran into them. They embraced. There in broad daylight, in front of the neighbours, in front of the workmen, they gave each other a long lovers' kiss, clasped each other as though never to separate.

Mo could not move. Her knees were buckling and she had to lean against a nearby railing. Derek and Issy were still embracing. She felt herself slide down, till she was half crouching, half sitting between the railing of one house and the hedge of the next. Her head was swimming. It felt so light. She retched, and watched a trickle of vomit trickle down the pavement. After a moment she pulled herself up. She grabbed the railing to steady herself. As she looked over she saw the two were moving into the house, arm-in-arm.

She leaned over the railing, took several deep breaths, telling herself she could do this, she was strong. She was Morwenna née Dobson who would lift herself by her bootstraps. Another wave of nausea passed through her. A pain was stabbing her chest. She could hardly breathe.

'I can do this,' she said out loud. She straightened up, did up the buttons on her cardigan. If she went now she could get to Victoria Terrace, bundle together her few remaining things and get the hell out of there. There was still time.

Back at the house Mo paced their bedroom, summoning that resourcefulness which had always stood her in good stead; she must be clear in what she did next. There was no point in raging against the tide: things would flow as they would. If Derek was in love with another woman there was no point in denying it. If it was a passing fancy it was another matter.

Perhaps she did not need to do anything right now.

Her breath had left her. She sat on their bed then curled herself into a ball. There was no denying they had quarrelled time and again in recent months. She had hated him as much as she loved him, but he remained her true north, the sounding board and haven to which she returned. She loved him. She desired him. Yes, there'd been times when she was too exhausted for love-making or too cross with him; when she sought to punish him, but even that was done with the ground plan of levelling the score between them. Now to observe his happiness, the lightness in his step as he ran into the arms of another woman, was a dagger thrust into her. How could he? How? She knew there had been other women in his life, but he had sworn off them, he'd said. He'd told her that she was the one, the only one. She was his anchor and his fire.

Her body was wracked with pain. She felt sick all over again. Derek, she murmured, you utter bastard cheat liar. Words tumbled through her mind. She got up from the bed and changed into something more becoming, donning the one silk gown she still possessed, painted her mouth bright red and swept her hair back. If he could do it so could she. Men still found her attractive: Bonnington and Knighton, to name but two. Besides. Besides. She was an artist just like him. It was high time she got out there and did something about it.

What she was wearing suited her. It was a shade of cerise, a dress which clung to her but was not vulgar as it shimmered in the light. She took her one and only coat, resting it on her arm. She left the house taking only a small bag with her: enough for an overnight stay.

Chapter Fifty *Eleanor*

Something about the school week with its periods of forty minutes, its regular recesses, its reviews and reports appealed to Eleanor's deep-rooted need for order. It got her up in the morning and made her so tired that she had no problem sleeping at night; it kept her sane and rendered her a valued member of society. This stability had seen her through Timothy's death and the funeral. But term was drawing to a close. At school, she grew listless. At home, the absence of Timothy was a dark ghoul dominating the house. She had seen neither Mo nor Derek in days.

To cap it all Guy had left her to chew the cud, as he put it. He was keeping out of her way, scuttling between lessons and cricket matches. Without him, she felt flat. But today he'd invited her to see Charlie Chaplin's latest at the local picture house. She couldn't wait to see him: she missed him more than she cared to admit. Today, though, she also feared their meeting.

As usual she was one of the last to quit the premises. She was surprised to see a small gathering at the school gates. A couple of her colleagues were talking to a third person. She was even more surprised to discover this third person was Mo. 'Ah, here she is,' she heard.

Mo nodded a greeting. 'I was asking after you. I thought I'd missed you.' Her colleagues departed as Eleanor drew level with them. 'Eleanor, can we talk?' Mo was looking nervous. 'Can we go somewhere?'

'Not home you mean? Has anything happened?'

'Yes and no.'

'There's a teashop just round the corner. But Mo I don't have a lot of time. I'm going out this evening.'

'With Guy?'

'Yes, as it happens.'

They walked in silence as Eleanor led the way to Mrs Jones' Teashop, an old-fashioned establishment, with patchwork cushions, Welsh dressers and pretensions to country living. They ordered a large pot of tea. Mo looked at Eleanor with unwonted directness. 'I didn't want you to worry. That's why I came…'

'What is it Mo? What's the problem?' A young woman arrived wielding a large tray. 'My goodness,' said Eleanor. 'That'll keep us going for a while.' The waitress offloaded the willow-patterned cups and saucers. 'It must be something important for you to come to the school.'

Mo tilted her chin towards her with a look of defiance Eleanor had not seen recently. Her eyes were gleaming with determination. 'I've left Victoria Terrace. And Derek – at least for the time being.'

'Oh!' Eleanor lurched back. 'Does he know?'

Mo's eyes shifted away, avoiding Eleanor's.

'Family is family. In times of trouble nobody else understands in quite the same way…'

'Look,' Mo cut in: 'it's like this: I've left. I don't think Derek will even care.'

'Mo, of course he'll care! What's got into you?' When Mo said nothing but stared sullenly ahead, Eleanor went on: 'You can't just go sailing off. What about the promises you made – don't they mean anything?'

Mo flashed her an angry look. 'Promises? Commitment? You better ask your brother about that.'

'What do you mean?'

'He's nothing but a cheat and a liar and – and I don't want to live in the same house as him no more.' Mo's face grew red.

She was struggling to find the right words. 'I've had enough.' Before Eleanor could stop her she had pushed away her tea and headed for the door. By the time Eleanor reached the street her sister-in-law had been swallowed up in the stream of passers-by.

Eleanor went back to the table, just as the waitress arrived to see if she could clear it. 'I won't be long. Just finishing,' she said. She pulled a cup towards her, and sat sipping, stunned and unable to piece it all together.

* * *

Guy was not surprised by the news. 'I saw it coming,' he said. They were walking towards the Kentish Town picture house where already a line was snaking its way round the block in anticipation of *The Gold Rush*. 'It's like watching two lions mate.'

'Can't say I've had that experience.' She made a stab at levity.

'Two sensitive and insecure people who love each other madly but are riven by jealousy, ambition…prickly as hell.'

'Is that how you see them?'

'When I've been in the same room as them it was obvious that they are too similar. Mo is more accommodating. She puts up with more and suffers more. With Timothy gone it's just too difficult for them.'

By now they had reached the box office. The black and white photos of the film promised spills and thrills, humour, romance and as ever the little man pitted against the goliaths of society. Guy put his arm round her shoulder as they walked into the brightly lit foyer where someone was playing the piano.

For the next hour or so they were lost in the dramas of the Lone Prospector. They laughed, sighed and applauded as the little man battled his way through blizzards, taunts of his burly fellow gold-seekers, icebound log cabins and encounters with bears. He was lost, rescued, teetered off cliffs and finally, in the romantic ending, grew rich and won the girl of his dreams. The audience was delighted.

When they emerged from the picture palace in the fading light it had been raining and the pavements were glistening. Guy drew Eleanor closer to him. 'So, Madame. You can't get away with it forever.'

'What are you talking about?'

'You know very well what I'm talking about.'

'Oh Guy, can't we just continue as we are?'

'Is that what you want?'

They walked for a while in silence. She stared down at the shiny paving slabs, at puddles that had formed and were draining away. She heard someone singing an Irish air in a nearby pub. She felt the warmth of Guy's arm. She could not bear the notion of being separated from him. But marriage? When Lance died the promise of marriage had gone with him. So, too, had all certainty. She had been struck by lightning, pierced from head to toe, every molecule shot through and forever altered. Couldn't Guy realise that?

A tear trickled down her face and she brushed it away, not wanting him to see. 'Everything seems to be falling apart,' she said weakly.

'Is it that you don't – don't care for me enough?'

His voice was thick with emotion. He was crossing over into the danger zone, into the face of the gun barrel. What courage did it take to do that! Whereas she wanted to hide in the shade, lurk in the protective ditch. She could hear him breathing heavily then inhaling, holding his breath, waiting.

'Eleanor...'

'Guy. I – I.'

'You need to be willing to take risks. Otherwise you're half alive. I don't want an in-the-shadows relationship.'

'It's complicated.'

'It's *not* complicated. Either you want to be with me or you don't. It's quite simple.'

'Your mother…'

'My mother is not at issue here. We'd find a solution. Get her a cottage. That really is a side issue.'

'Not for me it's not.'

'You think Derek's impossible. You're even worse. At least he gives life a try.'

They walked on, his words hitting her like blows: was she, in her own way, worse than her brother? Derek pursued life, embraced it, let it trample all over him. He was nothing if not an enthusiast.

'Just so you know… I'm leaving London. I've handed my notice in. I was hoping you'd come with me – as my wife. I've been looking at properties. Cottages. I've put my London property on the market. Even got a buyer for it…'

'That's a slap in the face.'

'If that's what it takes… look, I'm tired of drifting. I'd gladly tip a bucket of iced water over your head, give you a hefty shove into the gutter... anything to make you realise how much you mean to me.'

'You have a delicate turn of phrase.'

'With you it's the only way.' He paused. 'So you need to tell me whether I should go away and forget all about you or whether you'll join me in my crazy dream…'

'That sounds like an ultimatum.'

'It is. I've decided I have to have all or nothing.'

'Is that so?'

'That is so.'

'Can I at least think about it?'

'You've had time.'

'Another twenty-four hours?'

'Eleanor, don't you understand what I'm saying? I want to be with you all the time. I want to see your face every morning when I wake up and last thing at night.'

The words resounded through her, warming her, terrifying her, leaving her no way out but to make a clear choice. They had reached the turning into her road. She looked at him. Bit her lip.

'Yes, then yes.' She broke away, hurrying towards the shelter of her family home.

Chapter Fifty-one *Derek*

The next time she saw him Eleanor filled Derek in on what had happened. 'What did she say – exactly? Tell me what she said.' He felt the breath going out from him.

'She was furious.'

'But why – why?'

'You tell me, Derek. Perhaps she got to know about something she didn't like…' Eleanor showed little need to spare him. She looked angry herself. Derek slumped down into the worn wing chair by the empty grate. He stared into the blackened hearth. 'So, it's true, is it, what she suspected?' she persisted.

He shrugged. 'She's been impossible. In a world of her own.'

Eleanor banged her hand onto the table. 'Have you no sense of responsibility towards her?'

'She has frozen me out. You've no idea what it's like.'

'Don't I?'

'How could you have?'

'I know a lot more than you think I do.'

'So what are you telling me – that's it's all my fault? She's half crazy. You do know that? She imagines all sorts of things….'

'Like you in the arms of another woman.'

He snorted, got up and strode around the room. He sensed Eleanor watching his every move. 'There's more going on with her than you realise. She's eaten up with ambition.'

'I knew that from the start. But *you* didn't understand, did you? You were always so wrapped up in yourself, you couldn't see what was going on in front of your nose.'

'Meaning?'

'She was frustrated with her life and you didn't help. You didn't give her enough time, enough attention...'

'Sorry, but it wasn't like that.'

'Wasn't it?'

Words were useless to explain. He was growing exasperated. As always his sister would claim to know best and leave him squirming, feeling guilty as hell. He could not say that he and Mo loved each other but perhaps, for now, they needed to be released from the bond they had so hastily entered into. He felt drained, he was floundering; the last thing he wanted was to be berated by his superior sister. He did not want to lose Mo. He was not trying to teach her a lesson. He just wanted to keep his equilibrium, get his needs met: stop the blackness descending. And she was trying to prove a point and had pushed it too far. Why all of a sudden was she clamouring for independence?

'Where has she gone?'

'I have no idea.'

'For God's sake WHERE?' For all the brave, cold words he would utter to his sister, he needed Mo. Maybe she was a bird of flight, never to be trapped. But he would seek her out and bring her home, establish some accord between them.

'Derek, what have you been up to? *Is* there someone else? A serious someone else?'

'Of course not,' he almost barked at her. 'You believe everything she says.'

'No, I don't, but I wouldn't put anything past you.'

'Eleanor, can we drop the subject?'

'So there IS someone? You have been unfaithful to her. Now at all times! What's got into you?'

'For God's sake, leave me be. You understand nothing and never have done.' She breathed deep, as if suppressing anger.

Agitated, she got up and stalked around, stopped near him. 'In fact there is something I need to tell you.'

'And what would that be?' he said, at once unsure of himself, the ground slipping and sliding beneath him. She hesitated, sat down opposite him, re-arranged the sugar bowl and teapot on the table.

'I – I am leaving London. I'd like to put the house on the market.'

Dumbfounded, he stared at her.

'You seem surprised. You thought we would just go on forever?'

'Eleanor, I had no idea....'

'You wouldn't, would you. You take for granted everything will just stay the same. Only *you* are allowed to change.'

'No, I don't think that. But I didn't see this coming. What's happened?'

She coloured slightly. 'Guy and I are thinking about setting up a school.'

He gaped at her in disbelief. 'When did all this come about?'

She shrugged, looked evasive, shy almost; despite his troubles he was curious.

'We've come to a crossroads, Derek. Mo will not be back in a hurry. For now I suspect she can't bear to be in the same house as you.' Derek frowned, thrumming the table with his knuckles. 'Sorry if that sounds harsh, but you need to know.'

'I had no idea.'

She relaxed a little. 'Nothing is fixed. But I have decided I want to leave London.'

'With Guy?'

'Yes, with Guy.' Her voice sounded firmer now.

'But you love your job.'

'It's teaching I love. Staying on at Blundell's will get me nowhere. I need to move on.'

'Well. That does put the cat among the pigeons…' He sat brooding, staring at the bars of the empty grate. 'I don't know what to do,' he said quietly.

Eleanor looked across at him, her eyes softening for a moment. 'As far as Mo goes, I'd allow her time. Then you could put out feelers. You might both come to your senses.'

'You see this as an aberration on her part?'

She shrugged one shoulder. 'She was really upset when I saw her. She didn't have the words, didn't know how to express herself.' Eleanor had got up and was clearing things away from the table. She looked perturbed. 'Heaven knows you need each other now more than ever.'

* * *

The next day Derek could not settle to anything. He did not leave the house. It was time he took stock at Fingal's Cave; he needed to check what auctions were coming up and acquaint himself with the latest West End shows so he could plan ahead. Instead, he fell into mulling over recent days. His assistant would mind Fingal's Cave yet again.

Was it possible Mo had seen something she shouldn't have? Unlikely. But it was evident there was no retrieving the situation from one day to the next. He would have to think long and hard about what to do next. Mo, he thought: I shall have to live without you. The thought seared. It was not possible. I shall have to learn to, his mind insisted: I must. The funeral was past and Mo was back on her feet. If he wanted a clean break now was the time.

* * *

When Eleanor returned from school she said they should visit the solicitor in order to check the deeds of the house and make sure there were no impediments to a quick sale. On their parents' death the house had passed without hitch to them. No will had been left and as sole heirs they'd agreed a fifty-fifty split. Their father's life insurance had covered what remained of the mortgage.

At her words he felt more sluggish than ever.

'You're sure you want to do this?' He was shocked at her haste: she had always been the more cautious and grounded one.

'Derek, it's time you stood on your own two feet.' Though he had heard this from her before, there was a new fierceness in her eyes, which warned him she was in earnest. He had never thought he would witness Eleanor in love again. Even now he could not credit it. So used had he grown to the ice queen – the one who controlled and kept chaos at bay – that this emerging Eleanor seemed untrustworthy.

After supper he sat at the table, chin propped on his open palm, staring into space. He would miss this house. 'Are you finished?' He nodded. She took the plates to the sink.

He thought about his parents. Mariette, the melancholy, he'd once dubbed his mother in an irreverent mood. He recalled her soft voice, her wispy hair, her kindness and gentle intuitive intelligence. He had not thought about her in a long while. Next month would be the anniversary of her death. All too often while she lived he'd sought to distance himself from her. She had many ideas and was sensitive to what went on around her. Through her, he was pulled into areas of himself he would later develop. He had a lot to thank her for.

Father he'd always found stern. It dawned on him now how anxious his father would have been, with the war raging and gobbling up not only young men but most of his savings. With Lance's death the concerns of his parents multiplied as Eleanor sank into the deepest trough. When she resurfaced, albeit frosty with suppression, they'd heaved a sigh of relief. During the war his mother told him nightingales had once sung over the city parks but now they trembled in fear of bombardment. That, too, had passed.

Victoria Terrace contained so much life imbedded in its

fibre. How could he leave all this behind, stand naked in front of another dwelling with a jumble of other people's memories and have to call that place home? The house had held them all together. At times he'd been ashamed of its terraced respectability, its net curtains and window boxes. In the street there were the old working-class families like the Constables, who had been there long before them. Father had intended bettering their position, moving them up the hill towards Dartmouth Park, where the houses had front gardens and even names. But then came the war and it never happened.

To leave Victoria Terrace was to abandon what roots he had; it was to jettison any hope of continuity. He thought of Issy being pushed from Remington Square. That was a bad business. Leaving there was a wrench for her, harder, he sensed, than the rupture with Arthur Bonnington, for she'd become younger, lighter, without him. She had thrown so many parties there, she would be surely sad to leave.

He returned to the matter in hand. Eleanor meant business. Once she put her mind to it, she would be capable of upping sticks and disappearing with Guy, somewhere where he could not follow.

'You've decided, have you – it's definite?'

'Derek, you need to find your own place. A situation that fits in with your artist ways, a studio with space, light and the freedom to make a mess.'

He was only half listening. In his heart he vowed to find Mo and make her see sense. She would refuse to return to The Mare's Head: that would be an admission of defeat, regression to childhood frustration. 'I'm going to find her,' he declared. 'Wait at least until I do.'

'And what if she doesn't want to be found?'

'I'm not sure she knows what she wants right now.'

She smiled. 'One could say that was a very condescending male view.'

'And that sounds like a typical sister reprimand.'

'Has it occurred to you that she has a free will and right now she is opting to find her own way?'

'How can you possibly say that, knowing how confused, upset and bereaved she is? She needs protecting from herself.'

'Does she Derek?' She paused. 'Perhaps it's you she needs protecting from.'

Chapter Fifty-two   *Mo*

Her old digs at Riverton Road had changed little. Mrs Roberts greeted her with a smile of sympathy, asked how she was doing and offered her tea. Mo declined, wanting to push away sympathy. Mrs Roberts showed her into the front parlour, a privilege never granted when she lived there. Mrs Roberts shut the door respectfully behind her and went in search of Stella. Mo took in the porcelain dogs and ladies with parasols, the chintz-covered chairs and flowered wallpaper. A fake Empire ormolu clock ticked and tinkled. A picture of two Victorian girls on a swing stood above the mantelpiece. The room reminded her of a funeral parlour and set her on edge.

The door thrust open and there was Stella, face shining with cold cream. 'Sit down Mo. I'll get Mrs Roberts to make some tea.'

'I don't want any.'

'Yes, you do. Or you should do.'

Mo sighed and collapsed into a wing chair among the cushions. Stella moved swiftly out of the room and when she came back, shifted a chair close to Mo. She grasped her hand.

'I saw Derek with Issy,' said Mo. She put the corner of her thumb to her mouth and chewed on it. 'In broad daylight – like the fondest of lovers. I could kill him, I really could.' Stella said nothing. 'I wonder how long it's being going on. He must think me an idiot…'

'I don't doubt that he loves you,' Stella said quietly.

'Don't give me that. Why would he go off with her?'

'It might be a reaction – you know – to Timothy's going. Men are strange like that.'

'So what's this? Sticking up for him all of a sudden?'

'I'm just trying to balance the picture. Derek's had other women. You know that. I thought it was part of the appeal…'

'Stella!'

'In the circles he moves in they're all for free love and all that, though to be honest I thought he'd settled down.'

There was a rattle outside and a knock. Stella leapt up to take the tray from Mrs Roberts. She placed it on a little round table and began to pour. Mo watched as though through glass. She noticed Mrs Roberts had put out her best rosebud tea service. They sat sipping while outside the streets grew slowly darker. The clock ticked on. Mo found herself listening to it, soothed, despite herself, by its rhythm. It struck her that she had nowhere to go, no one to go back for. She gazed down at the swirls and circles of the Axminster carpet. Her eyes were watering, she sniffed loudly: 'So what am I going to do?'

'I'd get back to work if I was you. It's hard to think straight, but you must. You could go back to The Fox's Den – work behind the bar, sing in the night club.'

'Jonathon Knighton offered to take me on,' said Mo flatly. 'I went for an audition. I sang. I belted it out and they loved me…' She gave a dry laugh.

'Well there you go. Opportunities exist.'

'That was weeks ago …' She put down her cup.

'Look, there are a couple of rooms at the top of the house here. Mrs Roberts never lets them. She keeps them for when her sister visits. I could ask. As a stop gap.'

When Mo gave a desultory shrug of the shoulders Stella decided to take the initiative and sought out the landlady.

* * *

Up in the attic bedroom with its the sloped ceiling and bird's eye view over rooftops, Mo felt oddly at home. Stella smuggled up a half bottle of whisky, which they saw off between them. Mo went to bed woozy and had strange dreams where Derek was calling out to her down a long tunnel.

She woke with a heavy head. She and Stella had a breakfast of porridge and tea in the back scullery. 'You're right, you know. I need to get back to work. It's the only solution.'

Stella grinned. 'So what's the plan?'

'Anything really: singing, pub work, modelling. Ideally I'd like to do something that's going somewhere...'

Stella stared at her, saying nothing.

'Don't look at me with such alarm, Stella.'

'It sounds too good to be true. Too sudden.'

Mo gave her friend a wide smile. There was something dynamic about being with Stella. She was spiky and full of zest, some might say she was common, brazen even. She treated other women's husbands as fair game, but she had a deep streak of loyalty. She was the tonic Mo needed.

As Stella put the bowls in the sink, Mo looked around. The scullery was the same as ever. Only the vacuum cleaner was new. Mrs Roberts would be keen to show she moved with the times. Stella said she had come and gone from here twice in the last two years, always back to His Nibs as she called her sometime lover, Julius Peter. Riverton Road was always there to fall back on.

Stella was looking older these days. Her eyes had lost their hardness. 'Do you want me to make enquiries? Put in a word for you?' she asked.

'Wouldn't do no harm.' Mo drifted into a state of detachment. 'Right now I don't want to see Derek's mug anywhere near me.'

Stella laughed. 'That's what I like. A bit of gumption.' She rinsed the dishes. 'You could always come with me. See who's there.'

'I could and all,' said Mo. 'Don't know about taking my clothes off any more. Got too many lumps in the wrong places.'

Stella chuckled. 'You look fine. You've matured nicely.' They went up to Stella's room where she pulled a dress out of the cupboard. Mo eyed the grey number with indifference. 'Do you want it? You can keep it.' She looked at her wristwatch. 'We need to go. It's getting late.'

* * *

When she entered the college premises Mo felt a stone in her chest. The familiarity rendered her sad and anxious. Stella engaged with her own routine straight away and Mo sensed she was getting in her way. 'I'm off,' she said. 'See you back at the digs.'

Stella looked across in astonishment.

'You've hardly spoken to anyone yet.'

'It's not for me Stella. I just can't.' She wandered out into the street where the loudness of the traffic made her start. She stared at the passers-by, alienated. A sheet of newspaper floated up and flattened itself against a lamppost.

The Fox's Den, was a few minutes' walk away. She glimpsed herself in a shop window and adjusted the grey cloche hat Stella had lent her. Once there, she pushed open the etched glass door and thrust forward as though the most confident of women. The manager had changed. The bald, rotund man had given way to a serious young man with a dark moustache, and there was no sign of the skinny fellow with the hairy arms. 'I've come for a job,' she said. 'I'd like to sing in the nightclub. I used to work here.'

'And when would that have been?'

'A couple of years back.'

'A lot has changed since then.' He raised one eyebrow and peered at her. 'You are?'

'Mo Eaton.' One or two customers were taking in the encounter with interest. She caught the familiar stench of stale beer and ancient, nicotine-soaked walls. He eyed her from head to foot and did not seem dismayed by what he saw. 'You need a barmaid, too. I noticed walking through, it's not very tidy.' Before he could respond she carried on: 'I'm a good worker. My parents run a pub in Hackney. I know what needs to be done. I could work in the bar and then sing in your nightclub. That draws people in.'

'References,' he said. 'We would need two letters of recommendation. We can't have an unknown person handling cash.'

'The last publican knew me. I told you I worked here before.'

'He's long gone. Come round tomorrow night. I'll have a word with the boss. We can't pay you much.'

'What do you pay?'

'Come tomorrow. By the way, the nightclub's shut down.'

'Oh.'

Once she was back outside on the street she knew she would not go back. To return there would be to regress to Hackney and greasy, beery men grasping at her. She would move forward towards music, pursuing her lodestar. Buoyed up by that idea she decided to call round to The Athena. It occurred to her she might bump into Derek there then recalled he only worked there mornings.

When she asked to see Knighton she was ushered into a small space, crammed with scripts. She picked one off the pile. G.B.Shaw. *Joan of the Coalyards*. She struggled to read the resumé: a female miner takes on the colliery owners and fights for more money and modernisation of the pits. An unlikely tale: since when did women go down the mines?

Startled by voices in the corridor, she replaced the script as Jonathon Knighton strode into the room. His eyebrows shot up on seeing her: 'Ahh,' he said, 'Mo Eaton.' She nodded, unable to utter a word. He came across and took hold of her hand. 'I heard what happened,' he said. 'I am so very sorry.'

Mo who had been putting on a fair show of it, coughed,

almost choking. Overcome with pent-up emotion she thrust herself into his arms. Alarmed, he patted her back. Still finding no words she snuffled against his chest before pulling back. 'I'm so sorry,' she said. 'You caught me by surprise…'

'That's quite all right. You're a brave woman…'

'I need to work,' she said. 'I need a job …'

'Isn't it too…?'

'It's not too soon. If I don't do something I'll go crazy!'

'Sit down, won't you Mo – Mrs Eaton.' She glanced back at a chair laden with more scripts. He shifted them onto the floor and she sat down. 'Where's your husband now? I saw him this morning.' Knighton looked concerned.

'I don't know and I don't care,' she stated fiercely. Knighton looked surprised at this blast of defiance. 'I'm ready to work.'

'Look, I need to think about this. It's not just me who decides these things.'

She felt herself in danger of crumpling again. She leaned back into the chair. 'Mr Knighton, could I have some water please?'

'Of course.' He left the room and came back with a glass. 'Call round tomorrow, why don't you? I'll see what I can do in the meantime.' She sipped the cold water. When she glanced up Jonathon Knighton was staring at her in puzzlement.

* * *

Mo watched the glow of a summer dusk slanting through the attic window and thought of Derek. Would he be worried about her? She pulled out the one photo of Timothy she kept within constant reach in her handbag and smoothed it out. She switched on the side lamp and ran her fingers over the picture. It had been taken on the occasion of her father's birthday. He had insisted on a trip to see them; now she was settled, now she was respectable. He had forked out the money for them to go to the High Street photographer's.

Timothy looked so fetching in his little sailor outfit, with his plump dimpled legs. Light radiated from him as he faced the world. He exuded curiosity, joy, and eagerness. His little face stabbed her through, beyond tears, beyond self-reproach. 'Timothy,' she whispered. 'Oh Timothy.' She crept down to the bathroom on the floor below. She splashed cold water in her face, stared at herself. Did she kill him? The question assaulted her. Was she Lady Macbeth whose ambition was a dark bird clutching at her? Nonsense, she said out loud. It was nobody's fault. But she should have had him inoculated, whispered the darkness. Go to bed, she commanded herself. She crept back up the stairs and slid between the covers.

In the morning she put on the grey frock Stella had given her, primped her hair and added rouge to offset her pallor. She arrived at the theatre at eleven as Knighton had suggested. She had told him she did not want to bump into Derek and he insisted he was not due in that day.

She wandered into the auditorium, where she sat in the back stalls and pictured herself up front, in the limelight. When she heard steps across the boards and a light was switched on she moved towards the stage. Derek's drawing room stood out before her with its carefully rendered bookshelves and windows. She felt a tightness in her chest: he had done a good job. Jonathon Knighton's voice echoed in the wings as he moved off, back into the corridor. She found him in his office.

'Come in, my dear.' He was mellower than in class. 'We've got a second Coward revue coming up. Are you still able to sing?' The question took her aback.

'Of course.'

'I want to try you out.' He touched her face lightly with the knuckle of his middle finger. She flinched then smiled to conceal her unease. 'I know how hard it must be for you. Just take it easy…' She got up, ready to leave, ready to sing, ready to do anything rather than sit tense as a high wire in the airless room awaiting his next move.

'Do you have numbers you can sing unaccompanied?'

She rattled off the names of several popular tunes she knew. He told her to pick one. She cleared her throat and began. As she sang confidence seeped back into her.

'Look for the silver lining, where e'er a cloud appears in the sky,
Remember somewhere the sun is shining,
And so the right thing to do is make it shine for you.
A heart is full of joy and gladness will always banish sadness and strife,
So always look for the silver lining, and try to find the sunny side of life.'

He clapped with enthusiasm. 'Superb! A great voice you've got.' She exhaled in relief. 'You'll be in the chorus. But shouldn't you talk it through with your husband first?' Mo clutched the arm of the chair as anger bit into her.

'That won't be necessary.' When he said nothing she blurted out: 'I'm not with my husband any more. My husband and Issy Fontane are having an adventure. In some circles that does not mean much, but to me it does.'

He looked thoughtful. 'Listen, it's not the same thing for a man – I'm sure…'

'You're sure what? That he's just …' She broke off, unclear what she'd been about to say.

'If it helps, I'm an old friend of hers. She's not nasty. She just needs to get by – like most people. Look, let me take you out for lunch,' he said. She nodded. 'I know a lovely bistro on the edge of Soho.'

They left by the Stage Door. He held her lightly under the elbow and led down an alleyway into the street, which gave onto the Strand. He was humming *'Be my girl.'* She stared at the pavement, faint with confusion as she hurried along to keep pace with him. 'Ah, here we are.' Knighton pushed open the door in front of them.

'Can you promise me something, Mr Knighton?' When he looked baffled, she said. 'Will you keep it a secret – from my husband – that I might be working for you? I want to make sure our paths don't cross. Not right now at least.'

'Fair enough,' he said.

They entered a cosy restaurant with onions hanging beside copper saucepans and round tables decked in red check tablecloths, much as she'd seen in Paris. They were enveloped in an ambience of warmth, ease and bonhomie. The proprietor came over and seeing Knighton gave a quick bow. 'Today, monsieur, I can recommend *La bouillabaisse*.'

'Whatever you say, Albert.'

Mo could smell garlic and butter and hear the sizzling of a frying pan. Knighton plied her with cold white wine which made her feel calmer. She struggled to push away memories of Paris, memories of Issy's party. She was here. Derek had defected. This was her life now.

After several minutes the *bouillabaisse* arrived, steaming and smelling of the sea. She served herself from the tureen, pushing bits around on her plate to identify them and then plunged in. Seafood was not new to her. Often as a child there had been day trips to Southend in lieu of a week at a resort. The meal was long and leisurely. Only the moment was real, she kept telling herself. When melancholy threatened to intrude she quaffed more wine and turned her attention to Knighton, who was watching her the whole time. There was no going back to Bootles and Dukely's, no helping out at the bar in The Mare's Head. No... at least she was on the right side of town with a man who had eyes for her and could help her along in her career.

Chapter Fifty-three *Derek*

Derek left the studio – telling himself he'd be back within hours – and set off to find Mo. For once, Stella was willing to give him the time of day; he caught up with her in the corridor at Chelsea and coaxed her into a drink in The Cockerel Tavern. 'I was wondering when you was going to pitch up.' She tilted her chin towards him in defiance. Her lips were painted crimson. At college she'd always had a reputation as a fast young woman who liked a bit of fun, the kind who fitted in well at the Polytechnic.

When he told her his concerns about Mo she swilled her gin cocktail around in her glass and took a slow sip. 'I can assure you you're not the only one. She's been through the mill.' He sat in silence over his ale and suppressed his irritation with Stella. She had a way of grinding in home truths like broken glass on soft skin.

'Do you know where she is?' Despite his stab at self-mastery his voice caught. 'Is she staying at Riverton Road? I went round there but the landlady virtually slammed the door in my face.'

Stella smirked. 'No worse than you deserve, I dare say,' she said lightly.

'I know we haven't always seen eye to eye. But I need to know.'

'And what if she doesn't want you to know?'

'I need to see her. Talk to her.'

'Take it from me. You're wasting your time.'

'But where IS she? She is staying there, I take it.' He scowled into his ale, he was getting nowhere fast. Even if this demi-mondaine knew Mo's whereabouts she would not reveal them.

* * *

He had his work cut out keeping up with Knighton's demands. Another show was being put together and for that he had to produce an office interior and railway booking office. After visiting stations and calling on a friend he knew in the City, he drew up sketches. It was good to be busy and out of Victoria Terrace. Prospective buyers had come to look at the house but so far no one had snapped it up. As for Eleanor, she was inhabiting a world of her own: she and Guy were forever going to the picture house or down to Soho to eat. She looked younger by the day. He was glad for her, but afraid. Her insouciance spelt the end of his time in the family home.

In the studio he did sketch after sketch, compared, contrasted, drew up canvases as mock-ups for something larger. Garfield approved and told him to continue, even making warehouse space available near the theatre. Derek worked long hours, barely seeing anyone. Issy had left town for a while, visiting friends in the West Country. Every day that passed he felt the urge to find Mo. He needed to see her. Deprived of her company, he found he could not stop thinking about her. Only that morning, alone in Victoria Terrace, he'd cried out her name, clutching the pillow, murmuring, entreating her. He'd scrubbed his teeth till they bled then stared at his fierce eyes in the bathroom looking glass.

Chapter Fifty-four   *Mo*

'You could have a great career
And one day you should, my dear,
But you're too good my dear,
You're too good.
If you want a future you should get a past.

We're all alone, no chaperone
Can get our number,
The world's in slumber
Let's misbehave
There's something so wild about you
That's so contagious,
Let's be outrageous
Let's misbehave!

Mo was moving in a sinuating line around the stage, gently swaying her hips and turning her big, expressive eyes towards the audience, her voice as clear and confident and strong as it had ever been. In the otherwise empty auditorium Knighton leapt to his feet in the front stalls where he'd been sitting. He had wanted to try her out for a solo and she had seized the chance. He came up on the stage and kissed her hand. 'Star quality!' he said and she giggled in delight. He had kept his word to her and made sure Derek was not around.

When he suggested they might go for a drink to his flat, which was near the theatre, she hesitated for just two seconds then smiled her assent. In for a penny, in for a pound, echoed somewhere in her head. This man was a better bet than Derek anyway. Only when Knighton was leading her up the stairs to his two bedroomed place in Wardour Street, did she pause for thought. Was this what she wanted? She grew impatient with herself. Thinking too much would get her nowhere. She had to stay clear about her options.

The rooms were adorned with Egyptian motifs following the latest craze for Tutankhamen; in between were numerous signed photos – 'To my dear friend Jonathon' – of actors and directors. Noel Coward was there and even Ivor Novello, attesting to how well connected he was. With its waxed floorboards and severe art nouveau furniture and lamps, the place struck her as severe. He took her coat from her. When she used the bathroom, which had a white porcelain sink and dressing-room lights around the mirror, she had the uncanny sensation of being on a stage set. Her mouth, which she painted red, puckered in a pout. She squinted at herself and shrugged, as though to a friend.

'Come and sit down,' said Knighton when she came back into the salon. 'What would you like to drink?' He was standing by a drinks cabinet, which was replete with whisky, brandy and soda. He switched on a sidelight and pulled out a ruby-coloured flask, holding it up to the light. 'Shall I make you a cocktail? I'm rather good at those. How about a Champagne Cocktail?'

'Sounds fun,' she said. She watched him putting sugar and a lump of ice from the icebox in a tall thin glass, together with a dash of something dark, then lemon peel and slowly stirring. He popped open a bottle of champagne, poured the mixture into two triangular-shaped glasses and added the frothing champagne. He handed her a glass. The fizz tingled in her mouth and made her catch her breath.

'Another?'

'Why not?'

She glanced at a silver-rayed clock on the wall and sighed.

She should be getting back to Riverton Road. They talked. She asked him how long he'd been in theatre and what he enjoyed most about it. He in turn asked her about her family and what her greatest ambitions were. Her tongue was growing loose; she wanted, she said, to shine and bring pleasure to many through the power of her voice.

'And Mo, what is Mo short for?'

She grimaced. 'Morwenna.'

The question startled. It was a while since anyone, apart from family, called her Morwenna.

'Morwenna. MORWENNA. Such a beautiful, poetic name. A beautiful stage name. From now on to me you will always be Morwenna. It'll get you farther than Mo, I guarantee you.'

When she continued to look puzzled, he added. 'You shall sing as you wish. And I will help you! And now a little sup from the royal house of Armagnac, Morwenna?'

She sidled down onto the striped sofa. He poured a decent measure into two round glasses and came to sit beside her, putting one of the glasses on a side table. The other he cupped in his hand and tilted towards her mouth. 'Distilled in Gascony, the oldest brandy of France, medicine to the body, fire to the soul, warmth on the chilliest night.' She shifted back, alarmed. 'Come now, one sip and you'll be converted.'

She shifted back. 'I've had enough, I think.'

'I see you do not trust me.' He tilted the glass. 'Ahh! In former days they used it as remedy for all sorts of cankers and maladies.' He placed the glass on the table and moved closer. 'A gal like you won't be lonely for long.' She stared down at the Modernist style rug at their feet. She said nothing, smoothed her frock, which had ruched up a little, and sensed him brooding beside her. When she glanced up she noticed he had acquired the frown so familiar to her in the drama sessions.

For want of something better to do she leaned forward and

took the minutest sip from her glass. The brandy coursed through her, warming and calming her. It had an ancient subtle taste that reminded her of turf, old inns and country fires. She dared not try more. His hand brushed her thigh. 'Wasn't I right? A drink to soothe and warm you through. My dear Morwenna, don't look so alarmed.'

She gave an uneasy laugh. 'I should be going ...' Her voice sounded thin and unsure of itself. He began to run his fingers lightly over her shoulder blades. She stiffened. He sighed and got to his feet.

'I shall make you some coffee.' He disappeared into the kitchen. He came back in bearing a laden tray and poured black coffee into minute black cups with angular handles. The tongs and spoons were silver christening gifts. Everything in the place asked to be noticed, admired.

She spooned several cubes of sugar into her cup. 'You have a sweet tooth, I see.' Now he was moving around, restless, his eyes scanning her and the room all at once. He snapped open a gold cigarette case and offered her a cigarette. When she declined he took one himself and lit up, blowing out a long stream. It seemed to calm him.

She sipped her coffee and said: 'Maybe I will have a cigarette.'

He gave her one, flicked open his lighter so the flame warmed her cheek. 'Morwenna,' he began. 'I see a great future for you. You have the talent, the voice, I told you that already. But – but, well I know this is a difficult time for you. How can I put it, there's more to getting on in life than having determination. It is also about having the right attitude...' His words hung in the air. She felt awkward. She wanted to ask him what he meant exactly. But she already knew. She could hear Stella's voice crisp in her ear.

'They're only ever interested in one thing...'

'Look, I'm tired. It's been a long day. I think I should get back.'

He frowned. 'Yes, you best get home. I'll call you a cab. Can't have a young woman like you wandering the streets alone at this time of night.' Did she detect sarcasm in his voice? All of a sudden she was weary, so weary. How was a woman to make her way if she didn't play the game? She straightened her spine. She felt a flash of anger. She glanced around at the shiny objects in the room. Was all this a display: trappings to ensnare the quarry?

He helped her on with her coat, lingering and touching her shoulders. He turned her round to face him and took her face in his hands. His lips sought hers, tentatively, tenderly at first. She could taste the garlic on them. He was pushing against her, growing more urgent. Yet she could only think of Derek. If he can so can I… she tried to persuade herself. She pulled back and blinked hard. 'I want to go home.'

He laughed. It was a careless, casual laugh as though he was remembering himself and trying to change tempo. 'You are too adorable. I will come downstairs with you and hail a cab.'

Outside the air was cool in her face. Knighton beckoned to a passing cab and settled her into it. When he went to give her a few coins for the fare she refused. The cab drew away leaving him waving goodbye on the kerb. She waved back. When she reached Riverton Road she wanted to sink into her bed, into the deepest of sleeps and never wake up again. The cocktails and Armagnac were working their magic; to this came exhaustion from stress, anxiety, sleepless nights, uncertainty, lack of food, bone-aching grief, helplessness, anger, hope, self-recrimination, guilt, speculation, rootlessness and change. The mix had gone round and round in her frail frame, round and round in ever tighter spirals. One slim body could not contain it all. She needed a vacation from herself, from her life, from the responsibility of carrying her body along on the planet.

The blackness came and carried her away. She dreamed of

stormy skies, of boats without rudders and seas without end. The dreams startled her awake. She took more of the sleeping tablets she had stashed away and floated off again. Tomorrow was another day. For now, oblivion was calling her.

* * *

She woke with a thumping head and Stella banging on her bedroom door. Bemused, still half asleep, she grabbed her dressing gown and opened the door.

'Just came to check on you. It's past one o'clock. My class got cancelled. You were very late back here last night.'

'I know.'

'I saw Derek by the way.'

'Oh,' Mo clutched at the lapels of her dressing gown, pulling it closer. 'And what did he have to say for himself?'

'He was hot on your trail. I lied. I said you weren't here. And Mrs Roberts showed him the door.'

'What did he say?'

'Knighton's got him making another batch of stage sets. Likes the painterly effect of his work far … Derek was pleased with himself about that, but kept on about how much he needs to see you…' Mo leaned against the doorjamb and shook her tousled head, absorbing what Stella was telling her. She moved back into her cramped attic room and slid down onto the bed. Stella stood over her.

'Stella – what exactly did he say?' Hungry suddenly for news of the one she hated as much as she loved. Slowly, as she moved out of torpor towards awareness, the evening at Knighton's filtered into her mind. Knighton. Knighton was offering Derek more work? This was getting too tangled up. Knighton was hers now, surely? She'd been to his flat, he'd offered her work, kissed her on the lips even. What right did Derek have to keep blasting into her space, threatening her longing to sing?

'What's up, Mo? You look like you've seen a ghost.'

'I was in Knighton's flat last night.'

'Oh, I see.'

'We had a drink.'

'Is that all?'

'Yes, that's all.'

Stella glanced over to an unscrewed jar of tablets on the bedside cabinet. She picked it up. 'What've you been dosing yourself with?'

'Give that here?'

'What is it?'

'Nothing. Just to help me sleep.'

'Oh Mo, that's dangerous you know. Especially if you've been hitting the bottle.'

'I haven't been hitting the bottle.'

'Armagnac, if I'm not mistaken.'

Mo stared at her. 'How d'you know?'

'I had a fling with him. Way back. It didn't mean much to either of us, though I was more involved than he was. I wasn't head-over-heels. But I like the power of the man. But I haven't forgotten his tactics. Did he promise to get you work, tell you you have talent, but needed the right attitude?'

Mo felt herself go queasy. 'He said that to you and all?'

'Don't take it to heart. He wants to make you feel you're special but he's a womaniser through and through. The only person he keeps coming back to is himself. And Issy, I suppose. Though nowadays they're more good friends. He's taken up with Zara again, I hear.'

'Doesn't it mean *anything* to him?'

Stella laughed. 'Mean anything? My poor lamb, it means pleasure and satisfaction. Sensuous delight. Young body, fresh mind… he likes all that for a while. But it's all about him in the end. He even wanted a photographer to take shots of us in the buff. Not quite doing it, but almost. All for the sake of art. He's into something he calls Tantra. Sex as a way to the stars, he says. It's a wonder his dick hasn't fallen off…'

'Stella!' Mo could not help but laugh.

'Sorry. I've forgotten you don't like that sort of patter.'

'I was beginning to think there was something wrong with me. I wanted to. At least part of me did. But well, in my heart of hearts I'm still married to Derek.' They were silent for a moment. 'I can't bear knowing he might be in love with another woman. I'm breaking up inside …' Her back and shoulders began to shake. Stella sat beside her on the bed, took her in her arms and rocked her back and forth.

'Don't you worry, love. He's not worth it,'

'Who isn't?' wailed Mo.

She felt Stella hesitate. 'Well – neither of them.'

After a while Mo quietened down. She pulled back from Stella. 'I want to sing. I want to get on with things and forget. But it's hard.'

'I'll make you a strong cuppa,' Stella said, 'then we'll have a good talk and see what you're going to do next. All right?'

'Can you make me some toast and all?'

'Get dressed and come down to the kitchen. I ain't waiting on you hand and foot.'

Chapter Fifty-five *Eleanor*

Eleanor and Guy took a nine o'clock train out of Paddington, heading west, and arrived at Scadley on the Oxford branch line shortly after ten. They had an appointment with the local estate agent's, Whiteley's, at ten thirty. That gave them time to wander up and down the main street and get a sense of the place. Main street was an exaggeration: it was the only street. Either side of Whiteley's were neat shops with bow windows and old-fashioned signage; next door was a grocer's with rows of shiny apples. In all, the village boasted three public houses, including an ancient coaching inn with stone steps, an Anglican church with a moss-covered roof, a teashop and an undertaker's. At the edge of the village was a blacksmith's. Beyond the street stretched the green of arable land, copses and hedgerows. Eleanor looked around. 'Kind of quiet, isn't it?'

Guy took her hand and tugged her gently along. 'I want to show you. There's a stream down the end with a hump-backed bridge.'

The advertisement for a disused barn and outbuildings had caught Guy's eye. He knew the village from a cycling tour and thought it worth pursuing. They wandered down to the stream and threw pennies into the clear water. They leaned over and watched the flow where osiers from a weeping willow were dragged sideways like mermaid hair. On the way back up the street Eleanor noticed three middle-aged women eyeing them from behind the netted windows of the teashop. The place reminded her of trips to Oxfordshire she'd once made with Lance. The sun broke through clouds and lit up the weathervane on the church steeple. An old jalopy chuntered down the road. A post van was waiting at the corner by the church. Eleanor glanced at her watch. It was time. They entered the estate agent's.

'Ah Mr and Mrs Masteron, I take it? I'm Berkley.' A man bustled towards them holding out his hand. Eleanor was about to correct him when Guy spoke.

'Yes, I'm Masteron. This is my fiancée, Miss Eaton.'

'Delighted.' Berkley excused himself for a moment to collect the papers relating to the property. 'It's going for a good price. The vendor is looking for a quick sale.' Eleanor was sceptical: more like some wily farmer thought he could pull the wool over their townie eyes.

Mr Berkley took them by car to the premises, which lay two miles further out. As they passed hedges straggly with hawthorn berries and brambles, Eleanor grew more excited. She had forgotten the sheer beauty of deep countryside. They turned off down an overshadowed lane and came to a halt. In a field to one side stood a sizeable barn and surrounding it were low outbuildings. The door was hanging off one of them, roof slates were missing from the other. Guy whistled through his teeth. As Berkley got down from the car and opened the door for them, she adopted a neutral stance.

'There have been several interested...' Berkley started. 'The owner is moving to South Africa. As I said, he's looking for a quick...'

'Let's have a look at it then.' Guy strode ahead. Berkley unlocked the barn door. Eleanor caught an aroma of hay, seasoned wood and beneath all this a whiff of mouldering apples. The place would have been used for storage.

Her heart lifted as she gazed up at the hayloft and cruck beam structure. Viking banqueting halls and mediaeval churches had this form: it was as old as the earth. While Berkley was detailing the square footage and state of the rafters, her mind drifted. Something in her was warming to the place: she could imagine the space as an assembly hall or furnished with partitions to create classrooms. The height and the warmth of the wood enfolded her, made her feel safe. She paced to the side and back again, then surprised the two men by climbing up to the hayloft. From there the extent of the barn was even more apparent. Sunlight was peeking in through the open doors, illuminating and radiating the whole. It seemed a kind of blessing.

She clambered down. Guy walked towards her. They moved outside towards the outbuildings. As Berkley walked ahead she touched Guy's arm and whispered fiercely. 'What d'you think?'

He looked pensive for a moment before replying: 'It has potential.'

Berkley turned back towards them. 'It obviously needs refurbishment. What exactly were you looking for, if I might ask?'

Eleanor hesitated while Guy continued: 'The place has its merits, but you must admit in its current state it's vastly overpriced.'

Berkley coloured. 'It's a period barn. There aren't many like this remaining…'

'Left to wind and rain in months it would be good for nothing but swallows and voles.'

Berkley gave a professional smile. 'It's a gem of a barn, built in oak it has withstood frost and fire, damp and snow...'

'That may be, but unless you're a farm with surrounding fields – which is not part of the deal – the barn in and of itself is not valuable.' This straight talking of Guy was something she was not familiar with. She liked it. He looked as though he was not going to give an inch. She decided to keep her counsel and let him get on with it. She walked back over to the outbuildings. One had a pleasant southerly aspect with its tangle of bindweed and ivy glinting in the sun. Already she could imagine them converted into cottages. She pictured a kitchen garden there, a duck pond here. She let the two men carry on haggling and wandered back into the barn. Through the open door she glimpsed Guy's square shoulders and intelligent face in earnest discussion. From where she was standing she could not quite catch the drift of what they were saying. Am I ready for this? went through her head. Her body often told her things her head could hardly comprehend. Would they really be able to set up a school here? This was more than a way out of Blundell's: it was an uncompromising step towards an envisaged future. The middle-aged prattlers in the teashop she could cope with, as she could the bats flitting around the eaves at dusk or mice scratching in the skirting boards. The sharpest challenge was tying up her fate with Guy's.

She smiled to herself. The nights she had stolen with Guy, the weekend in Rye, the afternoons in the Imperial Hotel in Russell Square, the walks on Hampstead Heath, discussions late into the night. There was no turning back now. No prevarication on account of Derek, Mo and – her heart pierced with ice – Timothy. She strolled back to the others. 'I think Mr Berkley, Mr Masterton and I would like a little time to view the premises on our own, if you don't mind.'

'Of course,' Berkley nodded and returning his papers into his briefcase told them he'd wait for them in the car.

'So?' Guy's face was open and enthusiastic.

'Beat him down a bit. Ask about electricity and sewerage and all that stuff.'

'I did already.'

'It's pretty remote, don't forget.'

'Is that a yes or a no?'

'Let's take the plunge.' Guy took her hand and drew her towards him.

'We'll need to set a date.'

She hesitated, just for a moment. 'Yes, we'll need to set a date,' she repeated and smiled back at him.

Chapter Fifty-six *Mo*

'You made your bed, now you must lie in it.' How often had Mo heard these words, scalding like acid from her mother. The two of them were in the scullery at The Mare's Head. Already entering the place made Mo heavy with a sense of entrapment. Ma was looking tired, as always, but there was something else too: a spark of defiance, anger even. The sentence had been her chorus ever since Mo could remember, but she spoke it a little too fiercely, as though she feared its opposite. Mo felt dulled by confusion. Ma had never taken her part nor seen things from her point of view. There was a constant unspoken anxiety towards her, as though Ma feared this daughter would let her down or disgrace her in some way.

'I just wanted to let you know,' said Mo flatly.

'Now, after all you've been through, I would've thought you need each other.'

Mo groaned with impatience. 'You don't know the 'alf of it. 'E was, he was... there was another woman involved. An actress.'

Ma banged a pot onto the range. 'No excuse. You've got to 'old fast to what you got.'

'Well, I've moved on. We've moved on. If you must know I've got someone who's willing to act as my manager. He rates my voice, my singing.'

'Forget all that. It won't last. Believe you me. It won't.'

'And what makes you so sure?'

'It's the way of the world. The way things will always be between men and women.'

'But you performed, didn't you? Why didn't you never

wanna tell me about it?'

'That's my business, my girl.'

'You never told me, Ma. I was always dying to know. You just didn't want to say.' Ma shot her a dark look and shifted the boiling pot of potatoes on the hob. Her mouth was tight with Mo-wasn't-sure-what. 'Anyway, now you know. I didn't want you to hear about it from someone else.' She felt she had done her bit. Deception did not come easily to her. She did not want to lose her family all over again. For all their faults they reminded her of who she was, where she had come from. 'D'you want to meet 'im?'

'No bloody fear,' retorted Ma. 'You can keep your fancy man to yourself. I've 'ad enough of fancy men in my time. And good riddance and all.'

'Ma, what are you talking about? Who do you mean?'

'Never mind. All water under the bridge.' If Mo was not mistaken Ma's neck was tinged pink. She turned her back to Mo.

'Anyway, it's not like that. As I said, he's my manager.'

'We'll see about that.' She paused. 'Don't just stand there. Lay up the table then. Your father wants feeding.'

'I need to make my own way.'

Ma paused and looked across, almost wistful: 'You may be dazzled by the theatre lights now, but one day they'll burn you.'

PART 4

1928 eight months later

Chapter Fifty-seven *Mo*

'Yes sir, that's my baby…Yes sir, I don't mean maybe. You're my baby now…' sang Mo, eyeing her would-be audience coquettishly. *On with the dance* was drawing to an end and Knighton wanted to involve her in putting together a few dance and song routines before the next theatre piece. Her voice slid over the notes, delighting in the punchy rhythms of the song, its irresistible verve. 'Bravo!' applauded Jonathon from the wings. 'You go from strength to strength.' She bowed before the empty rows.

'Now try *Carolina Moon.*'

The thirst for American songs was unquenched: everything stylish emanated from Broadway or New Orleans. For the last week Mo had been working flat out, giving no time for rumination. She was only too pleased to be considered for the Revue. She was tired, though – suffering that bone weariness which never seemed to leave her these days. Joe Keaton, her accompanist, was leafing through sheet music. 'You know it, do you, Morwenna?'

'No,' she piped up cheerily, 'play the tune. We'll go through it bit by bit.' Knighton stayed for the first few bars then someone beckoned him backstage. Mo was relieved to be out from under his watch. Sometimes she longed for the disregard Derek would display. For though he liked to appear careless, hostile even, beneath it all she sensed his fervour; whereas she suspected Knighton's affection was skin deep.

Knighton continued to open doors for her. Through him she could mingle with those she had once envied. By now she had taken enough elocution and voice lessons to fit in, only when she was tired or angry did the adjustment slip. Never again would she be poor. Never again would she be out of work. Never again would she... oh, the list was too long.

It was over a year since Zara had resolved to reclaim the errant Laszlo and abandoned her ties to Jonathon. At first Mo had kept Knighton at bay, mindful of his reputation and Stella's warnings. But by and by they became friends, then lovers. He may have spun her the same line about talent as he'd uttered to other women, but he did not belittle her ambitions. He avowed he could not be bothered with stupid, commonplace or shallow women. Stella had talent, he argued, and had told her so. It was not his fault if she frittered it away. Zara, too, had talent and worked hard. But she, Morwenna, had the voice. It was a rare and distinctive voice, one that sent his spine aquiver.

'Let's go through it again,' said Joe. 'We can take our time. They don't need the stage for a while.' His fingers flitted over the keys.

'*Carolina Moon,*' she crooned, coaxing her voice into the glamour and romance of the song. They worked phrase by phrase until she had mastered it.

> *'Carolina Moon, keep shining,*
> *shining on the one who waits for me*
> *Carolina Moon, I'm pining, pining for the place I long to be*
> *How I'm hoping tonight*
> *I'll go by the right window*
> *Scatter your light*
> *Say I'm alright*
> *Tell him I'm blue and lonely.*
> *Dreamy Carolina Moon*
> *Oh how I'm hoping tonight*
> *Scatter your light*
> *Say I'm alright*
> *Tell him I'm blue and lonely*

Carolina Moon.
Dreamy Southern moon, keep shining.
Shining on the one who waits for me.'

When Knighton returned he stood stock-still, listening, then stepped forward. 'Well done!' Then he whispered. 'And now I'm taking you for a treat.'

* * *

In Claridge's they sat by a shining fender while a maid tidied their table. Above them gleamed a wondrous art nouveau chandelier. A waiter in an immaculate dining suit came to take their order for high tea. The tea, sipped from bone china, was a delicious Orange Pekoe. People were coming and going in the foyer in clusters. Outside it started to drizzle. He touched her hand. She leaned forward and popped a marshmallow into her mouth, then took another and popped it into his.

Others were heading for the fancily bedecked tables and placing orders for tea and scones. She took her clutch bag and disappeared into the Ladies where she sat before the mirror, powdering her face, settling the odd wisps of hair. She stared at her blank eyes, which to her consternation were filling with tears. She attempted to repair the streaked powder on her cheeks. Walking back along the corridor, she commanded herself to behave. She was the luckiest girl in the world, the most fortunate of the hopeful performers… Knighton got up as she approached. She sat down and stared at the fender without speaking.

'Morwenna,' he said gravely. 'What's got into you of late? You're impossible to read.' Her chest tightened. She assumed she was playing her part to perfection. 'It's not too much for you, is it – the sudden switch from chorus to…?'

'Of course not,' she said airily and pulled out her cigarette holder. He snapped open a silver cigarette case. She drew on the cigarette and gazed into the fronds of a nearby fern.

337

'Can I clear away, Madam?' asked the maid, who had appeared from nowhere. Mo could tell from her accent that she hailed from the East End. Mo caught the look of bated fear in her eyes, the desire to please and be unobtrusive. It gave her a shiver of apprehension.

'Yes, please do.' She leaned back, blowing out a long stream of smoke, which obscured the air between her and Knighton.

Chapter Fifty-eight *Derek*

Derek was forced to watch from afar as Mo became Morwenna, the rising star. It was clear she was Jonathon Knighton's mistress. At first he could only admire and quietly burn, knowing he had had his chance and marred it. The brittleness he so detested in Stella he now saw taking root in his beloved Mo, until she became a stranger to him and he could no longer bear to see her.

His own restlessness was driving him on. He agreed a deal with the freeholder of Fingal's Cave, sold his share of the business – which had picked up of late – and made a tidy profit. That, together with his proceeds from Victoria Terrace enabled him to buy a cottage and workshop. He moved to Merton. Eleanor and Guy were struggling to establish their school in the heart of the country. Never had he seen his sister so radiant, so energetic and so poor. She was thriving on the challenges she'd set herself, but he needed, for now, to create space between himself and her.

The scenery work had taken off, slowly at first, but then one contact led to another so the demand increased. He found he could pick and choose where and what he did. And so he avoided The Athena and worked elsewhere in the West End. Interiors became his specialism, and he accomplished them with growing facility, often with other painters working under him. This left him time for his own work. Patrick, who'd furthered his connections in the South of France, was often away, leaving him the choice of Chelsea or Merton. 'Don't stop and judge! Get the work out there,' Patrick had commanded. 'Think of your work less as an aesthetic product and more as communication.'

Derek did not need to be told twice. Years of self-suppression and trivialising his efforts, dissolved. His fellow painters, the ones he counted as friends, encouraged him, as he did them. Together they would fight their way out of the cave of mediocrity. They would break the mould, smash the form, meld together what had been kept apart. He used both studios. Large canvases, dark colours, oil lamps burning in the night were suited to the spacious studio in Merton. In Chelsea he gouged out of himself the horrors of recent months and threw them at the canvas. He thrust violet, raw umber, rose madder and Payne's grey at solid and soft surfaces; he reconsidered, drew, sketched, allowed himself to feel what he felt, raged, wept and rejoiced in his output. In time the paintings acquired precision, penetration. Coming from a place within him that he had previously only intuited, they moved towards the light. He spent hours alone in one of the studios, no longer restless.

There was no end to it.

Over time Issy began to fade into the background. They still met, supped and slept together, talked, encouraged each other and went their separate ways. She was getting more work now. She stopped playing the party girl, the bubbly socialite. The new modernity and maturity suited her: she got roles as mothers, widows, older *femmes fatales*. She stopped worrying about eating sugar and trying to acquire the boyish figure so much in vogue.

Shaughnessy grunted approval at what Derek was doing, while Derek himself cared less what people thought. 'Time to exhibit,' said Zara, one day when she came to inspect his latest work. 'You've got a style of your own now.' And it was true: his work was neither art nouveau nor stark realism, neither Cubism, Fauvism nor any of the other 'isms'. He was learning to trust his own love of line and hue, and listen more to the troubled workings of his spirit.

He would have a summer exhibition, hire space in Connaught Gallery or some such place and show his artistic offspring to the world. He would exhibit with Pierre and other painter friends. He returned to Paris. He savoured the Bohemian, carefree life where rubbing shoulders with street life and poverty was more poetic than in the East End of London. He stayed for weeks at a time, sharing lodgings with Pierre and visiting ateliers of other painters. He rose at dawn most days, in contrast to his former avoidance of the glare of morning.

The lower he dipped into his own shadow, the more he could pull it up and splatter it onto the canvas. He mastered technique. Crosshatching shading colour balance composition: he dared make mistakes, choices, uncertain combinations and clashes. A new language was opening itself to him. Devoid of romanticism and diversion, it was a confrontation. No longer did he evade his fears, lies, obsessions or remorse. Increasingly these came hobbling and creeping out of forgotten corners.

Rarely did he get drunk now; he did not feel the need. After initial disorientation he took courage from the energy that sprang up when he stopped fighting himself. Whether in Paris or London he could not stop painting. As he surrendered his daemon quickened, descending and visiting night after night with dreams, nightmares, hauntings and whisperings of things in the air, in nature, in the people around him. He received the whisperings and put them to work.

One weekend he threw open his studio in Merton, inviting people he knew and others he didn't, friends of friends. 'Superb!' said Issy when she saw his row of East End street walkers. Paris by night captivated Shaughnessy. Zara loved his take on Reading railway station in the rain; they were neither too harsh nor hackneyed, she murmured. 'Direct observation', thought Derek, glad he was at last able to dare the truth and let the world make up its own mind. More people started calling by. One or two collectors bought paintings and hung them in their homes or galleries.

* * *

The next time he was in Paris, Pierre mentioned that a former storage space on the Left Bank was available. It would cost next to nothing to exhibit there. Would Derek be interested in a joint exhibition? Pierre took him to see it. They wandered in silence through the dank space. It had a stone floor and the walls, once daubed white but now grey, echoed and ran on forever. A good airing was called for. They would need to work at the place to make it presentable. Derek gazed around, noting grime in the corners, while Pierre watched him with a mild air of anxiety. Derek grunted: 'Let's give it a go.'

'I thought you'd like it,' said Pierre.

'I'll have to fetch more works from London.' The ones he had completed here in a fury of activity were already stashed at Pierre's place.

Later, they put braziers in the place to drive off the damp and when, the day after, it seemed dry enough, Pierre called in a favour from neighbour, who set about scrubbing out the corners and giving the whole a fresh coat of paint. While they were still clearing it out, artist friends drifted in, murmuring approval, criticism and envy. Derek and Pierre started mulling over the paintings they already had, juxtaposing them, pondering themes and wondering how to intersperse words where needed. *Desolation* was one theme, *Struggle* another, but there was also *First Light* and *Liberation*. They sorted, rejected, reconsidered: the images covered a multitude of concepts. Derek fingered the walls, gazed at the light falling through the barred windows and wondered whether there was enough of it.

This was his first exhibition of any size. It was an artistic coming of age – stepping out from years of unease and self-doubt. He had enough hours behind him now to realise there was always a breakthrough if only he persevered. He'd acquired the patience to go over themes, pin down a subject from every angle.

He travelled to London and came back with a large leather case, containing his latest unframed pictures. As they viewed his works, side-by-side, he could see patterns he'd been unaware of. He was emphasising line and geometry, then darting back into colour and tone. When he stood back he could not help making judgements. He could see gaps and inconsistencies: gauche forays, which went nowhere. 'Nothing is quite finished or rounded off,' he murmured.

Pierre, pipe in hand, gave him a sideways glance. 'Don't look so glum.'

'They don't amount to much, seen together,' said Derek drily.

'I thought this exhibition was about experimentation. That's what we agreed.'

Derek continued to view his paintings. Pierre was right. This was about trying out new things, letting go of handed down notions of what were fitting subjects for artists. Besides, they would look better framed. And Pierre knew just the man.

He smiled to himself. Paris felt less elitist than London. The Cambridge-dominated Bloomsbury Set posed, conversed, painted, wrote, blurred genders, pontificated about the bourgeoisie and railed against patriotism and Empire while barring all but the select to their soirées. Bohemia, it seemed, was infinitely more palatable if you had assets and a country pile behind you. In Paris painters were more disparate and therefore, when they happened to come together, more generous. And also more outspoken.

Pierre returned with more of his paintings and placed them along the wall. The two men stood before the paintings. Pierre frowned and commented. 'There's more movement in your work. You're not the same painter you were a year ago.'

Derek sighed, wondering if Pierre knew about Timothy's

death. He had not talked about it with his French friends, wanting to draw a line and start afresh. In the event this was impossible. Everything he did came sweeping out of the past, a wind blasting over him beyond his control. 'My son died last year.' He stepped forward to adjust one of the paintings.

'I heard,' said Pierre. 'Very sorry…'

'Diphtheria.' He spat the word out. He had not uttered it in a year, the taste ash in his mouth. 'I was in Hell. It broke through whatever reserve I had…'

'War did that to me,' said Pierre.

Derek hesitated. 'But you pushed it away. You started playing safe …'

Pierre stared at him, eyes pools of intense blackness. Hate flashed through lightning fast, replaced by resignation. He walked away. Two minutes later he came back with another canvas bag, which he wrenched open. 'Like these you mean?' He cast two paintings down in front of Derek. They looked like an animal had been slaughtered on them. '*Designs for death*', they were called. Blood dripped over black hurtling spaces where stars crossed with abysses and purple shot skies. Pierre's face contorted with pain. But night ferments into something else, thought Derek: there is always the dawn breaking in, dew on grass. The men were sunk in a silence neither knew how to break. Mo would have thought of something to lighten it.

At that moment he had an urgent, unbidden desire to see her.

Chapter Fifty-nine *Mo*

These days an abundance of flowers arrived at Mo's dressing room; people loved her gamin, cheeky look, her clear strong voice, her youth and exuberance. The critics of *The Daily Herald* and *The News Chronicle* hailed her: 'A talent to be watched,' they wrote. They'd revelled in her rendition of *Poor little rich girl* in *On with the dance*. Her star was indeed rising and all those around her told her so. Knighton was pleased, bringing her to interminable cocktail parties and receptions, to show her off. Sometimes she baulked at being paraded like a pet Pekinese, but mostly she lapped it up. Who was she to question what she'd always set her sights on?

Derek be damned. He had let her down, chosen another. Mostly she thrust him from her mind when he dared intrude. This happened at the bookends of the day, at dawn and dusk, when her thoughts were less under her control. What had she become? She'd then ask herself. Come the morning she'd flick away the question like an irritating fly and arrange to visit the hair salon or answer some of the fan letters, piled up in her dressing room.

It didn't help that at first they had both been working for Knighton. When he left to pursue assignments elsewhere he was no longer that constant thorn. One day they came across each other at a theatre party. Her heart beat strangely. She could not avoid sneaking looks at him, wondering what he was up to and if he was still with Issy? She left the party without speaking to him but could not sleep that night.

The next day a bunch of deep red roses arrived without a card. Though she tried to push away the thought she wondered if they were from him. Most bouquets had visiting cards attached, but this had none. Knighton smiled when he saw them. He liked to take credit for her success.

That evening they'd been invited to yet another cocktail party.

They were in an apartment adjacent to the theatre, which was on permanent loan to Knighton as theatrical director and where Mo stayed for a peppercorn rent. She stretched out on the chaise longue and considered her pink toenails, one of which was chipped. She heard him shifting about in the room next door. She pulled the cigarette holder from her glittering evening pouch, pressed in a cigarette and began to smoke. 'Are you satisfied with the Revue?' she asked as he entered the room.

'Coming along nicely,' he said without looking at her.

'I'm over the moon about it,' she cooed. She meant it, but just for a second she caught the forced urgency in her voice. He slid down onto the edge of the chaise longue, caught hold of her hand and squeezed her fingers.

'What are you going to wear tonight, Morwenna? I think you could do better than the beige number you wore last time. It made you look pale.'

She shrugged, past caring right then what he did or did not want her to wear. 'What time do we have to be there? And more to the point who is going to be there?'

'Just make yourself pretty. I'm told some of our backers might come, so don't go putting your dainty little foot in it, will you?'

'Do you take me for a fool?'

'Hardly. You're the sharpest tool in the kit,' he said with a whisper of a smile. He planted a kiss on her right nipple. 'And the most beautiful.' She pushed him away.

'Do stop it! Look, go away and leave me in peace for five minutes.'

'Only if you promise to wear your blue dress – the one with the beads and diaphanous skirt. You'll have them falling over themselves.'

With that he kissed her swiftly on the lips and left the room. She watched him go, quelling a vague irritation. She lay back and closed her eyes, opened them and stared at the intricate ceiling moulding beside the chandelier.

* * *

When they walked arm-in-arm into the cocktail party, cast members swarmed round them. 'Champagne cocktail?' A girl from the chorus called to her. 'You look stunning tonight,' said another. Mo smiled, adjusting the blue headband, which matched the sea blue of her dress. Knighton handed her a bubbling coupe. She sipped and turned to the others in the room. All the cast were here, lined up against the wall, giggling and hooting around the piano, sitting squashed together and gossiping on the edges of chairs in their pinks and shimmering silver with their bobbing bobbed heads.

The cast had been working hard. Tonight was a mid-way pause and celebration. The show had only weeks to run, from now on there would be scarcely time to draw breath. She had worked as she had never worked before, rising at six, learning and relearning lines, doing voice exercises, stretching limbs, toning her body; her mind relishing it all. Theatre was what she was born for: how could she ever have doubted it? No time to think, no time to regret or remember what had gone before. Barely time to visit her family – a flying visit weeks before just to reassure them all was well.

But all at once, in the midst of the hubbub, she started: Issy was here. Suppressing an involuntary spurt of anger, she turned this way and that, laughing, tossing her head back. Yet she caught Issy's profile from the corner of her eye. Issy was wearing a cream shift and had her hair fashionably short. She had a contented, mature look about her. They avoided each other, yet Mo could not help but glance towards her. Through the grapevine she had heard that she and Derek were more friends now than lovers. Issy, it seemed, had a talent for friendship with men: enviable, because it put her on an equal footing with them.

Mo caught herself watching Jonathon Knighton's back as he talked, moved his hands in heated exchange about this or that. There was a fiery bullish intelligence in him, which now and then broke out into loud expressions of wit and criticism. She went up and slipped her arm into his. He looked at her in surprise. 'So, Morwenna, my sweet,' he said with an air of amusement. 'Another cocktail?'

Chapter Sixty *Derek*

Derek was back in London for a few days before the exhibition in Paris kicked off. Issy had invited him to the Kit Kat club in the Haymarket. The Kit Kat, which had opened in 1925, was the latest place for the fast set. Issy often went to the club on weekdays when Arthur was out of town. Arthur held an account there and they still recognised her on the door and allowed her free access. Nobody quibbled when she ordered a drink or two. She'd told him Knighton often went there and sometimes Mo. He knew this was his best chance of seeing her. At the theatre she had a virtual bodyguard. Only the night before he'd dreamt Mo was floating out of his life in a hot air balloon with Knighton. He could hear the roar of gas and saw her white hand waving. He'd woken in a cold sweat.

Now he stood by the wrought iron railings of the smart Georgian edifice and whistled. He pulled at his cuffs. In her time Issy had done well for herself: this was definitely a toffs' hangout. He looked down at the patent leather shoes salvaged from an auction box while he still had Fingal's Cave. He noticed that his trousers, also a hand-me-down, were on the long side. No matter. They fitted the formal dress code here. He'd become so absorbed in his work he cared little about his appearance.

Issy turned up late. She kissed him on either cheek and led the way. 'Can't stay,' she said. 'But thought I'd get you in there. It can be difficult'. She pressed the bell. These clubs, though eager to cast off the stranglehold of tradition, had, after all, standards to maintain. They couldn't let any riff-raff in, unless the riff-raff was the pet adoptee of some person of means.

'We're with the Bonnington party,' declared Issy with panache and walked in. They entered the main salon. The place was humming. Couples were dancing cheek-to-cheek. The merry-makers clustered round tables and in odd corners of the large salon. Laughter, snatches of talk and the clatter of glasses assailed his ears. Swirls of blue smoke hung round table lamps or below the ceiling lights. The décor was in ivory, gold and turquoise on Italian Renaissance lines. Tall royal blue pillars rose right up to the roof.

'Oh my dear, how lovely to see you!'

'About time! Where *have* you been hiding yourself?'

Above this din came the penetrating blast of a trumpet. The sound thrilled him. He looked around, scanning the dimly lit tables, the bar area and the glittering dance floor shaking under the impact of twirling couples. The women were wearing clinging, drop-waisted frocks in shimmering pastel shades. Their hair was cropped in the latest Eton cut. A few couples were shuffling while others gyrated energetically.

He danced with Issy but could tell her heart was not in it. She left soon after. After she'd gone he approached the bar, bastion of the unaccompanied male. He fished in his pocket for loose change and ordered a Scotch, which he downed in one. When he requested another the barman asked if he wanted to start a tab. 'Why not?'

'Name, sir?'

'Er. Arthur Bonnington.'

'Bonnington? I believe there is another Mr Arthur Bonnington that comes here.'

Derek smiled. 'My cousin, don't you know. We have a lot of Arthurs in the family. Now fetch me another whisky, my good man, before I die of sobriety.' The man nodded and poured a good measure. Derek swore off alcohol when he was working, but tonight he felt the need for it. He smiled to himself at his audacity but felt no guilt: Bonnington was an arch cad.

Three or four whiskies later he grew pensive. What was he to do about Mo? So much time had elapsed; she had a new life for herself with its own trajectory. Even now she was probably holed up somewhere with Knighton or treading the boards in The Athena. With a growing inevitability she had slipped away from him. And who had he to blame but himself? He had squandered her love. In his self-preoccupation he had ignored her needs. Last time they spoke she said their marriage was impossible. But she hadn't meant it, had she? Surely not?

He eyed the barman, who at that moment had shifted to the other end of the counter. He decided to distance himself from his growing debt and moved towards where the dance floor was most crowded. With a pang he told himself this was not one of Mo's nights.

Just then the music stopped. From across the dance floor he spotted a vision of glory, for there, laughing and moving around like a skittish deer, was Mo. She was laughing and bending her head this way and that. Her hair, backlit like a halo, framed her face. She was decked in a pale pink shift, which softened her and made her look delectable. Pearls dangled from her neck and sparkled.

He darted across the room.

'You! What are you doing here!' she cried. A couple of young men were leaning in towards her, exuding admiration. She seemed in her element. Knighton was nowhere to be seen. 'I didn't know you were a member.'

'I'm not.'

'So – how?' Puzzlement flitted across her face only to be quickly supplanted by her all-encompassing smile.

They were being hemmed in. All around were merry-makers, chatting loudly, swilling back champagne and fruit cup. Someone shrieked in merriment. 'You don't say! How positively sick making! What a nerve.' He glanced over her shoulder at svelte women who looked like actresses and at men in wide lapelled suits and dinner jackets. The scene swayed before him, a pulsating mirage.

At the next table were a group of theatre-goers discussing plays. 'Have you seen Shaw's latest?'

'Rather poor show if you ask me. Certainly not as good as his last.'

'Don't you mean Shaw?' guffawed another.

Someone suggested more brandy was needed in the fruit bowl.

'Scraping the bottom of the barrel if you ask me.'

'No, brilliant, my dear chap. Brilliant.'

The words cast so lightly away gave Derek pause for thought. It was a long time since he'd mixed with such people. He pictured Mo cooped up in their bedroom, poring over tattered magazines, and then gazed at her standing before him. Her eyes were gleaming, her dark hair catching glints from the chandelier. He glanced at her high round breasts and sighed.

'Nice place,' he murmured. 'Do you know many people here?'

'A few.'

'So what do they all do? For a living, I mean?'

She raised an eyebrow. 'What a boring question!'

Now couples were smooching to slow jazz while others lounged in the dark, smoke-filled corners. He longed to hold Mo in his arms. 'May I – would you like to dance?' He glanced towards her companions and whispered. 'Who are all those school-boys?'

She laughed. He could tell she was nervous. 'They're theatrical friends.'

He held her hand. 'Can I have the pleasure?'

'Just one then.'

He stumbled, crushing one of her feet. 'Ouch!'

'Sorry darling.'

'Don't you darling me.' They laughed again. 'You always did have two left feet!'

As the floor cleared he guided her towards the dance area. 'What are you doing here?' she asked.

'Seeking you,' he said.

She gave him a withering glare. 'Expect me to believe that?'

'Ah Mo, it's so good to see you.'

He held her so lightly, his hand clasping hers, her body so close. He wanted to murmur into her hair, tell her what an idiot he'd been. He needed her forgiveness. He didn't deserve it, but it was what he hoped for. He pulled her gently towards him. He could feel her heart beating, keeping pace with his. When the dance finished he asked if he could join her at her table. A tendril of hair fell onto her forehead. He longed to reach out and smooth it away. She glanced at her watch, looked hesitant, but gave him a quick, rather brittle smile: ''fraid not. Time for me to go. I have to be up early for a rehearsal.'

'No Mo, don't go.'

But she turned abruptly and strode back to her table, collected her stole and her two companions and without glancing back at Derek left the ballroom. He could only stare after her in consternation, knowing better than to try and follow her.

Soon he had other concerns. From the corner of his eye he saw two men peering across. Despite his alcoholic haze he started. The barman was pointing in Derek's direction. Next to him, with an expression of bemusement, was Arthur Bonnington.

Derek scuttled away, dodging past the swaying bodies. 'Excuse me! Excuse me!' A waiter passed with a fully laden tray. Derek's trousers were too long. He stumbled, almost tripping the man up before diving into the mêlée of dancers. He searched for a sign to the Gents and finally found an arrow tucked in a corner. He rushed towards it, hearing footsteps behind him. The passageway had several doors. He tried one after the other, opening on to a broom cupboard and storerooms until at last he found a door that led to a backyard. He scrambled through and thrust himself over a waist-high fence, tearing his trousers in the process. He found himself in an alleyway that ran into the road.

Minutes later, battered and with ripped trousers, he was whistling his way among the flâneurs of Piccadilly. He concentrated on walking a straight line down the centre of the pavement as the cold air hit him. He stumbled, righted himself and attempted to continue the straight line while frustration blurred his vision. 'Mo,' he murmured.

Chapter Sixty-one *Mo*

Mo could not afford to let her mind dwell on Derek and what might have happened had she stayed on at the Kit Kat club. It was dangerous even to think about him. He unsettled her in a way nobody else could. Besides she had so much on her agenda: run-throughs, rehearsals and then the unending receptions Knighton expected her to attend.

The next such reception was at The Savoy. She had never seen so much satin, so many flattened bosoms and bottoms. The boy's look was still in vogue, in shades of sea green and purple, a dash of the Orient in the mode of the *ballets russes*. She thought wistfully of Fingal's Cave. Knighton was holding a champagne cocktail towards her. Again! That's how she pictured him these days. A journalist from one of the evening papers, who'd interviewed her before, was edging towards her. 'Miss Eaton Mrs Eaton!' – still not able to determine her marital status. Mo gave a bright smile and turned away from both of them. She was not in the mood for publicity.

'Morwenna darling,' Knighton was touching her shoulder. She turned towards him. 'There is someone keen to meet you,' he whispered into her ear. She grimaced. These evenings were piling up, one after the other. They excited and tired her in turn.

'Herr Olmak, may I present the adorable Morwenna Eaton?' Mo found herself in the presence of a dark-haired man with a wiry frame and a firm handshake.

'I have been following your career. A haunting voice you have.' She detected a crispness in how he sounded his words – a Hungarian accent, she later learned. The man was a musician,

Knighton told her. For a moment the stranger's eyes searched hers. Mo started. She had met him before.

'Didn't you accompany me when I did an audition a while back?'

'That's right,' said Knighton. 'I'd forgotten. Sandor was helping us out while our regular répétiteur was off sick.'

'I have been following you. Great success in your last show. I'm an admirer – a fan…' His mouth was twisting into a half smile. She had a momentary sense of dislocation. Used as she was to praise, she found something too intense about this man. It was impertinent for a virtual stranger to have this effect on her. As soon as she could she shifted to the other side of the room, where a heated exchange on lowering the age of the vote for women was underway. Such talk made Mo wary. There was such vehemence on both sides.

She looked over her shoulder. Some of the cast were drifting into the room, chatting, laughing. From the other side of the room Sandor Olmak was watching her. She suppressed a sliver of anxiety, there was something all together too fervent about him. Yet she was fascinated too. There was an upright Bechstein in the corner. Now Knighton was talking to Olmak, indicating that he should play. Olmak bowed his head in a gesture of assent, seated himself at the piano, took a moment to collect himself and then his fingers flew over the keys like a hundred breezes.

Mo was transfixed: the music was from another world, somewhere wilder yet finer. Who was this man? Questions flurried through her mind even as the music soared and dipped, grew to a frenzy or became so slow and melodic that it seared into her. It was gipsies revelling in dance, setting the sky alight; it was the call of the exile, across the wide empty plains of Eastern Europe.

She wanted to tell Olmak to stop. Right now. Only she couldn't.

Béla Bartòk was the composer, she later learnt.

* * *

After her next performance the man, Sandor Olmak was waiting for her. He was often on the periphery of The Athena crowd, it seemed. Since they'd been introduced, he had become bolder, no longer taking pains to hide his fascination. And for her part, she was strangely affected by his attraction to her.

He cornered her. 'Brava, my splendid Morwenna!' He clasped her hands in his. She wanted to pull away: it was uncanny the effect he had on her. Yet he brought something of the wider world with him, something of continental Europe and the cabarets and nightclubs she recalled from Paris.

'The best ever,' he enthused. 'As I said last time we met, I have followed your career from away – afar, I mean.' But why, she wanted to ask, what am I to you, apart from a bright voice among so many?

'Music is in the blood,' he said. 'It delights me to hear you. To sense the path that lies ahead. But come, I speak too much. Let me buy you a cocktail.' They were in the bar area, near the foyer with its glittering globe. A crowd was spilling out into the lobby. The mood was high, the alcohol flowing.

'Do your family come to see you perform?' he asked. Mo was thoughtful. She shook her head. Any reference to family or Derek still disturbed. 'Have you had much vocal training?' he went on to ask.

'A few singing lessons.' She recalled her days with Miss Dawson in the airless room with the cluttered upright piano.

'You could do anything. Cabaret, opera. I think Cabaret. You have the – how shall I say – the liveliness. Have you considered more – serious training?' Now he looked earnest, a teacher taking his pupil to task. 'These shows will – will extend you. And nothing like Noel Coward to fit in with today's time spirit. He likes pretty surfaces but …' Mo turned away. She did not want to be reminded of her inadequacies or the shortfall in her repertoire. She had handed over her career to Knighton.

As if on cue Knighton appeared at her shoulder.

'There are more people who want to meet you, my dear.' Deftly he steered her away from the man with the penetrating eyes and awkward questions.

'Who are they?' she whispered. She was starting to tire and longed to be alone. Knighton had her by the elbow and was guiding her towards an earnest-looking huddle, which parted as they arrived.

'So what's to follow?' asked one man with light, frizzy hair. 'Coward is so prolific these days it's hard to keep pace.' She heard Knighton muttering about giving an airing to jazz. After a few minutes of smiling and feigning interest she touched his shoulder.

'Jonathon, I must retire now...' She made her excuses and slipped away to the Aldwych apartment where she could contemplate the evening's proceedings in solitude.

Chapter Sixty-two *Derek*

Back in Paris Derek had plenty to be getting on with. He was glad of it, as it helped push Mo out his mind. He could not afford to dwell on her as long as she remained inaccessible. Besides, he did not want to wallow. To show his paintings in this city had once been beyond his ambition. It was *the* place where innovation in art was allowed to flourish. From the generic to the specific, in atmosphere and practice, it remained the City of Light.

Outside, a dull grey sky: the last gloom, he hoped, although they were well into spring. The weather had been cool enough to drive Parisians indoors, into galleries and museums. A mist was lying over the Seine, with shadowy figures silhouetted against lampposts. Yesterday evening he'd passed an old tramp's nest under Pont Neuf and wondered whether the man would see out the year. He'd spotted anglers, perhaps after a perch for their families.

Times were getting tough here, too, no less than in London.

Before the opening Pierre was looking as nervous as he'd ever seen him. 'Do you know who's likely to come?' Derek asked him.

'Not a clue. There are too many workshops and ateliers, too many artists. Half of Europe has moved here. Picasso expressed an interest and threatened to call by. You can't imagine how jittery that makes me.'

Derek laughed. 'Steady on, it's only a show. Your life doesn't depend on it.' He attempted to calm him but Pierre did not look convinced. As for himself, he had been coming and going between London and Paris so much over recent weeks that he almost felt at home here. On more than one occasion he considered transferring over here all together. But when it came to it, he baulked.

The word had got out. At first the curious, the cold and the bored trickled in, so he and Pierre were no longer alone with their offerings. The two of them had put together a leaflet and this was what Pierre was referring to when he spoke, rather solemnly, of their manifesto. In truth, the leaflet contained little more than a paragraph setting out the *raison d'être* of the exhibition. Away from 'isms' it stated, whatever that meant. For him, it signalled not following a particular school, but he could not vouch for Pierre.

Now they were standing in the lobby. Over the last week they had done a fair job of cleaning the storage space and turning it into an avant-garde venue, just a bit rough round the edges. There was a lot of competition, of course. A decade before Amedeo Modigliani had set a new bold tone, painting nudes with pubic hair. An outcry ensued. The police moved in and shut down his show.

After that standards were changed forever. Anything was now permissible. Picasso was as ubiquitous and inventive as ever, though some said he was going through a fallow phase. The Spanish painter held centre stage always mutating, never allowing himself the comfort of the familiar. But that surely what it was all about? Norms were expendable; work and talent were not. In London Derek had been swimming upstream against a flood-swollen river.

'I am tired being overlooked,' declared Pierre. He was wearing a pin-striped shirt with a worn collar that made him look like an impoverished bank clerk. Derek picked up a leaflet and reread the manifesto. 'Out of chaos, order; out of carnage, rebirth; out of confusion, clarity.'

He suppressed a groan. It sounded so high-minded, not to say pretentious. It was even banal. All this had been said before. But Pierre had insisted on some statement, some declaration of intent. They must have been drunk when they wrote that, though he didn't drink much these days. He forgot just when they'd composed it.

'Surely a painting should be its own manifesto?' He stroked his month-old beard and noted Pierre's puzzlement. 'You Continentals are constantly trying to define yourselves. Declare what should or should not be the order of the day. Yet more often than not you fail. The Commune in Paris, revolution in Moscow, soviets in Germany – all come and go. Despite all that and the bloodshed in the trenches, Renoir painted dimpled ladies in dappled sunlight until the day he died.' When Pierre started moving away, Derek wondered if he'd offended him. Sometimes he shot his mouth off without thinking. Trouble was, he expressed himself more freely here than in London.

The first visitors came and left, saying little. By now, Derek was used to standing by while others viewed his work. Talk about thick skin, he'd grown a carapace over the last year. Besides, he'd already sold over twenty pictures in that time and for not inconsiderable amounts. That had to be worth something.

How was he to build a reputation here? He had done the groundwork, now he had to do the selling. Where to find that courage to release his work into the world and prevent himself becoming pensive? Let everything ferment, he mused. Let his unconscious bring to fruition that which was in the ether yet never expressed.

'There are no prices on these,' said a portly woman with a pork pie hat on. She was accompanied by a thin, surly-looking woman with the beginnings of a moustache. They seemed to have wandered in out of the cold. The portly one eyed his pictures critically and cast a glance towards him. He shrugged.

'We are always open to negotiation,' he said.

'Is that so?' She harrumphed and moved on, followed by

her companion, who was clutching a bundle of food packages. They walked the length of the rooms, their steps echoing. After several minutes they returned. The thin woman handed Derek a card. 'Do call on us one Saturday evening,' she said. Derek nodded, confused. When they had gone he glanced down at the calling card. 'Gertrude Stein.' He caught his breath. So the *grande dame* of the Parisian art scene had condescended to come to their exhibition.

Chapter Sixty-three *Mo*

Just days after she'd started her role in the Revue Mo found she could not get out of bed: a horse had dragged her through the town. In fact, it was a night spent alone. Increasingly, when they had two performances a day, she was only too happy to slope off into a solitary bed.

She could hear sounds from a neighbouring apartment: people arguing, doors slamming then silence, ominous in its suddenness. She glanced at the alarm clock. It was time to be up and about. Still she was unable to shift a limb. She groaned and turned over. She had no desire to get up and play the actress, for she had dreamt of Timothy. She was holding him in her arms, he was alive and wriggling, chirping like a fledgling, his eyes, tender and mischievous, gazing up at her. She could smell him. See the blue matinee jacket she dressed him in in the cooler months.

His wraith scattered as daylight broke, unwanted, into the room. She stared ahead, willing his return. A tear trickled down her face. She remembered it was Sunday: today she had neither rehearsals nor performances. With effort she made her way to the bathroom. The geyser growled into life. She dropped crystals into the bathtub and watched them bleed into the water, clouding it blue. She slid into the bath, gasping as warmth surrounded her. She lay soaking.

How would she fill her day? She had shrugged off Knighton's invitation to a trip to Surrey with the rest of the cast. She was tired of parties and jollity, tired of playing the mistress, the star singled out from the chorus to gleam beside the maestro.

She lifted the sponge, squeezed it, sidled down further into the water and squeezed it again, letting a stream of warm water sift through her hair, down her forehead, over her face. She tipped her head back, sinking, so the surface broke and met above her face, before she pulled herself up, breathing deep.

Today she would visit her family.

What else was there for her to do – alone, in the actors' flat, on a blank Sunday in the West End? She thought of Derek at the Kit Kat club several evenings before. She sighed. If she let him, he could walk straight back into her heart. But she would not allow it. She got out of the bath, dressed herself, choosing a slim-fitting sea-green frock, elegant yet respectable. Carefully she made up her face, the powder and rouge so subtle only a professional actor would spot them. Her hair she combed and trained flat to her cheeks and forehead. Her dead eyes stared back at her. She left a note for Knighton, on the off-chance he might call round before or after the outing.

She headed east on a tram. It rattled through Fleet Street and along Farringdon Road, she changed at Clerkenwell onto another and alighted near The Mare's Head. The pub seemed eerily quiet. She called round the back at the draymen's entrance. The back door was locked, too. She banged on it; paced around the yard where she'd once helped her mother with the mangling. Perhaps they were at Cissy's? Reluctant to confront a clan gathering, Mo wrote a note and wedged it into the door crack. She hastened back to the main street and onto a tram going west.

Not quite sure what was driving her, she found her way to Saint Paul's Cathedral. It was halfway through a service. She found a place at the back of the church. The choir was singing: *Panis angelicus.* The sweet high voices pierced her through. A shaft of light caught a pillar, scattering on the fluted surface, reaching up into the golden tesserae behind an image of an angel preventing Abraham sacrificing his first-born. She gazed up at the golden vault, the candles, the alcove pointing towards the altar, the golden pipes of the organ, winged cherubs and the flowering capital of the Ionian pillar.

Was it possible that Timmy existed in some other form?

The question, once put, whirred around inside her. She bent her head to the pew rail, uttered a helpless formless prayer to a Great Beyond she no longer knew whether or not she believed in and then tears came, wracking her chest. The woman alongside looked alarmed. She smothered them, gulped them down, attempted self-control. Only when the grief was safely put away did Mo sit back on the pew. Hope in the Risen Christ. She had heard the words before. Just words. Now the possibility of Timmy out there, in the ether, took hold. What if there were a life of the spirit, distinct from the body? She filed out of the church with the others. Many gathered on the steps, exchanging sunny greetings, chatting in clusters. She scurried away.

Later in the week she made time between rehearsals to visit the Spiritualist church in Islington. She recalled passing it months before. She lingered outside, saw from the noticeboard that a clairvoyance session was underway. With thumping heart she entered and found a seat. It was a stark, almost empty hall. There was a raised platform, with two chairs on it and a sparse bunch of flowers. A thin woman and an earnest-looking, bespectacled young man were presiding over the meeting. They uttered a non-denominational prayer asking for guidance from the power of Spirit and evoking the protection of those who had walked the earth plane and were now in higher realms. After this came a hum of expectation followed by silence. The thin woman announced she would now 'tune in'. She closed her eyes.

'I'm getting a man called David, Dunstan Duncan. Yes Duncan. He smokes a pipe and was fond of keeping pigeons. Yes, yes. There's a lady here. Yes, you Madam in the white hat.

He says, do you remember you brought in the last red rose to him. The day before he passed…' The woman in the white hat nodded and bent her head, stifling emotion. 'He wants you to know: it is all right. He says there was a disagreement – about money. Yes?'

'Yes,' answered the woman timidly.

'He says it is not important. He understands now why you couldn't trust him. He wants you to forgive yourself…'

'Thank you. Thank you.' She muttered, twisting her hands, shoulders shaking.

There was silence as the audience waited in expectation of another visitation.

'Now,' she cleared her throat. 'I'm getting a very young child. Passed away… his-his.' She coughed, coughed again, reached for water. 'A disease in his throat and chest… and I'm getting this lady here in the grey hat. Tom, John, Tim. Is it Timothy?'

Mo nodded, unable to speak.

'I sense – he can't say much. But he's at peace. He wants you to move on. Not to be afraid. I see a bird flying. Bitterness is wasted. He came to bring joy. Wake you up. Now he is in the spirit world. Watching…'

Mo could not hear any more. She gathered her bag and rushed down the half empty rows. 'Wait, wait… there's something else,' said the medium. 'A bridge you need to build,' he says. 'And there's a man – a stranger who is not a stranger. A foreigner.'

Mo hesitated at the threshold of the hall, took a deep breath and thrust out into the open air. Was she crazy to be delving into such twilight practices? Dizzy with confusion she hurried down the street.

* * *

In the week following her visit to the Spiritualist church Mo was troubled as never before. She had fractured dreams and tattered glimpses of other times. Her hard fought for psychological balance was under siege. When would she have that longed for sense of peace? Knighton was putting pressure on her: he wanted her to sign up for more parts, do more auditions at the theatre. The Athena was doing well for itself: they had to keep the supply of entertainment flowing.

To add to her confusion every time she came across one of Derek's pieces on stage she felt a twinge. In unguarded moments it was a twinge of regret, sadness, longing even; other times it was a spurt of anger, irritation that even now, when they no longer saw each other, he still impinged on her life.

On with the show. On stage, in full flight, stepping into the light, the burning light, circle of intensity – me before them, lamb to the slaughter. Dogged steps dogs barking, hounds of hell, yapping snapping at my ankles swollen with fear nowhere to go now, no place to hide, on with the show, the party goes on, doctor theatre, grin and bear it, stiff upper lip, feet twinkle toes dance now, dance now dance sing for your supper, sing out loud. March to the beat, onwards, upwards, no stopping now, no time for sorry, no time for grief. Timmy is gone, a blank wall where is he gone? My heart is with him. Where has he gone? Where are you Timmy? Where are those eyes so full of joy, the promise of things to come? Buried deep along with my heart. I can't do this – today dry as dust – heavy legs sinking down to the earth the soil where Timothy my Timmy is buried. The planks the boards of the stage are swaying towards me a ship at sea tossing me this way and that. Careening, careering towards no career rocking roiling listing out of all control the boards coming towards me I am so faint so faint no blood in my head in my neck…

It took a few seconds for the rest of the cast to realise that something was amiss with their soloist. Staring ahead with no sound coming out of her mouth, she was stricken: mid-song, mid-dance. The audience was agape, thinking it was part of the act and then she was sliding towards the floor, this waif, this slim young thing with the voice of an angel, was down there, flat out on the ground.

'Close the curtains!' hissed Knighton from the wings. 'Right now!' and together they came, swishing within inches of her. The audience was at first bemused then let out cat calls, boos and slow handclapping.

Mo came to into the dressing room surrounded by concerned faces, hands attempting to help. 'Out, all of you!' yelled Knighton. He was frowning down. He was holding a glass of water towards her. 'Someone make her a strong cup of tea with sugar,' he called over his shoulder. Someone scurried off towards the back-stage scullery.

Mo blinked towards the light. 'What happened?'

'You passed out,' Knighton mumbled. Even in her half-conscious state she could tell he was furious with her.

Chapter Sixty-four   *Derek*

They were said to look down on wives, Gertrude Stein and Alice Toklas, and Gertrude had once written with disparagement about the male homosexual act, which was odd, given their relationship. But if you were invited to one of their Saturday night gatherings, you went. No point in arguing against the wind: Gertrude held the reins of the English-speaking literary world and remained abreast of modern art. Though she had shifted her focus from painting to literature, she remained avid for novelty.

Some maintained that it was Leo, Gertrude's brother, who had had the more discerning eye and the sharper business sense when it came to acquiring modern art. The Steins had colonised not only Rue de Fleurus but nearby Rue Madame in Montparnasse. While Michael Stein, older brother and head of family, had done his best to bankroll the rest of the family, Leo and Gertrude had indulged their tastes in modern art and acquired pictures while the works of the old masters remained beyond their means.

That had been in the early years of the century, but now Gertrude was the one who needed to be impressed. It was just as well Mo was not around to be snubbed. Yet Derek could not help regretting her absence. It was here, after all, where they had first got to know each other. Here that Paris had opened itself to them as the city of lovers, of Spring, of eternal optimism, where you did not need money or connections to get by, where wine was cheap and there was always music in the bars and fierce talk and laughter in the air.

Derek turned up at 27 Rue de Fleurus ten minutes before

expected. Rue de Fleurus was a short street off the Boulevard Raspail on the left bank near the Luxembourg Gardens. He rang the bell and the concierge appeared and let him in without bothering to find out his name. A central archway led to a paved courtyard and the two-storey apartment, once shared by Leo and Gertrude. Alice Toklas had since turned it into a home that was always well dusted and fragrant with lavender.

Together Leo and Gertrude bought paintings by Matisse, Degas, Renoir and Gaugin. They were said to have acquired paintings in twos because they could never quite agree. Leo was reputed to have discovered Cézanne. He also was said to have brought to a head the ongoing fractious rivalry between Pablo Picasso and Henri Matisse. He had an instinct for what was different, what would stir people up; he'd been keen to make his mark and had done so. Eventually Gertrude and Leo fell out over Picasso and Gertrude's writing. In the end Leo could abide neither. Now the siblings were estranged.

When Derek eventually entered the salon he stopped short: he had never seen anything quite like it. The rows of paintings caught his breath. They were so many modern, colourful, jarring and unsettling images he did not know where to start. They'd acquired so many works that Gertrude had taken some of the pictures out of their frames. All this was in contrast with the heavy, Italian renaissance furniture. Here and there were plumped Eastern-looking cushions. It was warm there and, despite his misgivings, welcoming. He was relieved to see several other visitors. He recognised one or two of the artists from his rounds with Pierre. At times, these studio visits blurred into each other and he was more likely to recall artworks than the individuals who created them.

There were so many different directions. Still. While some lingered over the mutilated bodies of returning soldiers, others harkened back to portraits and landscapes, seeking reassurance in past forms. Yet others immersed themselves in the Machine

Age or *neue Sachlichkeit*. And here, on these walls, Cubism, Dadaism and Surrealism clashed and squabbled. Picasso sat next to Matisse and Braque.

'Do try our almond cookies,' said Alice. Her face was unsmiling but he caught an aura of deference. He picked up one of the cookies, which was crumbly to the touch. She moved on towards two painters whose heads were bent together in avid debate as they sat on the brightly coloured divan. Nearby Gertrude was stretched out on a sofa wearing a brown corduroy skirt and gondolier sandals. As he approached Gertrude pinned him with her authoritative, curious stare. It was hard to evade feeling judged. He attempted a smile.

'Your show has attracted attention. I hope that works for you. It's not easy being an artist in Paris. There are so many of you.' She got up and moved past him, ponderous, and stocky as a tugboat. He wanted to catch hold of her, ask her if she'd buy some of his larger and more adventurous pieces, whether she would put a word in for him where it counted. The pleas died in his mouth. She was a generous but shrewd person, an open-minded hostess who preserved fierce, unbending opinions; she was not someone to be persuaded.

Pierre had declined to join him here as he had not been singled out with an invitation. Now he wished Pierre was beside him as a comrade-in-arms to deliberate on the next tactic. He swallowed the last of the cookie, which was tastier than it looked, and began to wander through the rooms. Henri Matisse was there. Seeing him, he wished he'd *insisted* that Pierre join him for he was a fan of Matisse, adored his ability to appreciate and transmit colour and light. He'd even trained under Matisse a few years before. Tonight Matisse had an air of distraction about him. Derek knew better than to break his reverie.

Chapter Sixty-five *Mo*

After the incident on stage Mo could not face living in the Aldwych flat. Knighton had taken her back there that night and she'd spent another day there, but now she wanted distance between them so she could recoup her confidence. She'd caught his toxic mixture of frustration and suppressed rage and wanted to get away from it. Once she'd picked herself up, even a little, she insisted on a visit home.

* * *

Ma looked at her across the counter in the dimly lit bar. 'Wasn't expecting to see you so soon.'

'You 'eard what happened?' asked Mo.

'You were the talk of the town.'

'What?'

'I'm teasing you. But, yes, we heard. Someone from the chorus knows a neighbour. Said you was in a bad way.'

Mo vaguely recalled concerned faces but it had all blurred together. She'd been left with an overwhelming sense of confusion and shame: she'd let herself down; she was not the professional she'd made herself out to be.

Ma shook her head, looking at her solemnly. 'You look poorly, all right.' When Mo said nothing she continued: 'You can stay 'ere if you want. As long as you need to.' Mo hated to acknowledge it but right now mothering was what she needed. And however prickly and inadequate Ma's attentions might be, here she was, offering respite.

'Wouldn't do no 'arm I don't suppose,' she murmured. 'Maybe for a day or so.'

'Why don't you go and lie down. I'll make some broth for

you.'

Mo sighed and closed her eyes. She was both glad and sad to be here. It seemed an admission of defeat, sinking back into the past. But for now, just for a while, she wanted to crawl into bed and forget about the world. Upstairs, in her former bedroom, the old dresser and scraps of dolls had gone, as had the old bed. In its place was a new mattress, put directly onto the floor. With a pile of blankets and an eiderdown it looked cosy enough. Ma was being as kind as she was able. Who knew how long before the old resentment came creeping back. It always did. Then she would start persuading Mo to change her ways, change her job. Change into someone she could never be.

Mo lay down on the mattress, fully clothed. In a while Ma came with broth and bread. She hovered by the door, looking uneasy. 'Ma, what is it? You look sad,' Mo surprised herself by saying. As a rule they never talked about feelings.

'I 'ate to see you like this.'

'I'm fine. All part of ...'

'I was a singer once...'

'Ma – why don't you tell me about it? You hardly mention it.'

'It's all over now.'

'Why didn't you carry on?'

Ma turned towards her. Her lips were drawn tight, her brow closed. ''Ere, take this while it's still 'ot.'

'Ma?'

'It was for the best,' she muttered, putting the bowl on the little bedside table. She looked trapped: a prisoner in her own house.

'You've always been set against my singing. I never understood why.'

Ma leant down towards Mo, her gaze was clear despite the anxiety written there. 'You would never have believed it, eh, that I was in Music Hall?'

'What name did you go under?'

'Maisy Aurora.'

'Really? Why don't you tell me about it?'

Ma went to close the curtains. 'You'll be wanting to sleep. After you've finished that.'

'I'd like to know.'

'There are some things best left, Morwenna. And now there are things I need to see to.' Her voice was firm, after a momentary lapse the old resistance had flared back into life. Mo started to eat the soup. It was thin and salty but she caught a flavour of beef in it. No point in forcing the issue. She could not compel her mother to tell her story. Then almost in a whisper she heard Ma mutter: 'I was swept away. The music. I was a slave to the music, odd as that sounds now. There is so much you don't understand and never will.'

'Why not try me?' said Mo. But Ma had already left the room. Mo was on the point of calling after her, demanding details. But she did not have the strength to fight her mother. Never had had for that matter. She should take whatever was on offer, and be grateful, not push against the fences that had been so long in place. A cloud of weariness came over her and she surrendered to it.

She slept for twelve hours and so complete was the forgetfulness that when she did wake she was at a loss as to just where she was. When she saw the worn lino and the threadbare curtains it all came back to her. She snuggled back under the coarse wool blanket, pulling it up to her chin, smelling the slight mustiness of the covers in the room that always had a tinge of damp about it. She stretched out her leg, brushed her foot onto the cold lino.

Downstairs she could hear the clattering of crockery as breakfast was underway. She realised how hungry she was. She stumbled to her feet, splashed water in her face from the ewer her mother had left for her and pulled on her skirt and jumper. She couldn't remember undressing herself. Maybe Ma had done it; maybe she'd shrugged off her clothes herself in sleep. No matter. She ran her fingers through her hair and prepared to greet her parents. With the benefit of a clear mind she realised she'd need to say something, but she wasn't quite sure what. She had grown so used to perpetuating the fiction that all was well with her.

In the event she needn't have worried. True to age-old family tradition, neither parent displayed an iota of curiosity as to why she had pitched up in a state of nervous exhaustion. Her mother, of course, already had the gist. And perhaps that was enough. Porridge was bubbling on the range. The scullery was filled with a smell of toast. Her father was sitting, legs sprawled, one hand around an enamel mug, the other flicking through the pages of *The Daily Mirror*. He grunted when he saw Mo, gave her a quiet smile. 'Good to see you, gal. Fought you'd forgotten all about us.'

Mo sat at the scrubbed pine table. Ma filled a bowl with porridge and pushed it towards her. Mo helped herself to milk and sugar and started spooning the thick, lumpy mixture into her mouth.

'I 'ear you're with us a few days,' said Pa as he dived into the sporting pages.

Mo grunted. 'Not that long. Feel right as rain this morning.'

'That so? You look a bit pale to me,' said Ma, offering her a plate with a slice of toast on it. Mo wanted to protest that that was her natural colour, in recent times they'd only seen her with rouge on.

'Right then,' said father, folding his paper and tossing it into a corner. 'I best be getting on. The draymen will be coming. Need to open up the back.' He tousled Mo's hair and shuffled out of the room. She noticed how worn he was, from his shabby shoes to his patched jacket, to his lined face.

'Think I'll be heading back. If I stay away too long there won't be no role for me. They'll think I quit.'

Ma was slowly buttering her toast. 'And how is Derek these days? You never bring 'im 'ere?'

Mo's heart thumped. 'Ma I thought I'd explained. We've gone our separate ways.'

'Morwenna marriage isn't like that. You made a vow, remember?' Mo groaned. There was no way she wanted to get into this discussion. 'You've got to take the rough with the smooth. He's a good man, basically.' Her mother's voice cut into her. 'Do you still see each other?'

'He is working in other theatres these days. Our paths rarely cross.'

Ma gave her a searching, not-to-be-fobbed-off look.

'Well, Ma, you know what I'd really like, what would make me happy, is for you to come and watch me perform? Would you do that for me?'

Ma started tidying the breakfast things into the sink.

'Ma?'

'When's the next performance? I fought things was coming to an end? That's what you said.'

'It's got another few days to run.'

Mo watched her mother's sloped shoulders, trying to decipher what was going through her mind. Ma turned, wiped her hands on the tea cloth. 'Well, we'll see. I might.'

Chapter Sixty-six

By the end of the week Mo was back at work, fending off stabs at solicitude and incessant questions from the rest of the cast. She'd had a one-off turn, she insisted, but was now back in action and keen to get on with things. Knighton was watching her with a wary eye, but chose to keep his distance.

Sandor Olmak caught up with her by the Stage Door. Initially she felt a surge of annoyance, wanting to ask him what exactly he wanted from her, but by now he was becoming part of her entourage. Besides, she needed to see faces other Jonathon Knighton's, for she was not yet ready to deal with him. She found herself drifting with Olmak into a nearby pub. Why not, she thought carelessly, I could do with a little relaxation.

'So how are you, Mrs Eaton? You come back to work soon?' They had settled in a dark corner by a lamp fringed with red beads. She gazed at them then up at him.

'Oh, do call me Morwenna. And thanks for asking, I'm back in the saddle now,' she said cheerily.

'I was there, Morwenna. I saw it all. You were like a sheet. You looked as though you'd seen a spirit – a ghost.'

'I had a shock, but I'm better.'

'Are you?'

'Of course.'

'Your performance tonight was tiptop. I just worry about you. You mustn't push yourself too hard.'

'I'm fine. I really am.' Puzzled, she stared at him. What was her welfare to him? His concern struck her as intrusive.

'I heard what you've been through from Jonathon

WAYWARD DAUGHTER

Knighton.'

She shot him a fierce look. 'I said I'm better…'

'Are you sure?'

'Quite sure,' she whispered. They fell into a silence that grew like an intimacy between them. She struggled, wistful and desperate all at once. Why should she unravel her story to a stranger? 'I had a son…' she whispered, almost to herself.

A look of pain came into his face. He seemed unable to speak then murmured: 'I know. I know all about it. It broke my heart when I heard.' He touched her hand, his eyes softening. 'I would love to have known him.'

She pulled away. 'But what's it to you?'

He shrugged, gave a fleeting smile. 'I sense a kind spirit.' He looked over his shoulder as if seeking distraction.

'Kindred spirit, you mean?'

'Yes, yes. That's it.'

'Why should you…?'

'As I said before,' he hesitated as if searching for the right words. 'I'm an… an admirer. I watch you for quite a while.'

She leaned back in her chair, swilled the wine in the glass, noticing how it caught glints of light from the gas mantle. 'It all got to me.'

'What did?'

She drank more wine. 'I wanted to go … home but I no longer know where that is. I was at home – my childhood home, but that wasn't it. In fact I feel more at home in the theatre. That's why I stay there overnight sometimes.'

'Do you? Is that allowed?'

She laughed. 'The stage manager doesn't mind.'

'I know what you feel, Morwenna.'

Anger spiked her then. 'How – how on earth do you know what I've been through? How do you know what I'm talking about?'

'Because I have felt like that all my life. Never knowing

what place to call my own. Or where I'm – where I'm rooted.' He looked unutterably sad.

She drew back, considered his solemn face and was curious. 'So what's your story? What happened to you?'

'That's another tale.'

So he was as much a misfit as she was. 'Go on,' she said. 'Tell me more about yourself.'

'Another time.'

He went pour her more wine. She covered her glass with her hand. She was beginning to feel tired. He looked at her again, eyes sharp with challenge yet full of understanding. 'I wanted to say. Don't let this this setback be the end for you. It's just a – a stumble along the way. I believe in you.' He touched her hand again. She recoiled. Captivated by the exoticism of the man, she was also unnerved by him.

'That's more than I can say about my family.' She fiddled with the corner of an ashtray. 'My Ma never wanted me to sing…'

'Your mother?' He looked momentarily at a loss, almost startled. 'What would she have you do?'

'Heaven only knows. All I know is that she doesn't approve of me being on the stage. Never has done.'

He looked reflective then glanced over his shoulder. 'Drink up, Morwenna. They're wanting to close here. It's time to go.'

Chapter Sixty-seven

Sandor Olmak might have been correct in stating that's Mo's performance was tip-top but Knighton only gave her a small role in the upcoming Revue, which was, for the most part, a light-hearted Noel Coward medley. She had only one new song to perform. She'd also be allowed to sing *Carolina Moon* as she'd got it off to a tee. Anything American would do, said Knighton. The Charleston and the Shimmy were still in vogue and jazz was edging its way into London nightclubs.

Knighton could not afford to let Mo go. She knew that, but was still on edge, knowing her position was less solid than before. He was watching her, she noted, but still from afar. Was he growing tired of her, she wondered? Her recent collapse must have unnerved him.

She was preening herself in front of the dressing room mirror. It was true what Ma had said: she was not at her most dazzling. *'Carolina Moon keep shining…'* she murmured to herself as she removed grease paint from her face. Gently she stretched the blue-veined, porcelain skin below her eyes. Her mouth was drooping slightly. She grimaced, puffed out her cheeks, pinched them to restore colour.

'Night Morwenna,' called one of the chorus girls, as she made for the corridor. Mo heard a porter whistling outside, then a burst of giggles and high-pitched voices as more of the chorus tumbled out into the night. She brushed back her hair and opened her eyes wider, blinking at herself. She had lost weight in recent weeks and could ill afford to. She pulled on her day dress, adjusting the dropped waistline and smoothing out the creases. Tonight Knighton would not be waiting for her, but perhaps Sandor Olmak might be.

She started wondering whether Derek ever came to see her on the sly, but brushed away the thought. Knighton and she had not discussed 'the incident' as he dubbed it. Best left like that. She did not want to draw him into her doubt, her lingering grief. After all, Knighton and The Athena were part of her recovery. She had not lied when she told her mother that she could not afford to stay away from the auditions. So many starry-eyed hopefuls were always buzzing around Knighton. He always said her voice was special. But what if that voice was overcome by other singers vying for attention?

She twirled around to see herself from behind, turned this way and that to catch the best profile. The powder blue dress was becoming. She could pass muster at any gathering. But what if what she looked like and the voice were no longer enough? She adjusted into the bar-strapped shoes, which were a perfect match to her dress. She wandered through the auditorium towards the front foyer.

The rows of plush red seats were sunk in shadows, the stage curtains firmly drawn. Light glimmered from the foyer. Drawing near she heard the murmur of voices. As she entered it she saw a bunch of people huddled round the bar, laughing and raising glasses. She glanced over the shiny seal heads of the women, the slickly parted, smarmed-down hair of the men, searching for a familiar face. And there was Knighton, with a bevy of the chorus girls hemming him in. Next to him was Garfield, the Stage Manager, a head above everyone one else with his sinewy neck and close-cropped hair. Sandor Olmak was there, too.

He waved across at her. At almost the same time became aware of a figure hugging the relative obscurity of one of the pillars. It was Ma. She was holding back, as if at a loss what to do next. Mo rushed up to her in excitement. 'You came,' she could not help beaming. Ma looked embarrassed. She eyed Mo from top to toe and gave a whisper of a smile. 'I'm so glad,' continued Mo. She held out her hands to grasp her mother's but the latter's remained by her side as if she could not trust them.

'Morwenna,' she said quietly. 'You sang beautifully.'

Sandor Olmak had caught up with them. He had not seen Ma. As he reached Mo he came to a halt. 'Ma may I introduce…?' But Olmak turned away abruptly and brushed by as though he never had the intention of coming near her. 'Well,' said Mo. 'How rude.' Ma was stricken with confusion. 'He's a musician,' said Mo by way of explanation. 'Sometimes comes to watch me sing.'

Ma said nothing. 'Ma, can I buy you a drink? A gin and orange, a pink gin, or champagne cocktail?' Mo's voice was eager. She felt the need to fill the silence, to protect her mother from the unfamiliar environment.

Ma nodded. 'A large brandy,' she demanded rather to Mo's surprise, as she never usually went near the stuff. Olmak glanced over his shoulder as he moved towards the theatre exit and out into the street. Mo caught a whiff of fear, rejection in Ma's eyes. How could Sandor Olmak be so insensitive? Was he avoiding her mother because she looked so shabby, so lowly? Had he not said he admired the struggle and chutzpah of the working classes?

'I'm so glad you came,' Mo repeated. 'All this time… and now you can see for yourself.'

'Indeed,' mumbled Ma.

'Would you like to come to my rooms? Take some refreshment?' It felt as if she was dealing with a stranger. Ma shook her head and said she needed to be heading home. She had done what she came to do. Now she would know what Mo was talking about when she spoke of the show. 'Ma, are you okay? You don't seem to be yourself.'

'It's nothing.'

'Nothing? Are you feeling ill?'

'Best be going. The trams get few and far between at this hour.'

'Are you sure… is there nothing else I can get you?'

'You did good, Morwenna. It was a treat to see you up there…' Ma clasped her hand, knocked back the rest of the brandy and pulled her coat closed. 'You wait till I tell Pa. As I said: I'll be off now. When will you be coming to visit again?'

'There'll be more rehearsals. This revue is more of a filler. The director will be doling out roles and songs. I need to be around.'

'But are you up to it, Morwenna?'

'I'm fine. I really am. Work is the best medicine.'

'If you say so.' Ma sounded weary. 'And where's that husband of yours? You need him now more than ever.'

'Oh Ma, let's not rake over that again.'

Ma sighed. 'It's tough in this business. You need someone to look out for you. You shouldn't let pride stand in your way.'

Mo moved back. Knighton was throwing curious glances in her direction, looked set to come over and join them any minute. This was not something she wanted Ma to witness. She gave her mother's arm a friendly squeeze. 'I'll come when I can. Once I know what I am going to be doing.'

Ma started heading towards the exit. Mo watched her go, a familiar mix of resentment, fear and vulnerability oppressing her as it always did in the presence of Ma Dobson.

Chapter Sixty-eight *Mo*

The next evening when she'd finished her performance Sandor Olmak was waiting for her and when he suggested dining together, she did not hesitate. She'd been left uneasy in the foyer the day before and wanted to find out why. They headed towards a bistro in Covent Garden on the edge of the Strand. She watched the taxis ferrying people home or on to other parties after the theatres and cinemas had given out. They were shown to a table near the window where a large thick velvet curtain hid them from the other diners while allowing them to watch the bustle along the thoroughfare. Olmak ordered a bottle of Burgundy.

'I wondered if I upset you in some way?' she began, unable to contain herself. He started fiddling with the base of the candle that sputtered and dripped in the centre of the table.

'What do you mean?'

'Last night – after the show – you walked straight past me.'

'I was in a hurry. I had to get somewhere.'

'Did you? I thought you were coming over to see me. I was with my mother.'

'Your mother?' he hesitated. 'Your mother was there?' His eyes flickered.

'And you cut us.'

'I just said, I had to get somewhere.'

'Is that so?'

He glanced across at her; she stared back, determined not to let him off the hook. When he said nothing but made a show of reading the menu again, she decided to pursue the questions that had been nagging her.

'I know so little about you. Yesterday – I told you about myself. Before we go any further I – I want to hear about you.'

He shrugged, looked over his shoulder to attract the attention if the waiter. 'Not much to tell.'

'I'm interested.'

He sighed, looked into his wine glass. 'Do you really want to know?'

'You said something which intrigued me – about being rootless, that we were similar in some ways. That got me thinking...'

He sipped his wine, held the glass up to the table lamp. 'Not a bad vintage. They certainly know about wine, the French.'

When Mo did not reply he continued to ruminate for minute or two, then started speaking in a low voice, directing his words to the tablecloth as if he were afraid to look at her. 'I left Vienna when I was in my early twenties – a decade before the war. It was a wonderful place then and we – we Jews were part of that...'

'You're Jewish?'

'Yes, I am.'

For the next few minutes he described the city as he had known it in his youth – the magnificent Indian Summer of it before the plunge into chaos. It had been a place to be, a place for artists, but especially for anyone who loved music. It was the era of Bartòk, Mahler, Strauss, Kodály, Schoenberg and Janáček...' His voice filled with longing, nostalgia.

'The waltz. You've heard of the Viennese waltz? A dance so popular. It was *toll* – crazy. *Überschwänglich* – how do you say – exuberant. A symbol of old Vienna. And then Ravel came along and turned it into a frenzy, a dance of death, an ecstasy of longing and danger. That was my Vienna...'

Their food order arrived. He cleared his throat and looked momentarily at a loss. Mo cut into her steak, watching the blood ooze into a blob of mustard. 'So what about you? How did you fit into all that?'

'I didn't. Certainly not at first. My mother came to Vienna from a *shtetl* in Galicia in the nineties. I think she ran away – because of me. But there had been unrest. Pogroms, even, and refugees fleeing the Russian Empire. She hoped for a better life there. For me, at least. In Vienna things had got better for us Jews. The arts were an open area – field. So that's where we could work: in music, painting, theatre. You have no idea how hard it had been to be a Jew and now at last the doors had begun to open. But then – the war came...'

'How sad.'

'Not just sad, it was a tragedy. It destroyed everything. Finished the Hapsburgs. You see, for all its badness the empire was a kaleidoscope of peoples: Magyars from Hungary, Czechs, Eastern Orthodox, Muslims, Hassidic Jews, Serbians and Galicians. The police could be brutal. But you knew where you stood. And the *fin de siècle* – ah, a feast for any artist.' His voice had taken on the warmth of affectionate remembrance.

'So what brought you to London?'

'That's another story.' He shook his head, as though dowsed in cold water. 'Enough of all that.'

'Why England?'

Mo watched him as cut meticulously into his steak, seasoning it with juice and mustard. His actions were so precise, as though he were holding chaos at bay. He was lost in the past, staring down at his plate. He finished the remainder of his meal and placed his knife and fork carefully together on the plate. The waiter came to clear away. 'I wanted to learn English. The Anglo-Saxon world was a strange one to me. I was curious.'

'Where did you grow up?'

He sighed, played with his napkin.

'We lived on the outskirts of Vienna. But I soon moved to

the centre where I could get a job as a rehearsal pianist with an operetta company. I tried to develop my classical career. From an early age I loved music. Music allowed me to fly. Yes, to fly. I discovered that as a five-year-old.'

'Why, what happened?'

'I can't remember the exact occasion.'

Suddenly he glanced across at her, his face shadowed with pain.

He poured himself more wine. 'And then I moved to London.'

'You were here during the war?'

'No, ten years before.'

'Coming from Vienna became a problem?'

'I left before the war broke out. And then I was called up.'

There was something niggling at the back of her mind. Something he was not saying, something he was taking pains to conceal. It came to her as a churning in her gut, a light butterfly feeling in her chest. And then it pushed its way into her awareness: he and Ma *had* known each other.

'You recognised her, didn't you? You knew each other. Please don't lie to me Mr Olmak. This is important.'

He refused to look at her, his eyes cast towards the ground. At that moment he looked more distraught than she had ever seen him. It was clear he would admit nothing. As they were leaving the restaurant he said, almost in a whisper. 'You will perform, Morwenna. You were born to perform. But it will be to walk among flames.' He clutched her hand. 'Morwenna, follow your bright star wherever it leads you.'

Chapter Sixty-nine *Derek*

In Paris things were moving fast for Derek. The exhibition was drawing to a close. There had been several write-ups in the art reviews in *Le Figaro*, *Gil Blas* and elsewhere. Mostly they were favourable, though one critic was puzzled why Derek Eaton was moving in divergent directions at the same time. Derek put this quibble down to the French obsession with order and clarity. No wonder so many of the Dadaists and Surrealists blasted out of these traditional straitjackets!

The Saturday evening soirée at Gertrude Stein and Alice Toklas's apartment had led to another. Then the *grande dame* of art had let it be known that she would call by the gallery yet again. That she had noticed his work was remarkable, that she had invited him to her soirées was even better, but that she wanted to return for a further viewing was a clear sign of interest.

The exhibition had only hours to run. Already the crates were ready to box up the paintings. The signs outside had been taken down and he'd totted up their takings. Considering the relative haste and amateurish approach in putting the whole thing together, the yield had been good. He'd sold seven paintings and Pierre three. But more than that, word had got about that here were two artists worth watching.

Gertrude no longer had the backing of either of the Stein brothers when she acquired new pieces of art. She made her own deals. In terms of her own creativity, she concentrated these days on writing. She wrote herself, searching, she'd said, a new mode of expression, a way to manipulate language. Many saw in her work repetitive, unpublishable gibberish, while she and a few others were convinced of her genius. Derek was not about to engage in that wrangle. Literature was not his forte.

He saw the two women approaching. They presented a strange sight: Gertrude, striding ahead, solid and squat as a south Italian peasant, and Alice, small, lean and serious, holding back, following in her wake. Gertrude greeted him with a firm handshake. He led her into the body of the exhibition while Alice remained by the entrance where Pierre was tidying papers.

'I've been thinking about your work,' said Gertrude. She was not smiling but her dark brown eyes had warmth and intelligence. He could understand why people enjoyed her presence. Alice Toklas was talking with Pierre. Derek noticed his friend bending towards her, struggling maybe with her American English.

Gertrude lingered in front of *First Light*. A smile lit her face. She turned to him. 'This was the one. It's been on my mind. I love its in-the-momentness, the way it straddles the border between things and ideas. Has no real centre but it's built up in blocks. Has luminosity and transcendence while at the same time it's playful and full of surprise.' He said nothing. If she could see all that in them, who was he to argue? He had painted it as the whim took him, early morning, not quite awake and wanting to catch that dreamlike state.

'And this,' she said, pointing to *Dance of triangles*. Why, it's quite delightful.' Derek looked again at the juddering, dissolving forms of triangles overlapping each other. There was something in their arrangement, in the bleeding of colours and shades into each other that made for an overall effect of vibrancy, mystery even. He must have been half conscious when he did that, too. He could not have achieved it with deliberation. But for all that, it mirrored the metamorphosis he'd been undergoing in recent months.

Alice and Pierre had wandered into the main exhibition area and were moving from canvas to canvas, saying little. Alice carried a notebook and was making jottings as they progressed. 'Ah there you are, Pussy,' said Gertrude. 'These are the ones. I want to buy them. Make a note: *First Light* and *Dance of Triangles*. They are still for sale, I take it?'

* * *

Derek had been away from London for nearly three weeks. He was itching to be on the move again. He wanted to get back to London and flaunt his recent success to the gallery owners who'd not given him the time of day. Most of all, he wanted to get into a regular routine. At Pierre's studio there was not really enough room for the two of them.

It was time to develop his career back in England. The place needed shaking up. It needed new insights and a new way of relating to the world they were moving into. So much had been freed up. Militarism was on the run. The power grip of the fathers had been challenged and empires broken up. Father Freud was giving the lie to the veneer of respectability. Nuclear physicists were discovering the core components of matter. Women were coming forward: they even had the vote now. Not only had they thrown off their whalebone corsets but they were avid to express their opinions.

Not that he had the arrogance to assume he could shake up anything. But he could be part of a movement – he smiled even as he mouthed the word. He could stir the pot, throw in his works, and see what had changed in recent months.

Gertrude Stein had purchased the two paintings she'd taken a fancy to. They were installed in the stairwell leading to the upper floor of her apartment. Here they would get the best possible viewing. He would be talked about, invited to more events, meet illustrious painters and collectors. But for now he needed to retreat: above all, he should not let his recent good fortune go to his head. The danger of playing to an audience was always there. That was the devil's route. He had learnt through his own despair that the guiding principle in his work must remain his own instincts.

He took himself over to Pierre's studio in Marais. Pierre was in the process of clearing out debris. He was bundling together broken frames and other bits and pieces to build a bonfire in the courtyard. An impressive heap of wood towered two metres high and he was adding to it by the minute.

'No works of art in there?' said Derek, as Pierre came laden with more wood.

'Only yours,' quipped Pierre.

'That's okay then. Didn't realise you were keeping so much junk in there. No wonder there wasn't room to swing a cat.'

'Swing a cat?'

'Never mind, it's a daft English expression. Look Pierre, I came to tell you I'm heading back to London.'

'So soon? I thought you were enjoying your new-found fame.'

'Selling two pictures to Gertrude Stein doesn't mean instant acceptance.'

'You could have done a lot worse.'

'I know. I'm grateful. But I need to go. I just wanted to let you know. I'm going tomorrow.'

'So, it's all decided.'

Derek caught a whiff of jealous resentment from his friend. Or was he imagining it? They had had good times together. 'You can come over if you want. Come and work. I've got two studios at my disposal.'

'I want to follow through on the leads from the exhibition. I made a lot of new contacts.'

'I guess we both did. I'll be back.' Pierre shrugged and carried on loading up the bonfire, which was tilting to one side. 'Here let me help you. You don't want to set the building on fire.'

They made several trips to and from the studio until the space there was clear. Pierre threw some kerosene from a lamp over the pile and struck a match. Whoosh! There was a crackling and flare of light as the bonfire ignited. The two friends stood side by side and watched the flames soar. For a moment Derek had the oddest sensation of being in the midst of it.

He shook his head and began to think of his return to London. If he were honest he longed to apprise Mo of his success, he had a longing to see her and to let her see just what he was now worth in the eyes of the world.

Chapter Seventy *Mo*

Mo thought she had put on a good show. They took six curtain calls. Someone was throwing roses onto the stage, someone else stamping their feet. Knighton was beaming towards them. And then, all at once, she couldn't stand it. She couldn't stand him. He seemed so phoney, so preoccupied with what others thought, whether or not the cash registers were jangling. It was all – so out of joint.

Afterwards, in the dressing room, she reached for the bottle of whisky she kept in a cupboard to warm her when she needed to take the edge off the cold. She poured a good measure and sipped. She stared at jars of cold cream, grease paint and bowls with powder and puffs, at the silken gowns and peignoirs hanging on the rail. She eyed the rows of flowers and cards offering good wishes, not just for her these days, but for the whole line-up of chorus girls. A candle was flickering in the corner, casting shadows about the room, lighting up the screens and mirrors in colliding patterns. She yawned. She was feeling so tired. More than tired, weary into her very skull. She wanted to stretch herself out and rest.

In the room next door was a day bed where performers lay down when they were not on call. That would do. She carried the bottle through. Everyone had left by now. She lit a kerosene lamp there and settled onto the sofa. It was soft, yielding to her body. The pillow smelled of lavender – a nice touch by the wardrobe mistress, who liked subtlety. The aroma reminded Mo of a garden in Oxford she and Derek visited when first married. Lavender brought in a whiff of spring, of the countryside. She took another small swig of whisky, loving the fire-water down her gullet, the swimming in her head. It was so good to let go, view the world through a swaying, blurred distance.

Now the theatre would be empty. She had told the night porter to go. Here she was on territory she understood. It was comforting to have these empty rooms around her, here where theatre was a daily concoction of costumes, face paint, hopes and illusions. Edges were growing hazy, inner doubts muted and far away. She was a swan gliding through reeds, sure of its direction. She smiled to herself. The morning would take care of itself, the following week would bring rehearsals. Knots to be undone and configured. She folded her hands under her cheeks and tucked her feet up. drawing down a silk shawl from the back of a chair. It was so light and yet warm against the chill of night, as she drifted into a deep and dreamless sleep.

Chapter Seventy-one *Sandor*

Sandor Olmak sat brooding over a pint of ale in The Unicorn pub, recalling his meal the evening before with Morwenna. There was so much he'd left unsaid. So much which had to remain unsaid. *Wanderlust,* it had been and the need to get away. Europe was an overripe fruit, ready to fall. Without knowing it, had he sensed the war coming? Why England, she'd asked, and he'd replied he wanted to learn English. The Anglo-Saxon world had been a strange one to him. He'd liked its abrasiveness, its love of technology.

In Vienna, in those glory years when culture was appreciated and order valued, everyone knew their place; everyone, that is, except for him: Jewish, Hungarian, working-class. Poverty he knew and the indignity of not being respectable. His father he'd never known. His mother he knew only too well. He'd breathed and swallowed her atmosphere of pain, disappointment and shame – morning, noon and night. It was suffocating. She worked part time in a *Trafik,* a tobacconist's, and took in washing, though she hated every minute of it. She never tired of telling him she was born for better things. Ashamed of the circumstances of his birth, she'd hidden him from her better-off relatives.

Music became his religion, his father, his country. It loosened the bonds that tied him to his mother. It washed away her *oh weh*, the-world-is-a-terrible-placeness. He loved her, but she took away his freedom. He longed more than anything for the wide spaces.

He couldn't remember the exact occasion – only heavy mahogany furniture and potted plants and the magical black and white keys of the piano. It must've been at a relative's house – some rare invitation to a musical soirée. Someone muttering: 'Look at them – straight from the *shtetl*.' She let him have lessons after that evening. Seeing the glitter in his eyes, she'd scraped what she could – skipping meals, wearing shoes with holes.

His face shadowed with pain.

In London he could lose himself. Forget the poverty, the guilt. Be someone else. Someone he wanted to be. Music had taken him all over the place – into concert halls, into dark corners of pubs. Always led by music, he'd given himself up to it: to its variety, its chaos and its order, to the people who made it. He'd relished the humour and vulgarity of Music Hall, even as he found the music trite. He loved the lower orders breaking free and stamping their mark. They had confidence in themselves and despite all that was done to them, a *joie de vivre*.

Then there was Maisy. He sighed. Oh, how he'd loved her. And now there was Morwenna, edging ever closer to the truth. Just as well Morwenna had not pressed him on why he had returned to London when he did. That it was not just the sense of Vienna at war with itself, though that would have been reason enough. Vienna had indeed become dangerous. The Social Democrat *Republikanischer Schutzbund* and the rightwing nationalist *Frontkämpferung* were at each other's throats, crippling the city. Unemployment was growing. The toxic miasma of anti-Semitism pervaded the city. With so many opera and theatre companies going bust it had become hard for him to find work.

But how could he tell her that beyond all that he was desperate, as the years passed, for connection, for family? The time was not yet ripe. He had already written what he needed to say to Maisy. For now that was enough.

The bar was about to shut. It was well past midnight. Beer might have been watered down in the Great War and licensing hours restricted, but in this part of town around Drury Lane, publicans knew who their best customers were and bent the rules accordingly. This was never more so than in this, Sandor's local.

At first it was just a wisp above the rooftops, then a cloud growing to a wall of smoke, which billowed out. It seemed to be coming from the huddle of theatre land. It couldn't be *her* theatre, could it? Immediately alerted, a hound sniffing the wind and sensing blood, Olmak darted to the window. But that afforded him no better view. By now others had noticed. Someone yelled: 'Fire!' Someone else was summoning the Fire Brigade.

The smoke was building, thick against the night sky, and could no longer be ignored. Morwenna might be in danger – improbable, given the sheer number of theatres hereabouts, but not impossible. He had to find out. He dashed through the bar, letting the door swing behind him.

More anxious by the minute, he threaded his way down the narrow streets towards The Athena. From the Stage Door of The Athena swirled a pall of grey. Flames were breaking out higher up, in the second storey. 'Morwenna,' he gasped. The building was ablaze, the heat growing more intense by the minute. Any approach down the alleyway was hazardous. People were gathering to watch.

He had to get through. If Morwenna's life was in danger there was no question of not doing so. He pulled a handkerchief from his breast pocket, tied it over mouth and nose, squinted. The acrid smoke was everywhere and now came the sound of the fire engine bells clanging through the streets, far off but getting nearer. He got to the ground and crawled where he could under the thick smoke. 'Morwenna!' with superhuman effort he thrust forward, barely able to breathe. He blasted through the Stage Door. Here the fire had not yet taken hold. He could hear timbers creaking, cracking up, exploding, burning wood and plaster falling in all directions; a fierce crackling and crashing of structures, a curling twisting black and red creature devouring all before it. He managed to take several steps before the fumes overcame him. He let out a muffled scream as the heat hit him then nothing as the poisons in the air and the rush of oxygen, feeding the conflagration, swallowed all.

Chapter Seventy-two *Mo*

Mo coughed. Once, twice, the sounds of crashing – something falling – something heavy. Smell: she could smell acrid burning. Head dizzy, wanting to shelter in the pillow, lying down. No – pulling herself up, staggering to her feet. Something was not right. Wake up. Burning crackling smoke more and more smoke. Burning crackling heat, another crash. The Stage Door exit was impassable, swallowed in heat, clouds of grey. She dragged herself along, half-blind, coughing, head and heart pounding. Someone was calling her name. 'Morwenna!' On and on. She could scarcely breathe. All in blackness. Alone – no one around. Crackling growing ever louder, a fierce dragon. Smoke getting thicker. She grasped at the wall, staggering groping kneeling beneath the blast of heat. There was another way out, away from the smoke. Down away from the back towards the other side – where they put out the rubbish. Where there were sometimes rats. And then she was banging open the door into the alleyway with a blast of hot air behind her, pushing her through.

Stumbling now thrusting forward then only the blackness, the gutter, people around her, voices, hands, arms, louder voices people looking towards her coming nearer one last effort one last step no, she was already there, on the ground, collapsing, sinking down. Someone slapping her face, calling her into wakefulness, the stamp of yet more feet, a light flashing in her face, water splashed in her face, a glass of water held to her lips, being propped up from behind, spinning head going round and round out of control, lights, voices, an acrid smell in her nostrils, a whirring and whirling all around her.

What was going on? Oh how she longed for calm, to sink into oblivion, of not having to struggle. And now a gruffer voice was taking command. 'Let's get her up out of here. There are still fumes about. Where does she come from? Who is she?'

'Connected to the theatre, I guess.'

'One of the singers, one of the chorus. One of them from The Athena.' The Athena. Ah The Athena. Now she remembered, vaguely, through a veil, there was smoke, she was choking as the wind of heat crackled, caught hold, spread along the corridor coming closer. Choking. 'Get her up out of here.' The voice was calling again; others then were heaving, dragging her along.

'Keep awake miss,' a woman was saying, her voice softer, near her ear. 'Not long to go. The ambulance is coming...' More water. She was parched.

'Water,' she gasped.

The bright lights and rushing sound of an ambulance pierced the gloom of the alleyway where she was lying, surrounded by perplexed passers-by. The clang of the fire engine bells above that. She looked up at a hand-held torch flashing around her, more faces bent over her and more voices, some urgent now. She fainted clear out. Then someone was smacking her on the face, offering more water.

A tall thin man, who seemed to be in charge, said that as far as he could tell from a quick examination, they would probably not want to keep her in hospital long: she had not sustained serious injury, nevertheless it would be a good idea for her to be checked over. She came round, nodded and drifted off again. She heard the same man muttering that this drowsiness was not a good sign – perhaps she had banged her head and concussed herself. They should take her in as soon as possible.

The ambulance drove to University College hospital, she later learnt. Here she was placed in a general ward where they prodded, poked and took blood pressure and pulse readings.

They sounded her lungs. She seemed to be unharmed, the doctor said to the ward sister. My guardian angel called out to me, she whispered before drifting off again. How else to explain that insistent voice calling her? She could have sworn someone was shouting her awake, willing her out of the fiercely imploding building.

In the background, out of sight, she heard more voices. Feet coming and going in the corridor, doors swinging open and shut. She thought she could make out Knighton: his distinctive cough, the low register of his voice. She sensed rather than saw the presence of Ma amongst the cluster of doctors, was Pa there too? She couldn't tell. And Derek? More than anyone else she wanted to see Derek. But he was nowhere to be seen. Did he even care about her? She might have died. Outside, in the corridor there seemed to be some sort of altercation going on. She heard Ma's shrill voice raised in anger. 'If you cared, it wouldn't 'ave 'appened.' Or something like that.

Then there was quiet. She didn't hear Knighton anymore.

She felt her mother beside the bed. She was stroking her hand, smoothing down the rough hospital blanket, pouring water into a beaker.

PART 5

Chapter Seventy-three

Word soon spread around the West End, though accounts varied. A fire had started around eleven, they all agreed. At first it was a slow smouldering, not noticed by late night revellers on the Strand. Or if they did notice they thought someone was burning rubbish. A lot of scenery, flats and costumes – all highly inflammable – were stowed near the site of the origin of the fire. Some said it had started in a dressing room, probably from a candle burning into a pile of scripts; others said it was faulty wiring and still others maintained it was arson.

The building did not burn down in its entirety. Only the back part was affected, near the Stage Door, though management went on to say that the theatre would be out of action for several months. The police had ruled out foul play after they found a burnt-out stage light, which they assumed had been left on and overheated. The candle theory was discounted.

Luckily the fire occurred when the building was no longer in use. There was only one potential victim of the fire: Morwenna Eaton, the actress and singer who was sleeping in the building at the time, as actors sometimes did. She was lucky to have escaped alive. Some said she was overtired, others that she was sick, others that she'd had too much to drink. Although the worse-for-wear, she'd managed to make her way out through a seldom used side door.

But on the second day after the fire, when the police were mulling over the black debris of charred wood they came across the stumpy remains of a human body. It was located in the corridor leading from the Stage Door. This door had been levered open from the outside, which gave rise to further suspicions of arson. The corpse represented, as far as they knew, the only casualty of the blaze.

So far this fire victim had not been identified. All the police would give out was that it was of a man, probably in his late forties – from the teeth – and of slim build. The body was too fire damaged to provide any signs or papers of identification. The police made a few enquiries, asked anybody who might have information to come forward. Having looked at the available evidence they were about to close the case when the publican of The Unicorn public house presented himself.

'I 'eard you was looking like.' Ben Tulston stood before the counter sergeant in the local police station, looking sheepish. He'd gone over and over the night of the fire in his mind, confiding in his wife. She nagged him to go to the police. He brushed off his wife's demands for a day or two before conscience got the better of him. After all, the man, whom he knew only as Sandor, *had* gone to try and help. He gave the surly-looking sergeant in the station as much information as he could. He couldn't say much: The Unicorn bar was always dimly lit. Besides, he gathered not much of Sandor remained. He'd asked other habitual drinkers and one knew the deceased better than the others. This man identified him as Sandor Olmak, musician and keen theatre-goer. He even knew where Sandor lived.

The sergeant took himself off to the address he'd been given. It was a shabby Georgian house off Percy Circus. The landlady, looked apprehensive. 'I ain't seen Sandor in days,' she offered when asked. 'Owes me rent, too an' all, he does. 'asn't paid this week.' She confirmed that he had never gone missing before and that his comings and goings were usually regular.

Chapter Seventy-four *Mo*

'I'm lucky I still have you,' Ma whispered to Mo, tucking back a strand of her hair.

Mo had been discharged from the hospital. Still in a daze she'd let herself be taken back to The Mare's Head again: to rest and recoup, as the doctor said. Knighton had wanted to see her but Ma refused him access. For now Mo could not be bothered to find out the full story. She guessed it had something to do with the squabble she'd half heard when she drifting in and out of consciousness.

She and Ma sat over a strong brew of tea in the scullery. Mo watched a sheet flapping on the washing line. It ballooned out then flapped angrily in the wind. 'I was lying down to rest one minute, the next half choking to death. I 'eard someone shouting. I thought I was dreamin'…'

'No, you wasn't dreamin'. There was someone.' Ma looked down at the ground. She seemed even more buttoned up than usual.

'Do they know who?'

Ma became very busy then, aligning the big brown teapot with the sugar bowl, with the milk jug. Mo felt uneasy watching her, knowing something was struggling to emerge, knowing Ma would do her utmost to contain it.

Ma bent her head. ''E died.'

'Who?'

Ma shrugged.

'Where?'

'By the Stage Door exit. 'E came in from the alley.'

'It wasn't the first time I stayed over. When I was dog tired and wanted a bit of peace I'd stop there overnight.'

'Did anyone know that?'

Mo sighed. 'The night watchman. The stage manager – I asked him if it was okay. And another friend.' Her mind was struggling to piece together the time before the fire: who had been around, who might have come back for her... 'Do the police know who it was?' she asked again.

Ma looked suddenly very old, her face stricken with pain.

'Ma?'

Ma stood up and looked ready to be getting on with the hundred and one tasks that took up her day. She stood by the door. ''is name was Sandor Olmak,' she said and shut the door firmly behind her.

Mo stared at the door, examining the flaking paint on it, the boards that made it up, the scuffmarks by the floor, the pale mauve paint on the walls, patched now with damp. Her head was light with disbelief. Sandor Olmak. The man she was just beginning to know, the musician from Vienna... the man causing her to assess her singing, her career ... her ally and friend.

Too new, this information; too unexpected – it did not fit into the scheme of things. It could not be true. There must be some mistake. She felt numb. She found she was shaking. And how to explain her mother's reaction? She'd looked stricken. As though the life had been sucked from her, as though she'd seen... and the pieces began to slide into place. Ma did know Sandor Olmak. They had a connection, a shared past. The night in the theatre foyer flashed through Mo's mind. They had recognised each other and did not know what to do. He had walked straight past them, Ma had fumbled and fussed and sought the next best excuse to head home. They knew each other. They had not expected to see each other. But they had, they had. She felt sick. But more than that, an insatiable curiosity began to form in her.

Chapter Seventy-five *Eleanor*

Eleanor read about the partial destruction of The Athena Theatre in *The Western Echo* a day after it occurred. She tried contacting Derek but he was not picking up, then she remembered he was in Paris, still caught up in his exhibition. Many of his flats would have gone up in smoke too – months of hard work. That would be a hard blow.

It was only days later that she discovered, through a second article, that Mo had been in the building at the time of the blaze and that there had been a fatality – someone who'd rushed into the smoke-ridden back entrance, presumably in an attempt to rescue her. Eleanor did not question why Mo was overnighting there: it was really none of her business. Not that she'd given up on her sister-in-law, but Mo had always been a bit wild and unpredictable.

Enough for now that she was safe.

Numerous times she had invited her to visit her and Guy in Scadley. An ongoing invitation, she always said. So far Mo had not taken her up on it and she did not push her. Let her make her own way. In the past Mo seemed to have resented any suggestions she put to her. Yet Eleanor kept the channel between them open: no one could accuse her of barring contact or shrugging off her obligations. Mo irritated her. She always had to be different, special. She never seemed able to appreciate what life was offering her. Yet Eleanor could not help admiring her spirit, the ambition which had enticed her from the grubby East End pub to sing on the West End stage.

She wondered if Derek knew about the fire yet and whether or not he was back from Paris. She decided to call him again.

In the meantime she needed to prepare for the day ahead. She slid out a pile of exercise books for drawing and writing. Tomorrow they were going to take a nature walk. Here, as always, she felt ill equipped. The children from these villages and farms knew far more about birds and flowers than she did. They could identify a lark's call from a thrush's. They knew about the nesting patterns of reed warblers; they could catch a glimpse of a bird of prey in the sky and tell her instantly what it was.

She smiled as she pulled out the question sheet she'd typed. The Scadley project was becoming what they'd envisaged: an experimental school and a home for herself and Guy. It was the new beginning they'd promised themselves.

Chapter Seventy-six *Mo*

Ma was immersed in practical chores and was not keen to talk. Every time Mo glanced towards her, she looked away. Mo found her frustration mounting. What was she doing here anyway? She was not a child. If she didn't want to stay in the Aldwych apartment right now, there were other options. She could afford to rent a room somewhere. If that felt too lonely she could seek out Stella or one of her friends from the theatre. It was time to move on. She'd been grateful for the respite, heartened that Ma had shown her concern, but that did not mean she should feel obliged to remain in The Mare's Head longer than necessary.

But then there was Sandor Olmak. Throughout the day her mind kept circling back to him. To him and Ma, and the mysterious link she intuited between them. By late afternoon she had made up her mind. She packed her things, which amounted to a toothbrush, a nightie and a change of clothes thrown into a weekend bag after her discharge. She confronted her pale image in the stained upstairs mirror. What a sorry sight! She needed to get out in the fresh air, start moving and dancing again, belt out a few songs. Forget the past. And suddenly the words of Sandor Olmak were in her head, telling her that her recent collapse on stage was merely a stumbling. It should not deter her. Her throat caught. He had saved her life. Whether or not he knew it. The voice had woken her. It had cut through her desire to escape, her dissatisfaction. Her eyes filled with tears. He had cared enough to risk then his life for her.

She found Ma lining up glasses in the saloon bar before the

early drinkers arrived. 'Ma, I need to get back and get on with things…'

'Surely not this evening? I fought you was going stay and 'elp out like.'

'Another time.'

Her mother stared at her. Mo noticed that she was still looking more drained and listless than usual. 'The doctor said you need rest. I thought that meant a few days at least.'

'Ma, there's nothing here for me to do. I could help out in the bar tonight but I'm sure you could manage without me. You usually do.'

Ma clicked on the cash register button so it pinged and sent the drawer shooting open. She emptied some coins from small sack into the compartments. 'Pa was 'oping to see you. E's been down at the brewery sorting a few things.'

'Ma, I'll be back.'

Ma carried on tidying up the counter and wiping down the beer pumps.

'Ma,' Mo braced herself. 'That night – when you come to see me in The Athena – I could've sworn you and Sandor Olmak recognised each other. He was coming towards me. He'd smiled and waved. And then he just cut us. That wasn't normal. And you acted strange… You took off pretty sharpish. Went straight home when I was sure you was going to stay and have a few drinks with me…you looked … well you wasn't your normal self …'

'What you talking about?'

'Ma, did you know him from your Music Hall days?'

Ma continued wiping down the beer taps, avoiding eye contact.

'Ma?'

'You could say…'

'I want to find out more about him. He was always there after I performed. It became uncanny.'

Despite her busy movements Ma looked edgy. It gave Mo a strange feeling in the gut. 'He was a friend of mine,' she said simply.

'Ma, what was it?' Mo surprised herself by asking.

In fact she looked vulnerable. Ma who had always been so stern and reliable, the realist, the one with the firm hand on the rudder. Had she deceived them all? There were layers and layers to her. Did Pa know any of this?

'Ma, please tell me. I need to know.'

Ma gave her a long, hard stare. 'Do you? Sometimes we think we want the truth when we don't.'

'Ma, please.'

Ma let out a long sigh and threw the cloth to one side. 'So you wanna hear. You're sure about that?'

Mo suppressed a shiver of apprehension, sensing she was stepping towards a ravine. Ma walked over to one of the round tables, pulled out a chair. 'Sit down.'

Mo did as she was told.

Ma sighed and started speaking, slowly at first, then ever faster. 'Your pa had had his accident and I was back working. Singing like. And Sandor just happened. We 'it it off straight away. Never known no-one like him. Like an angel he was. Like he'd been dropped from the sky to light my way.'

Mo was shocked to hear such words. Ma was always so reticent.

'What happened?'

'I was moon struck, that's for sure. The moment I clapped eyes on him I knew I was a gonner, family or no family, husband or no husband.'

'Oh.'

'It was like lightning striking. I knew it was my one chance. I didn't recognise myself. The songs came pouring out of me, like there was no tomorrow.'

'So what was it like?'

'I could've sung all day and all night. And then – well – when you're swept away like that there's no nay-saying, no holding back. But we was careful we was. Didn't want to 'urt nobody. Even when the passion was in us… sweeping us along. We knew it wouldn't last. Couldn't. That made us all the more desperate. Every waking minute I thought of him. Couldn't wait to be with him making music, making love, making the stars sing. Not everyone gets that. And when it comes – I guess you've just got to catch hold of it.' She paused, looked down at the table, smiling to herself.

'But even then I knew something was not right. Not morally I don't mean. Though there was that too… I was a mother with a young child and a decent man for a husband.'

Mo felt a sense of dread, knowing she'd unleashed a force that was beyond her. The words were gushing out of her mother. Ma was lost in the memory. Once she started it was as though she'd blotted out all awareness of Mo sitting there, listening.

'But… but there was something he weren't saying, couldn't say… I knew he was never mine. Not really. Always some part of him held back. And then one day 'e wasn't there anymore… he just upped and left.' She paused. 'I had no choice in the matter. Didn't know what had hit me. Pa knew something was up but we never talked about it. I just couldn't. Would 've broke his heart if I'd just come out and said it. So I never did. I stopped singing and threw myself into the bar and the business and then well I discovered I'd fallen for you. I 'ad no choice. I just 'ad to keep going. But I was glad. Glad I had some part of him growing inside me. I knew then that you'd be different. That terrified me…'

'So what are you telling me Ma?'

'He was your father, Mo…'

'Why didn't you..? Did he know you were pregnant?'

'I was already married, Morwenna. Cissie was three years

old. We knew it would never work for us. Not in the long run.' Ma fell silent then, tears glistening in her eyes. She ran her fingers over the tabletop as if wanting to smooth out non-existent wrinkles.

'Why did you keep it from me?' Mo's voice was quiet.

Ma turned towards her. Her lips were drawn tight, her brow white and closed. 'It was for the best,' she muttered.

Chapter Seventy-seven *Mo*

Mo needed to be alone. After a morning's search she found a room above a shoe shop in the Strand and rented it on a weekly basis. Neither Riverton Road and Stella, nor The Mare's Head and Ma and Pa, and certainly not the Aldwych flat, where Knighton might call by at any time, were desirable. She needed to retreat, if only for a few days, to piece together the crazy jigsaw.

On the third day Cissy, who had been sniffing round the burnt-out theatre, came to visit. She was not unwelcome.

'Get that down you.' In the Strand Coal Hole downstairs bar Cissy was pushing a glass of whisky towards her. Whisky was the last thing Mo needed. She'd been feeling unwell for days, her body rebelling at recent events.

'Back to work soon,' Mo murmured. Though how that was going to happen she no longer knew.

'Will the company move somewhere else? I heard the repair work is going to take months.'

'Cissy, I haven't a clue.' She gazed at her sister. Of late she'd put on weight, which gave her face a slightly puffed, pasty look. But there was concern written there for her younger sister, the wild one who'd never settle down and toe the line.

'How did you find out where I was living?'

'Morwenna, it's no secret. One of the chorus girls saw you in the street and watched you enter.'

'Oh.'

Cissy was patting her hand. 'And where is Derek these days?'

Mo started, the name still an electric shock to her system. 'I don't know. Last time I saw him it was in a club…'

'Does he know about the fire an' all?'

'I don't want to talk about him.'

'What about this other bloke then – the one you was talking about before?'

'Sandor Olmak?'

'Who's 'e? No, Jonathon Knighton?'

From the sound of it Ma had said nothing about Sandor Olmak. Mo suspected that as always, despite her blurted revelation that day in The Mare's Head, Ma would close down and say nothing, ever again. Knowing that, made Mo tired.

'Oh him? That's just sort of professional.'

'What d'you mean?'

'Nothing. He's my boss.'

'Is that all?'

'Cissy – leave off will you? You're making my head go round with all your questions…' This disavowal of Knighton startled her. Was he really nothing to her? Did it count for nothing that he had helped her; that she had once enchanted and entertained him? Now that all seemed a long time ago.

'Anyway, look, I better get going… I've got a neighbour minding the kids.'

'Of course.'

After Cissy had gone Mo went back to her room. The sight of her belongings: a scramble of clothes and a few scripts stashed into three bags, depressed her. What a pathetic little heap! She made herself a cup of tea on the gas ring, got into bed although it was still early and pulled the covers up to her chin.

But the peace of mind she sought eluded her. Her heart was thumping with anxiety, her head dark with thoughts swooping like evil black bats. She heard a loud rapping at the downstairs door. At first she ignored it. It matched the erratic racing of her heart. But it went on and on. She threw back the blankets and impatient to put a stop to it, raced downstairs. Knighton stood in the street, looking red-faced and exasperated.

'There you are!'

Mo could only gape at him. 'Jonathon!'

'I had the devil of a time finding you. Look, can I come in?'

She glanced over her shoulder, recalling the tawdry upstairs room and her meagre belongings. 'I'd rather you didn't. Can we go somewhere else to talk?'

He raised an eyebrow. 'As you wish.'

She went back upstairs and quickly made herself presentable. They found a quiet corner café. 'What would you like to drink?' asked Knighton as a waitress hovered.

'Water. Just water.' Knighton ordered a pot of tea for himself.

Mo watched the retreating back of the waitress, looked out on omnibuses and taxis ferrying people to and fro along the Strand. This was not going to be easy.

'How are you Morwenna? You've been hiding yourself away. I understand that – after what you've been through. After your collapse on stage and then the fire, I was worried about you. Very worried.'

Mo nodded, trying to gauge from his tone just how authentic this concern was. Though he sounded more vexed than worried, she decided to give him the benefit of the doubt. 'I just need time to – to put myself back together.'

He gave a cursory smile, yet his eyes remained stern. 'I got the impression you were avoiding me.'

She hesitated. 'I let everyone down. I don't know what came over me on stage… And then – well, I thought I might have caused the fire…'

'That's not what the police think.'

The waitress approached with a carafe of water and Knighton's pot of tea and placed them carefully on their table.

Mo sipped then gulped the water.

'It was a shock to see you faint like that, I must admit. But nothing like what came after. Half the theatre going up in smoke and poor old Olmak! Bad business that, very bad.'

Mo found that she was shaking. She tried to stop herself but her hands and then her legs were moving involuntarily. She commanded herself to be still. She did not want Knighton to see her weakness. She swallowed more water, stared at the paisley patterned lino and summoned what determination she could.

'You were lucky to get out, is all I can say. Damned lucky.'

She grunted assent, unable to speak.

'The thought that I might've lost you shocked me to the core. You do realise that, don't you?'

'Yes,' she mumbled.

'I don't understand why you were staying there overnight.' She dared to look across at him. His dark eyes were searching hers. He covered her hand with his. She stopped herself pulling back from him. Too much complexity, too much entanglement – it was overwhelming.

He leaned back and sighed. 'Well, let's take one step at a time. I wanted to put you in the picture about what's happening. We've got shared use of The Apollo for our next production. I brokered a deal with them. They were going to have a gap of several weeks anyway. Most of The Athena is still intact, the auditorium and foyer are unharmed, smoke-damaged, but nothing a bit of decoration won't cure. The stage and dressing rooms need a total refurbishment. That starts as soon as the insurance money comes through. We've got a reserve fund so some clearing-up has started already.'

Again Mo nodded and felt the tremoring abate. She could tell Knighton was full of the immediate future. 'I'm glad the damage wasn't too widespread,' she said.

'I'm thinking about our next production and what we need

to do. I've had more meetings with The Apollo. And Noel Coward. We need to press on. I'd like to start auditions and then rehearsals in about ten days time. I've got a nice part lined up for you. As long as you're up to it…' Here he gazed at her in puzzlement. 'I never know where I am with you, Morwenna. Right as rain one minute, all jittery the next. I suppose I need some reassurance.'

Mo felt an old anger mounting in her. How dare he talk down to her? Did he know what it was to lose someone close, really close? Her eyes flickered towards him: 'Are you saying I'm not professional in my approach?'

'Not that, Morwenna,' he broke into a smile, rubbed the back of her hand. She drew her hands together, folded them, away from his. 'I'm not heartless, you know. But I do have to run a business. The show must go on.'

'Quite.'

'What I suggest is this: you go somewhere for a rest, a real rest. Probably out of London. Money shouldn't be a problem. I can give you something – as a retainer, if you like. Then you come back, hopefully refreshed, and we can make a new start. How does that sound?'

On the face of it she could not fault his logic. In fact he was being more than generous and giving her enough leeway to do whatever she needed to. But she continued to feel uncomfortable. Would she be ready in time? Would she be able to… the questions went round and round and she began to realise she did not have the scope now to deliberate. He was looking for a commitment. He was giving her a second chance. It might be just what she needed to get back on her feet.

'Thank you,' she murmured. 'That's a good idea. I'd like to get out of the city for a while, away from the West End.'

* * *

She decided to follow through on this and leave London as soon as possible. She would take a train west and book into a country inn. She wanted more than ever to get away from the place. She caught the Underground to Paddington and booked a seat on an afternoon train to Cheltenham for later that day.

First, she had some unfinished business.

The anniversary of Timothy's death was fast approaching. Before the fire she had been ticking off the weeks. Then, fearing that she would be paralysed with guilt and grief, she forbade herself to look at any calendar. She'd tried to immerse herself in her work. With the fire all that foundered. Now she could no longer make herself so busy that she fell into bed exhausted and scarce found time to eat, let alone think. She was numb with the immensity of what she'd undergone.

She would not go back to Timothy's grave in St Mary's churchyard. She was not ready. She'd been there only once. Only once read the stone inscribed: *Beloved son, taken too soon.* Already ivy was creeping up one side from the ground. She had bent to clear it, kneeling and putting her hand to the cold marble. Eyes blinded with tears, unsteady on her feet, placing a bunch of pinks against the pink-grey stone, clearing away the creeper and whispering a prayer. She had not been able to function for two days afterwards.

Timothy would have been a clamouring, delectable little chap getting into everything, exploring the world with his eager eyes and boundless energy. Her throat constricted as she attempted to stifle the image. The nightmare needed to disperse. But how to move forward when she had buried her heart along with him? The words of the medium came back to her now. Embrace life. He came to bring you joy.

Was that all just sentimental nonsense?

She heard it said that a year has to elapse before healing can commence, until then it is all the counting of days, the spring and summer of it. She had been dreading the approach of June. Now it was nearly there, only weeks to go. Winter days, short and filled with rehearsals, were a world away from that fateful summer day. As the days began to lengthen she'd found herself waking up to her pain.

And then Sandor Olmak had come into her life.

Though she had sworn to go nowhere near St Mary's, after Knighton's visit she decided she would return to Saint Paul's cathedral. Pay her son homage. Light a candle. This she could allow herself before her trip. Already she had packed an overnight bag, she was ready to leave London and its sorrows behind.

She sat in a back pew, letting the sonorous tones of the organ sweep over her. Was it Bach? The chords moved through her, on and on, lifting her, piercing her, as they circled back on themselves in a fugue, forever starting anew.

By the time the recital was over she was both stirred and strangely calm.

She thought of Sandor Olmak playing the piano, his hands flitting over the keys. She thought of how he had come from nowhere into her life and was now gone. Had he already been buried? How long now since the fire? She had lost track of the days.

Whenever she thought of him her head went round and round. No wonder she was so different from her sisters! No wonder she had grown up feeling strange, alien, at odds with those around her. She had foreign blood. She had Jewish blood. She was half Hungarian and God knew what else besides.

She had always thought herself Pa's favourite. He laughed more at her jokes, indulged her more. How could that be, when he knew her to be from another man's seed? He spoke of pride, of his daughters growing up proper – when all this time, eating away like a canker, was this cuckoo in his nest, this bastard-child, this intruder... harsh words ran through her mind. But then according to Ma, he didn't know, did he?

She was too exhausted to untwist the tangles, growing like

silted reeds in a river, choking it, altering its course of flow. A father she had always longed for, secretly, to confirm her sense of differentness; a man who'd taken an interest in her gift, her welfare; a man who'd sacrificed himself for her… yet Sandor Olmak had left Ma with his child and now, in dying, had abandoned Mo herself, just when she was getting to know him. He was unreliable, shiftless, a chimera… but for all that, he'd recognised her, loved her, tried to guide her.

Somehow she'd known the truth, without knowing she knew it, as soon as she set eyes on him, as soon as he met her gaze and advised her on her career. Those eyes claimed kinship. Those dark intelligent eyes of his, the spark and animation in them, that whiff she'd caught of other times and places. There was no doubting he was her father, her true father. And now, like Timothy, he was gone.

She caught left Saint Paul's and headed towards Paddington.

Chapter Seventy-eight

From her carriage window Mo watched the undulating countryside slip by. Terraced houses gave way to fields and farms, to waterways glinting in the sun. Branches over the rail escarpment were fresh with green leaves as sharp as lime. She looked at the faded prints below the luggage rack, horses and hounds at the hunt, bodies extended as they flew after prey. As a child the furthest she'd been from London was Southend to take the sea air and eat whelks. She stared out at sleepy railway stations with neat stationmasters' cottages beside toy town ticket offices and waiting rooms. After the bustle of London it all looked so civilised, old-fashioned even.

Cheltenham surprised her with its sandstone Georgian elegance of wide streets and pillared edifices. She booked into a hotel a stone's throw from the station and had an early supper of plaice and chips. Afterwards she walked round the town, gazing in through the bow windows of milliners' and posh frock shops. Once her feet started aching she returned to the hotel and had an early night.

The next day she was up bright and early. After breakfast, she wandered round Cheltenham again. She visited the town hall, the town library and the Pittville Pump room, all harking back the town's heyday as a spa town. She was growing weary of fine buildings. They made her feel so much the stranger, forever on the outside looking in. She longed for human contact. It was then she remembered that Eleanor and Guy did not live far from Cheltenham and if she were not mistaken she could reach their village by train.

Time and again Eleanor had invited her to spend time with

them: come and see the project, she'd written. Mo had been promising for months to do so, now might be the ideal time. Before she could change her mind she found a post office and sent a telegram warning of her imminent arrival.

Eleanor and Guy had married the year before, rather hastily, in Bath. Mo had been unable to attend the ceremony. At least, aware Derek would be there and not yet ready to face him, she'd declared herself unavailable. Now she was curious to see how they were getting on. In her letters Eleanor said she had no intention of returning to London. With time Mo came to realise how much she owed Eleanor. All things considered, Eleanor had been her ally in the difficult times. After initial suspicion, Eleanor had often taken her side, always urging her forward. Eleanor could not be pushed to one side in the forward scramble in the same way that Derek could be.

It was high time to visit her.

The branch line penetrated ever deeper into the countryside. Eleanor and Guy met her at the station of Scadley in what looked like a farmer's horse and cart, which, with so many motorised vehicles now on the road, she found distinctly quaint. Eleanor looked relaxed and bronzed from the sun. 'So you've come at last!' she exclaimed. Guy nudged the horse forward and it clip-clopped down the one street of the village. Mo looked round. This was true Hicksville, as they said in the flicks. She was bemused by what she saw, amazed at the scale of it, the snow-white lace curtains of the teashop, the carefully painted sign of the pharmacy, the women chatting in groups with their shopping baskets, who nodded a greeting to them.

'You know a lot of people here,' she remarked.

'Oh, everyone knows everyone here.' Eleanor laughed. 'You have to be careful what you say.'

'And you're happy with that?' She noted Eleanor's insouciance. Before, she'd been ever watchful, mindful of people's opinions. She looked freer. She had put on a little weight and it suited her. Guy had changed, too. He looked broader, manlier somehow. She guessed that was marriage.

'So how are things going? We heard all about the fire. That must've been a terrible shock?'

Mo said nothing. 'Can we talk about it later…?' she said at length.

'Of course. I'm sorry Mo. I really am. When you're ready…'

They passed out of the village, entering a narrow country lane with wheat on either side. The hedgerows were rich with clusters of purple and white flowers. Mo gazed at fields rising to the horizon before the cart plunged into an avenue of sycamores, which obscured the view.

'So how is the school going? Do you have enough pupils?'

Eleanor smiled. 'People were intensely curious at first. They're shy, country folk, but wily. They wanted to see whether we'd stick it out. After we'd braved the winter they knew we were here to stay. They came in dribs and drabs to see what we were up to. It's happening slowly.'

The lane dropped into a dell and Guy had to rein in the horse as it picked its way down. Sunlight broke through tall beech trees and cast a dappled light. 'Do you ever miss the buzz of London?'

'I thought I would, but our days are full from dawn to dusk, what with the building and getting the cottage and garden sorted out. We had men in to refurbish the barn. Guy supervised and pitched in. I kept tabs on the money, ran up curtains and sanded down floors. Did things I never thought myself capable of… now Kentish Town seems far away.'

The ground before them flattened out. Mo, who had risen early, found her lids drooping. The cart came to a halt before the barn, jerking her awake. Startled, she stared around. The barn was gleaming in the sun. The ground around it had been cleared. On one side stood a notice: School Entrance, on the other was the cottage: their living quarters. The oak-clad barn was a mellow grey-green as were its roof tiles, so the whole produced a tone akin to the bark of a tree. Mo gasped: 'It's a miracle!'

Eleanor beamed. 'Let's go inside.' Then, as if remembering something, she hung back. She glanced at Guy and said: 'It wasn't by design, Mo. You gave us no time…'

Mo wondered what on earth was going on. She got down, heart thumping, wondering what was ahead. She half guessed. The front door of the cottage opened. There, on the threshold, was Derek. She caught her breath. 'Why didn't you say…?' He stepped outside.

Guy cut in: 'Derek's been staying a few days – to help with the renovation. He said, you'd met up recently, that it wouldn't be a problem…'

'When we got your telegram there was no time to warn you,' added Eleanor. Mo said nothing. Derek was staring at her. She walked past him into the shelter of the cottage. It took a moment for her eyes to adjust to the dark. She glanced round the interior of the room. She took in the piles of exercise books sprawled in one corner on the flagstones, a chair which needed mending, the fireplace with an exuberant spray of wildflowers spilling out and bookshelves brimming with books of every shape and size. The sitting room led through to a kitchen where she could just make out herbs drying on a rack and a saucepan bubbling on the range.

She slid down onto the nearest sofa. She was unable to move. The others came in behind her. Derek took a seat nearby. He was careful not to come too close to her, but she was aware of him observing her. She found she could scarcely breathe. Eleanor filled the space with more chatter about the school and her pupils, last year's harvest and the late arrival of spring this year. She went into the kitchen to make them tea and came back bearing a tray laden with tea and scones. Guy brought up a little table to put them on.

Mo said no to tea. She glanced at Derek. Despite his dishevelled hair he looked well and more confident than she had ever seen him. He started regaling them with an account of his exhibition in Paris in between munching on a scone. During a lull in conversation Eleanor announced.

'We have some news for you.'

The words hung in the air. Eleanor looked towards Guy. 'We are going to be parents,' he said. Derek got up and gave his sister a hug, strode towards Guy and shook him vigorously by the hand.

Mo grew pale, felt herself sinking into the softness of the cushions: she was the bad fairy at the party, the wet blanket, the bringer of doom and despondency. And in the next moment she was getting to her feet.

'Do you mind if I take a quick walk – before it cools down?'

Derek looked at her with concern. 'May I accompany you?'

She hesitated then nodded her assent. 'Excuse me,' she murmured. She walked back out and crossed the courtyard where chickens fluttered out of the way. Derek was close on her heels.

'Mo?' he caught her arm. 'Are you feeling – alright?'

She continued walking. 'This way,' said Derek. He took off in the direction of the open fields and she followed. They said nothing, picking their steps along a narrowing path that dipped beneath overhanging trees and then rose into the breast of a hill.

'I felt ambushed,' she said. 'What was I supposed to do?'

'Mo, it wasn't intentional.'

On one side a row of poplars fingered the sky, on the other grew a riot of purple and yellow flowers. She caught the scent of early summer: cows parsley and honeysuckle. It grasped her by the throat. She breathed deep, not daring to look at him.

'I'm sorry,' he said. 'I didn't want to alarm you.'

'I shouldn't have rushed out like that. It was not very – civil,' she murmured.

'Mo, how are you? I just got back from Paris. I only just heard what happened,' he said quietly.

She said nothing, perplexed. 'Oh Derek,' she murmured at length, 'if you only knew.'

'You could've died. I can't bear to think about it.'

'I heard your work is going well. An exhibition in Paris, two in London, in the Grafton…' she was struggling to keep her voice even.

A slick of hair was falling over his forehead, darkening his eyes. 'Mo, I didn't realise…' He took hold of her hand. His hand felt firm, dry, protective. 'I didn't realise how unhappy you'd become…'

'Nothing as bad as what came after…' Her words faded. There was nothing more to say.

'Before the fire – were you happy with your new life?' he asked.

She shrugged. What was there to say that was neither a lie nor an evasion? She was singing. She had recognition, professional respect, and even money.

'And you?'

He sighed. He stopped by a vast oak tree and on impulse pulled her towards him. 'I never stopped loving you.' The sun caught the side of his face. She felt the warmth of it on her back. She was breathless from the uphill walk.

'You had a strange way of showing it,' she eyed him defiantly.

'There was no-one ever really except you.'

She glared at him and before she could stop herself gave him a hard slap on the face. He drew back.

He caught her hands, held them above her head. 'Listen, Mo, listen. I was wrong. I was stupid. I was distracted. I see that now …'

'You don't have to excuse yourself.'

'Hear me out. I was weak...'

She started back along the path they'd come on.

'Wait, Mo. Wait. Hear me out.'

She carried on walking, her voice taut. 'A leopard keeps its spots!'

No more words came, but a barrage of images and sensations: of all that they had had, all that they had lost. It attacked her gut, her heart, threatening to choke her. She coughed with this vastness of what had been between them. And the unspoken reproach: it needn't have happened, always on the brink of her mind, the tip of her memory.

He caught hold of her hand, pulled her back.

She threw him an angry, puzzled look but did not cast him off.

'It was about my work. In the end it was about my work. Once I found the – the courage to plunge into it, to stay in it, I came through. Now I know I can do it. It's me now when I work.'

He turned her towards him and kissed her gently on the lips.

'I was broken,' she murmured. 'And you broke me all over again...'

'Mo, Mo.'

'We should have had him inoculated.'

She heard him give a strangulated sob and before she knew it they were clasping each other, her body moulding to his in the long shadows of the late afternoon. The sadness and emptiness of loss entwining itself around them like the blue shadows of the tree bole even as the light of the sun and the crowns of the trees were bending towards each other above.

'I was just looking everywhere,' he murmured. 'When everything I needed was here, right in front of me.'

She glanced up at him, fighting a tremor of apprehension.

'Do you think…' he began, 'there could be hope for us. Another beginning?'

Her heart was drumming erratically. 'We have to be practical.'

'Why?'

'Why? Because we're not children anymore.'

'You are my heart and my soul.'

The gloom of early evening was falling slowly around them.

She looked at him, at his open vulnerable hungry eyes and saw the confused youth man that he had always been. She stared at the ground, steadying herself. 'Derek, would you come with me to his grave? It's his anniversary coming up.'

He nodded and went to draw her towards him but she hesitated. 'I've got so much I need to tell you that I don't know where to start.' She sounded firm, in charge of the situation, but her body was quivering. Was it fear, grief, or the stirring of a new possibility between them? The touch of his hand on her body, however light, however accidental, reminded her of all those other times before; her body remembered so much better than she did.

'We have time,' he paused. 'Do you think there a chance for us?'

She stared ahead. 'Perhaps,' she murmured so low he barely caught it. Then she looked around and said out loud: 'It's dusk. Let's go back to the house before the bats get us.' He laughed and led the way back across the fields.

THE END

Coming shortly:

Paris Shadow Dance

In Paris Derek finds his spiritual home on the Left Bank and becomes involved with Russian émigré artists, particularly with the enigmatic Tanya. Mo re-invents herself as a cabaret artist and finds a niche at the Scheherazade, a night-club run by the urbane Anton Lensky. They are caught up in the glamour and excitement of the city's night-life and its cutting edge arts scene. But there is a dark underside to the City of Light. Stalin's secret agents are lurking in the shadows and Mo is haunted by a mystery in her past.

THE EATONS, Vol 2

ABOUT THE AUTHOR

Brenda Squires grew up in London and Surrey and now lives in a restored Victorian Mansion in the deep countryside of West Wales, which she loves. Her background was in education, community work and psychotherapy but she has always had a passion to write. At first it was a background hum but it became ever louder, until irresistible. She was delighted and surprised when her first novel, *Landsker,* won the Romantic Novelists' New Writers Award. Her second book: *The Love of Geli Raubal* draws on her experience as a student of German and the exciting time she spent in a divided Berlin.

In the current trilogy: *The Eatons* she traces the ups and downs of a passionate relationship between two artists: a singer and a painter. She has always been intrigued by creativity: where it comes from, where it leads. Besides writing she has taken up painting recently and finds that the two art forms feed into each other. She likes learning foreign languages, walking in wild countryside and being by the sea. She helps run an arts and community centre in Pembrokeshire.

Printed in Great Britain
by Amazon

10195360R00253